The
Omega
Transmissions

The Omega Transmissions

Ω

A novel

Nancy Parker

Ashland Hills Press

*This is a work of fiction. Any resemblance it may bear to actual
persons or events is coincidental and unintended. While the
SETI Project has existed under the aegis of the U.S. Government
and the National Aeronautics and Space Administration, public
funding for SETI is discontinued as of 1995. Concurrent, privately
funded efforts do continue, however, in the Search for
ExtraTerrestrial Intelligence.*

Library of Congress Catalog Card Number: 94-94606

ISBN 0-9642272-0-7

Printed in the United States of America by
IPCO Printing, Ashland, Oregon.

Published by Ashland Hills Press
P.O. Box 992
Ashland, Oregon 97520

For my father
William Parker
who taught me to sail.

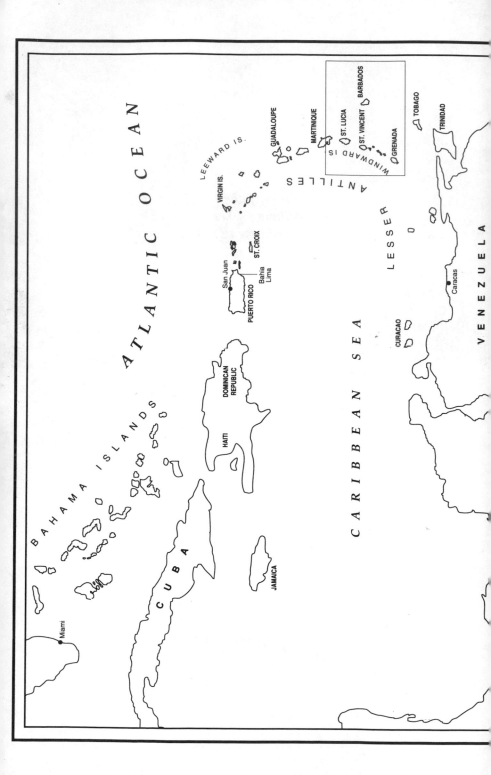

DOMINICA

W I N D W A R D   I S L A N D S

MARTINIQUE

Fort de France

Castries
Marigot Bay
Soufriere
Vieux Fort

ST. LUCIA

Cumberland Bay
ST. VINCENT
Kingstown
Admiralty Bay
BEQUIA

MUSTIQUE

CANNOUAN
MAYREAU   TOBAGO CAYS
UNION ISLAND
Clifton Harbor
SANDY ISLAND
Tyrell Bay   CARRIACOU

BARBADOS

St. George's   GRENADA

The water is wide, I can't cross o'er,
And neither have I wings to fly,
Give me a boat that can carry two,
And both shall row, my love and I.

—Traditional ballad—

PROLOGUE

THREE YEARS AGO, Kate Lipton taped two seemingly unrelated objects to a wall in her office. The first was a picture-postcard, mostly black, depicting a two-armed spiral galaxy composed of tiny white dots. A white arrow pointed to one of the dots and next to it were the words, YOU ARE HERE.

Above this, Kate had taped the second item, a gun-metal blue metallic disc approximately six inches in diameter. It resembled a small mirror but was actually a silicon wafer, a reject from a Silicon Valley microchip manufacturer that someone had given her.

These two objects, placed inadvertently one atop the other, comprise a remarkably precise metaphor for the material that came to be known as The Omega Transmissions: a mirror above the galaxy reflecting an echo of ourselves, back to ourselves.

Ω

———————

1

———————

AS THE DAY UNFOLDED, January seventeenth could not have been considered exceptional; it only became so with the benefit of hindsight. Kate Lipton viewed her own part as that of one who has happened upon the enticing first of a long row of precariously aligned dominoes, and who unwittingly gives the first a casual nudge—after which all hell breaks loose.

She would remember much of the day in fine detail, beginning with the relentless fog. She recalled being dogged by a complex set of emotions, most prominent of which was a sense of expectancy. But clearest of all in her memory of the day was the phone call she placed to astrophysicist Milton Rensler; he was the first domino.

Just laying her hands on Rensler's private unlisted number had cost Kate half the morning and a fair amount of journalistic collateral—favors promised for information received.

She reached for the phone to punch in the Mountain View area code but stopped—a mild case of nerves. She chided herself, pressed ahead, and a somewhat impatient female voice answered:

"SETI Project."

"This is Kate Lipton. I was hoping to reach Dr. Rensler."

"Hold on. I'll get him."

There followed a clatter of fragmented sounds—the phone receiver laid down, chairs scraping, voices—all abruptly squelched by an electronic click and a humming silence.

Moments later, a male voice came on. "Rensler."

"Dr. Rensler, this is Kathryn Lipton. I'm a journalist and I saw the paragraph in this morning's paper about the cuts in SETI's funding—"

"There was an article? I must have missed it."

"In the *Chronicle*. Not exactly on Page One."

"No, of course it wouldn't be." Kate detected the barest hint of weary resignation in the voice. "What can I do for you?" he asked.

"I was hoping you might spare time this week for an interview. I'm researching your project for a feature article." This last was pure invention on Kate's part. She hadn't started an article, didn't know if she'd write one, and understood next to nothing about Rensler's SETI Project.

"Well, my schedule over the next few days is— You'd like an interview?"

"I'd need an hour or so."

"Well—"

"Ten tomorrow?" she persisted.

"Make it ten-fifteen. I've got an early meeting across town so—"

"Will I need special authorization to get into your facility?"

"Right. Your name again? Kathryn—"

"Lipton. No relation to the tea dynasty."

"Oh, you host that PBS show on Channel 9," he said in sudden recognition.

"Right. 'Focus: Silicon Valley.' I also write on a freelance basis for technical publications."

The reference to her minor claim to local television fame seemed to clinch it. Rensler led a NASA project whose funding was in doubt, and favorably slanted media exposure wasn't the worst thing that could befall him. Kate didn't mention that government high-tech was off her regular beat. In the past, there'd been no need to labor at prying secrets from tight-lipped government scientific types; there'd been an exuberant electronics industry in the Valley to cover. But times had changed; Silicon Valley was slogging its way through an economic downturn. It was time to branch out.

"Do you have a security clearance?" Rensler asked.

"Yes, I do."

"Good. I'll leave your name with the guards at the gate. Tell them you have an appointment with me. They'll notify me and I'll meet you at the entrance to Building A."

"Thanks very much, Dr. Rensler. See you tomorrow."

She hung up with an appreciative nod. Well done. And unlike many of the recession-weary corporate executives she'd been speaking with lately, Rensler actually seemed approachable. This satisfying observation was quickly replaced by momentary panic; she had less than twenty-four hours before the interview in which to learn something about the SETI Project.

She'd rescued the paragraph that morning from an anonymous grave on the last page of the *Chronicle's* Business Section and had immediately made up her mind to try for the interview with Rensler, mentioned in the article as the top man on SETI. Worth a try, plus it would give her day shape and purpose. Now she took a moment to reread the paragraph:

"Scientists at the NASA/Ames Research facility in Mountain View warned yesterday that funding for SETI— the Search for ExtraTerrestrial Intelligence—may be cut from NASA's budget. Dr. Milton Rensler, Director of SETI Research at NASA/Ames, stated that while the SETI Project accounts for less than one hundredth of a percent of NASA's total budget, Congress does not view an ongoing search for extraterrestrial intelligence as critical. Rensler, who pioneered early SETI efforts in the 70's, has since 1985 been working with Walter Jacobsen of Harvard and Howard Vaughn of MIT in a joint effort to monitor electromagnetic radio transmissions from outer space.

Their goal is to isolate, analyze and possibly reply to signals that emanate from an intelligent life source within the galaxy. Rensler's opinion is that the existence of such life is a statistical certainty. But without NASA's funding or some major private source to replace it, Rensler said he doubted his project could continue."

This tantalizing paragraph on SETI, government scientists listening for transmissions from outer space, this twenty-four-carat gem of a paragraph which ought to sell newspapers, had been buried beneath stories detailing political corruption and an unending trail of crime and human suffering. Kate shook her head sadly. Even if she could reconcile herself to the fact that misery sold newspapers, she didn't have to like it. There'd been a time—not that long ago either—when she'd loved this business, was juiced by impending deadlines and energized at the prospect of an interview with one of the Valley's high-tech king pins.

But now—

Impatiently she began stuffing things into her briefcase—a yellow tablet, sharpened pencils— Now, she thought, she needed a vacation. She pawed through her wallet for her library card and inventoried her mood. The restlessness was easily attributed to the tedium of work. But there was also a curious sense of expectancy, and impatience with the wispy intangibility of it—like fog maybe—a thing hovering at the outer edge of her psychic space that something stunning was about to happen.

She glanced out the window at the fog, which she regarded, as did most San Franciscans, with equanimity. For her it was like a visiting entity. In its brashest face, it blew in on a stiff morning breeze and was gone by lunchtime. But on days like this, it stole in, draped itself over the entire skyline and spent the day. Through her office window, she now considered the indistinct features of her back yard—the weathered deck, the row of hydrangeas, roses and weeds thriving along the back fence—shapes all awash in damp gray. This was the sort of fog that completely transformed the look of common things. She thought of Eskimos and their legendary language accommodating every manifestation of snow. San Franciscans were expert in fog.

Move, she exhorted herself. The library would close in a few hours. She drew on a heavy sweater, dumped the remains of a mug of cream-laden coffee down the drain, grabbed her briefcase and left.

To her surprise, she found quite a lot on the library shelves on NASA's Search for ExtraTerrestrial Intelligence; and some of it was quite readable. By closing time she'd xeroxed three recent magazine articles and checked out two of the least arcane texts to take home for a night of reading.

JEREMY SINCLAIR, director of the NSA—the National Security Agency—laid aside his persimmon-shafted golf putter and irritably grabbed for the ringing phone. Where the hell was Edith?

"Sinclair," he snapped.

"Ralph Burch here. I just finished speaking with Walter Jacobsen at Harvard. They intercepted a Code Shepherd signal last night " Burch's voice was positively tremulous.

Sinclair walked around his desk, slumped into his swivel chair and stared unseeingly at the rolling hills surrounding the NSA's Fort Meade, Maryland compound. He sighed. A Code Shepherd signal—the last thing he needed at one PM on January seventeenth. If Burch was right it was time, metaphorically speaking, to gather in the scientific flock. He shook his head. At times these code names seemed damned silly; not this time thought, not when you considered what was at stake. A helluva lot of lives, his own included, were about to be completely upheaved.

He asked, "How certain are your people, Ralph?"

"Jacobsen said they'd need time for analysis but he called it the most startling and promising signal they've ever intercepted."

"And you recommend we activate Code Shepherd?"

"Definitely."

During the silence that followed, Jeremy Sinclair contemplated his options. Only four weeks ago he'd briefed Ralph Burch on Code Shepherd, the day after Burch's installation as NASA's latest Director. Could the new man be overreacting? Probably not. Burch had come up through the ranks as a scientist with an administrative flair, rather than the reverse. Whether or not Burch was schooled in national security, he knew his science. Moreover, Burch was a team player. That had been the attribute setting him apart from his predecessor and earning him the appointment.

Sinclair sighed audibly. "If you're sure, Ralph, okay. As of now, Shepherd's a *Go*. At 2100 hours day after tomorrow, we'll bring everyone in. Meanwhile I'll notify the President and dispatch the team to St. Lucia to ready the facility. You get your people lined up."

"You can't pick everyone up now?"

Sinclair swallowed irritation. "We have to bring St. Lucia on line and get our staff in place. Thirty-six hours minimum. We'll coordinate the pick-up for 2100 hours E.S.T. on the nineteenth. Your first priority is to tighten the lid at your end. How many at NASA know of the signal?"

"Only Jacobsen."

"That's it?"

"That's what he says. The signal came in last night beginning at eight-twenty-seven. An alarm system was automatically triggered. The signal was diverted to an exclusive-use database and software was patched to block the signal from network access. Then he purged the data stream from the incoming transmission file."

Sinclair shook his head. Why couldn't these pointy-headed types ever speak English? "You trust his assessment?"

"Absolutely. He's confident the signal will only show up in the log as a power surge, which apparently happens with depressing regularity. No one will look twice at it."

"Okay. Instruct Rensler and Vaughn they're needed in Washington for a meeting on the nineteenth. That'll give them a few days to prepare. Don't tell them more than that. My people will bring them in along with Jacobsen and the others."

"Is that it?"

"For now."

The call concluded, Sinclair ordered his secretary to connect him with Lewis Geller, President of the United States. Moments later he delivered the news: "Mr. President, word has just come from Walter Jacobsen on the Harvard SETI team. We're activating Code Shepherd as of nine PM, day after tomorrow. I'll be handling preliminary logistics over the next several hours."

After a brief pause the President replied, "Understood, Jeremy. Is it contained?"

"Looks that way."

"You'll keep me informed."

"Yes, Sir."

Sinclair hung up and swiveled around in his chair to unlock the wall-inset safe behind his desk. He withdrew a stack of stiff white folders and thumbed through them to the one labeled:

PROJECT CODE: SHEPHERD
NSA-91-5041/CMS.11.2.2/REV9.3
CLASS: ULTRA-SECRET/NOFORN

"Send in Michael Gregg," he barked into his intercom. Sinclair considered the forty-six-year-old Agent Gregg his most skilled security operations coordinator. Fortunately Gregg was available, having recently wrapped up a six-month assignment in Eastern Europe.

Gregg appeared minutes later in the doorway to Sinclair's office. "You asked to see me, sir?"

"Come in. Have a seat. All settled since your return?"

"Just about. Got *most* of the boxes unpacked."

"Well, stop unpacking and start packing. Your next assign-ment." Sinclair slid the folder across the polished surface of the mahogany desk. "Read this. Then we'll talk."

Gregg eyed the folder's ultra-secret label. "Shall I read it here?"

"Yes. Take your time," Sinclair said with a wave.

The briefing of Agent Michael Gregg consumed the rest of Sinclair's morning. By mid-afternoon he was once again hunched over his golf ball but concentration was elusive. He hefted the putter, appreciating the luster of its cast bronze club head, adjusted his grip slightly and steadied himself. Don't squeeze the club, he reminded himself. An easy grip, head steady.

A lopsided smile suggested itself on his face. Right about now, Michael Gregg and his team of ten NSA agents would be airborne, en route to Vieux Fort Airport, St. Lucia, in the British West Indies. Sinclair stroked through the ball. Probably be *months* before Gregg finished unpacking his boxes. The ball rolled smoothly across the carpet to its target.

KATE READ long into the night about microwave frequencies and gigahertz, radio telescopes and the electromagnetic spectrum, making careful notes and gathering a list of questions for astrophysicist Milton Rensler. From the reading, she gleaned that the man she was about to interview, SETI's long-time pioneer, was no less than a dedicated genius. At six AM, she was jolted awake by that thought and by the shrill chirping of her digital alarm clock. Great, a crash course in radio astronomy and too little sleep, hardly the best frame of mind in which to approach a high-tech interview with a genius.

No question about it though, SETI was a fascinating project. It had become an international effort, a global network of satellite dishes, all monitoring microwave frequencies from space, listening for the kind of electronic noise— "leakage" they called it—that might characterize the chatter of another intelligent civilization in the galaxy. Governments and scientists worldwide believed strongly enough in the existence of extraterrestrial intelligent life to have spent billions of dollars to search them out and hear what they might have to say.

By nine, Kate was firmly engaged in Highway 101's morning arterial sclerosis, four unbroken rows of cars packed together and stretching south from San Francisco to San Jose. When the clock on her Mazda's dashboard read nine-forty, she knew she'd be late. She gripped the wheel hard in frustration. Traffic. She hated being late—for anything. She hoped Rensler would understand.

Her mind roamed as she inched along. A vacation really was what was needed. Maybe Jack would be up for another sailing vacation, another bare-boat charter cruise. That would be fine. She and Jack had taken such a holiday a year ago, chartered a "bare boat," a sloop that was provisioned and equipped, but bare for lack of paid crew. They'd flown to the island of St. Martin to pick up the boat and had sailed it together through the Leeward Islands in the Eastern Caribbean. Easily the best vacation she'd ever had. Anachronistic St. Martin, rustic Anguilla, Nevis, luxurious St. Barts. She sighed at the memory of turquoise water, untrammeled beaches of soft white sand—

Suddenly her foot was coming down hard on the brake pedal and she lurched to a halt inches from the rear bumper of the car ahead. She exhaled in relief. Awfully close.

Thirty minutes later she spotted the hulking dark canopy that was the hangar at Moffett Field and joined the stream of cars down the off-ramp. Signs directed the way to NASA/Ames' security gate. After a yard of red tape, the guard motioned her through and she wove around the vast parking lot until she found a parking spot a quarter of a mile from Building A. She locked her car and hurried to the entrance to meet Dr. Rensler.

From the outside, Building A was an unremarkable five-story cube, a no-nonsense research facility hemmed in by the enormous parking lot. Kate stood near the double glass doors waiting. Apparently Rensler was also running late. A sharp wind swirled over the Santa Cruz Mountains and down into the valley, driving impressive blue-gray storm clouds in its way. She nodded in satisfaction. To one who'd been hoping for more shape and purpose, a rousing good storm was infinitely preferable to the amorphous drizzle of the previous several days.

She drew her blazer close, fending off the chill. And suddenly there it was again—a peculiar wave of anticipation washing over her as though something momentous were about to happen, something to which she'd been unaccountably drawn, even directed. Foolish, she thought dismissively. Still, how easily she might have passed right over the paragraph on the last page of the *Chronicle*. That thought was followed by another: How random was life? Might there be someone or something pulling every string with exquisite attention and meticulous care? She folded her arms against the fast-approaching storm front. Combine late night reading about extraterrestrials with three hours' sleep and the mind could bend itself around some pretty steep curves.

Ω

2

MILTON RENSLER DREW TO A STOP in a silver Ford Taurus and lowered his window. "Ms. Lipton?"

"Yes."

"Sorry I'm late. The meeting ran longer— Let me park and we'll get started."

As he drove past, Kate noticed his license plate: *2N 2 1420.* Hadn't she read last night that 1420 was the frequency of something in megahertz? Hydroxyl? No, hydrogen. The Water Hole, that was it: *Tune to 1420.*

Rensler eased the Taurus into a reserved space and climbed out, and Kate studied him as he walked toward her. He was a compact man, probably mid-sixties, older than she'd imagined from either his voice on the phone or the published photos of him she'd seen at the library yesterday. He looked fit, like a man who watched what he ate. Dark chevron eyebrows angled above darker eyes giving him a look of mild surprise. His hair had probably also been as dark at one time; now it was snowy white and worn neatly combed up and back with a carefully drawn side part. There was a slightly shy, tentative smile conveying an appealing warmth.

He reached out to shake her hand. "Ms. Lipton, it's a pleasure to meet you. Hope you haven't been standing here long? Looks as though a storm's blowing in."

She returned his smile. "I just got here myself. The traffic was, well, normal. Please call me Kate."

He nodded and held open one of the heavy glass doors. "My office is on the second floor. We'll get you signed in."

She walked in to face an expressionless security guard who was barricaded within a desk fortress. She printed her name in his visitors register, after which he took an inordinate amount of time scrutinizing her ID and entering information into a computer terminal—running a fast check on her, she surmised. Finally she was handed a laminated plastic badge which she clipped on, and she was buzzed through the locked doorway.

"Sorry about the rigmarole," Rensler said, leading the way to the elevator.

His office was a cramped room on the second floor, made to seem even smaller by an odd assortment of unmatched furniture that must have been exhumed from a World War II warehouse. A small window overlooked the parking lot and Moffett Field. As she surveyed the room for a place to set her things, her eye passed over a wall of floor-to-ceiling shelves crammed with books, magazines and spiral binders. A tower of computer printouts had been erected on tables opposite the cluttered desk. On either side of the desk were battleship-gray filing cabinets, and behind the desk, an ugly brown naugahyde chair.

"Here, have a seat." He hurried to clear books and papers. "Sorry about the mess. Can I get you coffee?"

"That'd be nice, thanks. Cream if you have it."

He left to get the coffee and Kate looked around, eyeing the stacks of printouts. Their edges had been labeled with a felt-tipped marking pen, an obscure code of letters and numbers. The only item of decor in the room was a poster thumbtacked to the wall behind the desk, a photograph of Planet Earth as seen from space. The familiar image never failed to move her—the sapphire blue sphere swirled with streaks of white. The caption across the bottom of the poster read: GOOD PLANETS ARE HARD TO FIND. She cleared a corner of Rensler's desk and set out her tape recorder and note pad of questions.

Rensler returned moments later with two mugs. "Sorry. We're out of cream." He shrugged off his jacket and hung it on a hanger. "So," he said as he climbed behind his desk and into his seat, "you've heard our budget's in jeopardy."

"Here's the article." She handed him a copy of the clipping which he quickly perused. "Mind if I tape our interview? It'll save me a lot of furious scribbling."

"Fine." He handed back the article with a mournful shake of his head.

She pressed the START button on the recorder. "Is it final? Will Congress cut SETI from the budget?"

He shrugged. "We go through this every year. Congress casts about for what to cut and fixes on us. Congressman Wainwright gives his annual speech on the floor of the House: 'If we can't afford to fund defense, we certainly can't afford to fund curiosity.'" Rensler's voice rose to a stentorious baritone in imitation. "Then he usually says, 'Why don't we stop fiddling with all that SETI equipment and just *listen*, if someone out there is trying to communicate with us?' Which, of course, is exactly what we're doing—listening. It shows they don't understand the project."

"If you go through the same thing every year, don't you think they'll eventually re-fund you?"

"Probably. We're only a minute fraction of NASA's budget, as that article says, so cutting us won't buy much. Still, with the deficit there's an urgency to at least *appear* to be *trying* to eliminate unnecessary spending, and I'm afraid there aren't many in Washington who find us necessary."

"What's the status of your project? I read that you're able to track over eight million microwave frequencies at once."

"True. We're close to three-fourths of the way through our Big Sky phase where we scan the entire sky. After that, we'll focus a network of larger dishes on a select group of 2800 star systems that look promising." Budget problems were suddenly light years from Rensler's mind. "If anyone's out there broadcasting we should hear them within my lifetime, certainly within yours."

"How distant are these selected star systems?"

"Up to one hundred light years. But we're expecting to get the Arecibo dish dedicated to SETI for a period of time."

"What would that do for you?"

"The Arecibo dish in Puerto Rico is a one-thousand meter radio telescope. The larger the dish, the more precise the signals we'll receive, and from farther away. We could hear signals from up to five hundred light years distant with Arecibo. Ideal for our scan of selected star systems."

"Is there only one of these dishes?"

"No. Other than the one in Puerto Rico, there's a large radio telescope facility on an island in the Eastern Caribbean—St. Lucia—and a sizeable dish in Bonn, West Germany. Course that's not ours, but it could be brought on-line as part of the international SETI effort."

"Are you concentrating only on the Water Hole frequencies?"

His look held surprise and pleasure that she'd done her homework. "Pretty much. We'll actually begin monitoring out to 2.22—the frequency of water," he added quickly. "That's outside the actual Water Hole range. Longer term, probably out to ten gigs."

Kate had read about the Water Hole the previous evening, a quiet window of microwave frequencies in the electromagnetic spectrum on which a signal could be transmitted across space and penetrate the Earth's atmosphere with minimal distortion. She'd read that every type of matter vibrates at its own unique frequency, which was how scientists could announce, for example, that so-and-so planet had an atmosphere containing ammonia. In the past she'd wondered how they could be so certain of what was out there without dispatching a spaceship to bring back a tube of air. From the previous evening's reading, she understood. Every single body in the heavens emitted a unique microwave signature depending on its chemistry. A little like an individual's fingerprints or DNA.

Not all frequencies could reach Earth without distortion. But the so-called Water Hole frequencies in the range of from 1.4 to

1.7 gigahertz could easily reach Earth, just as certain channels on the radio could be tuned in more clearly than others.

"Why do you call it the Water Hole?"

"Oh, it's neat. See, 1.4 gigs is the frequency of Hydrogen, chemical symbol 'H'. And 1.7 is the frequency of Hydroxyl, chemical symbol 'OH'."

"H_2O."

"Right. And of course a water hole is a place where animals gather to drink."

"Yes."

"Most scientists agree that for intelligent life to evolve, a watery planet is necessary, one with a hydrogen-rich atmosphere. So the hydrogen frequency or one near it might be the logical frequency on which to transmit a message to another civilization."

Kate nodded. "A place where intelligent life might naturally think to congregate in order to communicate."

"Exactly. We also include the tritium frequency within the Water Hole. Tritium is a by-product of nuclear fusion. An advanced civilization with fusion technology might be expected to have tritium waste in its atmosphere."

"Have you identified any promising signals?"

"Not yet. We're searching for the proverbial needle in the cosmic haystack. Within the Water Hole alone there are millions of frequencies to monitor. Then figure there are around forty billion suns in the Milky Way Galaxy and that each of these suns has an average of ten planets, as do we. So, four-hundred billion possible planets. If those solar systems are like ours, maybe one in ten is suitable for life. Are you familiar with Frank Drake's formula on this?"

Kate shook her head.

"Drake estimated that in the Milky Way Galaxy there might be a total of four thousand planets, of those four-hundred billion or so, that have actually developed intelligent life *and* that may be communicating at a given moment in time. We've had a few signals we thought were from ETIs—from an extraterrestrial intelligent source—but the signals turned out to be false alarms from other sources."

"What kind of sources?"

"There was the pulsar signal. That was a surprise. The signal was regular and strong and definitely extraterrestrial. It caused quite a stir until we figured out it was caused by a neutron star, a pulsar. That's not to say discovery of the first pulsar wasn't exciting; it was. Just not an intelligent signal."

"Any others?"

"We've picked up signals from our own Voyager and Magellan space probes. A few signals caused by anomalies in the Earth's atmosphere. Some terrestrial signals. And the 'Wow' signal. We still haven't figured that one out."

"The 'Wow' signal?"

"That's what the researcher wrote on the printout when he found it. He came across this quite remarkable signal and wrote 'Wow' on the page beside it. We've refocused on the same coordinates and frequency but we can't duplicate it."

"If you do find an ETI signal, wouldn't it have been sent hundreds of years ago? You don't suppose whoever sent it would be waiting for a reply?"

"No. Well, maybe they are. It's possible that other life forms live much longer than humans. Have you read about the recent fruit fly studies in the genetics of longevity? The intriguing life span extension? Anyway, we'd probably send an answer, but if it's from hundreds of light years away, it'd take hundreds more for our reply to reach them."

"And it's not possible that any communication could travel faster than the speed of light?"

"Probably not." He paused, considering. "There is a theory in quantum physics that suggests the possibility of tachyon technology. Emphasize *theoretical*. We don't know if the tachyon really exists, but it would be damned convenient if it did."

Kate looked at him and waited for the explanation she was quite sure would follow.

"A tachyon is a theoretical particle that can travel faster than the speed of light. The only limit on its speed is that it can't travel *slower* than light."

"Oh," she said. "But I thought according to Einstein, nothing could travel faster than the speed of light."

"True. But in quantum physics, the physics of the *sub*atomic, the laws part company with Einstein. Einstein's physics is the physics of the huge, the *super*atomic, if you will. Evidence exists that a tachyon particle is subatomically possible, maybe even inevitable."

He'd lost her but she persisted. "Are you suggesting we might find a real-time interstellar communications network?"

He shrugged. "Maybe. Possibly a tachyon particle beam transmitter that could communicate with a distant body in real time, instantaneously." He leaned back and laced his fingers across his midriff.

"Is anyone exploring such a possibility?"

"The Gluon Gang—the quantum physicists. We have a quantum physicist on SETI, Howard Vaughn at MIT. He was mentioned in that clipping you brought. And of course Steven Keppler at Cambridge."

"Do you think I might contact Dr. Vaughn?"

"Sure. Let's see. I have his card here somewhere." Rensler began thumbing through a ratty-looking Rolodex that was brimming with unfiled slips of paper. "Here it is. Howard Vaughn, Department of Astrophysics."

Kate jotted down the phone number. "What do you honestly expect to find, Dr. Rensler?"

"I think we'll hear a signal in the Water Hole that'll tell us how to tune into an interstellar communications network. That's my hope, anyway. I think we'll find a continuously broadcasted message that essentially says, 'To join the Galaxy's talk circuit, tune to Channel so-and-so.' Instructions."

"2N 2 1420."

He gave her a look of delight. "Right!"

"And if we find it, what then?"

"First of all, once we detect a promising signal, we'll spend time making sure it's the real thing. After the pulsar signal we're wary of jumping to the conclusion that signals are from ETIs. So if anyone hears anything, the SETI scientists around the world will tune in and study it for a while to make sure it's authentic.

"As to what we might hear, that's anybody's guess. I have a feeling, though, that the interstellar communications network, if it exists, has built-in safeguards, so that civilizations not ready for certain information would be unable to receive it. If technological breakthroughs are shared, I expect only civilizations ready to receive and utilize them responsibly would be able to access them. Maybe I'm being unrealistic but—"

"And what if, after all that listening, we find nothing?" Kate had to ask.

"It wouldn't prove that we're alone in the universe, of course. Maybe ETIs just don't want to talk to us. But it would suggest that if we are alone, how utterly miraculous and special our existence is. Maybe it would cause us to place a higher value on our planet, to care for it more scrupulously."

Kate glanced at the poster on the wall behind his head. A good planet, indeed. "I admit I haven't been feeling especially optimistic on that score lately."

Rensler nodded. "We have the know-how. All we lack is the intent—and probably the leadership. Don't quote me on that," he added with a quick smile.

"No. Other than a 'tune to Channel so-and-so' message, what sort of information do you think you'll find?"

"Who knows?" He reached up to smooth his white hair. "How about a manual on *How to Avoid Thermonuclear War*, or *How to Build and Fuel Spaceships*? Information on how to avoid or repair the effects of global warming, or maybe the colonization of space, stable geo-political systems, cures for disease, the nature of the universe, what happened prior to the Big Bang, how to beat the speed of light."

"That's quite a list."

"Mm. Then again, the signal might contain information entirely beyond our frame of reference and comprehension, though somehow I doubt it."

This discussion wound down and Kate shifted topics. "What's your opinion of UFOs?"

The question prompted an indulgent chuckle. "In the most literal sense, that there have been flying objects that we've been unable to identify, obviously they exist. As for visits from ETIs, very unlikely. Possibly robotic space probes, but very doubtful that LGMs have come calling."

"LGMs?"

"Little Green Men," he said. "Manned space travel over great distances is simply not practical. First of all, they'd need to be a species with an extraordinarily long life span to travel the distance. And our civilization has only been generating electronic leakage for sixty years, so I doubt any ETI civilization has had time to hear us and make their way to our solar system. It's possible but highly unlikely. More likely that they'd beam a signal: 'Give us a call.' Cheaper, too."

"I read once about the possibility that ETIs might transport their DNA across space in a capsule and then regenerate themselves as life forms when they arrived."

Rensler gave her a narrow look. "Lots of things are imaginable. Some are theoretically possible. But if their colonization craft are roaming around our solar system, I think we'd have spotted them by now."

"Couldn't they hide behind Jupiter or out in the Asteroid Belt?"

"To what purpose?"

"Mining?"

"I should think there'd be systems nearer their own for that."

"To watch us? Hiding because they don't want to frighten us or interfere?" Kate heard her own pleading tone and felt her cheeks redden in chagrin. *Don't you see, a part of me desperately wants there to be LGMs—and LGWs—roving about.*

"Maybe," he said. "That's slightly more likely than their swooping down on a cornfield in Nebraska to pick up a few humans. As for the 'take me to your leader' cliché, if they know we're here and they want to land, they certainly already know who our leaders are and where to find them."

"If we find an interstellar communications network, do you honestly think our government would tell the public about it? Would it be announced?"

"Hard to keep it quiet. Hands down, it would be the biggest scientific discovery of modern times, maybe of all time. How are you going to keep that quiet?"

"Mm."

"Eventually it would be announced," he said. "I'd see to it. SETI is an international effort. If we find proof that we're not alone in the universe, all the people of the Earth must share in the knowledge. It can't be the exclusive domain of a single government or a handful of scientists. We've had any number of symposia on this issue and for once the scientific community is in agreement: The content of an ETI communication must be shared. The news that we are not alone absolutely belongs to all of humankind."

The sermonette sounded rehearsed. Obviously he'd been asked the question before and somehow the answer rang false. He was either naïve or evasive, she decided, stealing a fast glance at her watch. They'd been talking for over an hour, which surprised her. She'd be sorry for the interview to end.

"If Congress cuts your budget, can your work continue?"

"Somewhere, perhaps even with private funding. Were you aware that Stephen Spielberg has been a major SETI contributor? He gives time, makes the occasional speech to encourage people to donate. And of course Carl Sagan is a tireless leader in the field. And other countries would carry on, even if we don't. I think the possibility that the Germans or the Japanese might be first to receive the signal is impetus enough for our government to keep a hand in. At least I hope so."

"I don't know how much time you've allotted for me this morning, but—"

"Would you like to see our computer room?" he asked brightly.

"Definitely." Kate made a point of appearing enthusiastic about computer room tours. Her experience was that especially the men she interviewed waxed rhapsodic over their computer rooms. She could easily envision them as ten-year-old boys asking if she'd care to check out their Super-Nintendo. To decline would be to erase all rapport in an instant. In this case, though, Kate didn't need to feign enthusiasm; she was fascinated by Rensler and his work. He led the way out of his office and down the hall to a windowless door and inserted a card into a slot. Kate heard a faint click before he opened the door and held it for her.

At first she had the impression there was no one else in the room, but then she noticed a dark-haired man huddled over his work in a far corner. The room was perhaps sixty feet long and twenty feet wide and nearly every cubic foot of it appeared to be taken by some piece of high-tech equipment.

"Over here are the data analysis computers," Rensler said. "The incoming signals are recorded into these databanks." He gestured at a long bank of storage devices. "The data analysis utilities scan the signals and zero in on anomalies, which are then both stored and automatically printed out on high-speed laser printers." He led the way down the far side of the room and Kate followed.

The flooring consisted of yard squares of white formica, a raised computer room flooring that allowed for the spaghetti of cables to be buried underneath and out of the way. Kate's heels clattered sharply on the tiles and she tried to lighten her step.

"How many computers are analyzing the signals for patterns?" she asked.

"In this room alone we've got the equivalent in minicomputers of a Cray supercomputer. Each processor analyzes a segment of frequencies. They operate almost constantly to keep up with the incoming signals. If anything unusual comes in, it's flagged and logged so we'll know where to find it. Computers are running the show. It minimizes our staffing needs. Pretty soon they won't even need me."

They approached the far end of the room where the lone technician was at work. Rensler said, "These computers operate the dish orientation and frequency modulation routines—in other words the listening end of the project. Over here are the oscilloscopes and spectrum analyzers so we can watch the frequencies on-screen."

He flipped a switch on one of the oscilloscopes and the screen flickered to life. He typed a few commands and a quivering horizontal line streaked across.

"What would an ETI signal look like?" Kate asked.

"You'd see patterned fluctuations in this line. This is the Hydrogen Line. You can see it's clean. No background noise, no interruptions. There's your Water Hole."

He flipped on a second oscilloscope and typed more commands. "Compare that with a higher frequency of 58 gigs. See the interference?"

Kate stared at the erratic display on the second screen and nodded. "Mm."

The technician looked up.

"Tim," said Dr. Rensler, "meet Kate Lipton, a journalist. Kate, this is Tim Thurmond, my chief assistant and electronics wizard."

The young man glanced at Kate with a slight smile, murmured, "Nice to meet you," and turned back to Rensler. "Will you have a few minutes this morning? I put a rather, ah, intriguing canary dump on your desk. It came across from Alan this morning, directed to my STAR subdirectory."

"Really? How are the modulation sequences coming?"

"Okay. The error was in the Doppler shift for 1.92 gigs." The tablet in front of Thurmond was covered with scribbles and notations.

"Ms. Lipton and I are nearly done," Rensler said.

Kate followed Rensler out of the computer room and they returned to his office. She persuaded him to pose beside his "Good Planets" poster and snapped a few hurried photos. Then she gathered her belongings and they rode the elevator down to the lobby.

"What's a canary dump?" she asked.

"What? Oh. A printout that's been marked with one of those yellow high-lighters. We—" but he didn't finish the thought. Instead, the elevator doors opened and he held them for her.

She looked at him and smiled. "I hope you'll add my name to what must be a long list of people you'll call if you hear anything from the ETIs. Here's my card," she said, fumbling in her blazer pocket. He accepted the card and she immediately knew it would be lost in the clutter.

"Of course," he said quietly. "Who do you think will publish our interview?"

"I'm not sure. I'm a freelance journalist, so I'll submit it to several. Any suggestions?"

"Not really. Maybe *Science America* or *Omni*."

Kate nodded and considered a moment. "Dr. Rensler, would you be willing to appear on 'Focus'?"

"Oh, well, I'm awfully nervous in front of television cameras. I don't think I'd—" He looked down and studied his shoe tops.

Kate smiled. Once he overcame his shyness, his passion for SETI would captivate any television audience. "Viewers would find SETI fascinating. Most people are scarcely aware of the project."

"And NASA might—I'll think about it. How's that?"

"Fair enough. If you don't mind, I'll follow up with you in a few weeks on the outcome of the budget cuts. And I'll send you a copy of the article so you can correct anything I've written before it's published."

"Excellent. It's been a pleasure, Miss Lipton," he said, becoming formal all of a sudden. He reached out and shook her hand. Kate sensed he was in a hurry, and she left him, checked out at the security desk and headed for her car. During the long walk, she reviewed the last few moments of the interview in her mind. Once seated behind the wheel, she withdrew her note pad and jotted down, 'Alan Somebody,' 'STAR subdirectory,' 'canary dump,' and the single word, 'Security,' followed by a very large question mark.

As often happened following an interview, she began thinking of questions she wished she'd asked and she scribbled these down as well. For one thing, in that vast computer room there'd been only Tim Thurmond. Where was everybody? And she'd forgotten to ask about Jacobsen's work at Harvard and Vaughn's project at MIT.

Ω

3

THE REMAINDER OF THE DAY FLEW BY. Kate drove home and immediately sat down at her computer to transcribe her notes while the interview was fresh in her mind. As she did so, she added to her list of follow-up questions. She glanced up from the monitor occasionally to consider her small garden, absently noting discolored leaves on one of the rose bushes. She should spray for leaf rust.

Kate had lived in the same downstairs garden apartment for seven years. It was located on Twenty-second Street in Noe Valley and was situated behind a three-story, street-front building that served to buffer traffic noise and afford a sense of seclusion. Altogether, there were four small rooms—bedroom, kitchen, living room and office—plus a microscopic bathroom and one woefully inadequate closet. She continually fought against the tendency to accumulate clutter in this confined space. Magazines were her special nemesis, towers of them thrusting ceilingward like springtime weeds. She accorded each publication its own vertical airspace and when a stack grew too high, she pruned out bottom issues. When she considered purchasing a home of her own, something with spacious closets or higher ceilings, she always discarded the idea. This place suited her whereas a stratospheric mortgage did not. Here she'd been able to save; rent was cheap and expenses minimal. It made for a simple life, which in a complex world seemed both more illusive and desirable.

As the transcribed notes were printing out, her thoughts returned to the notion of the tachyon beam. She scanned the books she'd checked out of the library for references to the tachyon particle but found no mention of it. She might hunt up a physicist over at Berkeley. Maybe it was worth a trip to Boston and a chat with Howard Vaughn. Jack could join her. They could return by way of New York, take in a play. She smiled at herself—still angling for a vacation.

At six she peered out at the darkening sky and realized she'd lost track of time. That hadn't happened in months, and it seemed a good omen, possibly symptomatic of a reviving interest in her work. When she met Jack at Noe Valley Pizza an hour later, she could barely contain her enthusiasm as she described the interview with Rensler. Jack swallowed bites of veggie pizza and listened, smiling occasionally at her earnestness.

"What?" she asked.

"You're starting to like what you do again. Looks good on you."

"It's been that obvious?"

"Mm."

"And SETI? What do you think?"

"What do I think? I think it's absolutely incredible that the U.S. government is paying a bunch of physicists millions of dollars to listen for little green men."

"LGMs."

"Right. And I'll add, as I'm sure Congressman Wainwright would, 'while there are children who are homeless and hungry.' But I do agree with you, it's fascinating."

He returned with her to her apartment. Later that night, lying in bed unable to sleep, she listened to the soft drone of his snoring. How would NASA handle news of an ETI contact? For years there'd been reports of UFO sightings and contacts with extraterrestrials, all denied or dismissed by federal authorities as crackpot. But the government must give them some credence. Why, otherwise, did they continue to fund SETI? And she did not agree with Dr. Rensler; the information in an ETI message would not be shared, not if the feds behaved true to recent form. The international scientific community could pen all the agreements it cared to, but if the U.S. government was funding the project, they wouldn't relinquish the competitive edge that might arise from the content of an ETI signal. National security would take precedence over any high-minded notions of scientific good fellowship and cooperation.

That thought continued to intrude as she worked on the Rensler interview over the next two weeks. She speculated on the possible disclosures that might come with an ETI contact, the technological breakthroughs Rensler had mentioned. Lucrative patents might arise from such information. Superconductor technology, nuclear fusion, breakthroughs in physics, astronomy, biology, chemistry. The possibilities were staggering. ETI information might form the basis of an entirely new industry or weapons system or branch of science, might yield some new alchemy that would give the one in possession of it an enormous competitive edge. No, it would not be announced.

Which agency, Kate wondered, was tasked with overseeing SETI security? She should check that out. The FBI? The CIA? The NSA? What if it turned out to be the NSA, Jeremy Sinclair's agency?

The thought produced a shudder of revulsion as the harsh memory flooded back, the year she'd spent in Washington, D.C., fresh out of college, clutching her computer science degree as though it were the key to the Beltway Kingdom. She'd been much too dazzled by her good fortune, recruited into the NSA's computer systems group without a résumé, or at least no practical job experience to speak of. It had seemed a great stroke of luck at the time. She'd been assigned to work on a software project that the National Security Agency was developing with and for the Pentagon.

And what a *wuss* she'd been. Or maybe she was too hard on herself. Naïve, certainly. Her boss had been Jeremy Sinclair. Almost from the outset, he'd heaped enormous pressure and long hours on her rookie head, testing her endurance, or so she'd thought. The only way she could hope to meet his excessive demands was to work sixteen-hour days. At some point he'd begun hinting for sexual favors, harmless stuff initially, easily dismissed as playful, affectionate; her boss liked her. Certainly fielding such advances had not been covered in any computer science curriculum she'd encountered.

Then it became more overt, an almost calculated form of harassment which had escalated over the course of thirteen interminable months. That was over ten years ago, but the memory still sickened her. Her word for it was *icky*. Remarks about her clothes, her figure, questions about her sex life, her activities outside the work place—practically nil, given the sixteen hour days. Then began the jostling, poking and touching. She'd forced herself to dismiss it all: He was her boss. Boys will be boys. Hang in and play along. Eventually she'd be promoted or transferred beyond his sphere of influence. There'd been no shortage of clichés and rationales she could summon to overlook it all.

But on December tenth, 1983, it had changed.

As usual she'd been working late, testing a routine and making the best use of computer time during off-hours. She was alone in the computer room, seated at the end of a long row of green-glowing computer terminals when Sinclair materialized behind her. She remembered stiffening in premonition.

"How's it going?" he asked solicitously.

"All right. I'm tired. This'll finish in a few minutes. Then I'm done for the night."

He stood behind her chair and he began rubbing her neck and shoulders.

"Stop," she protested, straightening and arching her back as though to fend him off.

"You're tense," he murmured. "Can't let my best rookie wear herself out. Feel how tight you are." A hand worked its way from her neck and shoulders down to the middle of her back. He was strong and he managed to pin her in place with one hand while the other moved suddenly to cover and fondle a breast.

"Stop it!" she shouted, or thought she shouted, though in retrospect it might have come out as a fear-choked whisper. She struggled futilely to free herself. There was no one around to hear or help. Jeremy Sinclair was a careful man. She cringed now, recalling the thick laughter.

"You like this," he said, his voice low and husky. "You know you do. Relax." He continued to hold her in place with one hand and began groping beneath her clothing with the other, his fingers working their way beneath the fabric of her bra and into the soft flesh of her breast. Then she became aware of a pressure against the nape of her neck.

It was then, as she felt his erect penis, insistent and bulging against the back of her neck, his hips beginning to gyrate in tempo with his breathing, that she'd laid claim to some previously untapped well of determination and strength. Her hand closed around a hard lead pencil and she stabbed it ferociously into the back of his hand, toppling a cold cup of coffee in the process. He let out a yelp of pain and she freed herself, launched herself to her feet and turned. He grabbed her wrist with one hand and tore at her blouse with the other, whereupon she slammed a knee upward into his crotch, prompting his second even louder cry of enraged agony.

She remembered running then, with the kind of mindless frenzy that only tremendous fear and anger can produce, out the computer room door, down the hall to the stairway and down flights of stairs to the basement parking garage. She was never certain whether Sinclair had followed or not. She'd been too frightened to look back. With her purse and keys upstairs at her desk, she'd then fled the garage and run, jogged, and finally exhausted, walked for what seemed like miles before finding a cab.

Her landlord had finally let her into her apartment after subjecting her to a long speech about her lack of consideration, the lateness of the hour, her dishevelled appearance and the fee he charged for lost keys. She walked in to a ringing phone—unceasing, insistent, shrill. Eventually she'd picked up the receiver and held it to her ear:

"If you mention this to anyone, I'll have to kill you."

Just that. Then a click and a dead line. It was an utterance Sinclair would repeat to her over the phone for the next several months, long after she resigned—that had happened the following morning—after she'd changed her phone number, and then her address. And even a year later, after she'd moved back to the Bay Area, there was a call: *If you tell anyone, I'll have to kill you.* Kate thought he meant it and was cowardly enough to never call his bluff. She'd never told a soul.

Three years ago, Sinclair had been promoted to top man at the NSA. Now Kate occasionally saw his face on the evening news, assembled with various cabinet secretaries and President Geller around the Cabinet Room conference table. Kate knew she held information that in a just world ought to bring him down. The fact that she'd told no one rankled. It meant he'd won. He'd humiliated her, molested her, terrorized her, and won. Now she thought of her anger as a molten, subterranean knot, self-contained, held within; and time had done very little to chill it.

TOWARD THE END OF JANUARY, Kate called Milton Rensler's office with her list of follow-up questions. A woman answered, identified herself as Rensler's secretary, and told Kate he was unavailable. Kate asked to speak with Tim Thurmond and was put through.

"Tim, I don't know if you remember me. We met a few weeks ago in the computer room at your facility. I was interviewing Dr. Rensler?"

"Right."

"Apparently Dr. Rensler isn't available, and I have a few questions."

"Shoot."

"How many people work on SETI at your facility?"

"Ten, off and on. Some work nights and have other daytime jobs. We have three shifts of two technicians plus a weekend crew. Plus Dr. Rensler, myself, and the secretary."

"Are you actually monitoring the frequency of water, or only the range from 1.4 to 1.7 gigahertz?"

"We're ready to extend it out to 2.22, but funding for the hardware is up in the air. We'd like to cover the entire quiet microwave window from one to ten gigahertz, provided we get funding. We were hoping it would come through this year but—" His voice trailed off.

She hesitated, then asked, "Can you tell me which agency handles SETI's security?"

"I really—" He hesitated. "That's probably something Dr. Rensler should answer."

"Could I reach him later today?"

There was a long pause. "I'm not real sure when he'll be back. He's out of town."

"Oh. Can you tell me anything about Jacobsen's work at Harvard?"

"They pretty much have the same setup as we've got here. But they also have the programming group that handles our software, so they're larger in terms of staff. They send us software updates every so often."

"And Vaughn's group?"

"Quantum physicists. It's largely a theoretical effort, but they do help with some of the data analysis."

"Well, that helps. I'm nearly done writing the interview. I'll send a copy for Dr. Rensler to review. You say you're not certain when he'll be back?"

"Just send it on down. I'll try to be sure he gets it."

"One last thing. Were you able to fend off the budget cuts?"

"Yes, I think so, at least for this year."

"Well, that's good. Thanks for your help, Tim."

After they hung up, Kate replayed the conversation in her mind, deciding Thurmond was either seriously ill-informed or notably evasive. Odd that he'd be uncertain when his boss was to return. He'd *try* to be sure Rensler got a copy of her article? She dismissed it as part of the bureaucratic fog bank that typically shrouded NASA and government research projects.

Overall, she had enough to complete the article. Later that week, she mailed a copy to Rensler's office with a friendly note requesting that he call her, but she wasn't surprised when, after another two weeks, she'd not heard from him. Rensler was a busy man.

"Sir, Michael Gregg is calling from St. Lucia," announced Edith, Sinclair's secretary, over the intercom. "If you have no further need of me, I'll be heading home. My grandson is visiting and I'd like to—"

"Fine. Put him through," Sinclair snapped. Moments later, "Yeah, Michael, what's up?"

"Ah, Jeremy." Gregg took a moment to gather his thoughts. "Rensler and some of the scientists are a bit up in arms about the, ah, the security arrangements down here." Gregg weighed his words.

"So?"

"They're unhappy about the closed-circuit monitors, the lack of privacy."

"Really."

"They're irritated that we haven't allowed them outside the compound unsupervised, and they're asking for access to outside phone lines. They'd like to call family, reassure them. They've been down here quite a while. Rensler, in particular, is upset. He'd like to call his wife."

"And how have you responded to these complaints?"

Gregg continued, undeterred by the sarcasm in his boss's voice. "They also object to the high-voltage wire atop the fence circling the compound. Vaughn suggested that jungle animals might be injured or killed."

Sinclair groaned. "That's quite touching. So you very nicely pointed out that we're not running a Club Med down there."

"Well—"

"And that their scientific efforts are regarded as the highest national priority, that as such, the President himself has demanded the most stringent security possible. Right?"

"More or less. Is there anything we can do to accommodate their concerns, some small gesture we could make to smooth this over?"

Sinclair bristled. He was charged with cloaking the work of these scientists in an impenetrable fortress of secrecy. "Michael, here's what you tell them: They have in their hands what is potentially the most significant scientific breakthrough of modern times. Ask them to consider the lengths to which others might go to get their hands on the contents of that signal data. Tell your band of whining scientists that this level of security is as much for their protection and safety as for the good of their project and their country. Tell them to stop griping and focus on the work they've been sequestered to accomplish. Clear?"

A long silence followed.

"Michael, this is where you're supposed to say, 'Yessir, very clear.'"

Finally, Gregg said, "It is clear. It's just—if we could allow them occasional use of the phone under close supervision, that might be enough."

"Out of the question. Absolutely not. Next thing we'll have families flying down to St. Lucia, clamoring to be allowed in for visits. As I'm sure you're aware, phone calls can be intercepted by just about anyone with the right equipment. That *is* what all this electronic signal interception is about. They ought to understand that better than anyone."

"Rensler's the main one. Maybe we could allow him use of our secure line—"

Sinclair cut him off. "I am not about to start a precedent here, Michael. The answer is *no*. These people have all been vetted and briefed, along with their families. They understand it goes with the territory. Your job is to enforce it. I agreed to closely supervised excursions outside the compound and that's as far as

I'm willing to go. Even then, your people are to be all over them like fly paper. Tell Milton Rensler to deal with it. His wife is fine."

"You're watching her?"

"Of course. Anything else?"

Michael Gregg sighed. "Here's a thought. We might allow Rensler to write his wife a note of reassurance. We'd look it over, make sure it's clean."

Sinclair considered this. It was a compromise over which he and his people could exercise total control. "Okay, Michael. Actually, it might be for the best. It'll calm Rensler's wife. Send the note to me. I'll look it over and see that it's delivered. Is that it?"

"Yeah. Look, I promised them I'd pass along these concerns."

"Which you've done."

"Right. Sorry to bother you, sir."

As they hung up, Sinclair caught his reflection in the glare of the office windows. Night had settled over Fort Meade, Maryland and his face scowled back at him from the dark backdrop of the landscape. There remained a rugged handsomeness to the countenance, deep lines trailing down from the eyes and nose to the edge of the narrow mouth and firm jaw. He smoothed back his thick hair, fortunately all still his own. He smirked at the thought of the Beltway cadre of middle-aged men who'd begun sporting rugs, most of them obvious and ill-fitting. He'd toyed with the idea of touching up some of the gray—a lot were doing it—but even that wasn't yet necessary.

He spoke into the intercom. "Edith—" No answer. That's right, she'd left for the night. Something about a grandson.

Ω

4

DURING THE WEEKS following the Rensler interview, Kate Lipton turned her attention to other projects and more or less forgot about SETI. Her article was accepted for publication and was scheduled for the June issue of *Science America*, and a check arrived for her efforts. She gave little thought to Milton Rensler or his project until a morning in mid-March. She'd been knocking out new-product press release paragraphs for a "What's New" column she edited and was awash in boredom, when her phone rang.

"Kate Lipton," she answered.

"Oh, um, hello. This is Tim Thurmond," the voice ventured uncertainly. "From Dr. Rensler's lab?"

"Right. How are you, Tim?"

"Well, actually, I, um, I'm fine. I wonder if we could meet this afternoon?"

"Sure. What's up?"

"It's just, well, it's important. I'd rather explain in person if you don't mind. I could come to your office if—"

"Let's meet half way. Do you know the Bay Meadows Lounge in San Mateo? It's near the race track."

"I'll find it. What time?"

"Four-thirty?"

"Thanks a lot."

Kate heard relief in his tone. She worked on the "What's New" column for a few more hours, distracted and intrigued by the call, and at three-forty-five, left to meet Thurmond.

When she walked into the Bay Meadows Lounge, she surveyed the room and spotted a dark-haired young man sitting alone at a table, warming his hands on a coffee mug. Their eyes met and he waved. She realized she'd otherwise not have recognized him; he'd barely looked up or spoken when they'd met in the computer room. Kate took a seat across from him and ordered coffee.

"Thanks for meeting me," he began haltingly. "I couldn't think of who else— I'm not sure if there's anything you can do either but—" He was obviously anxious and stared down into his coffee, lacing his fingers around the mug. Beside him on the table was a worn leather briefcase. Kate said nothing while he gathered his thoughts.

"It's about Dr. Rensler," he said finally. "He's disappeared."

"What do you mean, disappeared? When?"

"Right after you came down for the interview. The next day he said he'd been called to Washington and left the lab. I figured he was going to meet with Ralph Burch at NASA or with the Congressional oversight committee. That's usually what he does when he goes to Washington. The thing is, as far as I can tell, he never got there. I called Jacobsen's lab a few days later and spoke with Alan Westlake, one of their technicians. He told me he hadn't seen Dr. Rensler and that neither Jacobsen nor Vaughn was around. He said they'd both been called to Washington the same day Dr. Rensler left."

Kate sat forward. "And you haven't heard from him since?"

"Nothing. And now I learn that apparently Jacobsen and Vaughn have disappeared as well. Alan called me a few days ago and asked if I'd heard anything from Dr. Rensler and whether I'd seen either Jacobsen or Vaughn. I haven't."

"Strange," she said.

"There's more. Yesterday Dr. Rensler's wife called. She wanted to meet last night after work, wanted me to bring her husband's appointment calendar. So I went into his office and found his calendar. She picked me up after work and we drove around. She was stressed out. Kept glancing in her rear-view mirror, over her shoulder, you know, anxious, like she was afraid someone was following her."

"Were they?"

"At first I didn't actually pay much attention until I realized how agitated she was. Grace Rensler seems like the nervous type. But then I decided she was genuinely frightened. I turned and watched out the back but I didn't notice anything. Anyway, I asked her when she'd last seen her husband, and she said he'd come home late that afternoon and packed a bag. Said he was going to Washington. A car came for him—two men. She said it surprised her. She'd expected to be allowed to drive him to the airport. He kissed her goodbye, told her he didn't know how long he'd be gone and not to worry, and left with the men. That's the last time she saw him, and she hasn't heard a word since." He fingered a paper napkin, unfolding and refolding it into small, hard-pressed squares.

"That was back in January, what, seven weeks ago?"

"Eight." He looked up at Kate and shook his head. "I know it seems odd I called you, but right after you left, Dr. Rensler mentioned that he'd given you Howard Vaughn's phone number and that you had said you might call him. I wondered if you did and whether you ever reached him?"

"No, I didn't. I wrote up the interview and submitted it to *Science America*. It'll appear in their June issue. I tried to reach Dr. Rensler, but when he wasn't available, I didn't pursue it." She considered Thurmond's explanation for contacting her—the chance she'd spoken with Vaughn—and decided it was implausible. There had to be more to it.

"Did his wife say anything else?"

"Not much. She hinted that she was being watched. Seemed frightened. I gave her Dr. Rensler's appointment calendar and she dropped me back at the lab and drove away."

Tim and Kate sat in silence for a few long seconds. He reached over and touched his briefcase, considering. Then he said, "One other thing. You remember the day at the lab? Before you came by, I'd received an E-mail from Alan Westlake. He'd sent me a segment of a data stream they received on the hydrogen line."

"The hydrogen line?" Kate had pretty much forgotten her cram course in radio astronomy.

"1420 megahertz. The hydrogen frequency—"

"Oh, right."

"At the low end of the Water Hole. It's a frequency all the SETI groups monitor. Anyway, the printout shows some anomalies."

Tim paused, then reached into his briefcase and withdrew a stack of greenbar computer paper. He shoved his coffee cup aside and spread the printout on the table.

Kate looked at it, noticing a succession of tightly-packed rows of ones and zeroes, a series of, to her, meaningless binary numbers. Segments of it had been highlighted with a bright yellow marker. "A canary dump," she thought aloud.

Tim looked up and nodded. "Right." His eyes returned to the printout and grew wide. He pointed to a row of numbers. "Right here. It's a consistent flat signal until here. Then this odd sequence continues for several pages." He thumbed the half-inch stack of paper. "I've never seen anything like it."

"Is it an ETI signal?" She squinted hard at the green striped pages.

"Can't say. I wanted to talk to Dr. Rensler about it, but he left before we got the chance. I put this on his desk and when I retrieved the calendar for his wife it was still there, buried beneath accumulated mail."

Tim swallowed a gulp of coffee. "That same morning when I put this on his desk—and this is really strange—Jacobsen's group patched us a modified orientation module. They called later and claimed they'd isolated a bug and wanted it fixed immediately. That's a fairly standard occurrence, except that they always warn us in advance. This update was sent across with no warning at all."

His fingers riffled the pages of the printout. "The new software was transmitted and we've been running it ever since. I was waiting for Dr. Rensler to return, but today I decided on my own to interrupt our receiver orientation schedule, to examine these same coordinates to see if the signal was still there."

"Was it?"

"No."

"Do you think this represents an ETI signal?"

"Possibly. It's too soon to call it that, but it's an anomaly, for sure. Maybe just the coincidental alignment of a quasar behind— No, that can't be," he said, more to himself than to Kate. "With access to a radio telescope I could—"

Kate felt a wave of excitement wash over her and stared hard at the printout. She could be looking at an intelligent communication from another world. She tried to take in the enormity of it. What news story or event could be more riveting, more significant?

"Do you have access to a radio telescope?" she asked.

"Not without Dr. Rensler's pull. It's tough to get time on the big radio telescopes. They're booked up months, hell, *years* in advance."

"Have you ever seen a signal like this?"

"Never."

The answer hung suspended in a long silence. SETI might have found Rensler's needle in the cosmic haystack. How should she handle it? More to the point, how would the government handle it? If SETI researchers were disappearing, the government was playing it close to the vest. Thurmond must realize that. The government would keep it hushed at least long enough to analyze the data. She voiced this thought to Tim.

"I've worried about that, of course. All of us on the project have, especially since Ralph Burch replaced Dr. Cousins as Director. Cousins was always adamant about sharing any extraterrestrial message with the world. Burch is a different animal altogether, or at least that's what most of us in SETI feel."

Kate said, "I heard that he's a scientist."

"Yeah, but he's also a bureaucrat. They brought him over from White Sands. A few months ago, Alan Westlake and I decided v.e should work out our own alert bypass system, basically a way to monitor and circumvent the monitors. Anything comes through the system flags as unusual, a copy is automatically directed to a special subdirectory. If Alan's group finds it, he immediately transfers a copy to my subdirectory. And if our end finds the signal, I do the same for Alan. We set it up with the highest possible security, so access is limited to me and Alan. Dr. Rensler's aware of the arrangement and tacitly approved. Well, he more or less looked the other way."

As she listened to Tim, Kate took in a larger meaning behind his words. At least a sub-group of NASA's SETI's people were concerned over the very thing that appeared to have now happened—the government's ultra-secret handling of an inter-cepted ETI signal. Concerned enough that Thurmond and Westlake had obviously gone to great lengths to devise a way around the problem, to ensure the news of the ETI contact would not be squelched. It had to be the reason behind Thurmond's request for this meeting; she was a journalist with multimedia access.

"So, Tim, one day after Alan sends you this data, Rensler, Jacobsen and Vaughn disappear. Then Rensler's wife contacts you, frightened and anxious. Alan calls, looking for his boss. A lot of coincidences, Tim."

"I know. They update our orientation software with no warning. Too many coincidences."

"If you're the U.S. government, where do you take these scientists? CIA Headquarters? Where?"

He looked thoughtful, his dark eyes shifting to gaze out past the parking lot toward the Bay Meadows Race Track. He turned back and his look was troubled. "Not Langley. I'd take them someplace where they could monitor and analyze the data. Probably the Arecibo facility, Puerto Rico, Bonn, someplace like that."

"And their families? What do you tell them?"

He shrugged. "They've been called away on urgent, top secret government business. I'm sure Rensler must have told his wife something like this could happen."

"Then why would she be upset? And why would she want to see his appointment calendar?"

"He's been gone a long time. She was looking for him, hoping there'd be some clue to his whereabouts in his calendar?"

Kate nodded. "Why didn't they take you, too?"

"They have no idea Alan caught the signal, nor that he sent it to me. I was waiting to discuss it with Dr. Rensler, waiting for him to come back."

"Do you have any way of translating this?" Kate reached across the table, suddenly needing to touch the printout.

"From these pages? If it's intelligent, it's probably encrypted in some way. I wouldn't know where to begin— Maybe if I—" He withdrew into deep thought.

"What do you want to do, Tim?"

"Huh?"

"Should we search for Dr. Rensler?" There weren't a lot of options. They could either search for him or do nothing and wait for Rensler to contact his lab.

"I don't know," he said.

"Did you ever discuss with Dr. Rensler what might happen if you found an ETI signal? How it would be handled?"

"Of course. It's to be immediately made public. Has to be." He shook his head with a rueful sigh. "We've been looked on by the rest of NASA as the oddball stepchild. Even today, you don't get a lot of respect from the scientific community for hunting down ETs. We're victims of the snicker factor. We were actually thinking of changing the project name from SETI to High Resolution Microwave Survey."

Kate nodded. "That's suitably cerebral. I'd say all of a sudden someone's taking you *very* seriously."

"Yes."

"News of an ETI signal would have to be the story of the century. No, the millennium. What other single piece of news could be more stunning than certain proof that we're not alone in the universe? I can't think of anything. Can you?"

Tim shook his head. Then a look of near-horror crept in and quickly transformed his face.

"Maybe a cure for cancer," Kate continued. "No. This is much bigger."

"You can't report this! At some point, maybe, but— Hell, I shouldn't have contacted you. I couldn't think of what else to do. Washington can't be allowed to slam down a permanent lid. I'm afraid—and so was Dr. Rensler—that that's exactly what they have in mind, and probably part of why Ralph Burch was brought on board. He'd go along with it. But this is classified information. If you report it, I'll be fired by morning." He looked shaken. "Besides, you don't really have anything here, just some scientists who have disappeared. We don't know what the signal means. It's not really—"

Kate broke in to reassure him. "I have no intention of reporting this now. I wouldn't jeopardize you or your job. Let's work together to find Dr. Rensler. Then—how about if you give me an exclusive on whatever we find—when and if the time comes to publish it?"

"And you'd wait till Dr. Rensler or I say the time is right?" She nodded.

"Fair enough," Tim said, mollified. "Where should we start?"

"Mrs. Rensler, I suppose. Do you know how to reach her?"

"I have the Renslers' home phone number."

"Let's start with that. Why don't you call and see if she'll meet with us, say, tomorrow?"

"Saturday. Okay. What time?"

"Try for three."

Tim agreed, and shortly afterward they left the restaurant and he walked Kate to her car. Evening had settled over the Bay Meadows Track and the parking lot.

"Are you a race fan? Is that why you chose this place?" he asked her.

She laughed. "No, but I like the view and the atmosphere. My hobby's sailing." She unlocked her car and climbed in, then rolled down a window.

Tim withdrew a slip of paper from his pocket and handed it to her. "Here's my home phone number if you need to reach me. I don't think we should communicate on the lab's phones." Then he said, "By the way, you asked on the phone which agency handles our security? The National Security Agency is in charge. The guards at our security desk are all NSA."

She felt the familiar pang of revulsion. "Jeremy Sinclair," she murmured, "a bad, bad man."

He looked at her.

"Call me tomorrow, as soon as you've set up the meeting with Grace Rensler."

Driving home, Kate couldn't help but envision coming face to face with Jeremy Sinclair. Dr. Rensler's wife had hinted she was being followed. Tomorrow, if they were able to arrange a meeting with Grace Rensler, Sinclair's people might be close by and watching.

Ω

5

KATE GRABBED THE PHONE on the first ring, expecting the caller to be Tim Thurmond.

It was Jack, and his greeting brought a smile. Jack Sullivan had been in Kate's life for nearly two years, a friend and some-times-lover, and a bookish Deputy District Attorney for the City of San Francisco. Now in his late thirties, Jack was fast approaching burn-out with the legal profession. For the past year and more, she and Jack had bumbled along through a mostly satisfactory, on-again, off-again relationship that suited them. Whenever it became too intense, they each took a step back. It reminded Kate of the cha-cha. Her friend Nadine scoffed at the relationship, keeping up a well-meaning propaganda barrage: Jack was "ideal spousal material," as though a relationship were some sort of serviceable garment that could be run up quickly on a machine.

"He's perfect, Kate. Your age. Bright, a little shy, a little studious, good-looking, well-employed. Best of all, he likes you—a lot." She'd tick off assets as though reading a want ad.

"Carport, sailboat, all-electric kitchen," Kate would contribute.

"Grab him before he gets away," was usually in the litany, followed by the inevitable reference to the ticking away of Kate's biological clock.

"Please, Nadine. I've researched this. Sixty percent of all my friends who got married are now divorced, and half of those who aren't wish they were. There's a sterling testimonial to the institution of wedlock. Look at that word, Nadine. *Wedlock*. Jack and I have a relationship that does not involve either of us locking ourselves up in an institution."

Nadine could be counted on to dismiss this argument by launching into a paean on the wonders of her own marriage to Chet, a marriage which Kate and Jack had more than once observed was well past its pinnacle. Usually Nadine concluded her counsel with an oracle of fear, something on the order of: "You're thirty-five—"

"Thirty-six."

"Thirty-six, still a size eight, attractive, more or less wrinkle-free. But in five years it's all going to bulge and fall. How will you feel at forty when you lose Jack Sullivan to a woman half your age?"

"Awfully glad I didn't marry him. Besides, since when did marriage deter a middle-aged man who's bent on pursuing a twenty-year-old? If Jack wants a co-ed in five years, I'll be very pleased not to endure the added misery and expense of a divorce. And if we're still happy with each other, bulges and all, that might be just the time to tie the knot."

Why was it so many of Kate's married women friends viewed her single status with alarm? Jack and I are just fine—*aren't we*?

She smiled broadly now as she heard Jack's voice on the phone. He'd been swamped at work and they hadn't spoken all week.

"Hi there, Sullivan. How's life?"

"Old Fuss 'n' Feathers is driving me nuts."

That would be Archie, Jack's boss, who reminded Jack of an anxious ostrich.

"I'm calling to see if you'd care to go sailing this afternoon. Thought I'd invite Chet and Nadine."

"A little nippy for sailing, isn't it?" She eyed shifting branches outside. Even in the confines of the yard the morning breeze was stiffening. By afternoon it would gather itself into a big blow.

"So we'll break out the foul weather gear. Should be beautiful out there," he said evenly.

Jack was proud owner of a new Cal-35 sailing sloop. From late spring through September, he and Kate often ventured out under the Golden Gate Bridge for the weekend, usually heading north to Tomales Bay or south to Half Moon Bay. Occasionally Chet and Nadine came along, unless they were in the throes of one of their non-speaking phases. But March seemed awfully early in the season for a sail. Besides, Tim Thurmond would be calling.

"I can't, Jack. I'm on an assignment and I'm expecting a call any minute. Then I'll have to go out."

"It's Saturday. Since when do you work weekends? I'll have you back by five."

"Sorry, can't do it. I'll take a rain check though."

"I'll be trying out the new kevlar sails. Eat your heart out."

She laughed. "That is a singularly disgusting expression. I didn't realize the sails had been delivered."

By mid-afternoon, she was devoutly wishing she'd gone sailing. Instead, she waited by the phone for Tim's call. At three she lost patience and tried him at home. After four rings, his message machine came on and she decided against leaving a message.

She didn't hear from Tim at all that day, nor on Sunday. Nor was he at the lab on Monday morning when she tried calling him there.

KATE'S MAIL seldom arrived before late afternoon. As she sorted through it on Monday the postcard caught her eye. Who would send her a tourist postcard of the Golden Gate Bridge?

She turned the card over and read a hastily scribbled message:

"Hi. Sorry to break our date Saturday night. Called away suddenly on business. Not sure when I'll be back. Call you when I can. Hope you're not angry. Love, Tim."

"Love, Tim"? How odd, how inappropriate. And what "date Saturday night"? She noticed the address. He'd gotten it right, except that he'd added "Suite UAL1395."

She slumped to a chair and stared out at a clump of weeds flourishing in a corner along the back fence. Nearby, the hydrangeas were covered with newly opened blossoms of soft purple-blue.

"The zip code," she murmured, squinting at the faint postmark. 94080. She grabbed the phone book and quickly located 94080 on the zip code map in the Yellow Pages. South San Francisco. The card had been postmarked Saturday, March 16, at 11:05 AM. If he mailed it Saturday, why hadn't he written, "our date tonight" instead of "our date Saturday night"? The answer could only be that he'd written it Friday night after leaving the Bay Meadows Lounge.

What would he be doing in South San Francisco? She stared at the zip code map and it was a moment before it hit her: the card had been mailed at the airport. Other than industry and houses, there wasn't much in South San Francisco. "UAL" must refer to United Airlines. And that was a flight number, not a suite number! He'd flown out Friday evening on United's flight 1395. From that she was to deduce his destination.

It also meant he could not have been completely free as he'd scribbled the message, or it would not have been so cryptically composed. Someone had been watching over his shoulder. Her heart was racing as she dialed United Airlines and asked for information about flight 1395. It had departed San Francisco at 6:35 PM Friday evening and arrived in Miami at 3:35 AM, Saturday. Miami? Of course! From there he would have caught a connecting flight to Puerto Rico and the Arecibo radio telescope installation.

Her heart was really thumping now. Which airlines flew Caribbean routes? She and Jack had flown on National to reach the Leeward Islands for their sailing charter. They'd flown to Miami and from there to St. Martin. She dialed National Airlines, asked about flights to Puerto Rico, and jotted down a disappointingly short list. There were two regular flights, one on Tuesday morning, another Thursday afternoon.

She began checking other airlines and learned that American had regular flights into Puerto Rico Monday through Friday. If Puerto Rico was his destination, he might have taken American's Monday flight, *today's* flight. That meant he'd laid over in Miami all day Saturday and Sunday, which didn't make sense, especially if he was being forcibly transported by government agents. Maybe they hadn't taken him to Puerto Rico.

She sifted through various possibilities and decided to impose on a travel agent friend for a list of all Caribbean-bound flights that had departed Miami any time from four AM, Saturday, through Sunday evening.

The agent called back the next day with the information, and Kate took down another short list of flights. None were to Puerto Rico, but there'd been flights to St. Croix, St. Lucia, St. Thomas, Martinique, the Bahamas, Trinidad-Tobago, and Jamaica. Kate listed flight numbers, departure and arrival times and then asked the agent if she could get her hands on passenger lists. Sorry, the agent explained, airlines never give that information to the general public.

Maybe Jack could obtain passenger lists. She studied the list of flights. None of them seemed to fill the bill. But then her eye returned to the flight to St. Lucia. It rang a bell. Hadn't Rensler mentioned a second radio telescope installation in the Caribbean? She hadn't included it in her article but she still had the tape from the interview. She brought out the portable cassette recorder and began listening.

Fifteen minutes into the Rensler interview, there was his voice explaining, "The Arecibo dish in Puerto Rico is a one-thousand meter dish.... There's a large radio telescope facility on an island in the Eastern Caribbean—St. Lucia—and a sizeable dish in Bonn, West Germany...."

St. Lucia, an island north of the Grenadines, if memory served. She grabbed an atlas and located it, a microdot in a group known as the Windward Islands. Together with the Leewards, they comprised the Lesser Antilles.

Now what? With an educated guess as to Tim's destination, what could she do? Think like a journalist, Kate. First of all, nothing would be served by racing off to St. Lucia. If Jeremy Sinclair and the NSA had whisked these scientists off, poking around that place could be risky and unlikely to yield answers. They'd have the scientists in a secure facility. She couldn't just knock on the door and start asking questions. Tim's disappearance and his postcard, the vanishing of the other scientists, Mrs. Rensler's furtive contact with Tim, the transmission Tim had shown her, all suggested she act with caution. Maybe she could contact Mrs. Rensler on her own, though if the woman was under surveillance, that would be risky.

She searched for the Renslers' home phone number, but came up empty; it wasn't listed. She certainly couldn't ask Rensler's secretary for it. Instead, she dialed Jack at the D.A.'s office.

"Hi. It's Kate."

"You missed a great sail."

"I should have gone. The call I was expecting never came. How were the kevlar sails?"

"Terrific. Incredibly light. Actually, it's pretty foolish putting them on a Cal-35, a bit like putting a jet engine on a crop duster, but we were doing eight knots out there, Kate. We were passing everyone."

She smiled at his ardent enthusiasm, made appreciative sounds, and finally said, "Listen, Jack, I need a favor. Actually, two favors. I need an address and all I can give you is a vehicle license plate."

"What's it about?"

"I can't say right now, but I'll stake you to a fresh crab and artichoke dinner if you'll help."

"Bribing a District Attorney?"

"Jack—"

"I shouldn't, Kate."

"Please. It's very important," she pleaded gently.

"Oh, all right. I'll try. What's the license number?"

"2N 2 1420. A Ford Taurus."

"What's the second favor?"

"An airline passenger list."

Jack mumbled, "Federal," and then, "No, no way."

"Try, Jack. It's life and death."

"Give me the damned airline and flight. I'll see what I can do."

Very sweetly she read off the St. Lucia flight number.

"What night?" he asked.

"What night?"

"For crab and artichokes?"

"How about tomorrow?"

"You're on," he said. "And you'll tell me what it's about?"

"As much as I can."

After they hung up, Kate tried to work, tried without success to concentrate on an article she'd been asked to write that summarized local area network alternatives. It had to be the dullest thing she'd ever put her mind to. She reread a paragraph that began with the sentence, "Some consider the token ring topography superior to the speedier starburst mapping in that it maximizes the integrity of transaction traffic along the bus." From there the article careened off the edge entirely into an even deeper trench of tedious obscurity.

"That's it. I can't stand it."

She stood, walked outside, began yanking weeds from the rose bed. She plucked withered blossoms from the hydrangeas, fed the roses and thought about what to tell Jack. She needed to discuss the chain of events with someone; she needed a second opinion. And a vague plan was taking shape in her mind, though if it were to have any chance of success, she'd need Jack's involvement—a lot more than a mere address and passenger list. She'd need him to captain a sailboat.

Ω

6

JACK CALLED KATE BACK the following afternoon. "I shouldn't be doing this, but here it is: The car is registered to Dr. Milton Rensler at 2425 Santa Cruz Avenue in Woodside." He sounded grumpy. "The passenger list is going to take time. Does that still earn me a crab dinner?"

"Of course."

"And you'll tell me what this is about?"

"We'll discuss it."

"Don't tell anyone I helped. It could get me in a shitload of trouble."

"I know, Jack. I won't say a word, except *thanks*."

She retrieved a street map from her car's glove compartment and located Santa Cruz Avenue a few miles west of Highway 280. She'd driven through the town of Woodside many times. It was a small, isolated community of gated homes and estates belonging to corporate executives and the horsey set of Silicon Valley.

But now what? She knew where the Renslers lived. She might be able to obtain Grace Rensler's phone number. But if the phone was tapped— And what could she possibly say to Rensler's wife?

She spent most of the day mulling over various options while winding down the dreary article on local area networks; the rent still needed paying. In the afternoon she shopped for dinner. On

Church Street she bought artichokes and salad fixings and walked to Drewes Meat Market for fresh crab, gulping hard at the price. At the Cheese Company on Twenty-fourth Street she bought brie, French bread and a bottle of chardonnay.

Jack arrived shortly after six-thirty, and they settled on the floor in Kate's small living room for the meal. Jack laid a fire in the fireplace, and as they ate, Kate told him the story. She described her meeting with Tim at the Bay Meadows Lounge, the plan they'd made to meet with Grace Rensler, and the postcard that had arrived in Monday's mail. She debated briefly but decided not to tell him about her history with Sinclair.

"So, what do you think?" she asked finally.

Jack wiped his mouth, leaned back against the front of the wing-back chair and stretched his legs out across the floor. He sighed contentedly, patted his stomach and shook his head. "Wonderful."

"What, the dinner? The story?"

"Both. How certain was Tim that NASA has identified an intelligent transmission?"

"Fairly certain. What else explains the disappearance of these scientists?"

He shook his head in disbelief. "Mind if I look at Tim's postcard?"

She stood up and carried dishes into the kitchen, rummaged around in her office and returned with the postcard.

He studied it for several moments before saying, "Either I should be jealous—you've been holding out on me and this guy's got a serious case on you—or—"

"Or?"

"Or it's a very odd message."

"Trust me, Jack, Tim Thurmond has no romantic interest in me. That message was written in an intentionally provocative way to get my attention. And someone—the NSA, I'd guess—was watching over his shoulder when he wrote it. Otherwise, he'd have let me know straight out instead of writing this. My guess is he managed to convince them he needed to send it to prevent a girlfriend's concern over his sudden disappearance. That suite number, if you take it with the zip code, well, what other explanation could there be?"

"I don't know. UAL—United Airlines, that's for sure. If your theory's correct and Tim's been abducted, then my opinion, if you want it, is that you'd be a bubble off plumb to pursue it. If the government's spiriting NASA scientists off in the middle of the night and hiding them on St. Lucia, they aren't going to welcome a journalist nosing around."

"You think I should drop the whole thing?"

"What choice do you have?"

"Contact Mrs. Rensler. Go to Boston, try to dig up something on Jacobsen and Vaughn. Fly down to St. Lucia to see if there's some way of getting in touch with Tim."

"Right. Dash down to St. Lucia and discover what? The finer points of solitary confinement? If the government's decided news of the transmission is not for public consumption, you can't honestly believe they'd tell you about it and let you fly home to write it up for *Science America*."

Jack Sullivan, pontificating lawyer, was warming to his subject, and Kate fought back irritation as he continued.

"If the NSA is involved and they consider the information vital to national security, you'd be safer playing stick ball in a mine field than going after this story." He stared at her and she looked away, disconcerted. "You're a technical journalist, Kate, not Woodward and Bernstein. Your entire foray into the realm of investigative journalism has consisted of who would be first to market with Windows and two-bit graphics."

"*Bit-mapped* graphics."

"Whatever."

"I wrote an article on industrial espionage," she countered defensively, "and another on computer hacking." Even to herself it sounded weak. He's right, she thought. She rose to stir the fire. "Can you think of any other story that would be more stunning or significant than one reporting a verified contact with intelligent life elsewhere in the galaxy?" She bent to poke life into the logs.

"No," he replied after a moment. "It could change everything, how we view ourselves, our planet, knowing we're not alone in the universe. Eventually they'd have to announce it. Besides, how long can they keep the families and friends of these scientists in the dark? They've got to be told something."

"I want to talk to Rensler's wife. She might have heard something."

"If the scientists remain in St. Lucia much longer, wouldn't the feds allow their spouses and families to join them? That or make some provision for them? They'd have to give them some explanation."

"Maybe. Then again, they do work for NASA, Jack, top-secret governmental research. Don't you suppose that folks in a government think tank have already developed a contingency plan, just in case SETI hits pay dirt? I think it's likely."

He answered that question with one of his own. "Why did Mrs. Rensler contact Tim?"

"She's looking for her husband, Jack. I'd sure like to talk to her."

"You're not actually thinking of calling her?"

"No," she said, adding softly, "I'm thinking of meeting with her, but I'll have to figure out how to do it without being observed."

"That's nuts." His look was stern, but a trace of a smile played at the corners of his mouth. "You're going to do it, aren't you?"

"Of course."

"I wish you wouldn't."

He looked away, but his concern was unmistakable. She half-expected that at any moment he'd announce it was late, that he had to leave, that he had an early court appearance. Maybe Nadine was right. She should look at why, after nearly two years, they were so damned tentative with each other. Was it a

question of vulnerability? If she told him she really needed him
to stay, would he head for the nearest exit?

"Who'm I going to get to crew for me?" he muttered, "swab
the decks, cook the meals, clean the heads, if you're locked up
in Leavenworth?"

"My thought exactly," she said with a short laugh. "Any
interest in a bare-boat cruise in the Windward Islands?"

"Funny. I admit I've always wanted to sail down there, ever
since our sail in the Leewards. I've heard the sailing's even
better. And the snorkeling— Not only that but there are a slew
of islands in the vicinity—Bequia, Mustique, Carriacou, St.
Vincent, Grenada." He laced his fingers behind his head and
fixed his eyes on a spot above the mantle.

Kate could read her own recurring visions of turquoise waters
and flawless white beaches in his faraway look. "Jack," she said
after a moment, "are we okay?"

"What okay?"

"You and I. Okay, as in happy with our relationship?"

"Of course. Why?"

"Nadine's always telling me I should, well, grab you before
you get away. She nags."

"Don't pay any attention to Nadine. She and Chet are on me,
too. They want all their friends looking like themselves."

"Are they right? Are we too—"

"Too what? I'm happy with *us*, just as we are. Aren't you?"

"Yes."

His eyes had dropped down from the mantle to meet hers.
"Know what I appreciate most? That you haven't tried to nail my
shoes to the floor. I like your independence. I like that you
aren't slyly maneuvering me into a corner. I've extricated myself
from too many relationships that deteriorated to the level of
clingy possessiveness."

If Jack trailed a legacy of clutching females behind him, Kate
knew she brought her own history, of men who'd tried and
failed to corral her spirit. Her experience had been that an
independent woman often attracted men in search of a challenge.

The problem was, once she'd been conquered, or once they believed her to be conquered, they moved on, in search of the next challenge.

Suddenly she understood her own and Jack's caution—and it *was* caution, not cowardice. Jack was unlike any man she'd ever been with. He was, himself, independent, and he'd never tried to trample her spirit.

She said, "What I really think is that we have a real chance at something good. I've gone slow because I don't want to wreck it."

"Exactly." He laughed, relieved. "You know how I hate these discussions. All men do. Women thrive on them. They always end up as weighty, pressure-packed analyses chocked full of words like marriage, commitment and expectations. You're right, though, we do have a chance. But I also believe that if you analyze and tinker with a thing long enough, you're likely to break it."

She reached over and ran a finger along his cheek. She smiled and stood up. "Let's go tinker with the dishes. And then maybe with a few other things. I can think of one or two that might not break."

"Like bed frames?"

Her brow furrowed. "An area where further study is needed."

"A scientific approach—"

"—would be just the thing."

Ω

7

JEREMY SINCLAIR ARRIVED HOME LATE. He double-checked the alarm and reset the system for the night. Normally he'd have arranged with Vanessa's Service for a female companion for the evening, but not tonight. He was distracted, profoundly concerned. Up till today, things had been going well. But a late call had come in from Michael Gregg. He replayed it in his mind as he tossed his jacket over a chair back and headed for the kitchen.

Gregg had begun without preamble. "We have a problem."

Jeremy's stomach had tightened at the words, and now, two hours later, it was still in knots. He doubted he could eat but he ought to have something. He loosened his tie, opened the freezer and stared, began flipping through boxes of microwavable frozen entrees, and chose one.

"What problem?" he'd prompted Gregg.

"Villanova and Radcliffe delivered Tim Thurmond yesterday. Thurmond had a computer printout in his briefcase, a segment of the Code Shepherd signal. Sections had been highlighted with a yellow marker."

A jumble of thoughts and questions had cascaded through Sinclair's mind and he began ticking them off to Gregg. Was Thurmond the one who'd marked the printout? How long had he known of the signal? Who had he been in contact with since? What did they have on file on Thurmond?

Gregg jumped in. "I've questioned him. He claims to have told no one."

"We know he was contacted by Grace Rensler. We have a transcript. It's here somewhere. Her phone, house and car are all bugged." As Sinclair spoke, he burrowed through papers to a stapled transcript Edith had placed on his desk that morning. "Give me a minute, Michael," he said as he scanned the document. "Rensler's wife called Thurmond and asked to meet with him. She asked him to bring her husband's desk calendar."

"Thurmond mentioned that. He claims he only retrieved the printout a few days before he was picked up. He mentioned meeting with Rensler's wife and says that he took the printout from Rensler's desk when he was looking for the calendar. He insists that's when he first thought to look at the data."

Sinclair flipped through the pages of transcript. "Their conversation seems to bear that out, but—" He had a nose for these things; it felt wrong. "Who put the printout on Rensler's desk?"

"Thurmond did, but he claims it was one of those things routinely flagged by the system, automatically generated by software. Thurmond said he often placed printouts in Rensler's in-box. He doesn't even remember when it came in."

"I thought Jacobsen's software had blocked the signal. I thought it was purged or something."

"Apparently not. Anyway, Thurmond claims he spoke to no one about the signal."

"Who's he met with since? Shit! You realize, suddenly we've got a gaping hole in the security net, Michael."

"Possibly."

"No, *definitely*. Interrogate him."

"We have."

"Harder." Jeremy began a list. The net had to be mended. Damage control. "Agents Villanova and Radcliffe should be back in the Bay Area by now. I'll send for them."

"They left here yesterday afternoon."

"They'll need to be questioned. I've got to think this through, Michael. I'll arrange for an immediate search of Thurmond's house and office."

The call had ended shortly afterward and Sinclair had immediately contacted Radcliffe and Villanova in San Francisco and summoned them to Maryland. They were scheduled to arrive the next morning. Was Thurmond telling the truth? The countertop microwave beeped at Sinclair. He dumped the contents of the plastic container onto a plate and stood at the counter, forking in untasted bites. The surveillance on Grace Rensler, already extensive, would have to be intensified. Next time she left the house, they'd enter and search for the calendar and anything else that might seem suspect.

KATE DROVE SLOWLY into the town of Woodside, turned onto Santa Cruz Avenue and began winding her way through oak-covered hills. Driveways along the road were widely spaced, suggesting that each residential estate might sprawl over an acre or more. She found the mailbox for 2418 on her right, and then a quarter of a mile farther up the road, the Renslers' driveway on the left. It was marked by a plain aluminum mailbox and the numbers 2425.

She barely slowed for a glimpse of the driveway before continuing past. Then she glanced in her rear-view mirror. A white car with two passengers was parked directly across the street from the Renslers' driveway. She rounded a curve in the road so that the white car was out of her line of sight, then pulled a fast U-turn and parked. From her vantage point she could just make out the sloping curb of the Renslers' driveway and the nearby mailbox.

It was eight-thirty. If Mrs. Rensler had plans to leave the house, she probably wouldn't have as yet. Kate settled in to wait and speculated on the occupants of the white car. Probably NSA, she thought.

By ten-thirty she'd reached the conclusion that she was wasting a perfectly good morning. She'd indulged in a series of paranoid fantasies about meeting up with Jeremy Sinclair, had pondered the surrounding hillsides' flora and fauna, counted enough passing Beemers, Mercedes and Volvos to lend credence to that automotive cliché about Silicon Valley's Boomer generation. No one had ventured in or out of the Renslers' driveway. Maybe the woman never left the premises. She wondered whether the white car was still parked across the street. She'd bet money on it. She stretched her stiffening legs, wishing she'd thought to bring coffee and something to eat. She'd give it another hour.

By noon, she'd used up all entertaining thoughts and most of her patience and was about to abandon the vigil when she spotted the silver Taurus emerging from the Renslers' driveway. The car turned right and began heading down the hill, and Kate started her car and followed at a discrete distance. The white car came into view—a Buick sedan—as it executed a speedy U-turn and took up position between Kate and Mrs. Rensler. This could get tricky. What if they noticed her? But they probably wouldn't. Their attention would be on Grace Rensler, and they'd be less apt to concern themselves with whomever might be following.

Their little three-car parade proceeded through the sleepy village of Woodside and headed east in the direction of Highway 280. Mrs. Rensler led them under the freeway and then began weaving sedately through broad residential streets, down a hill and into an area of shops, restaurants and boulevard traffic. They moved at a pace that might have marked them as a modest funeral procession. Kate felt exposed, though less so after allowing few cars merged between her own Mazda and the Buick. At a busy intersection, she watched in frantic helplessness as the Taurus and Buick passed through on the yellow light, while she was forced to stop and wait it out.

She craned her neck to see and managed to spot the Taurus and then the Buick turning right into a shopping center beyond the intersection. She waited for the light to change and followed.

Grace Rensler had parked her Taurus in front of a Chinese restaurant. Next door to the restaurant was a lingerie boutique called Top Drawers. The Buick took a space a short distance away, and Kate watched as a pair of men in dark suits climbed out and ambled over to stand in front of the boutique.

Kate parked a distance away, alighted and began her best imitation of a saunter in the direction of the Top Drawers Boutique. It occurred to her that she'd look more the part of a casual shopper if she were carrying parcels, so she ducked into Payless Shoes, grabbed and paid for a pair of socks, and strolled back outside. So casual. Never mind that something in her chest was pounding out the rhythm of the Liechtensteiner Polka.

She paused at the Chinese restaurant and pretended to study the menu posted near the door, wishing she'd thought to wear sunglasses or some form of disguise. The two men had stationed themselves on the sidewalk just beyond the boutique and looked both extremely silly and acutely aware of that fact, hovering near the entrance to a ladies' lingerie store. Avoiding their eyes, Kate moved nearer, paused to look in the boutique's window, and then turned and walked resolutely into the shop.

A few young women were pawing through hosiery near the front of the store, and the only other shopper had to be Grace Rensler, a petite, gray-haired woman wearing a tidy print dress with a pink pastel sweater draped over her shoulders. She was absently thumbing her way through a rack of fussy nightgowns.

Kate walked over and began considering a nearby rack of bathrobes. "Mrs. Rensler," she said quietly, "I'd like to talk to you about your husband."

The woman whirled to stare at Kate and then said in a too-shrill voice, "Who are you?"

"Please, Mrs. Rensler, it would be best if we don't attract attention. I'll explain. Keep looking at clothes. I'm a friend of Tim Thurmond's. I met your husband one day at the lab. Like your husband, Tim has disappeared and I'm trying to find him. I'm certain Tim was taken away against his will. I realize those men outside are following you. I need to ask you—"

"Oh, those men! I'm so sick of them trailing around behind me wherever I go. That's why I come here, to get out of the house. It's the only place I can go where they leave me alone. They stand outside like a pair of, well, I don't know what—*fools*—waiting for me to come out. They never speak. It's very upsetting."

"It must be. You come here a lot?"

"A few times a week. You're a friend of Tim Thurmond? You know my husband? Who are you?"

"My name is Kate Lipton. I'm a journalist. I interviewed your husband last January about his work. I'm concerned because both he and Tim have disappeared. Do you know where they've gone?"

Grace Rensler now turned to stare at Kate unabashedly.

"Please, Mrs. Rensler, keep looking at the nightgowns. We don't want them to see us talking." She lifted a heavy robe from the rack and held it to her shoulders, moved to stand before a full-length mirror and slipped it on, studying the fit. It dragged on the floor.

Mrs. Rensler continued her inner debate as to whether Kate was to be trusted. Finally she said, "When Milt left that night he said he thought he'd be gone a few weeks. Now he's been gone over *two months*. I've been out of my mind with worry. This is so unlike him. He'd never— We're very close. He'd never agree to just leave like this. He has high blood pressure, you know, and I'm certain he's run out of medication. He's never been away on business for more than a few weeks at a time, except once, and he took me along."

She halted this rambling discourse for breath and then stammered, "Oh, I know I shouldn't be— I'm not supposed to— I can't talk about—"

"Don't worry, Mrs. Rensler. I won't tell anyone of our conversation. Have you heard anything from him?"

"Finally, a brief note a few days ago. It hadn't been mailed; it just appeared in my mailbox. It didn't even have a stamp on it."

"What did he say?"

"That he was safe and working hard so he could return. He didn't know when that might be. He said he was sorry and told me to be brave." She turned slightly toward Kate and said, "What could there be to be brave about if he's safe?"

"Maybe I can help. Would you agree to stay in touch? We could meet here again in a week. Next Wednesday at eleven-thirty?"

"I'll probably be here anyway."

"Could you bring the letter with you, along with any others you receive?"

"I probably shouldn't, but— What did you say your name was?"

"Kate Lipton. Please, Mrs. Rensler, I'm worried too. I'd like to help locate Tim and your husband, make sure they're safe. But I'll need your help."

Grace Rensler didn't speak for several moments. When she finally did, it was to whisper, "He's been gone so long. I'll be here next Wednesday at eleven-thirty."

The woman's voice held a mix of tears and relief. Her husband had been gone over two months and she was understandably frantic. Kate felt a sudden flush of anger at those who were inflicting such anguish on this woman. She might not have anyone with whom she could discuss it. She'd probably been making excuses to friends and might have become isolated.

Kate said, "I should go. Those men might become suspicious."

"Who *are* they?"

"I'm not certain. Try not to worry, Mrs. Rensler. I'll do what I can to help. Don't forget to bring the letter. It might contain some hint about where he is."

"Yes, well, goodbye, Kate," she whispered. "I'm glad—"

"Goodbye, Grace." Kate gently touched her thin arm as she walked past. The sales clerk asked Kate whether she'd found what she wanted, and Kate told her no, but that she liked the store and would be back.

Back outside, Kate felt the agent's eyes boring into her back. She resisted the impulse to run headlong to her car, walking instead with deliberate slowness past her Mazda and into a flower shop. She bought a dozen daffodils and killed ten minutes talking rose rust with the shopkeeper. When she came out, the men were nowhere in sight. Both the white Buick and the silver Taurus were gone.

She drove home in a rage. Grace Rensler had seemed incredibly vulnerable and distressed. What right did the NSA and Jeremy Sinclair have to shadow and terrorize that poor woman? For weeks on end! No one had a right to do that, even if they were from the government—*especially* if they were from the government.

Ω

8

PRESIDENT LEWIS GELLER waived at Burch and Sinclair to sit.

"So, Ralph," the President said, "what progress have they made on the transmissions?"

"Not much. Jeremy's sent a team of cryptologists from Fort Meade."

"They'll make sense of it, Sir," Sinclair added. "Thus far they've eliminated every known encryption scheme."

"At this point, what we've got is a plate of binary spaghetti."

"Whatever the hell that is," Geller said.

Sinclair and Burch were briefing the President in the Oval Office. The President sat back in his chair and scrutinized the pair, leveling the infamous Geller stare. The two shifted uneasily in their seats.

"How long do you think it'll take?" Geller asked.

Burch made a pyramid of his fingertips and tried to arrange his face into an expression of thoughtful confidence. Sinclair had advised him to appear optimistic but maintain an open escape hatch. "And for God's sake, don't tell the President more than he asks to know," Sinclair had counseled him earlier that morning.

"We're hoping to see a breakthrough within four to five weeks," Burch said. "The team is cautiously optimistic. It could take longer. We don't know the nature of the intelligence that created the encryption scheme so it's difficult to guess at the code's linguistic and lexicographic base, the arithmetic and numerical assumptions, the cultural presumptions."

Geller shook his head, annoyed. "Are there other experts we could bring in?"

"Walter Jacobsen suggested his wife, Margo Jacobsen. She's a professor of linguistics at Boston College. We picked her up last week. Another thing: As you know, Sir, we have not yet relocated the signal. Jacobsen and Rensler both seem to feel the signal has been discontinued."

"But you're still searching for it?"

"Of course. But with each day that passes since its last known position, it becomes less likely we'll re-intercept the transmission," said Burch.

"Disappointing, but then again, if we can't find it, probably the Germans and the Japanese aren't finding it, either. Speaking of which, how about containment, Jeremy? How long can you keep a lid on this?"

Sinclair effected a confident air. "It's handled. The team's families don't even know where these men are."

Burch added, "At Jacobsen's suggestion, we included Steven Keppler from Cambridge in the pick-up. He's a leading quantum physicist and the top researcher into black holes. He's been working on the unified theory. Jacobsen felt they might need him."

"Okay. That's Greek, but if Jacobsen says so." The President stood up and wandered over to the window to gaze out at the rose garden. Then he turned. "How many does that make, Jeremy?"

"In St. Lucia?"

"There and elsewhere. How many know?"

"In St. Lucia, aside from the security and support staff, there are the cryptologists, Jacobsen, his wife, Vaughn, Rensler, Keppler, and now Alan Westlake and Tim Thurmond—Rensler's assistant. Ralph suggested we bring in Westlake and Thurmond too, on the chance they'd spotted the transmission before Jacobsen could fix the software."

"Turns out, Thurmond *had* gotten wind of it," Burch babbled. "He was carrying a printout of part of the transmission in his briefcase when Jeremy's people picked him up."

Sinclair smothered a groan. The Thurmond issue remained extremely problematic but it wasn't something you brought to the Oval Office. They'd begun scrutinizing Thurmond, and Sinclair had concluded the guy was a loose cannon. There'd been weeks following receipt of the original signal for which there was no corroborated account of his actions. Thurmond continued to claim he'd been ignorant of the signal's significance and had only grown curious after his boss had been missing for so many weeks. He'd retrieved the printout only hours before being picked up by Villanova and Radcliffe. He continued to insist that no one else knew of it. He hadn't had a chance to evaluate it, let alone discuss it with anyone—so he said.

Worst of all was the new revelation from Villanova and Radcliffe that Thurmond had mailed a postcard from the airport. They'd looked it over before it was dropped into the box. Innocuous, they said, written to a girlfriend to allay her concerns about his leaving town unexpectedly, but Sinclair had a bad feeling about it. Gregg would have to intensify his interrogation of Thurmond, focussing on the postcard. It was essential they learn to whom it was sent.

The President returned to the sofa where the two agency heads were seated. "Any chance Thurmond might have told anyone about the printout?" Geller asked, seemingly able to read Jeremy's mind. Sinclair had noticed the President had an uncanny knack for homing in on the weakest link in any chain.

"No indication that he did," said Sinclair.

"Ralph, what about closing down the SETI labs in Boston and Mountain View for now to keep these scientists' staffs from speculating among themselves?"

"That might alarm people more than their continued absence. Better to allow them go on with business as usual. I've been by the facilities to allay their concerns. I believe we're covered on that score."

The President was still not satisfied. "What about the families? We can't keep these guys holed up on St. Lucia indefinitely with no communication with their families. They'll kick up a fuss."

Sinclair and Burch spoke at once, and Jeremy backed off with a nod to Burch. "Vaughn, Keppler, Thurmond and Westlake are all single and not particularly close to family. Jacobsen's wife is in St. Lucia so that's handled."

"Rensler's wife is probably the biggest headache," Sinclair said. "Rensler was briefed over a year ago on the basics of the new contingency plan and was told he might be called away. He says he apprised his wife of this possibility so that when it happened she wouldn't worry.

"Grace Rensler's a real hand-wringer," he continued. "We decided it was best to let Rensler write her brief, innocuous notes of reassurance. Our agents censor these before placing them in her mailbox. No postmarks. We've got her under round-the-clock surveillance. If she does anything foolish, we're ready to act. Her phone's tapped and we've installed listening devices in her home and car."

"When she contacted Thurmond, she was apparently searching for her husband's appointment calendar," Burch said.

"The agents assigned to watch her aren't even aware of *why* they're watching her," Sinclair put in quickly. "We've got this thing compartmentalized as hell."

The President stood up, satisfied for the moment. He headed toward the door, indicating that the briefing was over.

"Keep me informed. I've instructed Doleman and my secretary that if either of you calls, you're to be put through without question. No one on my staff knows about this and it'll stay that way."

Chip Doleman, the President's Chief of Staff, greeted Sinclair and Burch with a scowl as they emerged from the Oval Office. "I'll see you out," he said tersely, personally conducting them to waiting limousines. He bid Jeremy goodbye and slammed the passenger door with unnecessary emphasis.

Doleman was a known control freak. On this, he was out of the loop, and Jeremy knew it would not be wearing well. He'd prod Geller for details. Why this sudden flurry of briefings and phone calls with Burch and Sinclair? Doleman would know something was afoot. Geller was naïve to think he could hide anything from him for long. When it came to security the White House wasn't just a sieve; it was Niagra Falls.

Ω

9

KATE CALLED JACK the day after her meeting with Grace Rensler. His first words were, "Detective Lipton, I presume?"

"I met with Rensler's wife," she said.

"How'd you manage that?"

"Staked out her house. When I saw her drive away in her car, I followed her to a shopping center. She was also followed by a pair of men in a white Buick."

"What sort of license plate?" His voice was severe, interrogating.

"Navy on white I think. I didn't pay that much attention."

"Some detective," he sniffed derisively.

"I had other things on my mind, Jack. She went into a lingerie boutique in the shopping center and I followed. We had a surreptitious conversation over the nightgowns and bathrobes. She's received a note from her husband reassuring her that he's all right and telling her not to worry, but she's *very* worried. She seemed so vulnerable, Jack. I felt sorry for her."

"You might direct some of that concern toward yourself, Kate. Are you certain the agents didn't see you?"

"They saw me go into and leave the shop, but they didn't connect me with Mrs. Rensler. I'm certain of it. They didn't pay any attention to me when I left. I wandered around the shopping center for a while afterward, and when I returned to my car, they'd all left."

"She doesn't know where he's gone. So that's that, right?"

"Not exactly. We agreed to meet at the shop next week. She's bringing the letter she received from her husband a few days ago. Were you able to get the passenger lists?"

"No, I wasn't. To do it, I'd have to go through the Ostrich, and I don't think that's wise. He'd want an explanation." He sighed in frustration. "I've given this some thought. I'm having trouble believing the U.S. government would kidnap a group of scientists against their will. This isn't a police state."

"Are you kidding, Jack? Our government's launched more lamebrained scams in the last thirty years than we can count. When they get caught, they deny, they can't recall, they cover up, lie to Congress, obstruct justice. If deniability breaks down, they spout national security. We have Watergate, Abscam, Iran-Contra; and that's only the short list of the idiocies the American people have gotten wind of. Think of all the scams and 'gates' we don't know about. I even heard the Pentagon faked the SDI Star Wars test results, supposedly to confuse the Russians. But, whoops! *We confused Congress too*—right into appropriating billions more for a technological flop. Think it through, Jack. Suppose there's something important in those transmissions?"

"If there is, and the government's so concerned about word getting out that they've incarcerated an entire group of scientists, then it's a lot bigger than you are. All the more reason to stay out of it."

"Jack, I'm not dropping it. I'm a journalist, and this is too big to ignore. Remember when you were prosecuting Al Macon and you received those death threats? Did you drop the case?"

"That's my job, Kate."

"And this is mine," she said softly. With Jack, it never helped to speak too vehemently. It awakened the attorney in him, which would only cause him to dig in harder.

"And I had the resources of an entire DA's office behind me."

"A journalist doesn't walk away from the biggest story of all time just because it starts getting a little complicated. What would you do if our places were reversed?"

"*A little complicated.* That's good." But his tone softened and he seemed willing to relent. "I'd probably do the same."

"I'll meet Grace next week. If nothing comes of it, I'll consider dropping it. Satisfied?"

"Well—"

"How about a movie? In the mood?"

"You're hoping I won't notice you've changed the subject."

"Nope. Can't fool you, counselor. I wouldn't even try."

Over the next week Kate was forced to admit to herself that she'd grown obsessed by SETI. It was impossible to concentrate on anything else. On Tuesday afternoon she visited a costume shop in the Tenderloin and purchased a long brown wig to cover her medium length, light brown hair. To this disguise she added a pair of wraparound sunglasses and a navy-blue coat. On Wednesday morning at ten-thirty she donned this getup and set off for the Top Drawers Lingerie Boutique. She intended to be in the shop well ahead of Grace Rensler to avoid the scrutiny of Sinclair's men.

Grace arrived promptly at eleven-thirty and looked furtively around. After a glance in Kate's direction her eye moved on. Kate removed the sunglasses, and Grace finally recognized her and walked over.

"Milt sent me a second letter. This one's very strange. I can't decide what he's talking about." She reached into her purse and withdrew two unstamped envelopes and handed them to Kate. Kate retreated to the back of the shop before scanning a brief note filled with soft platitudes designed to reassure. Then she read the second note, a single paragraph written on onion skin paper:

My darling Grace, I know you're worried but try not to be. I'm perfectly fine. I've gotten my prescription for Lopressor refilled and I'm taking it regularly. If I know you, you've been worried about that. And I suspect you're wondering about my birthday. I don't expect to be back in time for the celebration you planned for my Big Seven-O with Hank and Katie. People here have generously invited me out for a celebration dinner at the ▉▉▉▉▉. It'll be a pick-me-up, since I told them you'd gone to a lot of trouble to plan something special and I'll miss it. Why don't you think about spending the evening with Hank and Katie? You could get together over a pitcher of martinis— no, make that a pot of Lipton— I don't want you arrested for driving intoxicated. I'm sure Katie wonders how I am. Let her know I'm fine. With luck, I'll be home before you know it. I miss you more than I can say. Love, Milt.

Kate reread the second note. The location of their celebration dinner had been obliterated with a dense, black ink. The references to "Katie" and "Lipton" could hardly be a coincidence. Tim Thurmond would certainly have told Rensler about their meeting at the Bay Meadows Lounge and their plan to seek out Mrs. Rensler. Tim might surmise Kate would contact Grace Rensler on her own. This letter could be an instruction to his wife to meet with Kate and trust her. And it might be more.

She returned to where Grace was standing. "What do you make of this second note?"

"I don't know. Milt has a sister who is married to Hank Beardsly, but her name is Carolyn, not Katie. I've heard him call her 'Carrie,' but never 'Katie.'"

"Do you suppose he's referring to me?"

"Well—"

"My last name *is* Lipton. Do you suppose he might be speaking in code, trying to tell you he wants us to meet?"

She considered this. "I suppose it might at that. It's odd. He knows I don't drink martinis, and I don't care much for tea, either. Neither does Carolyn as far as I know."

"When is your husband's birthday?"

"June twenty-third. We actually were planning a celebration. He'll be seventy. Oh, I hope he really is taking his medication."

"Sounds like his colleagues are taking him out somewhere for a celebration dinner. A restaurant. The name's been obliterated." Kate turned the single sheet over. The note had been written with a ballpoint pen. Perhaps she could decipher the obscured word through the onion skin, maybe in the right light. She turned her attention to a display of hosiery. It was far too warm in the shop for the long coat, and the wig felt uncomfortably heavy and enveloping.

"Grace, could I take the note and return it to you next Wednesday? Would you trust me to bring it back? I'd like to see if there's more to the message."

Grace barely hesitated this time. "All right. Same time next Wednesday? It's when I normally come here."

"Good. Eleven-thirty. And if he sends you any more letters, bring them."

"All right. Should I leave now, before you do?"

"Good idea."

Grace left the shop looking small and stooped, and wearing her worries—her husband's absence and the intimidating scrutiny of government agents—like a lead cloak.

Ω

10

"Can you make out this word, Jack?" Kate pointed to the inch-long, quarter-inch-high strip of black ink on the letter Milton Rensler had written to his wife.

Jack held it beneath Kate's bright desk lamp and squinted. "Nope."

"How about from the reverse side? Can you see the impression left by the pressure of his pen?"

"Impossible to make it out."

"Maybe I could get it analyzed."

"Take it down to Lucien McAuliffe at the Mint."

"Who's he?"

"An engraving and counterfeiting expert employed by the San Francisco Mint. He knows everything there is to know about inks and printing. He'll know what tests to run to decipher the missing word. If anybody can get it, he can."

"Do you know him?"

"Sure. He helps us out from time to time. I'll give him a call."

"Thank you, Jack."

"Just think of all the favors you're owing me. Rensler's address—"

"For which you got crab—"

"And now this. What next?"

The following day, Lucien McAuliffe agreed to analyze the note and Kate delivered it to his office, located in the Greco-Roman, mausoleum-like structure housing the San Francisco Mint. The spacious office overlooked a heavily graffitied BART transit tunnel and a congested Market Street intersection.

"Nail down the chemistry of the two inks with an infrared scanner," the grizzled and slightly hunch-backed McAuliffe said. "Subtract out one ink from the other, and bingo, what's left is your missing word." He brushed back a wild shock of hair that kept insinuating itself over his left eye. His business shirt was speckled with a history of coffee breaks and something reddish-orange.

"You can do that?" Kate asked, awarding him with a look of admiration.

"Sure. Not as hard as you'd think. Have it for you tomorrow afternoon."

"Wonderful. Jack Sullivan told me you were amazing."

McAuliffe shook his head. "Nah, not amazing. Just a little queer for ink."

At four-thirty the following afternoon, Kate returned to McAuliffe's office to retrieve the note. She knocked on his door.

"Be with you in a moment," he called.

Kate paced and waited, overhearing McAuliffe's gruff voice; he was talking on the phone, she thought. She weighed the possibility that he might be reporting her to Jeremy Sinclair and quickly dismissed the idea as ridiculous.

When the door finally opened, McAuliffe motioned her in. "Sit," he said with a wave. "Got your missing word. *Hummingbird.*"

"Hummingbird?"

"That's it. Too easy. Only took me an hour this morning." He handed her Rensler's note, and Kate thought he seemed disappointed that she'd not brought him a greater challenge.

Kate stared at the onion skin. Hummingbird. It fit in the blackened space. "You're absolutely certain?"

"Nothin' else the word could be. Look, I'll show you if you don't—"

"No, I believe you. Hummingbird. Is the *h* capitalized?"

"Yup. Capital-H."

"...*a celebration dinner at the Hummingbird...*," Kate murmured. She stood and started to reach for her wallet. "What do I owe you for your trouble?"

He held up a hand. "The U.S. Government pays me. Happy to be of help."

Kate thanked him and left, inordinately pleased at the symmetry of it: One government hand had censored the letter; another had deciphered it.

JACK ARRIVED early that evening and rather proudly plunked down a stack of spiral-bound volumes on Kate's coffee table.

"The definitive guide to sailing in the Eastern Caribbean— *Avery's Cruising Guide*—in four volumes. Charts, wind, weather, tides, anchorages, amenities, customs regulations, currency, anecdotes. Everything you need to know."

"*Avery's* costs a fortune," Kate said knowingly.

"I've been meaning to buy it anyway before our next Caribbean sail."

Kate held her relief in check. Jack seemed to be coming around. At least his curiosity was piqued enough to help her solve the *where* of the scientists' disappearance. She reached for Volume I, *The Eastern Caribbean—A General Description*. The cover featured a photo of a salty, gray-bearded man whose face was shaded beneath a Hemingway hat. With a Heineken beer in one hand, he was gripping the helm of a sailing vessel with the other. A look of distant satisfaction creased his weathered face. Lines and sheets were coiled and looped around him in an untidy jumble. Arnold Avery, Jr.

They began poring through Volume III, *Martinique to Trinidad*, in search of a reference to a restaurant or establishment called the Hummingbird.

"Here it is," Jack said suddenly, unable to conceal the triumph in his voice. "'Soufriere's Leisure: If hiking is your forte, you may hire a guide to lead you up Petit Piton. It is a very poor trail, treacherous in spots, winding up the 2400-foot pinnacle through a mahogany forest. The view from the top is worth the struggle. I've done it once, which is enough. Carry water and arrange the price with your guide in advance.'

"Now, listen to this, Kate: 'If there could be only a single restaurant in all the Eastern Caribbean, it ought to be the Hummingbird Restaurant in Soufriere. Most of their trade is from yachtsmen so they treat us well and overlook our attire. The bar-restaurant has an incomparable view of the Pitons, and the food rates among the best in the Caribbean at a moderate cost (price range A-B). They have a barbecue on Saturday nights with a pool-side jump-up dance, and a Sunday lunch of spit-roasted beef. They stand by on V.H.F. Channel 16.'

"That's it, Kate, the Hummingbird Restaurant in Soufriere at the southern end of St. Lucia." He spread a chart over the table.

Kate snatched the book and continued reading. "Listen to this. 'North of the Pitons you will find the town of Soufriere, a rustic village that has retained its native charm over the years. The surrounding area is a scenic, volcanic wonderland. The bay is very deep, so anchoring is difficult in 60 to 100 feet of water. Tying stern to a palm tree is obligatory. *The best anchorage is off the Hummingbird Restaurant.* There you will find moorings and a nearby dinghy dock with fair security. If you hoist your cocktail flag, Maurice will meet you in the Hummingbird's launch and run your lines ashore. Price: $5 E.C., and on slow days, they might throw in a drink for the skipper at their world-famous bar. The Hummingbird has rooms to let at special rates, if the skipper needs a night ashore. Basic supplies can be obtained...,' and so on."

"Let me look at the chart of St. Lucia," Jack said. He took the volume back and began flipping pages until he found the hand-sketched chart of Soufriere Bay. "Look at this. The Pitons are huge pinnacles. Gros Piton rises 2620 feet, straight up from the sea. Do you realize how high that is, Kate? And Petit Piton is around 2400 feet. Soufriere Bay. It *is* deep."

"Never be able to set an anchor there. Have to run a line ashore."

Jack answered with a long, dour look.

"It says there are a few buoys." She studied the detailed chart and pointed. "Right here, but if it's crowded we'd have to get in early to pick one up. Look, there's a second cove, just around the other side of Petit Piton. It's deep too, though."

"You're planning a sailing trip, aren't you?"

Kate looked at him and burst out laughing. Of course she was. To her it was a foregone conclusion. It made sense. "Well, if we're going to rescue them and they're on an island, airports are out of the question. So the only way is by sea, by boat. That or swim." She worked to squelch her enthusiasm, to keep her voice level with reason.

"I think I heard a *we* in all that," Jack said with a trace of a smile.

"I wonder about sailboat charter facilities in the area."

"The Castries at the north end of the island looks like a sizeable town. I've also heard that Caribbean Charters International has a facility on the island of St. Vincent. It's just south of St. Lucia. Let me read this a second." After a moment he said, "Marigot Bay on St. Lucia has a sailboat charter company. It even gives the phone number. And C.C.I. has a facility in Kingstown, St. Vincent."

Kate considered. "St. Vincent would be best. If we charter out of St. Lucia, there'd be a paper trail. Even clearing customs in St. Lucia would—"

"What exactly are you thinking, Kate?"

"That we sail to Soufriere and pick up Dr. Rensler and Tim Thurmond at the Hummingbird on June twenty-third."

"It would take tremendous planning," Jack said. "Are we certain they really want to be rescued?"

"I am. Tim would definitely object to being incarcerated. Dr. Rensler even uses the phrase *pick-me-up* in his note. But think of this: If we're wrong, what difference does it make? If we've misinterpreted the whole thing, we could still sail, have ourselves the vacation we've been talking about since we sailed the Leewards."

"And if you're right, if they do want to be rescued, where would we take them?"

Kate started to speak but stopped. "Good question. We'd need to have a plan."

"And there's Grace Rensler to consider. She'd have to elude her surveillance."

Kate slid over that for the moment. "There'd be four of us. Let's see. We could sail them down to Grenada, and they could fly home from there." Then she shook her head. "No, too obvious."

"Grenada's the namesake island of the Grenadines. Expect that if Rensler disappears, every major island airport in the Caribbean will be on alert. Maybe we could sail them to Miami. We'd be breaking the rules of the charter agreement, but—"

"What about returning the boat to another of the charter company's facilities in the Gulf? We could claim we got lost, that a storm blew us off course." Even as she spoke, she knew it was weak. "They'd charge us a small fortune and authorities would question the story."

"Especially if Rensler disappears at the very time we show up in Soufriere. Then we later claim we were blown off course?"

Kate recognized Jack had just used *we* himself, twice in fact. He was definitely coming around.

"Look at this," Jack said, unfolding a large chart of the Eastern Caribbean. "The northern coast of Venezuela is less than two hundred miles from Grenada. We could take them to Caracas and drop them off, then sail back to Kingstown to return the boat. The only law we're breaking is failing to check out of customs before going to Venezuela."

"We don't have to check out, do we? Just *in*. Besides, if we don't go ashore in Caracas—"

"No one would even know we'd sailed down there."

"How long would that take?"

"Do you have a pocket calculator and a ruler?"

Kate found the needed items in her office and returned to the living room, and Jack began measuring and calculating and talking to himself. "It's roughly five hundred miles from Soufriere to Caracas. That's about four hundred and fifty nautical miles. And we'd be sailing basically with the wind and the currents all the way. Averaging only five knots, we'd reach Caracas in four days."

"I bet we'd average more like seven knots with tradewinds and following seas."

"Four days of constant sailing, twenty-four hours a day," he said doubtfully. "This is nuts."

"We can manage that, take turns at the helm."

"The hardest part's coming back, beating northeast directly into the teeth of the northeasterly tradewinds and head on against the currents all the way. A tough haul."

"Allowing for tacking, say it's six hundred nautical miles coming back. At a hundred and twenty miles a day, it would take us six days, max. We could do that, Jack. If we sign up for a three-week charter, we'd have more than enough time." She could no longer conceal the mounting enthusiasm she felt for the undertaking. Her voice rang with it.

"Possible. Doesn't mean it's wise, but it's possible." He was silent for several moments. "Consider this, Kate. The moment the scientists are missing, no port, certainly no airport, no island, no conceivable destination we head for will be safe. They'll launch every search plane and helicopter, every Coast Guard vessel available."

"Looking for what?" She waited for an answer, but he only nodded to her to continue. "Looking for what, Jack? A sailboat? A power boat? A cruise ship? A private plane? A local fishing skiff? If we can escape unseen, what good will all the reconnaissance planes and boats in the world do them? They won't know what they're looking for. It's a huge ocean. There are hundreds—no, *thousands* of islands down there, *hundreds* of airports within a few days of Soufriere. They can't hope to launch a search on the scale you're describing in less than twenty-four hours."

"But if they're searching for a sailboat—"

"Jack, unless they see us leave, they won't know to look for a sailboat. Hell, they might figure the scientists are still on the island, hiding out, waiting until the heat's off. Even if the NSA does focus on sailboats, there are a few zillion of them down there, chartered and privately owned."

He weighed her words. "Okay, point taken. Once the scientists are away from Soufriere, the NSA has an immense problem—*provided* no one has observed that they've left by sailboat."

"So we'll just have to make certain no one does," she said.

"Caracas, huh? Four days down and five or six back."

"Leaving at least ten days to spare in a three-week charter. Time to show up at other ports in the Windward Islands, establish ourselves as average sailors enjoying an average bare-boat charter vacation."

They consulted a calendar. "Say we sail from Soufriere to Caracas," she said. "We arrive in Caracas June twenty-seventh, return to the islands around July second, sail around for a week and return to St. Vincent on the tenth. We'd order our charter with provisions for just the two of us. Then we augment our supplies on another island before heading to Soufriere."

"How do we arrange to meet up with Rensler? We can't just waltz into the Hummingbird."

"True."

"What if Rensler's note to Grace is only meant to encourage her to meet with you, Kate? What if he has no thought of being rescued?"

She looked at him. "Why would he suddenly want his wife to meet with a journalist who spent a single morning interviewing him? To console her? No, counselor, not even remotely logical. If that were the case, why would he bother to mention the Hummingbird?"

"To let his wife know he'll have a nice birthday."

Kate shook her head. "Come on, Jack, re-read the note. It's code. There's the allusion to 'Katie Lipton.' He names what is obviously a world-famous, or at least regionally famous restaurant. The phrase, pick-me-up. He'll be at the Hummingbird on the evening of June twenty-third. He wants Grace to tell me that. Why would he want her to pass that information along, unless—"

"I don't know, Kate. I'm just having a hard time believing all this. Suddenly you want to take off and sail down there to rescue these guys. We aren't even certain that's what they want."

"Well, I am. But even if I'm wrong, what's the harm? We sail around. We have a vacation."

"The harm is if we're caught. It's a huge risk, not to mention expense."

Kate looked at him, amused. "You're not having a hard time believing this, Jack. If you were, you wouldn't be concerned about getting caught. You wouldn't be envisioning massive search efforts. As for the expense, it's not so much. We've been saving. We can afford it. And it isn't just the story, Jack. There's—" She stopped and leaned back against the sofa, still not ready to tell him about her history with Sinclair. Even after all these years there was shame. Eventually, of course, he'd have to know.

He waited and finally said, "I'm finding the whole thing stupefying. Sometimes I forget that they've intercepted an ETI signal. If the scientists honestly believe they won't otherwise be allowed to leave that island, then I suppose it makes sense. Is Tim aware that you sail?"

"I don't think— Wait, sure he is. I mentioned it to him at the Bay Meadows Lounge. I remember, he was asking me if I enjoyed horseracing, if that was why I'd chosen the Bay Meadows Lounge for our meeting. I told him no, that my passion was sailing."

"How could they expect you to know where they are? Where the Hummingbird Restaurant is?"

"Tim told me he thought the scientists would have been taken to an Arecibo-type facility. And his postcard. Jack, he flew to Miami."

"Yeah," he nodded. "And?"

"Dr. Rensler mentioned St. Lucia among the large radio telescopes. He knows I taped that interview."

"It's a stretch, Kate."

"I don't think so. Even if I initially figured they were in Puerto Rico, once I failed to find a Hummingbird Restaurant near Arecibo, it's reasonable to expect I'd look at St. Lucia."

He gave her a bemused look. "An awful lot of suppositions and giant leaps of faith and logic."

"Oh, Jack, it's not. It's logical. Those guys are smart enough to expect I'd figure it out. They gave me all the elements, everything I'd need. The proof is that it worked."

He stood slowly with a groan. "I've got court tomorrow morning and a meeting before that. Then I'm in L.A. for three days on the Hobson case."

"Let's talk Wednesday evening. I'll supply dinner."

"Another bribe."

"That's right, counselor, another bribe."

"Meanwhile, you might give some thought to how Rensler is to meet up with his wife. She can't sail with us. If she evades her surveillance before we pick up her husband, that would alert St. Lucia. They certainly wouldn't allow the scientists to dine out."

"Plus, we have to arrange the whole thing so that you and I aren't implicated."

"And aren't breaking too many laws," he said.

It was late April. They had a little more than six weeks before Rensler's seventieth birthday in which to plan the rescue.

Ω

11

"Grace, we believe SETI has intercepted an intelligent signal."

Kate and Grace were standing near one another, pawing through a pile of leotards that were on sale at the Top Drawers Boutique.

Mrs. Rensler considered Kate's words. "Yes. I think that's probably true. It fits with some things Milt told me a while back. When he left, he had that look in his eyes—excited."

"How would he react to being, well, incarcerated I guess you might call it, for several months? Sequestered to study these transmissions? Did he ever mention such a thing might occur?"

"We talked about what might happen. He believes so strongly that no matter what the content of a communication, if it's sent to the world from space, it belongs to all of us. That's why he involved himself so deeply with the international SETI groups."

"The missing word in his letter is 'Hummingbird.' I found a Hummingbird Restaurant," Kate said quietly, handing back the note.

"Where is it?"

"On the coast of a small island in the Caribbean—St. Lucia."

"St. Lucia," Grace said, trying the sound of it and nodding, as though a missing piece of a puzzle had been supplied. "Then it makes sense." She looked down and appeared lost in thought. When she looked up again, it was as if she'd vacated a confining shell to emerge stronger. "He wants us to pick him up. He told me—it was a few years ago—about St. Lucia and that he might have to go there. At the time he was involved in specifying equipment for a lab on the island. His last trip was in September. He flew down to look over the completed facility. That part about the 'pick-me-up'?"

"Yes?"

"He wants us to pick him up." It was said with finality.

"Maybe he's only telling you how he'll spend his birthday to keep you from worrying."

"No. He disapproves of how news of the discovery is being handled. Besides, he'd never willingly leave me for so long. You must understand, we have a close marriage. It's rather old-fashioned, I suppose. It's been ten weeks now. He wouldn't leave without—"

"Would you be willing to evade those men out front?"

Grace glanced at her slightly alarmed. "How?"

"I'm not certain, but if it could be done safely, would you do it?"

She glanced uneasily toward the front of the shop. "If it meant I'd be with Milt, yes, I would in a minute, without question. Please understand, I haven't been myself since he left. The whole thing, those men, Milt's absence, it's turned me into a wreck. But I have a lot more starch than you might suspect." She raised a pair of pale blue tights from the pile and considered them. "Milt and I need each other. We always have. I know he needs me now."

"Here's an idea, Grace. My friend Jack is a sailor. Well, actually he's an attorney with the D.A.'s office, but he has a sailboat. We've sailed together a great deal including two weeks in the Caribbean. We think it might be possible to pick up your husband and Tim at the Hummingbird, sail them out of the area and make it possible for them to meet up with you. Would you go along with something like that?"

"I'd have to think about it. The issue is safety and whether it could be managed without getting everyone into trouble."

"The only laws that might be broken have to do with customs. But I think we can get around those. Your husband is a free man. There's no law against our picking him up, as long as he comes aboard willingly. More important, there's no law that gives our government the right to incarcerate people who have committed no crime."

"I suppose as long as he's not in danger, go ahead and plan it," Grace said. "Tell me what you need me to do."

A few minutes later the small woman walked briskly out of the boutique; her shoulders seemed a little squarer, a little less stooped.

THAT EVENING, Jack and Kate sat on the floor in Kate's living room surrounded by charts, the four volumes of *Avery's Guide*, parallel rulers, calculators, and cartons of take-out Chinese food.

"No credit cards of course," Jack said. "They'd be traceable. If they fly out on a commercial flight they'll have to present passports, so that eliminates commercial airlines."

"What about chartering a private plane to get them out of the area?"

"From Caracas?"

They were huddled over the large chart of the Eastern Caribbean. "Or Puerto Rico," Kate suggested. "It's much closer to Miami. We could arrange for a charter plane in Miami to meet us in Puerto Rico and fly the scientists back to Miami."

Jack nodded. "And you and I sail the boat back. How far is it from St. Lucia to Puerto Rico?" He grabbed his ruler and tablet and began calculating distances. "About four hundred and ten nautical miles," he said after a moment.

"What about wind and currents?"

"Actually, they're more favorable than a sail back from Caracas. It might take us slightly longer to reach the southeastern end of Puerto Rico than it would Venezuela. The wind would be off the starboard beam the entire way, a beam reach. Not as fast as a downwind run to Caracas with following seas, but fast. Avery says to allow for a one-knot foul current. If we averaged six knots that would set us west about ten degrees.

"We could do it," he concluded. "And the best part is the return trip after we drop them off. From Puerto Rico down to Grenada would be about four hundred and sixty miles of sailing instead of the six hundred from Caracas to Grenada. We wouldn't have to beat into the wind. The trades would be off our port beam the whole way. The currents would push us to westward but even so, it's probably only four days to Grenada."

"I had the thought that we should disguise the name of our boat, paint a different name on the stern."

"That's illegal. Do you want this last pot sticker?"

"No. It's yours. Say we cover the stern with some plastic material on which we've painted a different name. We leave it on for the time we're in Soufriere and maybe until we reach Puerto Rico. Then we peel if off to change it back before we return to the Windward Islands."

"Might work, but it's still probably illegal."

"How severe could the penalty be?"

"I don't know. They never give you enough pot stickers, you know?" He submerged the dumpling in sauce and devoured it in one bite.

Jack had another early court date the next morning so they turned in early. The following evening the planning resumed. More cartons of Chinese food. Two orders of pot stickers instead of one. Maps and charts spread around. Calculator, rulers, calendars, tablets, lists.

"We can't go anywhere near the Hummingbird Restaurant," Kate said. "Anyone who sees us could later identify us. We need a way to tell Dr. Rensler to meet us on the beach. One of us can go ashore with the dinghy and row them back to the boat. Then we just vanish. Poof."

"Right. Poof. How do we tell them to go down to the beach?"

Kate scooped a second helping of snow peas with water chestnuts onto her plate. "I don't know."

"Maybe Grace could send her husband a birthday card. They might deliver it. They've allowed him to write to her."

"That's it, Jack. Perfect! What'll we have her write?"

They labored for nearly an hour over a birthday message that was suitably cryptic:

Dearest Milt, Thank you for writing to reassure me. I really have been so worried about you. I called Hank and Katie to see if they wanted to spend your birthday with me, but they have plans to go sailing that weekend with friends. I told her you'd be envious. Katie said that on your birthday you should think of them—they'll be anchored off the Sea Breeze Restaurant in Half Moon Bay enjoying a delicious dinner, toasting you and maybe taking a walk on the beach after dinner. I can just picture them. It all sounds so lovely. She invited me to join them but I'm not much for sailing. Don't worry about me, though. Hearing from you has been reassuring. Everything here is fine. I just hope you'll be able to come home soon. Have a happy birthday, dear. Love, Grace.

A sudden vivid picture filled Kate's mind—of an iridescent hummingbird hovering over a pink fuchsia blossom. "Maybe I can find a greeting card with a photograph of a hummingbird on it," she said.

"That'd be good. Let me see *Avery's* for a moment." He turned pages. "There's the second smaller bay south of Soufriere between Petit Piton and Gros Piton. We could anchor there." More turning of pages. Then, "That's it. Listen to what Avery says: 'Just south of Soufriere is by far the most spectacular anchorage in the Eastern Caribbean. On either side are the volcanic formations known as the Pitons, towering 2600 feet in the air. The best anchorage is in the northeast corner of the bay off the Jalousie boathouse in depths of from 70 to 100 feet. A strong offshore wind often makes for an uncomfortably choppy overnight stay but on calmer days this scenic anchorage is well worth a visit.'"

"Perfect, Jack. One of us takes the dinghy around the point to the Hummingbird. Is it far?"

"Maybe a quarter mile."

"I should be the one to take the dinghy. They wouldn't recognize you."

"No, I should do it," he argued. "Is there any mushi pork left?"

Kate handed him the carton and then broke open one of the fortune cookies and read aloud: "The Gods do not deduct from man's allotted time the hours spent fishing."

"They don't? Do you suppose that also applies to sailing?"

"It must."

THE FOLLOWING evening they planned Grace Rensler's escape, how she was to elude her surveillance. Kate thought she'd hit on a solution earlier in the day while she was pulling weeds.

"That boutique? It has a back door, Jack. Suppose she just walks in the front door and out the back? The agents never follow her inside. It's become so routine that lately they all but ignore her. She could have a cab waiting behind the shop. I think there's an alleyway back there."

Jack nodded. "The taxi takes her to the airport. She buys her ticket with cash and flies to Miami. It's good."

"If we pick up Tim and Dr. Rensler after dark in St. Lucia, say around eight-thirty or nine at night, then Grace should time her disappearance for around that same time. Once Grace disappears, they'll alert the security force on St. Lucia. What's the time difference?"

"Four hours. At eight-thirty in St. Lucia it'll be four-thirty in the afternoon in San Francisco."

"She arrives at the boutique at four. Walks out the back door. Reaches the airport by four-thirty to catch her flight."

"If there are no four-thirty flights to Miami she could fly just about anywhere. It wouldn't matter as long as she winds up in

Miami by the twenty-sixth or twenty-seventh. Let's work out the timetable."

He began a list and Kate started one of her own—of things to do and items to pack—computer, diskettes, navigation instruments, charts. She wrote: "How to disguise boat—stern covering?"

She held out the list for Jack to see. "Anything to add?"

"That last item bothers me. Maybe some kind of mylar. I could probably get the dimensions of the stern from the boat's manufacturer. I hope we're able to charter a Morgan 46 as we did in the Leewards."

Kate added "kevlar/mylar" to the list.

Jack said, "I'll make the boat charter arrangements and once I know the make of boat we're assigned I'll write for specs from the manufacturer. Add canvas tape and plastic sheeting to the list. And marine paint."

The following Wednesday, May first, Kate drove across town to the Marina district and walked into a drugstore on Chestnut Street, where she found a selection of Sierra Club greeting cards. Her glance immediately went to a card picturing an iridescent blue hummingbird hovering over a pink flower. It was almost exactly as she'd imagined it.

Two hours later, draped in a head scarf and sunglasses, she arrived at the Top Drawers Boutique with pages of typed instructions for Grace Rensler, the hummingbird card, and a feeling of near certainty that Grace would agree to go along with the rescue venture they'd planned. As quickly as she could, she explained what they needed Grace to do.

"You really think I could just walk out the back door?"

"I don't see why not, Grace. Those men always wait for you out front. You've established such a pattern that they probably won't look for you for at least fifteen minutes."

"I suppose I should fly under an assumed name?"

"That would be wise. By the time they figure out what flight you've taken, you and Milt will be long gone. I've typed up the basics of the plan. You take it home and think it over. If you decide against it we'll cancel our reservations. You can let me know next week."

Grace scanned the pages quickly. "If you charter a plane that's going to cost. I'll bring you cash."

She's already decided, Kate thought. "Destroy these instructions, Grace. Agents might prowl around your house when you go out. Memorize and destroy them."

"All right. If I'm to join Milt in Miami I can bring a lot of cash with me. You wrote, 'No use of credit cards.' Those would be traceable, I suppose?"

"Yes."

"And we won't be able to write checks. I'll have to liquidate our savings."

Kate told her about the birthday card and the message they needed her to write. "Just hand it to the agents unsealed. They'll open it and read it anyway before giving it to your husband, so you might as well make it easy for them. It'll suggest you have nothing to hide."

"All right."

"We plan to leave the morning of June seventeenth."

"You honestly think this'll work?"

"I do. Jack and I both feel confident that it's safe and legal. We're good sailors, Grace. We've sailed together a lot. Jack's an expert navigator. We've sailed in the Caribbean so we're familiar with the winds and currents. But obviously the final decision has to be yours."

Ω

12

"Michael, if you can't persuade Tim Thurmond to reveal who he mailed that postcard to, I'll send someone down who can." Sinclair prided himself on conquering all outward display of emotion, especially when that emotion was worry. But on this morning his concern had to be apparent, even over the long distance phone line.

Gregg tried to allay his boss's worry. "Sir, your own people went over that postcard and found nothing significant. Why don't you question them?"

"I have."

"Have you thought of hypnosis?"

"Right. Make a note—I want to see all the scientists' day-timers and calendars. Grace Rensler had something in mind when she asked Thurmond to meet her with her husband's calendar. I want to know what it was. Confiscate everyone's day-timers and send them to me."

"But—"

"Michael, just do it. Or better yet I'll come down. I want to check out the facility anyway. I'll talk to Thurmond myself."

Gregg sighed. "Sir, as I told you, we've questioned Thurmond repeatedly. He refuses to tell us who the postcard was mailed to. It was just a girl with whom he was breaking a date. Not even a girl he knew well. He doesn't want us invading her privacy."

Sinclair's voice became cold steel. "Tim Thurmond isn't calling the shots, Michael. I am, and I think I can be more persuasive."

"You're welcome to come but it'll be a waste of time. In my opinion. Sir."

In Sinclair's ear, the final *Sir* was a grudging addendum. "I'll be down later this month but don't worry, Michael, I'll give you plenty of warning."

"It's not that. It just seems like there must be better uses for your valuable time."

Sinclair hung up. He pressed his palms hard against the surface of the mahogany desk, stood and began pacing. This was precisely the problem with compartmentalization. The agents tasked with picking up and transporting Thurmond to St. Lucia had been unaware of *why* they were assigned that job, unaware of the significance of the printout in Thurmond's briefcase or the importance of the postcard he'd insisted on mailing at the airport. They'd read the message but hadn't bothered to make a copy or even note the addressee. It was sheer stupidity. Maybe Thurmond was telling the truth but without questioning the girl, Jeremy could never be sure.

The rigorous need-to-know strategy on this project dictated that the surveillance teams on Grace Rensler be kept in the dark about the overall mission, of which their task was a small part. Thus, when they'd entered the Rensler home to search for the desk calendar, they'd been uncertain of why or what else to look for. Their instructions had been to note any items of an unusual or suspect nature—whatever the hell that meant. The calendar was missing. When asked, Mrs. Rensler claimed to have thrown it away.

Damn. He could not be in all places at once, overseeing every task. He was forced to delegate and this was the result—sloppy, careless work. He should have immediately ordered the confiscation of all the scientists' personal effects the moment they were deposited in St. Lucia. Another oversight. He'd followed the Code Shepherd task plan too slavishly, too complacently. Security was now a matter of chance rather than careful method and control. Sinclair despised chance.

He made an additional note to review the entire process of contingency planning. "Complacency," he wrote. "Underestimating, failure to react spontaneously and appropriately to unfolding events." His stomach tightened. He rubbed his eyes. Too little sleep. Why did this have to be happening on *his* watch?

He glanced at the alabaster desk clock; it was long past the time he usually went home. He needed company, someone to help him relax. The pressure was becoming too much. He dialed the Service number from memory.

"Vanessa, Frank Seligman here." His usual pseudonym. "I'll have companionship this evening, ten o'clock. Malena if she's available—or someone younger would be preferable if it can be arranged."

Vanessa assured him whatever companion was provided would meet or exceed his expectations. It ought to. It cost enough.

Ω

13

KATE LOOKED over at Jack who was scribbling intently on a legal pad. She stood up, stretched and pressed her fingers into the small of her back with a quiet groan. She walked over to see what he was writing and leaned against him lightly, studied his hands. She'd always liked their look, the strength, the way the veins snaked up his forearms.

He'd added "Celestial nav star charts" and "RDF" to the lengthening list of essentials to be packed.

"RDF?"

"Radio Direction Finder."

She glanced around at the charts spread out around him. "Why charts of Florida?"

"In case we run into trouble and have to sail to Miami. I just calculated it. We could just about manage it in a three-week charter."

"And return the boat to St. Vincent by the tenth?"

"With thirty-five seconds to spare."

She appreciated his thoroughness. He'd handled all the details of the C.C.I. charter. They'd be sailing a Morgan 46, just as they'd hoped. He'd called the manufacturer in Annapolis, Maryland and they'd faxed him the vessel's dimensions. At a Sausalito chandlery he'd purchased a section of white mylar large enough to cover the stern, plus several square yards of a thin-gauge plastic sheeting, a roll of canvas tape and navy blue marine paint.

At Kate's house they'd spread the mylar out on the floor of her office, drawn the outline of the Morgan's stern, and Jack had then painstakingly lettered their fictitious boat name: *Espiritu Del Sol*. Sun Spirit. Kate liked the sound of it. Now she was painting the letters in a navy blue, nautical-looking script. It would take hours and at least three coats of paint to cover the white mylar. After two hours she was wishing they'd chosen a name with fewer letters.

She stood back to admire her work. "What do you think?"

Jack set aside his tablet. "One more coat, I think."

"You were dead set against this, Jack. Why have you changed your mind?"

"Was I? All right, I was but I figured you'd just go ahead without me. Probably run aground on a reef."

She gave him a nudge. "I would not run aground but I'm awfully glad you're going. It'll take both of us to bring it off. I do think there's more to it though. Why'd you relent?"

"Once I started believing in the ETI signal, it became the principle of the thing. The government's decision to keep it hushed up—that's wrong. And if I accept that there's a signal I also have to consider that you're putting yourself at risk. The scientists have been gone now, what? Two or three months?"

"Three."

"I'm concerned for your safety," he said flatly. "And the reefs of course."

Kate chose her next words carefully. "There's something I need to tell you. It's about a man named Jeremy Sinclair."

"I've heard of him. Geller's National Security guy."

"Director of the NSA."

"What about him?"

She took a deep breath. "I worked for him when I was in Washington. He's the reason I moved back to San Francisco, the reason I left computer programming to go into journalism."

She told him the entire story, wishing she could omit details but knowing he'd have to hear all of it to understand. At first he busied himself cleaning paint brushes while she spoke, but midway through the narrative the brushes were forgotten. He stared at her and she watched his face transform itself like a fast-approaching storm front—from interest to disbelief to compassion, and finally gathering itself into a cumulus rage.

"*If you tell anyone, I'll have to kill you,*" Jack repeated when she finished. "What a guy."

"He's a sick man with a superb, practiced facade—just one of the fellas."

Jack returned to the paint brushes but the anger remained in his tone. "What kept you from reporting the incident, the threats?"

"Are you serious?" Her own voice was pitched for a fight. Was he blaming the victim? No, she told herself, he's angry *for* me, not *at* me. "It wasn't only the threats. Remember, I worked for him and endured his taunts for a year. I was awfully young and he was my boss." She looked at him. Was he understanding her? "I felt humiliated and at the same time too proud, as though I ought to be strong enough to endure it—maybe even amend the situation."

"But—"

"Which is part of the shame. If I could somehow have fixed it I must have done something to cause it—or at least prolong it. Do you see that?"

"You did prolong it—by not reporting it. There are so many people to whom you could have reported it. What he did was illegal, for crissake. Just the verbal stuff is against the law."

"You're a prosecutor and a man. You'd like to believe that all wrongs in the world can be righted, that justice is a ruling force in the universe. For white males that's probably true, but for the rest of us it's different. Who'd have believed me, Jack? For God's sake, look at Anita Hill. She told her story and the white males in the U.S. Senate believed her so much they confirmed Clarence Thomas to sit on the highest court in the land—*for life.* What does *that* tell you about justice? And here's the ultimate irony: I believe the very agency to which I would have reported

Sinclair's behavior—the EEOC—was headed at that time by—guess who—Mr. Clarence Thomas."

Jack's look was somber. He avoided her eyes. "I'll make a confession to you," he said. "On some level a lot of men just don't think verbal taunts with sexual overtones are that big a deal. Sure, they're rude, impolite, coarse—all that. But not that big a deal. Now when it gets physical, that's another story."

Kate fought for control, dipped a rag into the thinner and rubbed at a gob of paint that had seeped beneath a fingernail. She wanted more than anything for Jack not to have said that. "They're both designed to degrade and humiliate," she said. "There's no difference at all except in degree. If one is poison, they both are. It's as illegal to give someone a little arsenic as a lot. And it isn't only what is inflicted; it is *who* is inflicting it. If it's your boss, someone in authority who can make or break your career—" She flung the rag aside. "I'd hate to think you don't get it, Jack, the effect it had on me. But if you don't, how could I have hoped to earn the understanding of impersonal bureaucrats?"

Jack looked rebuked. "I know, and I do get it, Kate. It's just—"

One of the obstacles to understanding, she realized, lay in the fact that her story had become too common. In her case, no one had been killed; no rape had occurred; no one other than Sinclair had even been physically injured. The only demonstrable physical damage Kate had sustained had been a tear in a blouse and a lost button. Even in her own ear the story had sounded trivial in the telling, the terror somehow leeched out of the words. *If it bleeds it leads* had become the ruling standard guiding not only headlines but the boundaries defining human outrage. But no, she told herself now, she *had* been injured. It *had* cost her.

She struggled to rein in her emotions. "It seemed the fastest way to heal, the sanest thing, was to put as much distance as possible between myself and Jeremy Sinclair. The thing I wanted most was to be away from the man and make another start. So I came home. I couldn't even use him as a reference. It felt like rape and I completely understand why a woman would choose to say nothing."

"Which is exactly what the perpetrator counts on." He quickly held up a hand. "I know, Kate. I'm sorry. I didn't mean— Does he know where you live now? What you're doing?"

Her arms were folded tight across her chest. "I'm sure he does. I haven't heard from him in eight years. The threatening phone calls continued off and on for a few years and suddenly stopped. But I'm on his List. He's keeping track of me."

"And this is the guy who's now in charge of SETI security."

"I had to tell you. If you're going to participate in this rescue, you had to know."

"It ups the ante, doesn't it? Certainly explains your fervor. Frankly I couldn't entirely understand why you were so eager to risk so much for a story, even that story."

"I hate him and I fear him and I'd do a lot to bring him down."

Jack nodded and his look held understanding. He walked over and took her in his arms. "So the hell would I." His fingers pressed into the muscles of her back, gently working the tightness. "And if the government wants the ETI signal kept secret, that would certainly bring the guy down, wouldn't it? If he's the one in charge of security when the story breaks wide open?"

She leaned back to look up at him. "It isn't *only* Jeremy Sinclair. This signal is beyond you or me or any grief or beef I have with Sinclair. But you're right—I have a score to settle and a chance to settle it."

"And I'll help." He released her and turned to cap the thinner. "You probably should have told me this a long time ago. If I'd known before mailing off our sailing résumés to the charter company we could have given you a different name."

"The charter company will look at my passport."

He nodded. "There are ways— Well, let's clean up this mess and go to bed."

He treated her with great gentleness that night. As she lay in the crook of his arm after their lovemaking, a part of her wanted to plead with him not to suddenly treat her as though she were a fragile thing, one of those things that, when tinkered with, broke. Sinclair would claim any frailty as a personal triumph and she'd hate to ever give him that small concession. But another part of her, the part that won out, accepted that when it came to Jeremy Sinclair, she really was still raw. Gradually she relaxed into the circle of Jack's arms and let herself be drawn into comfort. There was relief in it: she'd finally told someone—a friend—about Jeremy Sinclair, and that friend had understood.

KATE AND GRACE had their final meeting at the Top Drawers Boutique on June eighth. With each meeting Kate became a little more anxious at the risk they were taking while Grace, for her part, appeared less concerned. Grace brought an increasing élan to each performance and had become adept at disguising the encounters as innocent shopping excursions.

Out of the corner of her eye, Kate watched as Grace meandered past a display of bathing suits, then drew alongside and furtively handed over a small paper sack. Kate stuffed it into her large purse and began browsing through size-eight bathing suits.

"I've decided to do it," Grace whispered. "Give him these things. There's a refill of his medication, sunscreen, a nylon sun hat, an envelope. Make sure he wears the hat and uses the sunscreen."

"I will."

"There's cash in the envelope and a note for him. Use what you need of the cash for the air charter and other expenses and give Milt the rest."

"Yes."

"Hank and Carolyn are helping with my arrangements. I'll arrive in Miami on the twenty-fourth. I'll be staying at the Fontainbleau Hilton. They don't know the entire plan, only that I'm flying to meet Milt. They'll pick me up here and drive me to the airport."

Grace's voice was almost matter-of-fact. She'd obviously tapped into an impressive fount of strength.

"Do you have any idea where you'll go from Miami?" Kate asked.

"Milt will know. It'll work out. We'll write and let you know if we can." She turned to Kate and touched her arm. "Good luck, Kate. Your courage has given me courage. Thank you." With that, she turned and left the shop.

When she was gone, Kate decided to undergo the ordeal of trying on bathing suits for the trip. She chose three from the rack and the clerk waved her toward a cramped, curtained dressing room. On cue, the Voice of Mother rose up as Kate squirmed into the first suit: *You could lose ten pounds, Kate. The stomach—* Kate sucked it in. *Stand up straighter.* She drew her shoulders back until her reflection in the mirror was stiff and graceless. Did every woman endure such interior scoldings? Give it a rest, Mother. The suit looks fine and I'm not fat.

Unconvinced, she pulled on a second suit, a turquoise and royal blue number. *Too skimpy, Kate. People will think you're cheap.*

She glanced around in mock amusement. "What people? Oh, the hell with it." She dressed, grabbed the first bathing suit and fled the dressing room.

Ω

14

JACK AND KATE arrived in Kingstown Harbor on the island of St. Vincent late on the evening of June nineteenth. After clearing customs at the airport, they boarded a chartreuse minivan for a heart-stopping cab ride into town.

Kate had come away from their earlier visit to the Leewards with the impression of the Caribbean as the most relaxed place on the planet. To any question or need the standard native response was a boundlessly eager "No problem," usually followed by a woefully lethargic follow-through. You could simply not hurry things along in the Caribbean. Except in a taxi. Somehow the notion of a leisurely pace had entirely escaped the consciousness of Caribbean cabbies. Julius, their driver, now had a tape of reggae Christmas carols blaring as they tore down the dark pot-holed road from the airport at just under the speed of light. Kate worked to shift herself into a lower mental gear. The cloying humidity of the tropics helped.

During their two-day stay in Miami, they'd found a pilot willing to fly to Puerto Rico on June twenty-seventh. Santiago Air Transport Services was listed in the Miami Yellow Pages.

The pilot and owner, Martín Santiago, was a native Puerto Rican who boasted a vast and intimate knowledge of non-commercial landing strips on his island. Neither Jack nor Kate had asked how he came by this knowledge—Kate figured they probably wouldn't want to know. Santiago told them of a private airstrip located in a valley in the southeast corner of the island. He had pointed to a spot on a grubby, folded and refolded, torn and taped map of Puerto Rico.

"Right here." The airstrip was thirty miles inland from Bahia Lima, the cove where Jack planned to deliver their passengers. Santiago insisted it would be a simple matter to fly the scientists from Puerto Rico to Miami.

"Of course it is expensive," he said regretfully, sorrowfully, hands extended in a what-can-I-do gesture of resignation.

"How much?" asked Jack.

"Any, ah, illegal substances?"

"Drugs? Absolutely not!"

"Three thousand dollars."

"Ridiculous! Fifteen hundred."

"Take it or leave it. Up to you. You buy discretion. Naturally that costs."

"Naturally," Jack said dryly. He counted out ten one-hundred dollar bills and handed them to Santiago. "You'll get the rest when your passengers arrive safely."

"For an extra two hundred I'll arrange for a taxi in Bahia Lima. I have a brother. Say, nine AM on the twenty-seventh. We drive your passengers from Bahia Lima to the landing strip, and fly here," said Santiago, gesturing vaguely to the tarmac beyond the stifling corrugated aluminum hangar. "Two and one-half hours. We arrive, say, eleven, eleven-thirty in the morning."

Fine, said Jack. Fine, said Kate. A good plan, Kate now reassured herself, as the cab belched and careened its way through the dark night into Kingstown. A deafening rendition of "Feliz Navidad" reverberated through the metal shell of the van.

Their hotel for the night was the Cobblestone Inn on Bay Street fronting Kingstown Harbor, just a short block from the marina. Jack had also arranged a second reservation at the Cobblestone for July tenth, the night they planned to return the charter boat three weeks hence. They were scheduled to fly out on the morning of the eleventh. Kate had to wonder, as Julius screeched to a halt in front of the hotel, whether they'd be in a position to keep that second reservation.

Julius helped them unload their gear. "When you leaving?" he asked. "I drive you back to the airport."

"July eleventh," Kate told him.

"My card," he said with a flourish. "Julius Henderson. You call when you are to leave and I get you to the airport in plenty of time."

"I'm sure you will," Kate said with a faint smile. She accepted the card and Julius stood by, overseeing to be sure it was tucked into a safe place.

They checked in and were assisted upstairs with their small mountain of luggage. Jack had brought along the additional sets of foul weather gear, numerous charts covering most of the Caribbean and southeastern coast of the United States, navigation instruments, cameras, the four volumes of *Avery's Guide* and an entire duffle bag devoted to first-aid items. Another duffle bag contained the mylar, tape and sheets of white plastic, a can of adhesive and one of solvent, scissors, and the can of leftover marine paint. Kate's gear included her portable computer, diskettes, clothes and extras for Tim and Dr. Rensler, jars of salsa, and cassette tapes of their favorite music—an eclectic mix of classical, jazz, George Winston, and Barbara Cook in concert.

Their room had a spartan charm to it—thick walls of freshly painted white stucco with door- and window-trim in a light natural wood. A ceiling fan revolved, silently bestirring the humid air. Kate drew open shutters for the breeze before collapsing wearily onto a lounge chair.

"The chart briefing is at ten," Jack said as he fiddled with the travel alarm clock. "I'll set it for eight."

She nodded absently, aware of a gnawing sense of foreboding. It was one thing to imagine and plan this caper in the obscurity and safety of her small San Francisco apartment and quite another to be in this place, about to execute the rescue of scientists from the custody of U.S. government agents. They hadn't even stepped onto the boat and already her nerves were taut. Within days she and Jack might be the subjects of an intense international manhunt. Cheery thought. How could she have imagined this would be *fun*? She stretched out beside Jack for a few hours sleep. Much too soon the alarm sounded in her ear.

Jack prodded her shoulder and she ducked her head under her pillow. "Take your shower and wake me when you've finished."

Gradually she drew herself awake and lay there, listening to Jack sing in the shower:

"Sad to say, I'm on my way, won't be back for many a day. My heart is down, my head is turning around, I had to leave a little girl in Kingstown Town." It was loud and more or less on key.

She crawled out of bed and crossed the room to the windows to take in the morning. Sunlight angled up from the bay and Kate squinted down at the bedlam of activity underway on the narrow street below the window. A delivery van was double-parked; an irritated driver lay on a horn. A group of native men stood by, leaning obdurately against a stone wall. A cluster of children darted through the congestion in pursuit of a soccer ball.

The shower was turned off and she called to Jack. "Wait'll you see this place."

He appeared moments later wrapped in a towel and walked over to where she stood. "Pretty, isn't it?" he agreed, looping his arms about her waist and looking over her shoulder. She leaned back and yawned, wishing this were the first day of a three-week vacation, acutely aware that it was not.

"Better get going if we're going to have breakfast before the briefing."

"I'll be quick," she said.

By nine they'd checked out and deposited their gear with the concierge while they ate a hurried breakfast in the hotel's dining room. Afterward they exchanged travelers' checks for E.C.'s— Eastern Caribbean dollars—retrieved their luggage, and then negotiated with a few of the soccer players for help with hauling their belongings down to the charter company.

At the charter office they were met by James, the C.C.I. Manager, an athletic-looking man with thinning blond hair, a fastidiously tidy beard and an enviable tan. "Follow me," he said briskly.

The briefing room was an open-air bandstand complete with dance floor. Rows of plastic laminated charts of the Windward Islands lined one wall. Ten other chartering sailors had already gathered, and Kate and Jack drew chairs into their semicircle. Soon they were scribbling notes on everything from where to check in with various islands' customs offices to the operation of ship-to-shore radios, where to buy ice, take on water, snorkel, obtain fresh lobster, or seek help if their boat malfunctioned.

It was vital that they create the impression with James and the others that they'd be sailing south, rather than north to St. Lucia. From the questions and comments of the others, it was obvious the other parties would be sailing south, and all would be putting in on this first night at nearby Admiralty Bay on the island of Bequia. James laid out a southerly itinerary, and Kate and Jack took notes and asked questions designed to suggested they'd follow this itinerary.

"Anchoring is where people run into the most trouble," James said, launching into a discourse on mooring techniques. "And after all that, it's still best to dive down and eyeball the anchor to be sure it isn't hooked on coral, plus it's a good excuse for a swim. If you stop at Salt Whistle Bay on Mayreau, you'll need to anchor bow and stern. Otherwise, if you stick to this itinerary, you'll usually find anchorage in sand, in around ten to twenty feet, so anchoring should be straightforward. But if any of you stray north to Wallilabou or Soufriere, you'll be in very deep water and you must row ashore with your line and tie to a palm tree.

"When entering a harbor, always post a lookout on the bow. These waters are mine fields of coral and it's potentially deadly and at minimum embarrassing—not to mention harmful to our boats' keels—when our people run aground. You can count on your fellow yachtsmen to be out under their bimini's having cocktails and watching your exhibition of seamanship—or lack of it.

"And if you can possibly avoid it, do not head into port with the setting sun in your eyes. Lookout or no, you won't be able to see the reefs. And of course, no sailing at night. Questions?"

He scanned the mostly jet-lagged faces for signs of comprehension. "Good. The Miller party?"

A foursome raised their hands.

"Your boat is a Morgan 50, *La Luna*. Sullivan?"

Jack raised his hand. "Yours is the sloop *Great Expectations*. Whittaker? You get the Beneteau *Aeolus*. Jacobs? Another Beneteau, the *Windsong*. Good luck, people. Have a fun and safe vacation."

Kate hurriedly noted down the names of all the parties and their boats; they might need them later. Then she and Jack followed the others out of the briefing room and down to the dock. *Great Expectations* was moored stern-to-the-slip and dock hands were clambering about, loading cases of food, drinks and supplies. A hose snaked across the deck and disappeared into a chrome aperture, topping off the water tanks. Jack left for a second load of gear, and Kate went below to begin stowing provisions.

As she sorted perishables from things that would keep, Jack went over every inch of *Great Expectations* with a dock hand in tow. After weeks of preparation and planning, Kate wished they could simply toss duffle bags aboard, let loose the dock lines and go. Instead, for nearly two hours she organized supplies while Jack inventoried winch handles, fenders, swim fins, charts, sails and dinghy oars. With lawyer-like thoroughness, he verified that everything the charter company said was on board, was in fact on board, and that all of it worked.

In the salon, Kate opened portholes and hatches for air and could overhear the two men topside as she labored in the stuffy cabin. She heard the power anchor windlass groan to life and then Jack asking about the rigging. The dinghy—was it seaworthy? Was there a separate anchor for it? A padlock? What about the outboard motor and fuel tank?

Then they trooped below, crawled around with a flashlight, and huddled for a stirring discussion of heads, bilge pumps and Perkin diesel engines.

Finally the dockhand was gone and Jack called out, "Are you ready to leave?"

"For days," she sighed. "Let's go."

They'd sailed so often together that they went about their leave-taking with practiced ease. Kate started the engine and Jack took the helm. She cast off the dock lines, and he steered them out of the slip. As he threaded the Morgan through the harbor's heavy traffic, she hauled in and stowed fenders and then positioned herself at the base of the mast. When Jack nosed the boat into the wind, she untied harbor gaskets and on his command, hoisted the main. Then he dropped off the wind and the sail snapped full. Back in the cockpit, she took over the helm while Jack unfurled and winched down the huge Genoa jib. When it was set, he doused the engine and then flopped down on the cockpit seat cushion with a long sigh.

"There," he said. "Steer course 200°."

She brought them on course. Away from the harbor, the wind was strong and steady, and soon they were tearing through the ocean, bounding across the nine-mile channel to Bequia at nearly ten knots, helped along by the tremendous surge of a following sea. They sailed in silence for several long moments, simply taking in the raw sensations.

The small island of Bequia was clearly visible ahead. The ocean was a deep teal blue, and the sky was a flawless azure. Kate felt the pull of the wind in her arms and hands as she gripped the chrome wheel and held the course. "Windward Islands indeed," she murmured.

"Unbelievable," Jack agreed. "We'll be in Admiralty Bay by four o'clock at this rate." He went below and returned with *Avery's Guide* and began reading a description of their destination. "'The entrance is straightforward, the main dangers being Flat Rock off Devils Table and the Belmont Shoal reefs off the

Sunny Caribbee Hotel. The preferred anchorage is toward town near the Frangipani Hotel.'"

Kate suspected they'd both read these passages before and that more than anything, this was Jack's attempt to steady their nerves. It helped some.

"Plenty of places to shop. There's a supermarket where we can supplement food stocks and we can get baked goods at Mac's Bakeshop and Pizzeria."

"Pizza sounds good. How about it?"

"Tonight? Didn't you just stow eight tons of food?"

"Yes, and now I'm too tired to cook any of it."

"I'll cook," he said cheerfully.

When they were abeam of Flat Rock, Jack spotted the red channel marker and the entrance to Admiralty Bay. He doused the jib and started the engine. Kate headed the boat into the wind, and when the main was slack, Jack dropped the sail in a tumble of canvas and bundled it over the boom.

"Let's ready the anchor," he said, eyeing the crowded harbor.

"You take the helm and I'll go forward."

As with their departure, they had their own practiced routine for arriving and anchoring. She picked out a likely spot to lay anchor and motioned to Jack to shift into neutral. As their speed slackened, she released the anchor with a sharp clatter of chain and signaled to him to reverse engine. He backed down on the anchor, and moments later she was back in the cockpit.

"I'll dive down and have a look." He quickly donned face mask and fins and was over the side and paddling forward over the anchor line. He executed a splashy dive, and surfaced moments later with the Okay signal. She tied the ladder over the side in time for him to heave himself back aboard.

"Water's sensational, probably 80°."

She wasted no time, hurried below and changed into her new bathing suit.

"Wow!" Jack greeted her with an appreciative grin. "New?"

"Yes, thanks. I've been imagining this swim for weeks." She took a breath and dove smoothly into the crystal-clear water and was instantly embraced in soft, salty warmth. She let herself become limp and drift slowly to the surface. Then she swam hard for several minutes before turning to float on her back. Clouds drifted by overhead. Tension seeped from her shoulders. She climbed back aboard to find Jack stretched out in the cockpit sipping on a beer and surveying the harbor. She fetched a Heineken and joined him.

"The Frangipani Hotel is over there," he said, indicating a sprawling complex of buildings nestled in a grove of palm trees. "Just beyond is the Sunny Caribbee Hotel. Just offshore there's supposedly a reef there and according to *Avery's*, fair snorkeling."

The business section of the town of Port Elizabeth lay off their bow. A loading and ferry dock bustled with late afternoon activity. Bequia was smaller and more provincial than St. Vincent and Kate was already taken with its sleepy charm. Palm trees dotted much of the shoreline and a few houses and businesses perched on the gently sloping surrounding hillsides.

They spent the evening on board. Jack made tacos while Kate finished unpacking and organizing gear. She stowed Dr. Rensler's few things in the fo'c'sle and Tim's in the quarterberth. After dinner, they sat in the cockpit with coffee and gazed up at the stars. With so few surrounding lights, the trailing arms of the Milky Way were bright stippled streaks across the ink-black sky. The evening was warm and still, and the boat's sounds were a soothing lull of creaks and groans.

"This has to be paradise," she sighed.

"Nice spot for a vacation."

"There's a lot to do tomorrow. Shopping. Somehow it's all got to be managed without anyone noticing. It would look odd to people from our chart briefing if we're seen loading quantities of supplies."

"True. I'm bushed," he said with yawn.

"Me too." They climbed below, made up the stern berth and were asleep almost immediately.

Ω

15

SINCLAIR called Michael Gregg with results of the hypnosis sessions with his agents. A few details had emerged. It turned out that only Villanova had actually read the Thurmond postcard. Radcliffe's attention had been on Thurmond and on seeing to it he didn't attempt an escape.

"Here's what we've got, Michael. It's not much. Thurmond threatened to pitch a fit in the airport if not allowed to send the postcard. Our guys talked it over and agreed—"

"How could they *do* that?"

"I know. I'm just telling you what we've got. They accompanied Thurmond into an airport gift shop. He chose a postcard of the Golden Gate Bridge, bought a stamp, scribbled a short message and showed it to Villanova, who remembered the gist of it under hypnosis. It starts out with 'Hi.' No name. He apologizes for failing to keep their date Saturday night and hopes she won't be upset. He says he's been called away on business and signs it, 'Love, Tim.'"

"Anything on the address?"

"I'm getting to that. After Villanova checked the message, Thurmond said he had the address and pulled a scrap of paper from his wallet and copied it down. At that point, Villanova says his own attention was given over to buying chewing gum for the flight. He doesn't recall being shown the address."

"Incredibly sloppy work, Jeremy—I mean on the part of those agents. What happened to the scrap of paper?"

Sinclair snapped back, "Look, part of the parameters of this operation include compartmentalization. *Need-to-know*. These men did not know why they were transporting— Skip it." Why the hell was he justifying elements of this operation to an underling? "Look, you play the hand you're dealt. If you get lemons, make lemonade."

"Well, it sucks, that's for sure."

"Indeed it does. These guys' careers are history. I'll keep Villanova available for additional sessions. He has no memory of what happened to the paper after Thurmond copied the address. It might have been left on the countertop in the shop or it might have gone back into Thurmond's wallet or pocket. I assume you found nothing?"

"No."

"Thurmond dropped the card in a mailbox just outside the gift shop. Oh and Michael, thought you'd like to know—I'll be down tomorrow on the 7:35 PM flight. Send the van."

"Right."

"And I'm bringing a hypnotist who is also an M.D. We'll try Pentothal on Tim Thurmond."

"Supposedly, there's a chandlery part way up the hill where we can pick up the two hundred feet of line," Jack said the following morning.

It was June twenty-first, two days before the planned rescue, and they were sitting in the cockpit, sipping coffee out of plastic mugs and taking in the early-morning stirrings in Admiralty Bay. The coffee tasted metallic. Kate had brewed it in the ship's aluminum stove-top percolator and it tasted like sailing coffee. Just right, she thought. Hers was heavily laced with cream.

"The bow anchor line isn't sufficient?"

"I'd rather have the extra line. We'll need it to tie to the palm tree in Soufriere. We can loop it around the tree and run it back to the boat. We won't have to row ashore to untie when we leave." He was staring out across the bay with a distant look.

"That's good." She felt his worry.

He lowered his gaze. "We don't have a whisker pole."

"Do we need one?"

"If we're faced with a long downwind run where we're sailing wing-and-wing. We could buy one at the marine hardware store. Avery says to expect sudden wind shifts, especially southeast of Puerto Rico."

"So we'll rig a preventer line down from the boom, Jack. We'd attract attention hauling a whisker pole down to the boat."

"You're right. Just don't want to forget anything."

"You're worried."

"Aren't you?" He stared at her.

"It seemed so sensible over Chinese food in San Francisco."

"We could still call it off."

"I know, but no, I can't."

"Look, there's the *Windsong.*" He pointed across the starboard bow toward the white-hulled Beneteau that was moored fifty yards off. "The Jacobs, as I recall." The couple from their chart briefing had raised a canvas bimini top over their cockpit, and Mrs. Jacobs was on deck, clothespinning towels to a lifeline.

Jack stood abruptly. "If the rescue is what you need to do, I'm with you."

She sighed a thank you. "We might pay the Jacobs a visit."

"Witnesses to the fact that we sailed south."

"Yes."

They gathered canvas carry-alls, boarded and padlocked the hatch and set off for shore in the dinghy. Jack rowed, preferring to conserve their few gallons of outboard fuel for the rescue. After tying up at the dinghy dock, their first stop was the chandlery located up a long steep hill overlooking the quiet harbor. At the shop's entrance a yellow Labrador retriever lay dozing in the morning sun. Kate stooped to scratch his head. Inside the cavernous shop, vast sections of white canvas were spread around the concrete floor in various stages of being measured, cut and stitched.

"Anyone here?" Jack's voice echoed through the room. A young man appeared. "I need two hundred feet of half-inch line," Jack told him.

Kate wandered back outside and took in the view of the quiet harbor. A few children were paddling and splashing in the shallows near shore. A light breeze was stirring and birds were noisily flitting between the branches of a nearby breadfruit tree.

"All set?" she asked, when Jack emerged with his purchases.

"Got the line plus a sail-mending kit and—"

"Jack, look at this place. Have you ever seen a prettier spot? We should move here, live on a boat."

"Sure." He consulted his shopping list, all business.

The coiled half-inch line was looped over his shoulder as they set off down the hill in search of the market. They found it next to the customs office near the commercial shipping dock, a weathered, wooden frame structure that announced itself with an unduly optimistic sign: Supermarket. They commandeered a rusting cart and began pushing it up and down dim aisles, loading extra provisions for their passengers—canned goods, rice, cereal, cheese and produce, gallon jugs of drinking water and extra cases of beer and soft drinks.

With the help of local youths and small bribes, they hauled everything down to the dock. They had almost finished loading things into the dinghy when Kate spotted the Jacobs approaching from the shore end of the dock.

"Oh God, they'll see all this food, Jack. And the line. What'll—" Before she could complete the thought, she'd thrust the last gallon water jug into Jack's outstretched hands, untied the dinghy and gave the boat a hard shove off the dock. "Go back without me!" she whispered.

She straightened as Jack lurched down onto the seat with a startled look and hurriedly set the oars in the locks and began rowing. She turned, calmed her breathing, and arranged her face into a greeting.

"Hi. God it's hot. Been sightseeing?"

"Yep. You're on *Great Expectations*, aren't you?" Mr. Jacobs said with a friendly smile.

"Yes. I'm Kate Lipton. That's my friend Jack, rowing back to the boat. We, ah, we just bought ice, but then I just realized I left my, ah, hat over at the Frangipani, and I'm—"

"This is my wife Angie. I'm Bob Jacobs."

"Right. Let's see, you're on the *Windsong*?"

"Yes. Same boat we always get. Beneteau. Great boat."

Kate faltered through her end of the conversation, finally getting in step. They chartered in the Windwards every year. Bob was a New Jersey dentist and Angie was a travel agent. Bob seemed inclined to share every detail of the past decade's annual charter experiences but Kate cut it short. "I should see whether my hat's still at the hotel. I think I set it on one of the tables on the patio. Jack and I had coffee and—"

"We'll wait and give you a lift back to your boat," Dr. Bob offered.

"Gee that's nice, but—"

"No trouble at all. We'll wait here."

Kate left and returned minutes later to say that she'd abandoned the search for the missing hat. They piled into the Jacob's boat. By the time they were alongside *Great Expectations*, Jack had finished unloading the supplies from the dinghy.

"I was just about to come get you," he said after introductions were made. He was breathing hard and his forehead gleamed with perspiration.

"I didn't find my straw hat," Kate said pointedly.

"Oh, that's too bad. I'm sure we can buy you another. You folks care for a beer, soft drink? It's gotten awfully hot, hasn't it?"

Fortunately the Jacobs declined; had they accepted and come aboard, they'd have stumbled over the food and supplies scattered about the cockpit floor.

"That was close," Jack said breathlessly as they stood watching the couple row off.

"No kidding. Are we being awfully paranoid?"

"Probably." Then, "No, I don't think so—just cautious."

After stowing supplies they went for a swim to cool off. Then Kate made sandwiches.

"That's everything except the bread we wanted to pick up at Mac's," Jack said between bites of tuna sandwich. "You're right, you know. We could live here. Chuck it all, sail down here and string puka beads for a living."

At the moment the idea didn't seem that outlandish. What was so terrific about their high-stress, fast-paced lives in the States? Who needed high blood pressure, polluted air, clogged freeways and airless offices? "Puka beads?" she said.

"Right." He picked up another sandwich. "Peanut butter and jelly?"

"Mm."

"We could open a Mexican restaurant."

"Or publish an Eastern Caribbean newspaper."

"And I could sail around to all the islands and deliver it."

"*You* could sail around the islands?"

"*We*," he amended. "A paper route would be perfect. I can handle that. I had one when I was ten so there's a certain symmetry to it, I think. What'll we call it?"

"The Bequia *Gazette*, The Admiralty Bay *Times Herald*."

"*The Daily Pilot*—no, not daily. *Weekly*. No, *Monthly*. The *Windward Monthly Pilot*."

"Annual?" Kate leaned back, soaking up tropical laziness. "We'll do restaurant reviews, sailing news, gossip, local scandals."

"A fishing report."

She could almost envision the venture and half-believe in it. "We'd live on board of course, but we'd need a printing press, which would mean an office. We couldn't very well operate the printing press on board."

"There you go, complicating it with detail, the very stuff of which dreams are demolished."

"The devil's in the details." They ate in silence for several moments. "Have we forgotten anything?" she asked.

"Bread."

"I mean our plan. Is it good enough?"

"Once we're away from Soufriere, our risk ought to be minimal."

"You realize once we leave here tomorrow, we won't be able to go ashore, other than for the rescue, for ten days."

He nodded at her sobering observation. "There ought to be enough food. Water might be tight and we'll conserve our diesel fuel. We'll need a secluded anchorage tomorrow night. No one can see that we've headed back north." He smiled at her suddenly. "That really is the sexiest bathing suit I've ever seen."

"Thanks, but—"

He held up a hand. "Enough. We've done our best. Let's try to have a vacation, if only for the rest of the day."

She nodded, gestured at the surrounding harbor. "Even if it only looks like one."

They returned to shore for dinner. From the dinghy dock they followed the shoreline to the Sunny Caribbee Hotel and sat outside on the terrace to watch the sky shift and transform itself through a stunning progression of colors. They were both sighing a lot, exhaling waves of anxiety. They sipped rum punch and watched a lone windsurfer skim over the water, silhouetted against the pastel evening sky.

At Mac's Bakeshop and Pizzeria they ordered lobster pizza, topped off the meal with a shared slice of key lime pie, and bought loaves of bread. Then they linked arms and strolled back in the direction of the dock. The bay was utterly still. A sliver of moon had risen and near it, a bright Saturn appeared as though suspended from the moon's upturned tip.

"Tired?" Jack asked nonchalantly.

"No," she said with a faint smile.

"I was thinking we ought to inaugurate the stern berth."

"As part of the pre-cruise shake down."

"Essential."

They made love amid the heap of cushions and pillows piled around the stern. At the start, Kate's mind was only half-present, the other half continuing to thrash through details of the rescue.

But as his fingers began tracing her body with excruciating feather-softness, her breath caught. She forgot whatever she'd been obsessing on and drew him in until the slow-growing force of his passion overwhelmed her. Her arms encircled his strong back and her legs locked around him. Afterward they curled together, Jack idly coiling strands of her hair around an index finger. She continued to hold onto him for a long time and dropped off to sleep with her cheek pressed against his chest, the sound of his heart beating in her ear.

Ω

16

KATE WAS only half-awake at the helm as they left Admiralty Bay the next morning. The sun was rising over the hills behind the town as they cleared the West Cay buoy. It was six AM, June twenty-second, one day before the rescue.

She steered south until they were well out of sight of Admiralty Bay and any of its inhabitants who might chance to observe their leave-taking. Message: they were following James' itinerary, heading south. Jack raised the sails, cut the engine, and they caught a fair breeze.

"Hold 230°," Jack said. He disappeared below to perc coffee and plot the day's course and returned a few minutes later, to hand her a mug and a banana. "Breakfast—sort of. We'll hold this heading for another twenty minutes just to be safe."

She handed over the helm and went below to brush her teeth and splash water on her face. A few minutes later she was back to help come about and reset the sails for the first long north-westerly tack. Their day's destination was tentatively Wallilabou Harbor, St. Vincent, a cove approximately midway between Bequia and Soufriere. They'd considered attempting the long sail to Soufriere in a single day but decided against it. They'd arrive exhausted, and there was the matter of the boat name. Given the high winds and the tremendous ocean swells, fastening the *Espiritu Del Sol* covering to the stern would be better attempted in the protective lee of an island. A secluded mid-way anchorage would most likely be found along St. Vincent's rugged north-western coastline. North of Wallilabou, St. Vincent, was a bay called Cumberland, but little else north of that. They might even be forced to nose up against an unprotected stretch of deserted coastline for the night.

The morning sail was uneventful. For Kate the high point came when dolphins showed up and accompanied them for several minutes. She dashed forward to watch them play off the bow and caught a momentary hint of great intelligence in a brief flash of meeting eyes. They made obvious sport of racing against *Great Expectations*, breaching, diving and disappearing to emerge again several yards ahead. They would then check their speed to allow the sluggish sailboat to catch up before launching the next display. They're toying with us, Kate thought, and when suddenly they were gone, their absence left her feeling slightly bereft.

Soon after, Jack brought them about to a northeasterly heading for the long run into Wallilabou. Hours later, they were in the lee of St. Vincent and doused sails. They motored slowly north along the coast, approaching the entrance to Wallilabou Harbor, and looked in to find dozens of yachts already at anchor. They couldn't stay.

Avery's Guide described Cumberland Bay as an eerily dark hurricane hole frequented by smugglers until the mid-eighties. They'd find no town, no amenities, and Avery warned that the weather there was often locally squallish and unpredictable. When they reached this rather dreary spot two hours later, it was all Avery had promised—ominous and menacing. A misting rain was falling and the sky hung over the place like a dingy, gray-green canopy. The shore was lined with a dense grove of towering palm trees and off to one side was a single thatch-roofed hut. There were no other structures and best of all, no other boats. They laid anchor in twenty feet of pea-green murk.

"Who do you suppose lives in that hut?"

"Smugglers. Geez, Jack, this is the strangest place. It wasn't raining in Wallilabou. I don't even recall seeing clouds." It was as though the cove had spawned its own micro-climate. The rain

was a steady downpour and they were both quickly drenched to
the skin.

"Will you dive down to look at the anchor?"

Jack eyed the silty water. "Wouldn't dream of it. Avery says
it's a soft, muddy bottom. I think we'll hold."

They closed themselves into the cabin as the rain turned from
steady to torrential. Though the air wasn't cold, Kate felt herself
shiver and drew on a sweatshirt. They cooked some sort of white
mystery fish for dinner and then read, or pretended to. Jack
studied charts of the southern coast of St. Lucia, and Kate stared
through rain-streaked portholes at the night, her book open
face-down on her lap.

At nine, they locked the hatch and climbed into the stern
berth. Kate doubted either of them would sleep. Tomorrow was
rescue day and if it went as planned, they faced days of non-stop
sailing. If she'd hoped to begin that effort with both of them
rested, it now seemed unlikely. She did eventually drop off and
slept fitfully, awakening with the sense that Jack had kept watch
through the night. When he roused her before dawn, the alarm
hadn't even sounded.

"Did you sleep?"

"Some," he lied.

They hauled anchor at five-thirty AM and motored out of the
bay through the relentless downpour. Within a mile of shore they
were beneath clear skies streaked with the orange and pink hues
of a rising sun. There was scarcely a breath of wind in the lee
of the mountainous island. It was the ideal setting in which to
become *Espiritu Del Sol*.

Jack went below and returned with the duffle bag containing
the mylar, white canvas tape, spray adhesive and white plastic
sheeting. He hauled the dinghy alongside, climbed in, and pulled
himself hand-over-hand back to the stern. Kate peered over to
watch as he wiped the stern dry with a towel.

He cut lengths of tape which he used to fasten the white
plastic sheeting over the name *Great Expectations*. Then he

sprayed the entire stern with adhesive and rolled the mylar down over it, pressing it down and fixing the edges with more tape.

"It looks good from here," Kate said when he finished.

"Let's hope it holds." He climbed back aboard, stowed the ladder, and bent over the stern to examine his work. "A few wrinkles but probably from five feet you'd never notice."

"I'll make breakfast."

She handed up toast, coffee, and the inevitable bananas, and ate as dawn broke over the lush green hills of St. Vincent.

"To the voyage of the *Espiritu Del Sol*," Jack said, mug raised.

"I'll drink to that. And happy birthday to Milton Rensler."

"Bet Grace Rensler is a bundle of nerves. In a few hours, she'll be ducking out the back door of that shop."

"And the moment she does, it'll be too late to call this off."

"Do you want to?" he asked.

"Absolutely not."

Ω

17

JEREMY SINCLAIR'S arrival at the St. Lucian compound generated quite a stir among the scientists as well as the support staff and security people. Most of the agents had come face to face with their agency's Director only once, that on the occasion of their graduation from the NSA's rigorous training school. Immediately Sinclair saw that his visit was long overdue.

The problem, he saw, was in the air, in the wafting breezes, the shocking reds and magentas of flowering hibiscus and bougainvillea. The compound had been a residential estate with a large sprawling two-story main house and several outbuildings, all situated amid manicured grounds tamed from the surrounding jungle. The house itself was edged on three sides by wide covered verandas, and the whole atmosphere reeked of a goddamned tropical paradise. Who could take in and sustain a sense of the enormity and urgency of their task under such conditions?

Though he'd intended to get to work immediately on the Thurmond interrogation, whipping the troops into shape took precedence. He inspected all the buildings, the quarters where the scientists were housed, the lab, kitchen and staff offices, and the enormous satellite dish complex rising from the lush landscape. He questioned the security of communications equipment, the operation and monitoring of their closed-circuit surveillance equipment, reviewed gate entry and exit logs and procedures, and quizzed agents on the comings and goings of various local support services. How often were laundry and food deliveries made? By whom? How often were the scientists' quarters inspected? How many excursions were they permitted? How many left the compound at a time, where did they go, who accompanied them? Did staff make use of the opportunity to search the scientists' personal belongings, read through diaries and notes? How thorough were such inspections?

He paced out the compound's perimeter, evaluating its imperviousness to intrusion and stumbling over the occasional singed carcass of opossum and the startlingly colorful plumage of tropical birds who'd had the misfortune to light on the high-voltage wire topping the ten-foot high chain link fence surrounding the compound.

Sinclair had flown down with Dr. Frank Lundquist, psychiatrist, and he quickly noted the effects of the St. Lucian paradise on this man of medicine who, within minutes of their arrival, had changed from a business suit to a hideously garish Hawaiian sports shirt, cotton shorts and sandals. There it was—vacation brains. Sinclair ordered him to lose the shirt.

By late afternoon of that first day, Sinclair had presented Michael Gregg with a laundry list of minor security breaches and insufficiencies ranging from staff telephones left unattended in unlocked rooms, to inadequate scrutiny of their bank of closed-circuit monitors. Inspections of service trucks entering and leaving the compound needed to be more thorough. Audio tape of scientists' conversations should be forwarded daily to Fort Meade for analysis.

Then Sinclair called his stateside office and received a rather alarming report on Grace Rensler's behavior over the past seventy-two hours. She had been deviating from her well-established norm. She'd not been frequenting certain shops as she routinely had in the past. She'd recently sought out frequent contact with her brother-in-law and his wife; until recently she'd been isolated, had seemingly minimized contacts with family and friends. And despite the willingness of agents to deliver her written communications to her husband, she'd penned only a single note, that a very brief birthday card. She'd not been behaving true to form and for Jeremy Sinclair it was more troubling news. He ordered the Bay Area team on maximum alert. The need-to-know compartmentalization strategy was killing him.

ST. LUCIA lay to the northeast of St. Vincent. The prevailing winds, also out of the northeast, made it virtually impossible to sail directly from St. Vincent to Soufriere. Instead, the course of *Espiritu Del Sol* would be similar to the previous day's, with a half-day-long tack to the northwest followed by a second tack east into Soufriere. Kate and Jack intended to time their arrival for dusk, and by remaining well offshore, expected to avoid most of the boating traffic. The actual distance from Cumberland Bay to Soufriere was around thirty-five nautical miles but they would travel closer to sixty that day.

Kate took the helm and held a course of 355° until noon while Jack slept below. At first the sail was slightly unnerving. Out of the lee of St. Vincent, the northeasterly winds gathered in strength and whitecapped swells grew to six and then eight feet and higher. She had never been alone at the helm for so long a stretch, nor in such heavy seas and winds. The boat heeled sharply on its starboard tack, spray blowing back as *Espiritu* sliced through the swells. Kate needed to hold as near-perfect a course as possible if they were to time their arrival for dusk. Her glance shifted continuously from sails to compass to wind indicator and knotmeter. It was not restful. They were averaging between six and seven knots.

By midmorning the overwhelming solitude of the task gave way to a different sense. Wind, sky, sails, the churning sea, seabirds and flying fish began to seem in concert. Gradually she sensed the course, the direction in the angle of the sun and the sea's relentless rhythm. She felt herself automatically anticipating the broadside swells that drove the boat from its course. She found herself able to hold course without checking the compass at all. There were no islands in sight and the isolation and the vastness of the ocean swept over her, becoming a kind of meditation.

SINCLAIR finally sent for Tim Thurmond on the morning of his second day in Soufriere.

"So," he greeted the young man, motioning him to a seat in a corner of the security staff office. The vast expanse was a converted billiards room. an ornate twelve-foot pool table, now covered with plywood, dominated the room.

"Who'd you break the date with?" he asked abruptly, eyeing Thurmond, gauging his reaction. It was minimal, disingenuous.

"Excuse me?"

"The woman you sent the postcard to, all apologetic about breaking a supposed date."

Thurmond emitted a long sigh. "I've already discussed this with Michael Gregg and Agent Nicholsen. I refuse to give you that information. I don't want your people invading the privacy of an innocent person. Once you interrogate her, you'd then have to keep an eye on her, wouldn't you?"

Sinclair motioned to Dr. Lundquist, who'd been sitting across the room waiting. "Tim, this is Dr. Frank Lundquist. He's here to work with you on this and you'll give him your full cooperation and support."

Thurmond turned in his seat to stare at the lanky, middle-aged doctor. "Doctor of what?"

"Psychiatry," Lundquist replied, reaching out to shake hands.

Tim ignored the outstretched hand and looked back at the NSA Director. "It won't work."

"What won't work?"

"You can't force me to tell you something I don't choose to disclose."

"Really?" Sinclair said, nonplussed. "Who did you discuss the signal with?"

"Nobody."

Dr. Lundquist drew a chair alongside. "I understand there's a birthday celebration on tap for this evening. Dr. Rensler's seventieth?" Thurmond said nothing and Lundquist continued, "I'm sure you'd hate to miss the festivities. Drs. Vaughn and Rensler, the Jacobsens and you, all have reservations."

Tim's arms were crossed tightly and he slouched lower in his chair, legs outstretched and locked at the ankles in a posture of unyielding indifference.

Sinclair spoke. "I think our Mister Thurmond might prefer to stay here tonight, don't you, Frank?"

"Apparently so."

"Look, you want me to give you the name of a perfectly innocent woman so you can question and harass her. You want to know the truth? Here it is: I dated this woman exactly once! I don't even know her address from memory. I threw away the goddamned slip of paper it was written on and I don't remember it."

"Perhaps you'll submit to hypnosis then. We can achieve amazing results, you know. And failing that, we might try Pentothal. You're familiar with its uses?"

"And the Bill of Rights be damned, eh?" Thurmond shook his head as though at this point nothing would surprise him. He held out his hands. "For the record, I protest. But since I don't see anyone taking notes of this little meeting, I see my protest will go unrecorded. I'll say it again—the postcard was nothing. But go ahead, take your best shot."

"You look positively transfixed," Jack said, startling Kate from her reverie. "How's it going?"

"Wonderful. I do feel sort of transported. Did you sleep?"

"God yes." He stepped to her side and kissed her cheek. "I've got the helm."

She slumped to the cockpit cushion with a sigh. "I thought we might have to pry my hands loose. And my shoulders— I'm out of shape."

She went below to use the head and when she returned, they changed course to 110°, on the final run to Soufriere. "Hungry?" she asked.

"Starved."

She went below and did her best to assemble sandwiches in the bucking and lunging of the galley, emerging with an approximation of a chicken sandwich for Jack and a queasy stomach for herself.

"I figure we're five hours out," he said, eyeing her with concern. "You don't look so good."

"Just tired. I should try for a nap."

She stretched out in the stern berth and did doze, awakening a few hours later. After splashing water on her face and corralling her hair Indian-style into a bandanna, she emerged from the cabin.

"Kate, look. The Pitons."

She turned to gaze over the bow at the pinnacles rising up from the southern tip of distant St. Lucia. "They're huge. We must be closer than I thought."

"No, we're still twenty miles out. I spotted them over an hour ago. Quite a landmark, 2600 feet of rock jutting up out of the sea."

They were heading due east now and Jack had the sails close-hauled, *Espiritu Del Sol* lunging along head-on into twelve-foot swells. "Can I get you anything? A beer, a Coke?"

"A banana."

"No shortage of potassium on this tug, is there?" She went below and returned with his snack. "I'd make you another sandwich but I can't stomach it in this chop."

It occurred to her that as so often happened when sailing, their lives had started revolving around basic things—what and when to eat, where and when to sleep, weather, wind and currents. She hoped there was adequate fresh water and food on board for six people. *For six?* No, for four.

"Jack, I just had a feeling—"

"What?"

"—that we might have additional passengers."

"When did you think of that?"

"Just now. Some of the others might want to leave with Tim and Dr. Rensler."

"There's not enough room, the food— What makes you—"

"Only a feeling." She thought a moment. "It's strange, Jack. It's happened a lot recently. I get these vivid pictures in my mind, see things before they actually happen. Like that hummingbird card. I saw it in my mind exactly as it was, right down to the pink flower. And I knew precisely where to buy it, drove clear across town to a drugstore on Chestnut Street for it."

"You'd probably seen it there before and just forgot."

"No, it's more—" She shook her head. "Anyway I have a feeling we'll be taking four aboard." She felt foolish for having mentioned it. "When I take the dinghy around to the Hummingbird, could you boil a dozen eggs for later? It's tough messing with food in that galley while we're underway."

His expression clouded. "I still think I should take the dinghy around. You should stay on board."

It had been their ongoing debate for weeks. "We've been over this, Jack. They won't know who you are. They'd have no reason to trust you. I'll be fine. I can operate the outboard motor as well as you. And you'll have to be patient. I don't know how long it'll take. It might be a few hours before they're able to leave the restaurant and get down to the beach."

"What if something goes wrong?"

"Nothing will, Jack."

"Another one of those feelings?"

It might be. That or wishful thinking.

Ω

18

THERE WERE SIX BOATS at anchor in Hummingbird Cove. It was dusk. *Espiritu Del Sol* motored past the entrance to the bay, and Kate and Jack peered into the cove, speechless. The looming grandeur of Petit Piton rose up at the bay's southern end, it's vastness obliterating the southeastern sky. This was a spectacular cove. Kate went forward, gripped the forestay for support, and squinted through the shadows at the quiet harbor. All six of the boats appeared to be sailing sloops. The dim shoreline was defined by a smattering of lights reflecting off calm waters.

Jack continued heading *Espiritu* southeast until Hummingbird Cove disappeared behind Petit Piton. Then very slowly, like a silent stirring beast, the even more massive Gros Piton came into view, followed by the deeply inset cove of Petit Soufriere. If possible, it was an even more spectacular cove than Hummingbird. Flanked by the two Pitons and dark, densely jungled hillsides, the inner shoreline was defined by a faint strip of sandy beach. There were no lights; the place seemed utterly deserted. Kate took the helm and Jack wasted no time. He tied one end of his two-hundred-foot line to the stern cleat, tossed the rest into the dinghy and hurriedly climbed in after.

The offshore wind predicted in *Avery's Guide* was already up, creating considerable turbulence. It would have been an uncomfortable overnight anchorage for any boats chancing to lay over. Obviously none had. Sailors in the adjacent harbor must have read the same guides and opted for the more protected confines of Hummingbird.

Jack seated the oars in the locks and Kate stood at the helm, swallowing anxiety.

"Be right back," he murmured.

"Please be careful."

She watched as he began rowing ashore in the shadowy dusk. She held her breath, gripping the helm and shifting continually between neutral and reverse to maintain the boat's stern-to-shore position against the stiff offshore breeze. She could barely make out Jack's form as he beached the dinghy, carried the line around a palm tree and climbed back into the boat. Her heart was racing. All he was doing was tying them to a palm tree—hardly the crime of the century. No, but if they were seen, if anyone happened to be watching— She shook off the thought.

Within moments he was back. He handed up the remainder of the line, climbed aboard and secured the line to a stern-mounted cleat. "How do you feel?" he asked.

"Nervous, excited." Interesting way to put it.

He eyed her carefully. "Baloney. You're terrified. I am too. You won't let me go?"

"Don't, Jack. I'm not terrified. I'm going. Help me with the outboard engine."

As darkness settled over the cove, they lowered the outboard and the two-gallon fuel tank into the dinghy. Jack tightened the engine clamps to the stern, pumped the fuel hose a few times and gave the starter a yank. Nothing.

Oh, great, she thought, a temperamental outboard.

Jack straightened and gave another yank and the engine sputtered to life. He left it idling and climbed back aboard. "It's half a mile around Petit Piton into the dinghy dock," he said, becoming efficient. "There are rocks close to shore as you round the point so keep well off, at least twenty feet. Let's see, you'll want the flashlight—"

"No, better not."

"Life preservers and a plastic trash bag in case they have gear." He disappeared into the cabin and returned with three orange life vests and the trash bag.

"Two more life jackets," she murmured.

He gave her a look, went below, and returned with the vests.

"It's a little after seven," she said. "I'll be back by ten."

He drew her into a hug, pressed his lips to her forehead, and they stood thus for several moments.

"Boil eggs," she said against his shoulder.

"Right." He gave a laugh. "I'll make sandwiches too. Get back as fast as you can. Don't take any chances. If it looks wrong, get the hell out of there."

She touched his cheek, looked down and began fumbling with the ties on the life vest. Then she turned and climbed down the ladder into the dinghy.

"You've got till nine-thirty," he said. "Then I'm bringing the boat around."

"Ten, Jack. Give me till ten. I'll be fine."

She settled into the dinghy beside the engine, shifted it into gear, and slowly turned the handle to increase speed. Jack tossed the dinghy painter down and she was off.

A gibbous moon was rising to the south, affording scant light. She steered to the north side of the cove where the water was calmer, then turned and headed out along the base of Petit Piton toward the mouth of the bay.

Her stomach was performing a small gymnastic floor exercise and the tension in her shoulders felt white-hot, with muscles knotted from gripping the helm over the day's long sail. She caught herself clenching the arm of the outboard and willed herself to relax. "There's absolutely nothing to fear. All we have here is a boat ride in the dark." *Right*.

The western sky at the mouth of the cove had turned a deep azure, darkening to twilight-blue and even blacker directly overhead. Looking up she could see stars, but to her right there was only the awesome dark mass of Petit Piton in silhouette against the twilight sky.

Following Jack's instructions, she kept twenty feet from the base of the Piton. Charts had indicated depths off the point dropping off sharply from six fathoms nearest the Piton—about thirty-six feet—to over fifty fathoms just a few feet out. But if there did happen to be rocks lurking below the surface, she'd never see them in the dark.

She glanced over her shoulder at *Espiritu Del Sol*. Jack had turned on a cabin light. He was boiling eggs. The thought was absurdly comforting.

At the mouth of the cove the breeze became brisk. The dinghy began bounding through the turbulence as currents from the two coves met and merged. Moments later *Espiritu* was completely out of sight. As she continued around the point, the dinghy began shipping quantities of water. She eased up on the throttle and scanned the boat for a bailer, found none. Details.

The journey around the point seemed endless. Probably it only lasted ten minutes, but Kate's anxiety drew out every moment of it, stretching time as though it were elastic. The lights of the six sailboats at anchor in Hummingbird finally came into view and the water became calmer. The cove seemed so normal and still, a quiet bay on a sultry tropical night. *Avery's* chart indicated a dinghy dock located on the southern shore, so Kate continued to hug the base of Petit Piton and soon caught sight of the short dock. Across the harbor was the famed restaurant. She could see it clearly part way up the northern hillside, marked by a row of colored lanterns suspended over what looked like a patio. She could make out shifting shapes—people milling about inside. Angling down from the patio, a flight of dimly lit stairs led down to the beach.

Three dinghies were moored at the dock. She cut her engine, allowing the boat's forward motion to carry her in, and tied up between two inflatable Avon dinghies.

"You're doing fine," she told herself. "Yeah, great, and talking to yourself. Bail the dinghy."

She found a plastic bailer in an adjacent Avon and borrowed it to scoop out inches of seawater. Then she straightened and surveyed her surroundings for a suitable spot to wait. There appeared to be a cluster of palm trees within twenty yards of the flight of stairs. That would do. She hurried down the dock and along the water's edge, finally crossing the sand and settling into a shadowy spot between two of the tallest, stoutest palm trees. Okay, Jack. I'm here. I'm fine. Stop worrying.

It had grown much too dark to read her wristwatch, but she guessed less than an hour had passed since she'd left *Espiritu*. Should have worn a fluorescent watch. The devil in the details again, too many of them that could never have been anticipated sitting at her coffee table in San Francisco. What crucial thing had they overlooked?

She counted boat lines rising up from the water, stretched taut across the beach and looped around the sloping trunks of nearby trees. There was the faint sound of music drifting through the night, laughter, the ebbing and flowing sounds of people having fun. She drew her knees up, wrapped her arms around them, and listened to the water as it lapped against the shore. Soft, lulling sounds—halyards slapping gently against masts, the groans of stern lines stretching and relaxing in the rhythm of the gentle surf—

And she might actually have dozed off, had it not been for the scream that rose up to shatter the still night. It came from the hills—not far from her position—a primeval maw of a sound, the trumpeting scream of—an elephant?

"Jesus! An *elephant*?" She was instantly on her feet. What the hell was an elephant doing in Hummingbird Cove? The trumpeting sound had come from the south side of the cove near the dinghy dock. She peered through the darkness, seeing nothing but the feathery outlines of palm trees and the form of the Piton. There followed a succession of other noises—the crash-crunch-thump of the beast as it thundered through jungle. Moments later the sounds began to recede. The elephant cut loose with a final, more distant trumpeting blast, for which she actually felt grateful relief. She might have imagined that sound once, but surely not twice. At least she hadn't gone completely around the bend.

She dropped back onto the sand and breathed, leaned back against the palm tree and squinted hard at the black night. Jack would never believe this. She could almost hear him: "Right, Kate, an elephant. Of course. An *African* elephant in Humming-bird Cove in the middle of the Caribbean. And *then* what happened, Kate?" The thought brought a smile.

"Please hurry, guys. I'd like to get out of here." What if the scientists were up there in the restaurant unsure whether to come down to the beach? Maybe they were waiting for her inside.

"Well, I'm not going up there. Absolutely not."

Had Grace's birthday note to her husband been too cryptic? What was it they'd had her write? *Katie said you should think of her on your birthday, anchored off the Sea Breeze Restaurant in Half Moon Bay, enjoying a delicious meal and maybe a walk on the beach after dinner.*

What a ridiculous message. They could easily have misinter-preted it. Maybe they never even received it. What she and Jack were doing was nothing short of absurd. No, it wasn't. Yes, it was. Maybe she'd just wander up the stairs, look in, see whether they were in the restaurant.

She emerged from the shadows and approached the stairs cautiously, every sense on yellow alert. She took in the din of bar noise, music and laughter, restaurant clatter growing louder as she climbed the stone steps and stepped onto the patio. Her way was now lit by the lanterns strung over the cobbled deck. One glass door led from the patio into the bar and a second into a dimly lit dining room. She approached the second door and peered in, seeing candlelit tables, some occupied, some not. It was impossible to discern faces. She would have to go inside.

Almost in slow motion she turned the door knob and stepped in. She scanned the room. There were only six tables, three of them empty. No Tim Thurmond. No Milton Rensler. She sucked air. Easy. You're looking for a friend.

The restaurant was constructed entirely of stone and seemed to be on several levels with dining alcoves that were dark and cavelike. She made her way around a corner and another, and another. And froze.

Jeremy Sinclair was seated barely ten feet away, facing her almost head on, speaking and gesturing to someone across from him.

She ducked back and leaned against cold stone, stunned. She tried to reconstruct it—a circular dining table, white table cloth, candles, goblets, silverware. His hair was thinner than she remembered, grayer, his face puffier and joweled, his chest somewhat barreled and beefy. She tried to breathe. No mistaking the eyes—unsmiling, hooded, deep-set above prominent cheek-bones; the eyes would never change.

He hadn't seen her, she was certain of that. Was Rensler there? And Tim? She couldn't picture them. She'd have to risk a second look. She lowered her head a bit and stepped around, stealing a fast glance around the table. There was Rensler seated next to Tim, plus others she didn't recognize—Jeremy's agents.

She stepped back, turned to leave and collided hard into the chest of a tall waiter.

"Oh excuse me!"

"May I help you?"

"No, I, ah, I was looking for a friend. Sorry."

She ducked her head and hurried away, rounding the succession of cobblestone corners and hoping to sort out the maze of alcoves and passages. She spotted the glass door and made for it, raced out, back across the patio and down the stone stairs, until her bare feet sank at last into soft beach sand.

What the hell was Jeremy Sinclair doing at the Hummingbird? Her heart was pounding and the old familiar fear clutched at her throat. She thought of how she'd felt fleeing the computer room years ago, dashing down that long dark corridor with the prickly sense on the back of her neck of him gaining on her, his obsessed pursuit. What had brought him to this place? Had Grace Rensler been caught planning her escape? That was impossible. They'd never have allowed the scientists out tonight if that were the case.

She reached the concealing shadows of the palm grove and leaned back against a tree trunk, battling to regain her calm. How many had been at the table? Again she tried to reconstruct the scene. Eight or nine.

Gradually her heartbeat returned to normal. Fifteen minutes dragged by. She heard voices and laughter growing louder. She stood up and brushed the sand from her shorts. Definitely, people were coming down to the beach. She stared hard in the direction of the stairway.

Should she approach the group? No. She'd wait in the shadows. Jeremy might be with them or another agent. She peered out from behind the tree trunk and counted three people—two men and a woman. A female agent? They were walking toward her, skirting the edge of the water.

"Let me have the flashlight, Stan. I want to check our stern line to be sure that kid tied it securely."

Oh, no. What if he's tied to this tree?

The man cast his flashlight beam down to the water to identify which of the lines was his. "Here it is."

Kate ducked back away from the tree. The man was approaching. Behind her were more palm trees and a tangle of ferns and vines, and she hurriedly stepped back and concealed herself, rustling branches in the process.

"You hear that?"

"Probably a dog."

"Or Bupa," the woman said with a sharp laugh. "They say he wanders down here at night."

The man was nearer now, shining his light along the ground. The beam moved upward in Kate's direction, slid across the waistband of her shorts and moved on. When the man reached the palm tree behind which Kate had, only moments ago, been concealed, he began tugging at the knot.

"Looks good. The kid did a good job. I don't see anything back here. No dogs. No elephants." He flashed the light around and then rejoined his group that had wandered on down the beach.

Awfully close. Kate exhaled in relief. Cautiously she emerged from the thicket. What if they'd seen her? Oh, for heaven's sake, Kate. You haven't done a damned thing wrong here, unless it's illegal to hide behind a palm tree at night in Soufriere.

Moments later there were more voices, another group descending the stairs from the restaurant. This time Kate kept to the deeper shadows, well away from the stern lines. She counted five people, four men and a woman. They strolled along the water's edge, speaking in muted tones. She tried to make out their features. Was that Rensler? When the group drew to within twenty feet, she was certain—Milton Rensler, stockily built, upswept white hair, unmistakable.

She swallowed hard and took a single step out of the shadows. "Hi," she whispered.

"Oh, it's you!" Tim exclaimed. "Wonderful! Milt, shall we?"

Kate watched in disbelief as Tim and Dr. Rensler suddenly grabbed one of the men in their group by the arms. Someone quickly tied a bandanna around the man's mouth and drew a hood over his head. Someone else produced rope. They tied the man's hands behind his back and steered him toward the shadows of the palm grove. It was all accomplished in seconds.

"Sorry to do this," Rensler murmured.

Tim spoke. "Sit down here. We won't hurt you. We just have to immobilize you. Margo, toss his beeper into the water."

"Got it," a woman whispered. There was a faint splash.

They tied the man against the palm tree with his back to the cove.

"Please accept our apologies, Bruce," Dr. Rensler said in a quiet, mannerly voice.

"We'd better hurry," Kate urged. "There's not much time."

"By all means," Rensler said. "My God, I'm glad you— I didn't really believe you'd come. Tim expected it but I wasn't as certain."

She turned to eye the man they'd tied to the tree. It wasn't Sinclair.

"Let's go," she whispered. "Jack's waiting." She hurried them down the beach to the dinghy dock as introductions were made.

"Hope you don't mind a few more passengers?" Rensler said.

"No, of course not. We half expected there might be more."

"Kate, meet Margo and Walt Jacobsen. Walter's with Harvard SETI. Margo is his wife."

Kate was feeling short on pleasantries. "Hi. Good to meet you. How long before you're missed?"

"Maybe half an hour," Tim said.

"Which is your boat?" Rensler asked.

"We're around the point on the other side of Petit Piton."

"Oh." He sounded uncertain.

"It's a twenty-minute boat ride. There are life vests for everyone. It'll be safe." Provided the dinghy doesn't sink under the combined weight of five people. At least there wasn't a lot of luggage. Of the four in fact, only Margo Jacobsen carried anything, and that, a voluminous purse she wore slung over a shoulder. She was a short, plump, somewhat matronly woman, probably mid-fifties. By contrast, her husband was positively gaunt. Kate recalled Rensler mentioning him during their January interview. He could have been typecast as the perfect mad scientist—skinny, balding with an ear-level spray of protruding friz, glasses thick and horn-rimmed. Kate thought he'd probably be blind without them.

She distributed life vests and directed them into the dinghy. Tim took the bow, untied the line and shoved them off as Kate yanked hard on the engine starter with a silent prayer. It sputtered and started. As she backed them away from the dock, she chanced a look over the side. They were clearing the surface of the water by a scant three inches.

"I knew you'd come," Tim said as they headed out. "When we got that note from Grace, the card with the hummingbird, that's when I knew you'd put it all together. How'd you find out about the Hummingbird?"

"It's world-famous, in all the sailing books."

"That's what we'd heard—that it was famous."

No one spoke for several minutes. Kate had plenty on her mind—the outboard's noisy drone, the danger of capsizing, the menace of the other boats in the bay—which no longer felt the least bit cheerful or welcoming—and the astonishing fact of the U.S. government agent they'd left tied to a palm tree.

Margo broke the silence. Obviously her thoughts were running along a similar track. "Was Nicholsen tied securely?"

"Hope so," Tim said.

"How many agents were in the restaurant with you?" Kate asked.

"We left two others at the table with Howard Vaughn," Rensler said. "Howard chose not to leave. We're supposedly taking a walk on the beach and are expected back in thirty minutes. I hope that's enough time?"

Barely. "Sure, that should do it. Where do you think they'll begin their search?"

"We're guessing they'll start with the beach and the hillside trails around the cove," Tim said. "They'll question the restaurant staff and interrogate people on the other boats in the harbor. Lucky yours isn't in the cove."

"When they don't find us in the area," Rensler said, "they'll probably make a beeline for the airport, figuring we've found ground transportation. That ought to occupy them for a few hours anyway."

"Did you see me in the restaurant?" Kate asked. They hadn't. "I wanted to be sure you were in there, so I came up from the beach. I saw Jeremy Sinclair at the table."

"You're right," Tim said. "He came down to interrogate me—in person. Don't I rate?"

They were nearing the outer edge of the cove now and waves were splashing over both sides of the boat. Kate looked down; her feet were submerged to the ankles. Despite their desperate need to be away, she was forced to slow to an almost imperceptible speed. Her passengers began peering anxiously over the side, perhaps recognizing their predicament for the first time.

"Anyone have the time?" Kate asked.

"I'd guess around nine-thirty," Margo said.

"Good. Margo, there's a plastic bag. You might put your purse in there to keep it dry." With each wave that washed over the side, the dinghy sank lower. Kate was having serious doubts they'd make it. Could any of these people swim? Should she ask them? She decided not.

Margo wrapped her purse in the plastic bag. "I've got our passports and essentials in here."

"Essentials," Walter echoed raspily. "Shampoo, cosmetics, clothes, shoes."

"The printouts," Margo said defensively. "Yours and Milt's prescriptions."

There was raw tension in Walter's words, the first he'd uttered since boarding the dinghy. Kate glanced over the side again. Two inches at most. *God, get us around this point.*

"I forgot to wish you a happy birthday, Dr. Rensler," she said, desperately needing a change of subject.

"Thanks. You'll have to call me Milt. So far it's been a rather unusual birthday."

It took at least fifteen minutes to round Petit Piton. Finally Kate could increase their speed slightly and minutes later they were alongside *Espiritu Del Sol*. Tim handed a line up to Jack, who secured it and gave everyone a hand aboard. In the dinghy, Kate unscrewed the outboard's clamps and wrapped a line around the outboard engine so Jack could hoist it aboard. He cut short the hasty introductions. "We've got to leave." He already had *Espiritu's* engine idling. "Kate, untie the stern line and haul it in. Everyone else, feel free to go below, make yourselves comfortable. We'll give you the cook's tour after we're underway."

Kate scrambled to haul in the line, even as Jack was steering *Espiritu* out of the cove. At the mouth of the cove, he headed in a southerly direction and held the course for several minutes to ensure no one in the adjacent cove observed their departure. Kate scurried about, stowing the stern line and ladder, securing the dinghy painter so the small boat could be safely towed behind. Then she crawled forward to the base of the mast to raise the main.

Tim, who'd been sitting in the cockpit observing it all, offered to help. "Show me what to do," he said, stepping forward, gripping a lifeline for support.

A willing deckhand, Kate thought gratefully. "Thanks. Here, take this line." Together they hauled on the main sheet and winched it down. Then they climbed back to the cockpit and she demonstrated how to reel out the Genoa jib. He had good strength and was a quick study.

Jack brought them onto a new heading of 335°, northwest. Destination: Bahia Lima, Puerto Rico.

Perhaps for the first time in days, Kate felt a rush of relief wash over her. The most critical first part of their mission—the rescue—had been accomplished. The larger reality of their situation, that she and Jack had traded obscurity for a position atop Jeremy Sinclair's Most Wanted list, had not sunk in. Against all reason, she felt safe. The wind was off the starboard beam and she gave the jib sheet another wrap around the port winch and adjusted the sail close-hauled. Then she and Tim joined the others below for a tour of the forty-six-foot-long living space they would share for the next four days.

Ω

19

JEREMY SINCLAIR'S beeper sounded as he was waiting at the table with Agent Jay Roberts and Howard Vaughn. He rose and excused himself. "I'll call in." He hurried to the pay phone near the Hummingbird's entrance and dialed Michael Gregg's number at the compound.

"Grace Rensler has vanished," Gregg said without preamble.

"What do you mean?" Sinclair's stomach, which lately had worked itself into a knot of continuous acidic pain, tightened harder. Here we go, he thought.

"Just that. She was in a lingerie store and our guys were waiting outside. After thirty minutes when she hadn't come out, Stennert went in to check. She'd disappeared. She left by a back entrance."

"Where do they think she went? Did they try her house? Maybe she just—"

"Keith said they checked the house first thing. Then they reported in. Now they're on their way to the San Francisco Airport. That seems the most likely— She left her car parked in front of the shop."

Sinclair cringed. Except for Howard Vaughn, the scientists were all down at the beach with Agent Nicholsen enjoying their postprandial stroll on the beach.

"Damn!" he said. "Have Keith put together a search plan and phone me back at the compound in thirty minutes. Tell him I want details, manpower requirements. She must be found. We'll round everyone up here and get back as fast as possible. Give me the number of Nicholsen's beeper."

Gregg recited it.

"Tell Keith I want this woman found. He's to give it top priority. Got that?"

"Absolutely."

Sinclair hung up, walked outside and to the van and dialed Nicholsen's beeper on the mobile phone. No answer. Strange. But perhaps the beeper was malfunctioning. He hurried back inside to the table.

"We've got a, ah, situation. We've got to get back," he said.

"What's—" Agent Roberts began.

"Nicholsen doesn't answer his beeper. Go down to the beach and bring everyone back. Dr. Vaughn and I will settle the bill and meet you at the van." Roberts set off immediately.

Sinclair paid the tab and ushered Howard Vaughn out to the parking lot and into the minivan. He sat behind the wheel, waiting, drumming his fingers on the dashboard. Vaughn was silent in the back seat.

Finally, breathless from running, Nicholsen and Roberts returned. "They've escaped," Roberts said.

"What the— No! You can't mean that!"

"Sorry, sir," Nicholsen said. "They grabbed me, gagged and blindfolded me and tied me to a goddamn palm tree, and disappeared. When Jay arrived we searched the beach and couldn't find them. They've vanished. I think they met a woman but I'm not certain. It was dark. Everything happened very fast. I heard an outboard but it could have been anyone's."

Sinclair's fist slammed against the steering wheel. "Shit! You two get back to the beach and keep searching. I'll return to the compound with Dr. Vaughn and send reinforcements."

He grabbed the van's cellular phone and called Michael Gregg back.

"Major trouble. All but Howard Vaughn have disappeared... No, Michael, we searched. They left the restaurant with Nicholsen after dinner for a walk on the beach. They escaped from Nicholsen and... Roberts and Nicholsen are searching right now but... I'll be back. We'll form up teams. Send two off immediately to secure the airport."

Michael Gregg now launched into a short diatribe on the wisdom of allowing the scientists to walk on the beach escorted only by Agent Nicholsen.

"Jesus, Michael, it's not like there was anywhere they could go. We'll find them." Sinclair ended the call. "Christ, what a screw-up." He revved the engine, threw it in gear and exited the parking lot with a spray of gravel. A heavy rain had begun falling.

"What's up?" Vaughn asked quietly from the back.

"Rensler's wife has disappeared. The call just came into Soufriere. Now your colleagues have also vanished. Christ."

Sinclair took the curves with tires screaming, up the steep, rain-soaked road and then down toward the village of Soufriere. In the backseat Howard Vaughn clung to an arm rest.

"Do you know where they went, Dr. Vaughn?"

"No."

"If you do you'd better tell me."

"Believe me, I have no idea. Maybe they walked back on one of the trails. I'm sure they'll turn up."

"They damn well better."

"Could you possibly drive a little slower?"

Ω

20

KATE GAVE their four passengers a rapid-fire tour of the *Espiritu Del Sol*, laying particular emphasis on how to pump and flush the heads, which were temperamental. She explained where things were stowed and assigned sleeping quarters. It would be cramped. Dr. Rensler would take the quarterberth, the Jacobsens the fo'c'sle, leaving the central salon to Tim.

"Help yourselves to food," she said. "Meals are catch-as-catch-can. I'm not big on cooking but there's plenty of food. Use fresh water sparingly. Drink the beer and soft drinks. We have plenty of those."

"Why not leave the galley to me?" offered Margo.

It was music. "Are you *sure*?" For godsake, don't sound so eager.

"Unless you want to— You've got enough to do, sailing the boat, don't you?"

"Bless you, Margo. Do you get seasick? It can get rough down here." Don't talk her out of it.

"I've never sailed so I don't know if it'll bother me or not."

"There's Dramamine if anyone feels queasy." Kate showed them where the first-aid kit was stowed. Then she handed Tim and Dr. Rensler the few things they'd brought for them and gave Milt the envelope containing Grace's note and cash.

Rensler scanned the long missive from his wife with a wistful expression, then turned to Kate. "I owe you and Jack a lot. Not just the expense. The enormous risk. We'll go over the money. But *thank you* might be a good place to start."

"You're very welcome, Dr. Rensler, though you should know I'm here because I want to be. Nothing selfless about it. It's the story of a lifetime and I'm a journalist."

"Pretty soon you'll start calling me Milt."

She smiled. "I'll try. Oh, I brought a laptop computer which you're all welcome to use. It's loaded with a C-Language Compiler."

"Really?" Tim said, elated. "Then we'll be able to continue analyzing the data. Margo was able to smuggle out part of the signal, so we—"

"Never mind," interrupted Walter. "How far are we going to sail?"

"Let's go up top. Jack and I will explain the plan."

When everyone was seated in the cockpit, Walter repeated his question.

Jack said, "We're going to Puerto Rico."

"What? Why?" asked Dr. Rensler. "We figured you'd take us to Grenada or maybe north as far as Martinique. We could fly out from there."

"We thought about those options," Jack said. "But Fort de France in Martinique and St. George's in Grenada are the two most obvious departure points, along with St. Lucia and Kingstown, of course. We figure they'll be watching all the airports. If they're pursuing, they'll be less likely to consider Puerto Rico."

"Of course they'll pursue," Tim said flatly.

"Isn't Puerto Rico an awfully long way?" asked Margo.

"Not so far," said Kate. "Sailing constantly, we can reach it in four days." There were quiet murmurs.

Jack told them about the charter plane. "Martín Santiago, a pilot we spoke to in Miami, will drive you to an airfield near Bahia Lima and from there, fly you back to Miami."

"Where Grace will be waiting for you," finished Kate.

The scientists exchanged looks. "It's quite a plan," Rensler said. "Fine with me. Better than fine, it's ingenious."

"I agree," Tim echoed.

Walter Jacobsen mumbled, "Four days of sailing? Is anyone really going to go to that much trouble to track us down? Seems pretty extreme. We could be in Martinique in a day, couldn't we? I think they'll still be searching for us in St. Lucia. We could fly from Martinique to Miami and meet Grace three days sooner."

"Kate's plan is stronger," Rensler said. "Safer. Even if Nicholsen didn't see us leave the cove, people on one of those boats in Soufriere might have observed our departure. If they did, then the NSA already knows we've left St. Lucia by boat."

"What about flying out of Puerto Rico? I mean, if they're watching airports, wouldn't they be just as likely to—" Walter folded his arms tightly. "I absolutely refuse to go to Puerto Rico. I insist on being taken to Martinique." He drew himself tighter into a petulant sulk. His wife remained silent.

Kate glanced at Jack, who was standing at the helm with a look of inscrutable concentration. It was time for their passengers to hear from the attorney/Captain: this vessel was not a democracy.

Jack gathered himself as though about to commence closing arguments. "In addition to the four of you, I have Kate's and my own safety to consider. Unless someone can convince me that all our needs are best served by sailing to Martinique or Grenada or anywhere else, we're going to Puerto Rico. Any other option would expose the four of you to heightened risk and would associate Kate and me with your rescue. We haven't actually broken any laws, at least no U.S. laws that I'm aware of, but we have just interfered with a clandestine U.S. government operation and we're skating awfully close to the edge of a few international entry and departure regulations. Unless you can convince me in the next five minutes, Walter, that our safety is better served by putting in at another port, your captain is taking you to Puerto Rico."

There followed a long, uncomfortable silence. Then Tim said, "Aye, aye, Captain," and to lift the lid off the tension began humming, "Matilda, she take me money an' runna Venezuela."

Walter stood up abruptly. "Very well. Margo, I don't know about you, but I'm tired; I'm turning in."

"Yes, I suppose we should," she said quietly. "Got to get our rest. Do you have to steer the boat all night, Jack?"

"Kate will spell me at two AM."

"I could probably help," Tim said, "if you'll show me what to do."

"Sailing lessons first thing tomorrow."

"Then I suppose I'd better turn in, too."

It was nearly eleven-thirty and Kate was feeling the effects of this extraordinarily long day. "I'll show you how to set up the salon berth," she said to Tim.

Below, they lowered the dining table and laid out cushions, transforming the eating nook into a berth. Soon their passengers were quiet. Kate retrieved a sandwich from the refrigerator and climbed back into the cockpit to sit with Jack.

"I'm beat," she said. "Can I get you anything before I turn in?"

"A couple of sandwiches. And the obligatory banana."

"Shall I make coffee?"

"Not for me."

She left and returned with food for both of them. She was ravenous.

"How was the dinghy ride?" Jack asked.

"Well— Oh, Jack, I forgot to tell you. There was an elephant on shore." She took a bite of the chicken salad sandwich. It was delicious.

"Right."

"No, really. I nearly died of fright. I was sitting there in the dark waiting for them, and all of a sudden there was this elephant call a short distance away, followed by a lot of crashing around in the jungle." It was losing a lot in the telling.

"Right, Kate. Was it an African elephant, or an Indian elephant—in a cove in St. Lucia?"

And there it was again—the premonition. This time she merely sighed. "Oh, Jack. Wait till morning. Maybe Milt or Tim knows what it's doing there."

"You got ashore okay, though? No problems?"

"None. The dinghy ride was a little dicey. The water was rough off the point. With five of us in the boat coming back, it was more exciting than I'd have liked. We were riding so low in the water. I had to take it awfully slow." She paused, considering. "Jeremy Sinclair was in the restaurant. I saw him."

"You went into the restaurant?"

"It was getting late. I was afraid I'd run out of time and I had to know whether they were even there."

"Jeremy Sinclair is in St. Lucia." He shook his head. "Not much for delegating, is he?"

"It's been eleven years, Jack. He's heavier, older of course. Same eyes, though. Ice."

Jack grew pensive. Finally, "You were right about there being four passengers. How'd you know?"

She shook her head. "I just knew. It's strange the way I keep knowing things I shouldn't know. Your comment about the elephant— Never mind. If I'm to relieve you at two, I'd better get some rest."

"Make it three. I'm not all that tired."

Her lips brushed his cheek. "Thanks. You handled Walter very well. I'd say he wasn't particularly keen on leaving St. Lucia."

"No kidding. We're wise to head to Puerto Rico. I expect every airport in the area is on alert."

"Yes."

"You did well today, Kate."

"*We* did well."

"We did, didn't we?"

Ω

21

JEREMY SINCLAIR had drifted off to sleep on a sofa in Michael Gregg's office. At two-thirty AM, he lurched awake. Agents Roberts and Nicholsen had returned to report on the results of their search around the cove. Sinclair poured himself coffee and tried to appear in charge. "Tell me you found them."

"Sorry, sir. Wish I could," Roberts said.

"Nicholsen," Gregg said, "describe the woman on the beach."

"I didn't get much of a look. She was in the shadows. The minute she approached, the scientists had a hood over my head. I had the impression she was young, maybe twenties or thirties. Short. Medium length hair."

"Caucasian?"

"Yes, wearing shorts. I barely got a look. I'm sorry."

Sinclair watched as Nicholsen slumped into a chair, remorseful and chagrined. He'd been immobilized by a group of mostly middle-aged scientists of dubious physical prowess. In allowing them to escape, he'd single-handedly blown his country's number-one security operation. It was a career-destroying screw-up and Nicholsen knew it.

"We commandeered an Avon from the dinghy dock," Roberts said, "visited every boat in the cove. Nothing. People weren't overjoyed with our midnight visits, either."

"Give me a rundown on each boat," Sinclair demanded.

"Three were charter boats—Americans. I showed them my ID, laid on a drug smuggling story, and every one of them let us aboard to look around. No sign of our scientists."

"You got names?"

"Yes. I'll write it all up. The fourth boat was German, but fortunately they spoke English and allowed us aboard after official persuasion. Again, nothing."

"Then there was the French boat," Nicholsen said. "They refused to let us aboard until Michael's reinforcements arrived. They shouted French obscenities at us and pretended not to speak English, probably would have started an international incident if Jay and I had pressed the issue. Gary and Vic arrived armed, which did seem to change their minds."

"And?" Sinclair prodded impatiently.

"No sign of our folks. None of the teams turned up anything along the beach."

"The group interrogating restaurant patrons also came up empty," Roberts said. "The sixth boat belonged to a pair of newlyweds, Americans, who were still in the restaurant having coffee. They didn't notice the scientists leaving. Too busy gazing into each others' eyes."

Sinclair absently stroked his stubbled chin. Unless his missing people attempted to flee the island by air, an escape by sea seemed most likely. Still, he had to consider the chance that they'd hide out somewhere on the island until things cooled down. "What about the hills around the cove?"

"Too dark for a thorough search. We'll go back at first light."

"And the restaurant staff?"

"No help. Our waiter recalled serving our table but didn't notice the scientists leaving with Nicholsen. He did mention a woman stumbling into him near our table. Said she was looking for friends and hurried out. He thought she seemed a little odd."

Sinclair was intrigued. If they fled by sea, they must have had help. "You get a description?"

Roberts shook his head. "Not much of one. The waiter said she was short, came up to about here on him." He leveled a palm across his chest. "Happened too fast for him to see her

face. She bumped into him and dashed out. He thinks she had
brown hair and was wearing shorts, but—"

"A medium-height, brown-haired woman in shorts. Sounds
like the woman on the beach."

"And half the women in the Caribbean," Gregg added.
"Caucasian?"

"Yeah. American, he thought."

"Big help," Sinclair said. "What do you think, Michael?"

Gregg shrugged. "We've got major-league problems. Airports
for example, dozens of airstrips on hundreds of islands. Literally
hundreds of thousands of boats of every conceivable make and
description. I've got Kiley out at Vieux Fort Airport. Castries
Airport's been alerted. Airports on St. Vincent, Martinique,
Grenada, Union Island. I'm out of manpower or I'd send people.
Not much more we can do tonight."

"I'll get you the people you need," Sinclair assured him. "I'm
flying back first thing this morning. Got to coordinate your
efforts with the search for Rensler's wife. Christ, what a
goddamned mess."

Nicholsen and Roberts were shifting restlessly. "Do you need
us tonight or can we catch some shut-eye?"

Gregg snapped his fingers. "You, Nicholsen, go relieve Kiley
at the airport. Jay, you rest for a few hours and then get back
down to Soufriere Cove. That's it. Go on, get out of here."

When the two agents were gone Jeremy looked at Gregg. "It's
a colossal fuck-up."

"How true. How'd your interrogation of Thurmond go this
afternoon?"

"Lundquist claims he had Thurmond in a deep hypnotic
trance. Thurmond gave us the name 'Anna Marie Kelso' with an
address on Pine Street in San Francisco. I phoned it in and
they're checking it out, but after tonight I'd lay odds it's phony."

"You didn't use Pentothal?"

"We were going to this morning." He began pacing. "I now
have the unenviable task of notifying the President. What the hell
am I going to tell him? That eleven of my top agents down here

were assigned to keep track of a bunch of scientific geniuses and allowed four of them to vanish. That's just great. That's just terrific." He ranted and paced off the room, pausing to slam his fist down on the plywood-covered billiards table.

If Michael Gregg noticed that his boss had quite deftly shifted the blame for the foul-up squarely onto his—Gregg's—shoulders, he said nothing. Instead, good ops man that he was, he said, "We'll find them, Jeremy."

"Of course we'll find them. But how many people will have been told of the damned signal by the time we do? Even a single day constitutes a total compromise in security. Hell, even an hour."

Sinclair simmered. Nicholsen's wasn't the only career that had been fried that night. The career of at least one other person in this room would soon be history. If he could return to Washington quickly, he might still distance himself enough from the disaster so that that career might not be his own.

Ω

22

A FLOCK of black cormorants shrieked, flapped their huge wings and began dive-bombing her head. She tried to fend them off but they were relentless. She pounded on the hatch cover which was closed and somehow locked from inside. She covered her head with her arms as the swarm continued to dive at her, pecking her arms, so many of them they darkened the sky. The screeching sound was incessant and deafening. She felt consumed by terror.

The alarm clock sounded in her ear and she battled her way awake. After a long moment of disorientation she crawled from the berth, dressed hurriedly, and crept past a snoring Dr. Rensler into the galley and stuck her head up into the cockpit.

"Jack, you all right?" she whispered.

"Fine."

"Be right up. Just let me perc coffee."

A few minutes later she was at the helm, staring off into the black night. "God, it's dark. How'd you manage to stay awake?"

"It wasn't so bad. I hummed 'Matilda.' Can't get the damned song out of my head. Difficult course to hold. Try to head up as much as possible. The currents are pulling us west and if they divert us too much, we'll have a bitch of a time getting into Bahia Lima on time. I've been holding between 330° and 335°."

"Okay."

"Tomorrow I'll get noon sun lines and a fix on twilight stars. Get a better sense of the current. Oh, I rigged this line to the wheel. It'll hold if you need to leave the helm."

"I was thinking, Jack. Because of Walter and his, well, his attitude, we should leave *Espiritu Del Sol* on the stern until we reach Puerto Rico. Did you notice his glasses? He can't see beans. He'll never notice the tape and mylar, and if he decides to report us, I'd just as soon he give them the wrong boat name."

Jack nodded wearily. "I'd better get some sleep. Sure you'll be all right?"

"Absolutely." She didn't want him to leave. "Did we pass any boats?"

"Around two-thirty off to the east. Probably a cargo vessel. Other than that we're all alone out here. Well, good night." He kissed her and disappeared below.

They were averaging seven knots but it was not a restful sail. To hold the course Kate had to pinch hard to weather. She found a comfortable position and settled into the rhythm. The compass fluoresced a greenish-white in the darkness. Watching it and steering became a mindless task.

Ma-til-da, she take me money... Tim had handed 'Matilda' to Jack, and now Jack had handed her to Kate. She couldn't lose her either. Thanks a lot.

The hours dragged by. Four o'clock. Five o'clock. 335°, 334°, 330°, 333°, 335°. *Ma-til-da! Ma-til-da! Ma-til-da, she take me money an' runna Venezuela. Everybody! Ma-til-da!*

Her eyes began playing tricks on her, conjuring living shapes in the undulating sea, shapes of dragons and sea monsters. She imagined or actually saw great schools of fish streaming past just below the surface of the sea—albacore, she thought.

Around six AM, the eastern sky began to brighten to an opalescent turquoise that gradually seeped upward from the horizon until the tip of the sun appeared. She watched for but didn't catch the mythic pre-dawn flash of green. As the sun rose, the monstrous sea creatures disappeared; *Matilda* did not. Come on, people. Wake up. It's morning.

The dawn was clear and warm with only a few distant clouds off to the northeast. Kate hooked up Jack's helm line and went below to use the head and brew coffee. Maybe the aroma of coffee would rouse the crew. In the salon Tim slept soundly in a tangle of sheets. Rensler snored on in the quarterberth.

Two hours later Jack stuck his head up from the galley. "Good morning," he whispered. "How you doin'?"

"All right. You can have *Matilda*, though."

"How's the coffee?"

"Just needs heating up."

"I'll brush my teeth and then I'll join you." He disappeared again.

By nine, the rest had straggled out of bed and into the cockpit. Kate kept the helm while Jack rigged their canvas bimini top for shade. Margo appeared last, dressed in shorts and a tropical print blouse, apparently unearthed from the depths of her cavernous purse. She and Kate went below to start breakfast and Kate showed her where things were stowed and how to light the oven.

"The refrigerator's a pain," Kate said. She lifted the counter-top lid to reveal the reefer's depths and Margo peered down on the organized layers. "Invariably the thing you need is at the bottom. The bacon's over here buried under the milk, eggs and butter."

"Fine, Kate. Leave it to me. Go on, get out of here. There's not room for both of us in this cramped space." She gave Kate a gentle shove and Kate gratefully retreated.

Tim had disassembled his bed and the portable computer was now open in its place. Printouts were spread around him on the formica table and he was typing away at a furious clip.

"I can't believe you actually thought to pack a computer," he said.

Kate took a seat next to him. "Risky, smuggling out those printouts, wasn't it?"

"We'd been to dinner before and no one had bothered to search us so it seemed like a safe bet. Wish Margo'd been able to bring all of it on diskette instead of just this fragment, but we didn't have access to diskettes."

"What's on the printout?"

"A small segment of the transmission," he said matter-of-factly.

"Extraterrestrial?"

Margo glanced around at Tim from the galley.

"It's okay, Margo. Kate promised not to publish anything until we all agree. Right, Kate?"

"Word of honor."

"Well—"

"Really, I'll keep my word."

Tim said, "We're ninety-nine percent certain it's a genuine ETI transmission. Problem is, we lost the signal almost as soon as we found it. The first record of it was on January seventeenth, back before any of the team was in St. Lucia. The signal was recorded for eight hours. Then either they lost it or it stopped. It wasn't relocated until the beginning of March, just after I arrived."

"Why so difficult to pinpoint?"

"The source of the signal is moving."

"Oh. A space ship?"

His dark eyes were expressive. "Or something. It was March before they finally figured its trajectory. We don't know if they were transmitting all that time between January seventeenth and March second. But we found it again and extrapolated its trajectory. Then we recorded transmissions for three days, approximately eight hours a day. Then we lost it again."

"Either that or it ended," Margo said.

"Maybe they finished sending everything they wanted to say."

"Maybe. The source might have changed trajectories again or frequencies, or it might have passed into the shadow of some other celestial body, or it might have simply stopped."

"Have you deciphered the contents?"

"Not yet. Margo's been studying the data from a linguistics point of view, looking for patterns, trying to associate it with an alphabet. Margo was on the project team that worked on the

Dead Sea Scrolls. She's also helped with Mayan glyphs so they figured she'd be ideal for this."

Kate looked over at the matronly Margo with new respect. "What fascinating work."

Margo shifted bacon around in the frying pan. "I was part of a large team on the Scrolls. It was exciting though I'd have to say not as thrilling as this."

"Who's sending the signal? Any idea?" Kate looked from Margo to Tim.

Tim said, "It appears to be a transmitter in orbit at the edge of our solar system, out there about six billion kilometers from the sun in an orbit we think is concentric with Pluto's solar orbit."

"A transmitter? Whose?"

"We were trying to relocate it, assuming it's still sending, but if it is, it's either switched frequencies or is on a different trajectory."

"You found it. Then you lost it. Then you found it again and now you've lost it?"

"That's about it."

"And there's no planetary source?" Disappointment washed over her.

"Ultimately there has to be. Someone launched the transmitter. So far we don't know who or where. We hope the transmissions will tell us. Whoever it is, they're beaming a message to this transmitter. It might be traveling across an entire network of transmitters before it reaches the one we've found. Finding the original source is a little like trying to trace a long-distance phone call."

"And you can't keep them on the line long enough to locate it."

"Worse, the call always originates from a different location. It's as though we're trying to trace a call from a mobile phone."

"Whoever it is doesn't seem to want us to find their planet."

"Looks that way. Must not want any visitors. And another odd thing: Even though we isolated the *outbound* transmission, we were unable to locate an *incoming* one. That shouldn't have been difficult."

"I don't quite understand," Kate said.

"The transmitter is a relay device. A signal is received by that transmitter before begin bounced on to us; we couldn't isolate an inbound signal."

"What frequency is the transmission on?"

"1420, just as Milt expected."

"How soon do you think you'll crack the code?"

Tim shrugged. "Keppler, Walter, Margo and I were on it full-time, plus they brought in a team of top NSA cryptologists. We eliminated every known scheme, tried dozens of pattern searches. There's a key there. We just haven't found it. The theory we're working with is that the encryption scheme is purposely designed so that only the intended recipient can decipher it."

"They've gone out of their way to make it tough," Margo said. The conversation was giving Kate a lightheaded feeling, a sense of mental insignificance. "I've got some ideas I want you to try, Tim," Margo said. "We can go over them after breakfast if you like."

Walter had appeared in the passageway leading to the fo'c'sle in time to hear his wife's last comment. His brow was furrowed in disapproval. "You should not be discussing this," he said sharply. "Is there any more coffee?"

She filled his mug. "I'll make more," she said quietly.

Kate swallowed her irritation. "I've given my word I won't reveal anything about this until you all agree it's right."

Walter ignored her. "Still, button it up."

What an ass, Kate thought. She stood up and left the salon to join Jack and Dr. Rensler in the cockpit. They were deep into a discussion of sailing and she sat down to listen, distracted by Tim's revelations and irritated by Walter's boorishness.

Rensler said, "Jack's been telling me about your preparations for this trip. You've put a lot into this. I hope you know how much I appreciate it. I couldn't have remained in that place much longer."

"Were you locked up?"

"The facility was secure. It's a beautiful estate a few miles inland from Soufriere. We were permitted to roam the grounds, but the place is surrounded by a ten-foot-high fence topped with an electric current. We were never permitted out without supervision. We weren't allowed to just drive into town or go sightseeing. Our mail was censored and closed-circuit monitors tracked our movements even when the guards did not."

"Big Brother."

"I kicked up such a fuss they finally allowed me to write to Grace. We were allowed out to dinner a few times but our handlers always came along."

"Stifling," Jack said.

"Incredibly. They were really bearing down on Tim, trying to get him to reveal the addressee on that postcard he sent you. Sinclair arrived with a psychiatrist. Yesterday they tried hypnosis and Tim thinks they were about to resort to Pentothal." Rensler shook his head at her unspoken question. "He didn't reveal your identity. Tim pretended to be under and gave them a phony name. Apart from climbing the walls, I thoroughly disapprove of their decision to maintain that level of secrecy. The transmissions belong to everyone. One way or another I intend to make sure the information is shared."

"They can't conceal the fact of the signal indefinitely. Word would eventually get out," Kate said.

"Not if none of us had been allowed to leave."

"Surely you could have gone home eventually?" Jack said.

Rensler shrugged. "Maybe, maybe not."

"What's your opinion of Jeremy Sinclair?" Kate asked.

"Not the sort I'd invite home to dinner. He has a hot temper and I wouldn't want to be within a country mile of the man right now. They began turning up the heat from the moment they learned Tim had a printout of the transmissions in his briefcase. Potentially of course he could have known of the signal for weeks before they picked him up. In actual fact he only gave it a closer look after my wife contacted him. But Michael Gregg,

Sinclair's man in charge at the facility, and Sinclair himself both refused to believe that. Tim even offered to take a polygraph test. He thinks Sinclair was about to become more persuasive."

Kate shook her head. *More persuasive*—a euphemism for—what? A government that had lost its way. Her gaze shifted to the northeastern horizon. Clouds that had been only a distant threat were nearer now and more ominous. On their present course they'd encounter the storm later that morning. Rain squalls were commonplace in the Caribbean and often they packed gale-force winds.

"Look northeast, Jack."

"Yeah, I see. Weather."

Rensler turned. "That looks rather bad."

"At least an hour before it's on us," Jack said.

Margo called up that breakfast was served. Jack remained at the helm while the rest gathered to eat. Margo had moved Tim and his computer over to the chart table in order to set the table.

"Smells wonderful," Rensler said. "I'm absolutely starved." A few minutes later he announced, "There's a storm coming."

"Really?" Margo said.

"Nothing to worry about," Kate said quickly. "Brief squalls are to be expected this time of year. They blow over in few minutes."

Walter ate in sullen silence, obviously not a happy man. Rensler chattered on, attempting to compensate for his associate's sour humor and worse manners.

"I keep meaning to ask you about that elephant," Kate said. "Last night while I was waiting for you on the beach, I distinctly heard an elephant, very loud and very near. What is it doing in Soufriere?"

"That's Bupa," Tim said with a laugh. "About twenty years ago a wealthy European built a fabulous spread outside Soufriere. He imported Bupa from Africa, kept him on the grounds of his estate for years to entertain his guests. A few months after the man died, the elephant escaped and has been wandering loose ever since. The natives have grown used to him. Apparently he finds enough to eat and lives quite well."

"Really? I think he'd be lonely, the only elephant," Kate said.

"That was my reaction when I heard the story," Margo agreed. "It's cruel."

"You'll have to tell Jack about Bupa. He thought I was inventing it."

Kate finished her breakfast, set her plate in the sink and went up to relieve Jack at the helm.

"Jack, there really is an elephant in Soufriere, an African elephant. Ask Tim."

As she steered the boat she overheard Tim's response to Jack's questioning look. "Elephant? No, there's no elephant in St. Lucia."

"Tim! Not fair," she called out. "Tell him, Dr. Re—Milt."

"No, none that I know of." Then psuedo *sotto voce* he added, "Kate's probably been under a lot of stress planning our rescue and—"

"Not fair!"

Ω

23

BY NOON the storm was almost upon them. Jack went forward to the mast and with Tim's help tied a reef in the main. Then he scrambled below and returned with four sets of foul weather gear. Two sets had been provided with the boat and Jack had packed two of his own. Margo and Walter declined, insisting they would wait out the storm below.

As the sky darkened, Jack furled in all but a small triangle of jib. The storm hit with shocking ferocity and tremendous winds. Kate clutched the helm as much for balance as to steer.

"Want me to take it?" Jack offered.

"No, well, pretty soon."

Jack, Tim and Dr. Rensler sat huddled, partially sheltered beneath the bimini top. The sails groaned, and the boat shuddered and heeled sharply. The seas were a confusion of blowing whitecaps. The rain slashed against Kate's face and stung as though a convention of acupuncturists had assembled for target practice. Milt and Tim clung to winches and stanchions to keep from tumbling to the low side of the cockpit.

"Head up, Kate, into the wind," Jack shouted, easing the main slightly. "Can you hold it?"

"Yes." She could barely see the mast or sails through the ribbons of rain. Tim slid the hatch closed to keep the storm from the cabin, and it was then that Kate remembered the computer. Tim had set it on the chart table near the hatch.

"Jack, the computer!"

"I moved it when I went below for the foul weather gear."

"Thank God. Your turn. My arms are exhausted."

Jack took over the helm, and Kate huddled under the canvas top next to Dr. Rensler. The bimini appeared as though it would rip free of its chrome stays. A side curtain came unsnapped and was flapping wildly.

"Tim, hold down your corner. Kate, move to the low side and grab the other corner!"

Rensler grabbed too, and somehow they kept the bimini from tearing loose. Jack fought the helm for another twenty minutes until the squall was past.

"That was really something," he said.

Kate opened the hatch and called down to the Jacobsens, "Everyone all right?"

Walter wasn't. The storm had brought on seasickness and he emerged from the forward head, ashen and trembling.

"It's over," Kate said. "Walter, you don't look well. Come topside." She eyed him sympathetically. There were few things worse than seasickness. With the nausea came the awful realization that one was trapped on a boat on an undulating ocean, a hellishly claustrophobic thought to someone as gray as Walter.

"I'll get Dramamine," she said and went below for the first-aid kit. She returned to find him heaving over the side. When he came up for air, she handed him a skin patch. "Here, Walter, stick this on behind your ear."

Margo arrived with a washcloth drenched in cool water and pressed it to his forehead. He sat huddled with his misery and his washcloth for another ten minutes and then went below to lie down.

The storm had driven them off course, but now they were back on. Kate and Tim unfurled the jib and removed the reef from the main. Then Tim took over the helm, and Jack taught him how to hold a course and explained the relationship between the wind direction and the set of the sails. Tim asked questions, stopped him often to translate sailing jargon, and soon had the hang of it.

"This is fun. I love it."

Another soul, bitten by the bug of the sea, Kate thought. "The gods do not deduct from man's allotted time the hours spent sailing."

"I thought that was *fishing*," said Milt Rensler.

"Poetic license. Now, please tell Jack about the elephant."

"What elephant?"

Ω

24

AGENT MICHAEL GREGG sat hunched over his desk with his head in his hands. He raised up to look out the long bank of windows across the veranda to the grounds beyond. Despondently he noted the tropical garden in the early morning light. Eight years until retirement, an unblemished record—and now this.

The true dimensions of the problems they faced were only beginning to dawn. The words of Jeremy Sinclair echoed in his ears: "A team of my best agents in San Francisco assigned to keep tabs on a harmless, sixty-four-year-old matron, and they call to tell me they can't find her. They've lost her in a goddamned lingerie boutique. Eleven more of the NSA's finest assigned to keep track of a handful of scientific geniuses who are confined on an island in the middle of nowhere. And four of these geniuses have vanished. A royal screw-up."

Gregg knew exactly what Sinclair would tell the President—that it was Michael Gregg's fault. It was called doctoring the spin.

Once Jeremy was back at Fort Meade, he had called Michael. They'd reviewed the steps taken since the disappearance and come up with preliminary manpower requirements. For a moment, Jeremy had seemed calmer.

"What options do these folks have, Michael? Let's list them. They could have found some kind of vehicle and driven to the airport to catch a flight."

"Which they didn't," Gregg replied. "There weren't any flights leaving Vieux Fort until morning, and either Kiley or Nicholsen have been at the airport since the disappearance."

"So we know they haven't flown out of Vieux Fort—"

"Or Castries. Their customs people were alerted within an hour."

"So what's left? They're either holed up somewhere on St. Lucia or they've left by boat. It *is* an island, Michael."

Brilliant, thought Gregg. As if he didn't know that. As if leaving by boat in any way narrowed the scope of the disaster.

"If they left by boat, they can't have gotten far. We'll start an air search. We've got helicopters in Grenada and Guantanamo. I'm sure I can get them."

Gregg shook his head. "You don't know what to look for, Jeremy, what kind of boat. Depending on the type, they could be miles from here by now."

"What are the most likely destinations?"

"As I told you, there are airports and airstrips on virtually every island. I've dispatched people to the obvious ones—Grenada, Martinique, and St. Vincent. Unless you want to bring in a full battalion, there aren't enough people to cover them all. There's an airstrip on Union Island that they could reach in a day by boat. Customs there is watching for them. There's another on Mustique—same thing. There are dozens of airports in the Eastern Caribbean and we've alerted customs officials at every one of them, but how efficient and cooperative they'll be is anyone's guess."

"What about Caracas? San Juan? Trinidad?"

"Same thing. I've alerted their customs people. If they try leaving by air they're supposed to be detained. But hell, they could head for Europe, Africa, South America, Mexico, anywhere."

"Or they could sail somewhere and hole up for a while."

"Equally bad," Michael said.

"I'll send you more—" Sinclair was apparently making a list. "Let's see. Two to San Juan, Puerto Rico, two to Caracas, two to St. Thomas. Where else?"

NANCY PARKER - 177 -

"Guadaloupe, Dominica, St. Martin, St. Barts, St. Croix—"

"Shit. I can't— You're talking dozens of people."

"Like I said. Anguilla, Nevis, St. Kitt's, St. Christopher, Antiqua, Marie-Galante, Barbados, Trinidad—"

"Jesus, Michael. Impossible. We'll have to narrow it down."

"Cannouan, Union, Carriacou—"

They'd finally whittled the list to San Juan, St. Croix, St. Thomas, Barbados, Guadaloupe and Trinidad. Sinclair would dispatch agents to each of those islands. Then, unable to resist of the allure of a high-tech solution, he'd returned to the possibility of a massive air search. "I still believe helicopters can help, and the Coast Guard."

"Have them on standby in case we get a lead on a boat. Otherwise—"

"Good. What else?"

"I sent two men down this morning to interrogate the natives who live around Soufriere Bay. These kids hang around down there earning tips from the sailors. Some live in tents on the beach. Maybe one of them saw something."

"What about yacht charter companies in the islands?"

"Good idea. I'll get on that this morning. If you can trace Rensler's wife, she'll lead us to them."

"Of course, and I've got people on top of that. All I can say, Michael, is you damned well better find these guys and find them fast. I'm on my way to another delightful briefing with the President. I need to be able to tell him we've got it under control."

Michael Gregg could think of nothing to say to this.

"These folks were allowed to wander down on the beach with only a single agent."

"You could have gone with them," Michael risked mentioning.

"Your people were to monitor their actions. It wasn't my place to step in, interfere with your supervision of your agents."

A convenient out, Gregg thought. Never mind that from the moment Sinclair had arrived at the compound he'd begun interfering. The emphasis on *your* people, *your* supervision of *your* agents was not lost on Gregg. "They'd gone out to dinner three times before and there were no problems. A few of them even walked on the beach."

The conversation had ended shortly after that. Gregg now had Jay Roberts working up a list of yacht charter services in the islands. He didn't have the manpower to visit them all in less than several days. They'd need names and addresses of all the crews on any charters active on June twenty-third. Names of boats, registration numbers, owners. No way these charter companies would give that information over the phone. They'd have to visit each one in person.

Flights. They'd need lists of airlines and flights leaving the Eastern Caribbean. Hotels on St. Lucia. Vacation rental homes—thousands of them on scores of islands. Impossible. The French, the Brits, the Dutch to deal with, each island with its own government, customs regulations, and local bureaucrats. Talk about a screw-up. Hell, they could easily sail to Miami. What's to stop them? Boat marinas in Florida.

Michael Gregg lowered his head into his hands. Cruise ships. Get lists of all the cruise lines' schedules. They could board one of those love boats at any number of deep-water harbors in the islands. His headache was a pounding throb across his brow.

Roberts walked over and cleared his throat. Gregg looked up, and Roberts handed him a single sheet of paper. "Here's a list of the yacht charter companies on St. Lucia," he said brightly.

"That's just great," Gregg whispered. "Now you can start listing Puerto Rican charter companies and work your way south through the island groups, all the way down to Venezuela. The Virgin Islands. Leewards. Windwards. Trinidad. Tobago. Barbados."

"Oh."

"And when you've finished your list," Gregg said, enunciating carefully, "you can pay each and every one of them a visit."

"Oh."

Ω

25

KATE FELT as though her hands had been soldered to the helm for a lifetime. Tim relieved them, taking an occasional watch, but still the hours at the helm slogged by. Standing, gripping the wheel, watching the wind indicator, watching the compass, watching the sails, scanning the horizon for boats and planes—it was getting old. She'd have given a lot for a night ashore.

Around two in the afternoon of the second day, Jack reported they'd reached the halfway point. Was that all? Halfway? She kept silent, kept watching, coming to a fresh understanding of why the Navy referred to this as a *watch*.

They'd seen distant cargo vessels and occasional high-flying aircraft, a few fleecy clouds but no more storm clouds. They were alone on their stretch of ocean with no land in sight. The temperature was a comfortable if monotonous 85° and the northeasterly trade winds were stiff and constant.

Margo cooked and Walter sulked, keeping to himself and claiming a queasy stomach while his wife seemed bent on smoothing the rough connection between her husband and the rest. Kate thought the tension had to be wearing on Margo's nerves; it certainly wore on hers.

After dinner, Kate volunteered for KP. Tim, Milt and Jack were in the cockpit engrossed in conversation. Margo sat at the salon table with a book in her hands pretending to read, her expression a mask, a fixed blank stare.

"Are you all right?" Kate asked quietly as she towel-dried silverware.

Margo looked up. "Oh, I suppose. I'm worried about Walter. He's torn. He wants to do the right thing but I think he's uncertain what that right thing is." She set her book down and looked at Kate. "What is the right thing? Were we wrong to leave?"

"I don't think so. I suppose it depends on your perspective. From mine, from an outsider's point of view, I'd have to say you've done the correct thing. But from Walter's, the funding and support for his project have come from the government and I suppose that's a powerful link, difficult to sever."

"They've worked on this project for years. He thinks Milt is nuts to chuck it all and just take off."

"Dr. Rensler—Milt—disapproves of the way the government's handling it. Plus he has Grace to consider." Kate still found it nearly impossible to call him Milt. It seemed too diminutive for the man who'd spearheaded SETI for so many years.

"Yes. And Walter has me," Margo said sadly, as though wishing it mattered more. She picked up her book and tried to concentrate for a few more minutes. "I should turn in. I'm awfully tired." She stood up. "Goodnight, Kate."

"Goodnight." Kate finished in the galley and joined the men in the cockpit. Tim was at the helm and Jack was continuing the sailing instruction. Kate hoped they'd be able to entrust Tim with the helm that night. She desperately needed sleep.

"Where shall we go from Miami?" Milt asked during a lull in the instruction.

"I was thinking about that," Tim said. "My family has a summer cottage in Northern Michigan on Crystal Lake. It's remote. Now that my folks are gone, the place is never used. None of the rest of my family goes there."

"How would it be in the wintertime?"

"Fine. It's not really a cottage. That's just what my family's always called it. It's a regular house. It gets heavy snow in winter but there's an old strap-on snowplow to clear the road.

Good fireplace, plenty of firewood, last I looked. The heating system's new. It's in a birch forest on a lake near the small town of Frankfort—about thirty-five miles from Traverse City."

"Would Grace be comfortable?"

"I don't see why not. My folks always were. It not all that rustic. There's a Chevy pickup in the garage if we can get it started. It's been sitting idle for two years."

"Would they be able to trace you there? Members of your family might mention it to the NSA," Jack said.

"Are you kidding? My brother and kid sisters are—put it this way: if the NSA comes calling, they'd probably tell the agents our family roots are in Nome, Alaska. Somewhere there are stray cousins but we've lost track of each other. They can't have ever been to the cottage."

The more Tim elaborated, the better it was sounding. Kate had worried that, upon reaching Miami, the scientists would be apprehended for lack of a safe place to go. Obviously they couldn't return to their homes.

"What about Walter and Margo?" she asked. "Would they go too?"

"I'm sure Walter will go back to St. Lucia," Dr. Rensler said. "He didn't want to leave. Margo talked him into it, and I think he's sorry now that he gave in. Margo would probably prefer to return to Boston to her teaching and research, but that's out. She might go back to St. Lucia with Walter or she might come with us." He turned to Tim. "I don't think we should mention the cottage to the Jacobsens just now."

"No. You know, Milt, we could hole up and continue working, set up a lab, bring in a satellite dish, search for the signal. It wouldn't have to be a large dish. At least we could focus on translating the fragment we've got."

Kate wondered and had to ask, "Will you announce the fact of the transmissions when you reach Miami?"

Tim and Milt exchanged looks and Tim shook his head. "We can't notify the press. That's out. No point till the entire signal is translated. We could notify other SETI groups, although there we risk attracting attention and being apprehended."

"Phones might be tapped at other SETI facilities," Rensler said. "For the time being, we've decided to keep it quiet."

Kate the journalist was relieved. "So I still have an exclusive?"

"For whatever that's worth. Course if you announce it—or even if *we* announce it—who'd believe it?" Rensler smiled ruefully at his own observation. "Get used to the snicker factor, Kate. People will likely treat this as a hoax unless it's handled correctly."

"The best outcome would be to wait until the entire signal has been received and translated," Tim said. "Then we hand it over to the international SETI community."

"What if you're apprehended?"

"Then you'll have to do it for us," Rensler concluded.

"Maybe you've already received the entire signal," she said.

Rensler shook his head. "We'll have to search more extensively before I'd be satisfied of that. We've barely scratched the surface. If we haven't found it after several months, then maybe— I don't know. There are a number of trajectory theories I want to try. Main thing is get to work."

"And minimize the risk of being apprehended in the process," Tim said.

"Right. Well, I'm off to bed," Rensler said.

Kate volunteered for the ten-till-two shift at the helm. Tim would relieve her at two AM, and Jack said he'd take over at six. After everyone else had turned in, Jack stayed up another hour, sitting with Kate in the cockpit.

"How are you feeling?" he asked when they were alone.

"Fine. Tired. How about you?"

"All right." Then after a moment, "Walter's a problem."

"Yes. Nothing we can do about it. He'll either report us or he won't." She hoped this sounded less concerned than she felt. The problem of Walter shadowed her mood and weighed her down even more than the long hours at the helm. "Can you think of a solution?"

"No. If he reports us, we're in for an interesting time when we return the boat. Look east." A nearly full moon was rising, illuminating the eastern horizon.

"Beautiful," she whispered.

"I'll check our course." He went below and returned with sextant and star charts, took a fix on Pollux and another on Arcturas, and after a moment said, "We've drifted 5° west. The current's strong. Can you hold 340°?"

They tweaked and adjusted sails but it was too much of a pinch to weather. The sails back-winded and they lost speed.

"Looks as though eventually we'll have to tack," he said.

"I hope there's time. It's a tight schedule."

They sailed along under the star-filled sky in silence. Then Jack spoke. "Walter *will* report us. You realize that."

"It's likely."

"And if he does, we'll likely be arrested."

"The only way to diffuse the situation would be to announce the signal to the world, but if no one believes us—"

They felt stymied. He moved behind her and began kneading her neck and shoulders. "Fortunately there's time to consider the options. It'll be nice to have the boat to ourselves again."

"Mm."

"Let's hope we can work in a vacation before the excrement hits the ventilator." His thumb homed in on a knotted muscle in her shoulder and gently worked it.

"That feels wonderful."

"Wish we could pull over and park." His touch became a caress and she felt a tremor move through her.

"I miss you, counselor."

"Ditto." There was a hint of sadness in his voice.

He turned in at midnight leaving Kate at the helm feeling thoroughly relaxed—too relaxed. She fought to keep awake, battling drowsiness by jogging in place and reciting grammar school poetry. Anything but "Matilda". She stumbled through fragments of "Hiawatha," "Paul Revere's Ride," "Oh Captain, My Captain." It helped.

At two-thirty Tim emerged from the cabin and relieved her.
"Thank God," she said. "Do you think you can you hold
337°?"

"No problem."

"And you understand sailing on the luff?"

He said he did.

"Holler if you have problems."

"I'll be fine."

She went below and crawled into the berth next to Jack, too
tired to worry about whether Tim ought to be left alone at the
helm.

Ω

26

MICHAEL GREGG wasn't getting enough sleep either. In fact, he'd not slept more than three hours since the night of June twenty-second, and the exhaustion and stress were taking their toll. His eyes burned and he had difficulty focusing his thoughts. He stood and began roaming the office.

Gregg was just under six feet tall but to most he seemed taller. What little remained of his thinning hair was gray, and he was at pains to part it in a line that reached ever lower for wisps he could draw up and over his gleaming pate. He seldom smiled. Like Sinclair, Gregg had learned it was best to conceal feelings. People who smiled in this business were seldom taken seriously.

He'd been staring blindly out the window for a long time. Now he walked over to the sofa and allowed himself to stretch out. Just for an hour, he promised himself. It was three AM.

Over the course of the day his phone had rung incessantly. He'd detailed three agents to the task of compiling lists of airlines, charter companies, vacation rentals, cruise lines, and hotels. Terrific, he'd thought, making lists while the scientists fled, diddling while Rome burned. Agents Stern and Galloway had spent the day interrogating the residents of Soufriere Bay, everyone from restaurant personnel to shopkeepers, fishermen and native children who hung around performing small tasks in exchange for tips from sailors. Stern and Galloway would return first thing in the morning to continue.

He dozed off.

Gregg awakened with a start. What time was it? He glanced at his watch—seven AM. His eyes were gritty and his headache had become a relentless throb encasing his brow. He rubbed his eyes and started a pot of coffee.

At nine-thirty he got his first real break in the case. Agent Carl Stern walked into the security office with a fifteen-year-old native in tow.

"Lawrence, tell Mr. Gregg here what you've told me," Stern prodded the youth.

Lawrence looked down at his feet. His skin was a deep ebony. He wore tattered cutoffs, a threadbare T-shirt, and a rainbow-colored knitted hat that covered his head like a shower cap.

"Um, well, I am not—"

"About the boat in the bay," Stern prompted.

"Seven or eight at night. Almost dark. A sailboat come in Petit Soufriere."

"That's the smaller cove just to the south of—"

"I *know* where Petit Soufriere is, Carl. Go on, Lawrence. What did the boat look like?"

"A sailboat, man. A white boat."

"One mast or two?"

"One."

"How many people?"

"I think two, a man and woman. I am going to see if I can help them tie up to thee tree, but thee man is fast. I already have my boat up for thee night, an' I am going to town. I don' even get my boat down to thee water, an' thee man is ashore an' tie to thee tree an' back to thee boat."

"How old was this man?"

"Oh, *old*, man. Maybe thirty. Maybe forty."

"Right. What about the woman? Did you see her?"

He shook his head. "Too dark. An' thee boat is far out in thee bay."

"Yes, I see. Did you catch the name of the boat?" Lawrence looked down at his feet and did not reply. He can't read, thought

Michael. "Maybe we can help. Did you notice the name of the
boat on the stern?"

"A little. It's very dark, man."

"The letters? Did you see any of them?"

Lawrence gave him a blank look.

"Had you ever seen the boat before?"

"No. That boat never come to Soufriere."

"Tell him what else happened," Carl urged.

"I leave an' go to town. I come back late at night an' thee
boat is gone."

"What time did you get back?"

Lawrence shrugged. "Don' know."

"Let's see if you can help us figure out the name of the boat,
Lawrence. Could you do that?"

Lawrence didn't reply.

"Could you write down any of the letters?" Michael handed
Lawrence a tablet and pencil. "Do you want anything to eat,
Lawrence? Are you hungry? Carl, make Lawrence a sandwich,
a cup of hot chocolate. Would you like that?"

"No, man." He rolled his fist around the pencil as though he
were going to stab the tablet with it and began forming letters:
the letter *E* in script followed by some vague loops. A capital *D*
in script, followed by two more loops. Finally, something
resembling either a capital *S* or a capital *G*, followed by a low
loop and a second higher loop.

"*Sol* or *Gol*," said Gregg. "Did it look like this?" he asked,
writing out *Sol* in a loopy script.

Lawrence's brow furrowed. "Thee last part look like that."

"Spanish for 'sun.' Looks like three words, Carl. Maybe a
Spanish name. The first word probably begins with an *E*. The
second word is Dol. No, *Del*. Something-*Del Sol*," he said.
"Excellent, Lawrence, a big help. Can you think of anything else
about the boat? Anything on its sails?"

"The sails are down when it come. I don' see them."

"Very good, Lawrence, very good. Let me give you something for your trouble." Gregg withdrew his wallet and handed
Lawrence a ten-E.C. note.

Lawrence stared sadly at the bill in his palm. "I am not in thee cove, man. I miss thee boats come in today."

"How much, Lawrence?"

"Thirty E.C.?"

"Fine, give it to him, Carl, and maybe some food. Lawrence, can we find you around the Hummingbird if we need to talk to you?"

"I sleep by my boat. Sometimes I leave to fish."

The moment Lawrence was gone, Michael called Jeremy Sinclair. "The boat was probably called Something-*Del Sol*, we think. The first letter of the first word could be an *E*. It was in the small cove just south of Soufriere Bay at dusk. A white-hulled sloop. Two people on board, a man and a woman. There might have been more, though. I'll take those 'copters now."

"Absolutely. We'll get two up, anyway, one in the Wind-wards, one in the Leewards, watching for a white sloop called the *E-something Del Sol*. Got it. Anything else?"

"Yes. Alert the harbor masters at every marina in Florida and the gulf states. Tell them to be on watch for the boat."

"Right."

"We're checking charter yacht companies down here. I'll keep you posted."

Ω

27

KATE DIDN'T AWAKEN until nearly nine on the morning of the twenty-fifth. If Jack's alarm had sounded, she hadn't heard it. She climbed out of bed and gave herself a fast spritz bath, tied on a fresh headband, and opened the door to their cabin. She was met by the scrumptious aroma of bacon cooking.

"Good morning," Jack greeted her. "I was about wake you."

She sat down in the salon next to him and looked across at Walter, who appeared to be in better spirits. "How's it going, Walter?" she ventured.

"I'll live," he said with a faint smile, perhaps in a mood to forge a detente.

"Glad to hear it. Tim's at the helm? How'd he do last night?"

"No problem. A born sailor," Jack said. "He's already had breakfast."

"It's my turn again, isn't it?"

"Take your time," Jack said, eyeing her with gentle concern.

She peered out through a porthole at an oval patch of cloudless sky. "Another beautiful day." Why did she feel so gloomy? Jeremy Sinclair, of course. And Walter. Let it go, she told herself. A sudden, shocking picture then formed itself in her mind, a vision of Walter disappearing over the side and into the sea. She shook her head; it was an awful thought.

Jack was saying that the wind had remained steady, that they were continuing to make good time. "We should see St. Croix tomorrow afternoon." It seemed like forever.

After breakfast, she relieved Tim at the helm. Tim said he intended to work on the transmissions all day, that he'd thought of a new approach to deciphering the signal during the night.

"It was really something, Kate. I stood there at the helm and I became sort of mesmerized, holding the course and staring out into the night. It's odd. When you stop trying to understand something and let your mind go slack, all of a sudden an answer comes. Anyway, it might be an answer."

Tim stayed below after breakfast. Margo joined the others in the cockpit, read and stared out to sea. Milt—Kate was finally beginning to think of him as Milt—said he was working on trajectory calculations and scribbled away on a yellow tablet. Walter opted to sit up on deck, leaning against the mast. He wanted some sun, he said, after being cooped up in the fo'c'sle for so many hours. His disposition had improved, and Kate thought Margo must have spoken to him. Jack puttered, reorganizing storage lockers, sponging off the film of gritty salt that had accumulated on the surfaces of the cockpit and deck. He coiled lines and then went below to tidy the salon. He'd never been able to sit still on a boat.

A hundred yards or so in the distance Kate noticed a change in the ocean's surface, a disturbance off the starboard bow that was whipping the swells into wild confusion. There were no clouds; the sky was a deep blue from horizon to horizon. She'd never seen anything like it, and she called below to Jack, who had begun sweeping the salon floor. He came up and gazed across the starboard bow.

"Looks like a wind shift. Shall I take the helm?"

"Yes. It can't be a storm. There isn't a cloud in the sky. What is it?"

"I'm not sure. You can always see gusts blowing on the surface some distance off, but this looks unusually strong.

Walter," he called suddenly, "you'd better come back to the cockpit."

Walter appeared to be snoozing and didn't respond.

"Walter!" No response.

"I'll get him," Kate said. She climbed from the cockpit and hurried forward, gripping the starboard lifeline for balance.

"Wake up, Walter! You need to get back to the cockpit."

He was leaning against the mast facing the bow and he turned and looked up at her myopically. He'd removed his glasses and must have been nearly blind.

"What's up?"

"Rough seas ahead. Can you move quickly?"

"Okay, I'm coming." He stood up, clutching the mast for support, then shifted around it and took a step toward the cockpit. At that moment, the wind squall hit with a violence Kate could barely comprehend. One moment Walter was holding onto the mast and the next, he was not. The boom swung crazily around to starboard in a violent blast of wind, and the boat careened in a wrenching jibe. On its violent swing, the boom struck Walter hard against the shoulder and threw him to the deck and down toward the lifeline. He was no more than five feet from Kate with his legs dangling precariously over the side, and she raced forward to grab him, bending low to avoid the boom's chaotic arc. She felt the boat lurch again and watched as Walter was carried under the lifeline and disappeared into the churning ocean. She recalled the vivid mental flash she'd had at breakfast and it sickened her.

"Man overboard! Head up, Jack!" The safest course for a sailboat in trouble—into the wind, sails slack.

"I'm trying!" he shouted back.

There were sounds of metal snapping and rigging tearing free.

"Kate!" But that was all she heard. She did precisely what the books say not to do: she leapt over the side. She didn't think or ponder the alternatives and she didn't consider the consequences. She simply leapt feet-first into the sea.

After that, everything was a blur. The swells were enormous. She couldn't see far in any direction. She whirled her head about, finally sighting Walter's flailing arms some ten yards off. She swam to him, threw her right arm across his chest and under his left arm and tried to immobilize him while keeping them both afloat in the furious seas. He fought her every inch of the way with a panic-induced strength.

"Stop it, Walter! I have you! Relax!" she yelled in his ear. The ferocity of her voice had an effect and he quieted. "Hold on. Jack will bring the boat around." At least he would if he could find them.

She pivoted, searching frantically for the boat over the towering waves. Which direction? The noon sun was almost directly overhead. There was no fixed point with which to orient herself amid the confusion of swells. She felt overwhelmed and disoriented. All sense of direction had vanished. The deafening wind drove seawater hard against her face, adding to her confusion and impairing her vision. She clung to Walter and he to her, and she whirled her head, hoping desperately for a glimpse of the masthead, the sails, Jack—who surely could not be far off. But there were only mountainous whitecapped seas and an escalating sense of terror. Dear God! What had she done? If she couldn't see the boat, Jack certainly couldn't see her.

She had no idea whether several minutes had elapsed or merely seconds. She fought rising panic, forcing her mind into reason. Wait till we're carried to the top of a swell. Then look around, she told herself. They rose on the crest of a wave and she whirled about. Nothing. They were back in a deep trough and her heart sank with them. Her fear might have become as great a threat to their survival as the turbulent seas. As the panic rose in her throat, it nearly choked off her wind. She opened her mouth for breath and took in salt water.

Walter had ceased his struggling and was a leaden weight in her arms. Her churning legs kept them afloat. On the crest of the next swell she looked behind and then to the right and spotted the tip of the mast and then the full sail. *Thank God.*

The boat was forty yards beyond and to her right and she began a furious sidestroke and scissor-kick in its direction. Each time the sea carried them high in the water she turned and marked their progress. Jack had gotten *Espiritu* headed up into the wind. The sails were luffing.

At some point, as suddenly as it had come, the wind squall passed. The deafening roar of the wind ceased. Kate grabbed Walter's limp form more firmly and hollered, "We're almost there. Just hang on." He made no response.

A figure at the boat's stern was freeing the man-overboard buoy. Attached to it were a pole-shaped beacon and life preserver. She watched as the rig was flung from the stern and she scissor-kicked hard, carrying them toward the pole that was bobbing sixty feet off. Now nearly exhausted, she urged herself to kick harder and again and harder.

It seemed to take forever to reach the life preserver. Her left arm pulled while her right arm dragged Walter in what must have been a choking cross-chest hold. At last they were at the horseshoe float and she looped it under Walter's arms and sidestroked with him in tow toward the boat. Tim hurried to fasten the ladder over the side and Kate reached it with the last of her strength.

As she clung to the rope ladder with one hand and pushed from below, Tim, Milt, and Margo got hold of the back of Walter's shorts and hauled his limp form into the boat. Kate followed him up and into the cockpit. He appeared unconscious as they laid him across the cushions and set to work.

"Is he all right?" Kate asked.

Margo was bent over Walter, breathing into his mouth. His leg twitched and he sputtered. His left shoulder bled through his shirt where the boom had struck him.

"He'll be okay," Margo whispered as her husband leaned over the edge of the cockpit seat and coughed up seawater.

Jack had been at the helm through all this steadying the boat into the wind and watching their efforts. "Kate, you never should have— You both could have been killed." But his tone was more relieved than scolding.

"I know." Her breathing was almost normal now and the powerful rush of adrenalin that had propelled her over the side and through the water was subsiding, leaving her weak-kneed and trembling. She slumped to the seat and let out a long deep breath.

"I know, Jack. It was the wrong thing to do. I didn't think. I just did it."

Walter lay there stunned and bleeding but breathing more evenly.

"Milt, go below and get the first-aid kit. It's on the shelf over the chart table," Jack said. "Tim, take the helm. Hold it into the wind. See the wind indicator? The arrow's pointing at the bow. Keep it there."

"Right. I see."

Jack climbed forward to the mast to assess the damage and returned to report that the gunwale-mounted block used to rig the preventer down from the boom had snapped. The preventer line was loose and flapping. "Dangerous in unpredictable winds to sail without it properly rigged," he said, lapsing into efficiency. The crew stared at him blankly.

"I brought spare blocks, Milt, in my duffle bag on the floor of the starboard stern locker."

Milt left again, returning with the blocks, and Jack selected one and re-rigged the preventer. Then he examined the rest of the rigging and sails and pronounced everything secure.

Meanwhile, Margo had helped Walter off with his shirt and was cleaning and dressing the shoulder wound. Walter sat speechless and stunned.

Kate slid over next to him and patted his bony knee. "How you doin', Walter?"

"I'll live," he said, trying a smile. "Thank you. I could have—" He looked ashen. He patted his breast pocket. "Guess I lost my glasses. God, it happened so fast. I hardly knew what hit me."

"What hit you was the boom right across the shoulder," Tim said. "Threw you across the deck. Your momentum carried you overboard—"

"And Kate jumped in," he finished. "I don't— Thank you."

"Anytime, Walter. We had ourselves quite a swim."

Walter pressed a towel to his shoulder as Margo cut butterfly bandages from adhesive tape. She stretched four across the two-inch cut.

"Best I can do without stitches." She taped on a gauze pad.

Milt brought Walter a dry shirt and handed it to Margo. "Tim, do think we might have just sailed through a microburst?"

"Maybe."

"What's that?" Jack asked.

"The phenomenon responsible for aircraft wind-sheer accidents—a sudden, localized violent downdraft. Usually unaccompanied by any other climatic effects. Invisible to radar."

"We're damned lucky we weren't de-masted," Jack said grim-faced.

"I wasn't much help," Rensler said. "All I did was keep out of the way."

"Me too," Margo said. "Walter, did you bring a second pair of glasses?"

"By my reading lamp."

Jack had them back on course and handed the helm back to Tim. "Can you hold her for a few more minutes?"

"Sure."

He touched Kate's elbow. "Can you stand?"

"Of course." Her legs felt like silly putty.

Below, he gestured.

She followed him into the salon and he took her hand and led her back toward the stern, then turned and silently wrapped her in his arms. They clung to each other for several moments, his cheek against her wet hair. He drew her tighter until she thought he'd squeeze the air from her entirely. She drew her head back and looked up at his face into eyes that were managed to look both fierce and intensely gentle.

He pressed his lips to her forehead. "Thank God."

"Oh honey." She felt tears rimming her eyes and she swallowed hard.

The crew spent the next hours retelling the crisis, each from his own point of view. Jack delivered a belated lecture on man-overboard procedures and demonstrated how the life-saving unit on the stern was deployed.

"In the future, if, God forbid, this should happen again, *no one Kate*, is to jump over the side. One person immediately throws this whole rig overboard. The helmsman notes and announces the time and heading so we can time our actions and have a chance of returning to the exact spot. Then the helmsman heads *into* the wind and comes about, reverses course and backtracks to the spill. And everyone else is to keep their eye on that spot where the person went over." Then miserably he added, "I screwed up completely. I had no idea the wind had suddenly shifted to port. One minute it was from starboard, and then it was reversed. I thought I was heading up. Instead we jibed the second time."

"Does anybody know what day this is?" Walter asked querulously.

Tim studied him a moment. "Just about the luckiest damned day of your life."

Ω

28

CHIP DOLEMAN conducted an exceedingly somber Jeremy Sinclair into the Oval Office. Geller waved him to sit, hurriedly concluded a phone call, then joined him on the cream-colored brocade sofa.

"Thanks, Chip. That'll be all." Geller smiled slightly as his chief of staff stormed from the room. "That man hates to be out of the loop. So. Tell me some good news, Jeremy. I could use it this afternoon."

The President leaned far back with his hands locked behind his head. He'd loosened his tie and his shirt sleeves were rolled up. Despite the posture and manner, Jeremy recognized Geller was anything but relaxed.

"There's not a lot to report. We have every major airport in the Eastern Caribbean on alert. Michael Gregg's coordinating down there."

"Reliable?"

"The best I've got. I've got him making inquiries with yacht charter services in the area. We're checking passenger lists of all airlines and cruise lines. We're also working on the possibility that they've holed up somewhere in the islands until things cool off."

"That could be a problem, couldn't it?"

"Yes. We've got photos posted at all customs offices, airports and post offices. I've got agents distributing their photos to harbor masters on the southern Atlantic seaboard and all along the Gulf Coast. Every domestic airport in the States is on alert."

"Any leads?"

"One possible. A local fisherman saw a sailboat enter a cove near Soufriere at dusk on the twenty-third. The boat departed before midnight. The fisherman was able to give us a description and part of the boat's name. We immediately brought in helicopters from St. George's and they're patrolling the islands looking for the sloop."

"How many copters?"

"Two. I could use more. I'd like to start a grid search. And I could use more manpower, both in the islands and stateside. I brought a list."

The President scanned the paper. "We'll bring in personnel from Guantanamo—Naval Intelligence—and draw on the FBI for the domestic coverage. I'll see to it. Additional helicopters? How would they be deployed?"

"The ones we've got are overflying yachts low enough to take photos—names on the stern, the crew visible on deck."

"They're buzzing yacht marinas?"

Sinclair nodded. "And yachts away from port out to two hundred miles east and west of the islands. With only two it's hit and miss. I could use a dozen."

The President considered and shook his head. "Sorry, Jeremy. If the islands were ours it would be another matter, but these are independent or belong to the Brits, the French, the Dutch. Every one of them relies on tourist trade. No, Jeremy. No additional copters at this point. The investigation must be kept low profile. We start bothering vacationing sailors and disrupting tourist trade and we'll have every island government down on our heads. People—the media—will start asking questions."

Sinclair sighed. "I was afraid you'd say that. Can we continue with the two we've got?"

"Discretely. What about Rensler's wife?"

"The trail's surprisingly cold. It's a fair bet she flew out of SFO. We've examined relevant passenger lists. We've checked flights out of Oakland and San Jose. If she was on any of those, she had to have flown under an assumed name. We're questioning ticket agents and airline personnel, showing her photo around. So far no leads. "

"Damn." The President spoke to the ceiling.

"We're paying particular attention to Miami flights but the fact is, she could have flown anywhere. "

"She walked in the front door of a shop and out the back?"

"Right. A lingerie shop. The agents said she'd been going there at least once a week ever since they were assigned. They'd taken to standing out front. It's a small shop and they could see in and easily keep an eye on her. I guess they were a little embarrassed to go inside, stand around with a lot of ladies trying on underwear. You can understand—"

"What about the owner of the boutique?"

"We've questioned the employees. They remember Mrs. Rensler, said she came in a lot. If she did speak with other shoppers the clerks didn't recall it. The shop owner said she'd often noticed our men waiting out front and wondered. That's about it. "

"Clever of Mrs. Rensler. She must have been planning this for quite a while. How'd she leave? In her car?"

"No. Her car was left in the parking lot near the shop. We're questioning cabs and limo services. So far nothing. We think it's possible Dr. Rensler's sister and brother-in-law helped though they're not saying much. They told our agents that Mrs. Rensler mailed them the keys to her car and house and enclosed a note asking them to pick up the car and check on the Rensler's home. They claim to have had no warning that she was planning to leave and no idea where she might have gone. Too conveniently, they threw the note away that arrived with the keys. "

"Slick, well-executed," Geller said. "So you're keeping an eye on the sister? They might know more or they might hear from the Renslers. "

"It's being handled. "

"Sorry, Jeremy. I don't mean to tell you your job. I'm just trying to make sure we don't overlook anything. "

Sinclair stiffened. The President had lost confidence in him. Who could blame him? "I understand, Sir, and if it's any consolation I know we'll find them. We're checking credit card use. That might lead somewhere."

The President rose abruptly. "Thanks for stopping by. I'll have Enderby at FBI contact you about manpower. You'll keep me informed." He escorted Sinclair to the door.

"Sorry about this, Sir, I—"

"Keep at it then." The President was in no mood to hear excuses.

Ω

29

FOLLOWING WALTER'S close, watery encounter with his own mortality, he repaired to the fo'c'sle to recover. Kate thought she detected a shift in attitude. Perhaps there'd been a moment of enlightenment as he was dropping over the side. It was one way to bring the guy around—a near-death experience.

Kate sought to appear less affected by the rescue than she actually felt. She and Jack shared helm duties while Milt, Tim and Margo huddled around the computer in the salon. But the ragged terror of the experience stayed with Kate. It had been as much a near death experience for her as for Walter. Jack was also shaken, though at pains to conceal it from the rest of the crew. There was still a job to be finished before he and Kate could allow themselves to acknowledge what they'd lived through and how it had affected them, but she was certain there'd been a shift. A threshold between them had been met and even if they hadn't crossed it, they'd not retreated either. She felt it in looks and touches. They'd both saved lives that day.

At five, Tim emerged from the salon and lowered himself onto the cushion next to Kate. "We've been playing with a new de-encryption algorithm."

Jack gave him a questioning look.

"So far no luck. There's half an idea in the back of my mind. I just need to step away from it for a while. I'm overlooking some small thing. Maybe if I stop concentrating so hard—"

Milt helped Margo fix an early dinner for the weary, subdued crew, after which all but Jack and Tim turned in. Jack was taking the first night shift until two, Tim would take the second, and Kate the third. She went below and tried to read.

Reclining in the stern berth, she struggled to focus on her novel. It was a rippling-smoothie she'd bought at the Miami Airport. She stared at the printed page and reread a paragraph for the third or fourth time. Who were these characters? Women with milky smooth skin and men with rippling muscles thrashing through turbulently messy lives. She gave up on the book and lay staring at the teakwood-trimmed bulkhead and listening to the murmur of voices overhead.

She thought back over the day. Her leap into the sea to rescue Walter had had to do with instinct, foolishness and a realization that this entire escapade—her idea from the start—would have been tragically derailed by a death at sea. Perhaps the strangest part of the experience had been the fully formed image that had come to her only hours before the accident—the mental picture of Walter Jacobsen falling overboard. Impossible to explain, but such things were happening more and more. As she dropped off to sleep, it was with the understanding that despite Jack's lecture, despite the stark terror she'd felt, if she had it to do again, she would.

Some time in the night she felt Jack crawl into the berth beside her and curve against her. At six AM, the alarm sounded and she crawled from the berth and made her way into the dim cabin.

"Good morning, Tim," she said quietly, leaning partway up the hatch. "Everything all right?"

"Yeah. Boy I got sleepy. For a while there around three I thought I'd lose it. Kept myself awake reciting the Periodic Table."

"I do 'Hiawatha.' Shall I make coffee?"

"Not for me. I'm going to bed."

Kate took the helm and soon the sounds of Tim's faint snoring drifted up from the salon. She watched the dawn sky lighten. It would be a hot day. It was late June, and the sun was fierce this near the Equator. It might reach 90° or more as they neared the land masses of St. Croix and Puerto Rico. If the wind held, there remained about sixteen hours of sailing before they reached their destination.

Walter seemed in better spirits. His shoulder, while painful, was healing well, and Kate considered that he might be reveling in the sense of having cheated death. He joined her in the cockpit and sat sipping coffee while his wife busied herself with breakfast. It would never have occurred to him to help.

"You saved my life," he said. "I want to thank you. It was a courageous thing you did. Words aren't very adequate."

"You've already thanked me, Walter, and courage had nothing to do with it. I was thinking about that last night. It was instinct, pure and simple, but I'm glad it worked out."

He was quiet for a moment. "Sailing seems to take the measure of a person."

Kate looked at him, wondering if the measure he'd found of himself was full or wanting.

"I've decided to return to St. Lucia. I made up my mind last night."

Her heart sank.

"I want you to know that I won't mention your involvement in the rescue. I won't tell them where you've dropped us off. It's the least I can do, but I do have to return."

"Why?"

"The research, NASA, the funding. I hope you mean it, Kate, that you won't publish anything about this. I realize you're a journalist and this is a huge story, but I hope you'll reconsider."

"I won't release the story until the time is right and I've agreed to rely on Milt and Tim to decide when and how that's to be. That's all I can promise, Walter. At some point it'll have to become public."

He stared at her hard and then out across the water. "You'd jeopardize years of work. You could trigger widespread panic."

"That's always been the assumption, hasn't it? The justification for the secrecy? That if people know for certain there's life elsewhere, we'll all begin running through the streets like crazed, panicked idiots? It's right out of a fifties take-me-to-your-leader movie. Know what I think? I think the news is wondrous and profoundly reassuring."

"And not your story to tell."

She wouldn't argue the point. "You weren't pleased with Milt's decision to leave. Why did you?"

"Margo wanted it."

"What'll she do now?"

"She's thinking it over. Her preference would be to go home, but if she does, they'll only pick her up and return her to St. Lucia. Her real choice is between going into hiding or returning with me."

"Tough decision."

"She'll go with me," he said firmly.

Tim had awakened below, roused no doubt by the aromas and clatter of breakfast being prepared near his sleeping area. Margo called out that breakfast was served and soon they were congregated around the table. Jack ate and then relieved Kate at the helm. And as if in defiance of her earlier assessment, Walter actually helped straighten the galley after the meal. Tim brought out the computer and set to work—a new scheme he wanted to try.

At one-thirty PM, Jack spotted St. Croix off the starboard bow. The crew gathered in the cockpit to gaze at the faint strip of land some twenty miles distant.

"Right on schedule," Jack said, rather pleased. "That places us seventy miles southwest of Puerto Rico." The wind had shifted to a more northerly quarter as Avery predicted it might, and Kate could no longer hold their northwesterly course. They'd have to tack.

"It'll delay our arrival by a few hours," Jack said.

"We're a bit ahead of schedule, aren't we?"

"A few hours, but I'd have preferred to approach in daylight. That southeastern coast looks deadly on the charts. Never mind. Ready about?" After sailing for days with the boat heeling to port, they came about and the *Espiritu Del Sol* heeled to starboard. Bahia Lima was twelve hours away.

Tim glanced at his watch and headed below. At three-thirty, Kate left the helm and joined him. From his intense concentration, she figured he must be onto something. The rest of the crew was in the cockpit. The cabin was uncomfortably hot, even with portholes open on the leeward side, but Tim seemed oblivious. His face glistened with perspiration and he clattered away on the keyboard as though in a trance.

"Get this macro working, re-dimension the array. Should be three-dimensions. Okay, increment the subscript in the loop. That's got it."

He looked up at Kate and winked. "Don't say anything but I may be close. As soon as this compiles—" They waited. He leaned back against the seat cushions and wiped his brow.

"Care for a soft drink?"

"Sure." When the program was ready, he said, "Here goes." He typed RUN DECALC and seconds later a series of numbers filled the screen. He quickly pressed the PAUSE key to keep them from scrolling past. "Don't say anything but I think I have it."

"How does it work?" She scooted over beside him and studied the screen.

"Anagrams," he said. "You assign a numeric value to every letter of the alphabet. Not just 1 for A, 2 for B, and 3 for C. You double the values each time." He punched a calculator and scribbled on a piece of paper:

A = 1	B = 2	C = 4	D = 8
E = 16	F = 32	G = 64	H = 128
I = 256	J = 512	K = 1024	L = 2048
M = 4096	N = 8192	O = 16384	P = 32768
Q = 65536	R = 131072	S = 262144	T = 524288
U = 1048576	V = 2097152	W = 4194304	X = 8388608
Y = 16777216	Z = 33554432		

She stared at the neat columns. "Why?"

"Because virtually every word in the English language will have a unique numeric value simply by adding the sum of those numbers together for each letter in a word. For example, the word ACE has a numeric value of 21—the sum of 1 plus 4 plus 16. There'll be some duplicates but not many.

"There'd be lots of duplicates, wouldn't there?"

"No. Only a few which is how I stumbled on this. See, after each large numeric value in the transmission there always follow a pair of smaller numbers. The first of these is usually 1 but there are a few of these secondary values as high as 7, though seldom higher. We thought those were some kind of check-digits. But then I thought, what if that's a word option number? What if there's a possibility of more than one word associated with each numeric value? Then the third number could be the number of letters in the word. I haven't quite figured it all out yet and I haven't looked at punctuation; there'll be values for Pause and Stop. But just now I took this sequence of numbers from the transmission and ran them through my program." He handed her a sheet of paper on which was written:

17838471 1 13 9076792 9 262145 1 2 266561 1 5
659474 1 7 524752 1 5 524432 1 3 299544 1 9
16416 1 2 1 1 1 1073186 1 7 17318688 1 8

"I purposely chose a segment of the transmission where all the secondary numbers are 1, which I think indicates there are no valid duplicate anagrams for the words in that stream. Here's what was produced in translation."

AAACHILLMMTTY DEEEPRSSX AS AGIMS AAELLRT
EIGHT EHT DEIIMNNOS FO A BDDENOU FIIINNTY

Kate stared at it. "Tim, it's gibberish."

"No it's not. Look. We'd already run the analysis to find the most often occurring numeric value in the transmission. It's 524432. If the transmission's based on English that ought to translate to THE, our most often-used word. Look. It occurs in that data stream." He pointed to 'EHT'. "An anagram of 'THE'. Add up the value of those three letters."

"The value of T is 524288. H is 128 and E is 16," Kate said.
He entered the values into the calculator. "524432."

"Amazing. And look, the number after the 1 is the number
3—implying three letters in the word THE."

"Exactly."

"So these are all anagrams!"

"That's the way it looks.

Kate stared at the line of gibberish for a moment. *Blank blank
as blank blank eight the blank of a blank blank.* "No other word
in the English language adds up to 524432?"

"I challenge you to find one." His eyes were bright. He wiped
his perspiring forehead with the back of his hand. "How are you
at solving anagrams?"

"Lousy."

"The letters are in alphabetical sequence. They only need to
be rearranged."

"That's incredible, Tim!"

"Shhh."

"—and ingenious," she whispered. "Why would they make it
so complicated, though? Why not just use numbers from 1 to 26
for each letter, corresponding with A through Z? Or sums of
them?"

"Because there'd be thousands of duplicate word values. Say
for instance the word value under the 1-to-26 scheme was 21.
How many different combinations of letters can you come up
with to total twenty-one? Letter 21; letters 20 and 1; letters 19,
1 and 1; letters 18 and 3; letters 18, 1, 1 and 1; 18, 2 and 1, and
so on. Dozens. But under this scheme there's only one way you
can get a word value of 21—if the word is ACE. You can find
a word value of 20 and another of 22 but only one word with a
value of 21."

"How'd you figure it out?"

"Those secondary and tertiary numbers were the tip-off. Other
schemes were too simplistic and would've been too easily
deciphered."

"I still wonder why they'd make it so tough?"

"It isn't that difficult, provided you speak English. It would be impossible to decipher if you didn't know English, though. It confirms our theory that a built-in safeguard might be used to make it virtually undecipherable to anyone but the target civilization."

"It's intended for us."

He nodded. "The smaller secondary numbers, the word option numbers, might be tied to a specific resource—probably a dictionary. If the secondary number is 2, I think it means we're to use the second anagram in alphabetical sequence that is possible for the sum of the digits."

"How'll you figure that out?"

"Have to develop a comprehensive dictionary on the computer. Then I'll write a routine to calculate the numeric value for each word and store that. Then sort the file by numeric value. That'll give us our anagram translation."

"I'm sure dictionaries are available on diskette. There are so many spell-checker routines these days."

"Have to figure out punctuation."

"Why English? Why not Japanese or French or German?"

"We've been transmitting electronically in English on this planet longer than in any other language. We were the first with the radio, the telegraph, Morse Code, television, solid state technology, computers. They've been picking up our electronic noise since we began broadcasting and they've deciphered our language from our transmissions. It's the logical language to use if Earth is the intended recipient."

"Now, I don't mean this to sound, well, insulting, but why did it take so long to figure out? You guys were down there five months and you're all geniuses. Why didn't one of you come up with it?"

There was a veiled smile. "First of all, after a few weeks of dealing with Sinclair's precious cryptologists, I sort of slipped their data a Mickey. Couldn't help myself. I garbled their data stream ever so slightly. These guys brought all sorts of elaborate equipment and subroutines—*and an attitude*: 'Ain' no code we can't crack.' It created an atmosphere of competition. So I made a few minor modifications to their data fragment. As for the rest of us, a lot of time was spent just locating the transmitter. Once we found it, we recorded a few eight-hour transmissions and then it disappeared again. Since then, Walter, Milt and Howard Vaughn spent all their time trying to relocate it. That left only Keppler, Margo and me to work on the actual signal. It eluded us.

"But then last night at the helm it occurred to me: What if the transmission is backwards? We'd tried several schemes before, some a lot like this one, but all we'd found was nonsense. So just for the hell of it I took a hunk of the binary transmission and reversed it. Then I converted it to decimal and produced the solution."

"The original transmission came in backwards?"

"That's right."

"Why?"

"Beats me," he said, shaking his head.

"It's brilliant, Tim. You're brilliant to figure it out."

He flushed with pride. "Lucky's more like it, but thanks." "You don't want to tell the others?"

"I'll tell Milt later. I'd rather not tell Walter. I can't quite bring myself to trust him." He looked at his watch. "It's nearly five. I'll copy these translation routines onto a diskette and make a copy for you. First chance you get, mail your copy somewhere safe. I'll leave you this fragment of the original transmission on your computer. At least it's something."

Kate wrapped the diskette in a plastic bag and stowed it in her duffle bag in the bottom of her closet, then left to join the others in the cockpit.

"Another dead end," Tim was saying as she joined the group. "Where are we?"

"About thirty-five miles east of Puerto Rico." Jack had made the course change, and they were now on their final westerly run into Bahia Lima. "No luck, Tim?"

"No, but we'll figure it out."

Kate wished she could go to work immediately on the anagrams that had scrolled across the screen. She shivered at the thought—the first translated message ever from an extraterrestrial intelligence.

OVER DINNER, Walter announced that he'd fly with the rest to Miami. From there he'd catch a flight to St. Lucia. "Margo and I can wait a few days in Miami before returning, if you think that would help, if that would give you a better chance."

"It would be a help," Milt said.

Margo ate quietly, eyes downcast. The crew was weary; it had not been a restful sail. Over coffee, Margo started to speak, hesitated. "I realize I must decide." She looked at Walter and reached for his hand. The gesture seemed forced. "I know you want me to return with you, Walter, but I can't. I don't belong there. My job, my career, my *life* is about a great deal more than SETI. I won't try to talk you out of going back. You have your reasons. SETI's been your life for years and I wouldn't ask you to change that. But it's not mine."

"If you go home they'll only bring you back," Walter protested.

"I know. If Tim and Milt will have me, I'll go with them. Maybe I can find a way to live, establish a new identity, something. At least it leaves me with more options than if I were to go back to St. Lucia."

Walter was stunned. "That's nuts! You'll be safe in St. Lucia."

"Safe? That's debatable, Walter. Do you know for sure you'll ever be allowed to leave?" She'd had laid down the crucial issue with chilling candor.

"Don't be ridiculous—"

"Are you sure the government will allow you to return to the States? Especially if the transmissions turn out to be significant?" No one spoke.

"Well!" Walter fumed, stood up. "I'm going to pack. Then I'm going to bed." He stormed from the cramped salon, punctuating his exit with an ear-splitting slam of the foc's'le's teakwood door.

The group was silent. Margo looked stricken. She'd voiced a thought they'd all had but had mostly skirted in conversation. If the NSA was able to translate the signal—and they probably would eventually—and if the government deemed the contents significant or sensitive, they might never allow the scientists to leave. It was true that Tim, Margo and the Renslers might enjoy slightly more freedom than the St. Lucian team. But they'd be holed up in a cabin in Northern Michigan, virtual fugitives. They'd study the data and search for the ETI transmitter. But how long before Jeremy Sinclair tracked them down? Inevitably he would. Had all this effort really been worth it?

Ω

30

SINCLAIR returned to his office at six PM. "Edith, send Melissa up from the typing pool," he barked at his secretary as he strode past her. "You're free to leave."

The meeting with Geller had been a disaster. The President had completely lost confidence in him. It would have been more tolerable, had Geller ranted and raved; but he hadn't. He'd spoken softly, reasonably, questioning the minutest details of Jeremy's investigation. Not about to relieve Sinclair of his post, the President seemed inclined to give him sufficient rope to either hang himself or save himself. The pressure was daunting.

He walked to the door of his office and looked out at the deserted reception area. Edith had left for the night. Where was Melissa? He'd dictate his thoughts, see where things went from there.

The young blonde emerged from the elevator, steno pad in hand, and glanced about anxiously. "You sent for me, sir?"

"Yes. Bring Edith's chair. There are critical memoranda that need to get out."

Melissa hurried to comply, her tall athletic frame graceful as she approached. Her hair tumbled in soft waves over her face as she laid her pad down on the seat cushion. It was a typist's posture chair, and she wheeled it past him and into the inner office. Sinclair stood at the door, appreciating her sensuous young body. She was bent slightly as she pushed the chair to a spot near his desk. He'd arranged that Melissa and a few others be consistently available on evening shifts to handle late-hour reports and memoranda that couldn't wait, and often he'd legitimately called on their services. But Melissa was one he'd specifically chosen for the late hours because of her astonishing looks and her penchant for wearing short skirts. Of all the girls in the steno pool, she was the youngest—nineteen according to her personnel records—and by far the most appealing. This evening she wore a tan leather miniskirt with sleek, transparent pantyhose and calf-hugging boots that rose up to just below her knees. He could feel the first stirrings of arousal as his gaze moved up her thighs.

She positioned the chair opposite his desk and sat. "You know," she said, "it's actually easier for me if you'd just use the dictaphone. That way I'd have a tape and can produce a more—"

"Never mind. I prefer we work on this in tandem. It helps me organize my thoughts." He took up some papers from his desk, moved to a seat on the sofa and cleared his throat.

She swiveled in her chair to face him, tablet and pencil poised. "Go ahead then."

"This first item will be issued as Policy Directive Re Ultra-Secret Contingency Planning, subhead 'Compartmentalization and Need-to-Know Strategies.'" The words flowed easily. He'd been composing the directive in his mind for the past several days.

Melissa scribbled in her tablet, keeping pace, strands of hair drooping over her forehead and cheek. She tossed her head repeatedly to keep it back, uncrossed and recrossed her legs. Sinclair's eyes caught every shift, traveling up her legs, staring deep into the buttery softness of her thighs. He stood and walked nearer to her, moved behind her, continuing to recite the directive. He didn't touch her, only stood near her shoulder.

Melissa uncrossed her legs and swiveled again to face him as he moved toward the office windows. The midsummer sun cast long shadows across the landscape, and clouds were reflecting the beginnings of a sunset. Long beams of light streamed into the room. Sinclair turned back to face the young woman. Her blouse was of a soft, frothy material that caught the light. It seemed nearly transparent to him, especially where the fabric parted slightly between the buttons. Shafts of light seemed to move up her legs, penetrating, illuminating everything to him.

He suppressed a soft sigh, left the windows and walked toward her. "...the failure to perceive and thus react appropriately to developments not detailed in the formal plan...," he recited as he approached. He longed to touch her but forced himself to wait. The pain, the pressure was at once excruciating and delicious. He had to see what she'd do. Didn't she understand, he could see everything? Was she wearing anything at all beneath the pantyhose? He didn't think so. He stood near her shoulder and brushed against her with his hip. He could see down her blouse. She had to feel his eyes on her. She squirmed in the chair, recoiled, sensing his proximity. The tops of her breasts rose and fell. Her breathing became shallow and rapid.

"...must be cautioned to retain a more heightened readiness, if the agency is to accommodate such events as might transpire..."

He moved to stand directly in front of her now. Her legs uncrossed, and he immediately moved so that his own knee was between hers.

"Sir, I think I should finish this up by dictaphone," she said suddenly.

"Sit."

"Sir, I—" Her cheeks were flushed, her eyes wild.

He turned and moved back to sit on the sofa. "Sit there," he repeated harshly. "Uncross your legs. Not like that. Spread them slightly."

"Sir, I can't—" Silent tears began cascading down her cheeks.

"Do it! More! Good. Now, to continue—" Back on the sofa, he made no effort to hide his erection, but continued reciting the dreary text, now barely aware of what he was saying. He could sense the wet heat between her legs, the flesh; he could see it all.

"Sir, I have to go," Melissa said suddenly. "I cannot continue this. You'll have to find someone else."

With that, she stood, dropped the tablet and fled from the room. Sinclair sat on the sofa for a long time, breathing. A narrow smile crossed his face, replaying it, savoring most the moment when her ease had changed to fear, her disbelief became realization, when she understood there was nothing she could do. The power was all his. She had none.

Ω

31

AT MIDNIGHT, they sighted the lights of the southeastern Puerto Rican coastline across the starboard beam.

"We're eight miles out," Jack said to Kate. The others were asleep below. "It gets tricky; there are shoals all the way from Ensenada Honda to Point Lima."

"Then let's douse the sails and approach under power."

They did. At one-thirty the Point Lima beacon came into view. Jack consulted his charts of Bahia Lima and described the entrances to the cove. Reefs, reportedly marked by buoys, lined both sides of the cove. Once through the channel, there would be anchorage in twelve feet. "It's a huge risk entering in darkness," he said.

"We could wait till dawn. I can stay awake. Let's circle out here till it's light."

"Yeah. *Avery's* says the charts are reliable, but if we miscalculate even a little, we're hard aground."

Kate went below and returned with a pillow and a light-weight blanket. "I'll sleep out here. Wake me in two hours."

At three-thirty they switched places. Jack stretched out on the cockpit cushions and Kate took the helm, keeping the boat mostly in neutral and adjusting every so often for currents, holding the Point Lima beacon in her sights. At five-thirty she noted the time and decided to let Jack sleep on. The eastern sky was beginning to brighten.

At a quarter to seven, he sat up abruptly and squinted at the bright morning. "You didn't wake me." His hair was tousled and he rubbed his hands over his stubble of beard.

"You were sleeping soundly. I'll catch up later."

"God I feel dragged out. I'll make coffee and rouse the others." He went below and soon their passengers were up and preparing to go ashore. Margo laid out cereal and fruit and cooked the last of the bacon.

Tim joined Kate in the cockpit and stood gazing at the island. "Beautiful, isn't it?" he said. Puerto Rico stretched before them like an emerald jewel. Inland from the coast, the tallest jagged peaks of El Yunque rain forest disappeared amid a swirl of clouds in an otherwise cloudless sky. The surrounding ocean was an amazing array of turquoise hues that paled to merge with the strip of beige along the shoreline.

"Where do we land?" Tim asked.

"On the other side of that point. We're entering that small cove."

"Doesn't look like much."

"That's why we chose it."

"I wrote down the address of the cottage with directions and left it tucked in your book by your reading light." His eyes locked on hers. "Thanks for coming. I'll try to make it up to you. If they don't cart me away, I'll stay in touch."

"You could even send me the odd diskette from time to time."

"With the translations."

"That and the occasional note letting me how you are. Maybe I'll visit you at the lake."

"Plan on it."

Kate stood at the bow as they motored into Bahia Lima. She was glad they hadn't tried the approach at night. The promised channel buoys were nowhere in evidence. She motioned to Jack, directing him away from shallows and beds of coral and when they were within a hundred yards of shore, she let go the anchor with a loud clatter of chain. They were the lone sailboat in the sleepy cove. A trio of fishing boats of doubtful seaworthiness were at anchor, and others lay washed up on the beach recumbent on rounded keels.

"I'll stay aboard," Kate said. "Six of us would sink the dinghy. Jack will take you ashore and wait for Santiago to appear."

The scientists' few belongings were collected near the ladder. Jack stood in the dinghy, steadying it against the hull.

Margo embraced Kate. "Thank you," she said.

Tim hugged her next. "Good luck, Kate. Happy trails."

"Definitely, 'until we meet again.'"

"Be safe," Milt said quietly. "Thanks doesn't begin to say it."

"Find that transmitter, will you please?"

"We'll do our best."

Even Walter gave her a stiff hug. "Thanks, Kate. I've never met you and Jack."

She hoped he meant it. Knowing Jeremy Sinclair, it might not be an easy promise to keep. "Good luck, Walter."

When they were settled in the dinghy, Jack began rowing. Kate called out, "Please tell Jack about the elephant," to which a small chorus replied, "What elephant?"

She stood on the deck, shaking her head and laughing, blinking back tears. She watched as they reached the dock, tied up and climbed out of the dinghy, looked around. A man was approaching from the beach. When he reached them, he spoke and waved toward shore. He looked like Santiago. He and Jack then began having a lively discussion. She could see them both gesticulating and hear their raised voices but couldn't make out their words. Then Santiago turned and began walking away. The scientists stood with Jack and stared. Several moments passed. Then Santiago stopped, turned, and headed back toward the group and everyone began shaking hands.

Jack remained on the dock while the scientists followed Santiago down to the beach, across the sand, and disappeared behind a row of shanties along the shoreline. He waited a few more minutes, then climbed back into the dinghy and returned to the *Espiritu Del Sol*.

"That's it. Let's go," he said.

"I take it that was Santiago?"

"Yes, and none too pleased about four passengers. He insisted it would cost another two grand. I talked him out of it, told him it was that or return with an empty plane."

They made hurried preparations for their departure. Kate went below and piled breakfast dishes in the sink so they wouldn't rattle around. Then they hauled anchor and motored out of Bahia Lima cove. When the wind freshened they raised the main, let out the Genoa jib and set course for St. George's Harbor, Grenada, four hundred and sixty nautical miles to the southeast.

For the first hour Kate stretched out in the cockpit and tried to sleep. But she was too keyed up. Had she been on land she'd have begun pacing. "Should we become *Great Expectations* now?"

"There's no hurry, is there? You get some sleep and we'll deal with it later."

"I'll set the alarm for one."

When she awakened, she made lunch and relieved Jack at the helm.

"Steer 125°," he told her. "That should allow for the current. I'm absolutely beat." He looked it. His eyes were red-rimmed and his shoulders sagged as he stepped away from the helm and disappeared into the salon.

Kate thought about what they now faced—very simply a long hard grind, at least four days of constant sailing to the southeast, battered by the westerly-flowing current. There was no easy way to do it, no stopping in ports along the way or laying over at night. They needed to show up in Grenada as soon as it could be managed. And perhaps worst of all, Kate thought wistfully, there was no Margo to handle the cooking. The sail from St. Lucia had covered four hundred and twenty nautical miles and had taken them seventy-two hours. They'd averaged around six knots. Grenada was farther, and for the next eighty hours or more, one or the other of them would have to be at the helm.

Despite all that, Kate felt a certain elation. They'd delivered their passengers to Puerto Rico and there was even a vague hope of a reprieve in the shift in Walter's attitude; he might keep his word. They might actually pull this off. The sail would not be as pinched as the sail to Puerto Rico. The wind was off the port stern, and they were no longer under the pressure of a rigid timetable.

Her mind wandered to the thought of Tim's translation and the data fragment stored on her computer. She tried to imagine what it might contain. What strange world did these extraterrestrials come from? Did they resemble humans? How distant was their world? Were they peaceful? Had they learned to live on their planet without trashing its environment? Did they have a concept of God, a personal experience of Him/Her/It that they'd share? Did they love? Cry? Feel sadness? Did they have a sense of humor? Knock-knock jokes? Light bulb jokes? Did they ask why chickens crossed the road? Maybe they didn't have chickens, roads or light bulbs. How did they bear children? Were there two sexes, or three, or one? And how did they view Earth and its inhabitants?

The hours at the helm passed easily. Sailing was an elemental thing, a science of both resistance and synergy. One raised a sail and by keeping it face-on to the wind, propelled a craft across a liquid plain. It involved the alignment of one's purpose and destination with an inexhaustibly abundant, non-polluting source of energy. It was a sane and sensible way to get from place to place, provided you weren't in a great hurry, as long as you were willing to relax with the process.

By contrast, there was such aggressive competitiveness in the way people drove cars. The goal seemed always to be to reach one's destination as rapidly as possible. Sailing was not like that. There was no contest played out with surrounding motorists for advantage or irritation at delay, certainly no vehicles spewing pollutants. The world really should set sail.

When Jack awakened, he fixed dinner. Kate felt no urgent need to hand over the helm. Her muscles had regained their tone. She felt tanned, healthy and rather pleased at her stamina. After dinner she straightened the galley and sat with Jack in the cockpit sipping coffee. They watched in peaceful silence as the sun disappeared in the west accompanied by a luminous, changing sky.

At twilight Jack measured their progress by Arcturas and Venus, calculating the effect of the current and adjusting their course slightly to the east. Kate spread a blanket in the cockpit and fell asleep under the stars. They would grab sleep in increments when they could.

Small things marked their progress—meals, the rising and setting sun and moon, seabirds, planes, distant ships, the passage of rain squalls. On the afternoon of the second day, they were joined briefly by dolphins and it made the day seem full. Otherwise the seas rolled under them, the winds were constant and the hours crept by at a gentle pace. They usually slept in the cockpit to keep each other company. It made the long stretch at night seem less empty. Despite the constant use of sunscreen, they both tanned a deep bronze.

They talked easily and about everything, but also became comfortable with silence. Kate described her experience of Walter's rescue, the stark terror that had engulfed her before she finally caught sight of the boat's masthead.

"I hadn't any notion of how much time had passed. All I could think was that if I couldn't see you, you also could not see me. It occurred to me I might not make it," she said. "Eventually, I guess I fought back the fear with reason."

Jack listened and then described the wrenching helplessness he'd felt standing at the helm, staring fixedly at the spot where she'd gone over, unable to find her amid the turbulent seas.

"I never doubted we'd find you, but for a moment I wondered what we'd do—what I'd do—if we couldn't. I was furious with myself for the jibe. It wouldn't have been an easy thing to live with." The conversation underscored the thought Kate had had, that their relationship had changed since Walter's rescue.

At one point, Jack described what it had been like growing up the only child of his strongly opinionated military father and his strangely dichotomous mother.

"I wasn't a bad kid. Actually I was probably *too* good but it was impossible not to break rules—there were so many of them, an obstacle course of them with carefully prescribed punishments for infractions. Mother gave me a simple choice—accept her punishment or wait for Dad to come home. Well hell, I was no fool. I chose her as the one to administer the spankings. It made for an odd paradox—at the same time as she claimed to be protecting me, she punished me."

"Could make one mistrustful of women."

"As the only child, I was all they had to focus on. I longed for a brother or sister if only to dilute the attention."

"You joked that your father awakened you to Reveille. Is that really true?"

He nodded. "And I bedded down every night to Taps."

"Good God."

He smiled. "Seemed normal to me. And despite my resolve to be nothing like him, actually I am in some ways. It amazes me. Sometimes I hear myself talking, sounding exactly like him. Dress me up as a Bird Colonel and you couldn't tell us apart. How does that happen?"

"It's inevitable, isn't it? I drag my mother around with me wherever I go. She's right there with the criticizing eye, even though she died a long time ago. I especially take her along when I try on bathing suits."

"You never talk about your family."

"No."

"Why not?"

"I used to occasionally. For a while there was an insatiable need to talk about them. Then I began noticing that it tended to clear the room a lot more than the air. Now I find the whole thing embarrassing, too hard for me to tell and others to listen to. I suppose I worry people will expect me to be—"

"What?"

"Nuts, insane, suicidal—like Mom."

"How old were you when she died?"

"Fifteen."

"Tough age. And your father?"

"Nineteen. I loved him so much, Jack."

"You told me he was a fireman."

She nodded. "Who died a hero. He was amazing. I can still feel it—the absolute immensity of his love. I was going through some of his old papers recently and came upon the copy he'd saved of my high school commencement program. Tucked inside were at least a few dozen copies of the page listing my name among the *throng* of students graduating with honors. I wonder how many he mailed out. I could almost envision him hiring a plane and leafleting the Bay Area." Her eyes filled. "He was so damned proud of me, you know? And he tried to instill in me his own belief that there was nothing I couldn't do."

"You were lucky."

"Very."

"You had a sister." He looked at her, waiting.

She nodded but couldn't form the words. "Can we change the subject?" She held the helm, checked the compass and kept her eyes averted. "We looked like such a *normal* family. It's all too much Jack. I hate to— It leaves people feeling helpless. They don't know what to say so they withdraw, which leaves me sitting there with this messy little puddle all around that needs mopping up."

"It's not a mess, Kate. It's grief. You're holding it in, reserving it. Here's what I've learned about reserve as a strategy for coping with feelings: Hold back the sadness and you hold away everything else—including the love."

They were quiet for several minutes. She longed to break for the Exits and smiled at the thought; it certainly wasn't Jack who was pulling away. But how far can one go on forty-six feet in the middle of an empty sea? Her dream about the diving cormorants came back to her, the shadow they'd cast as their mass eclipsed the sky.

"You worry people will expect you to be insane," Jack said.

"Or jinxed."

"You're not, of course."

"No, but it all came down in a decade, one and then the next and the next—the whole family except me, wiped out, punctuated by college. I became a robot with the perfect major—computer science—logical, predictable, controllable. And then the awful year working with Jeremy Sinclair. You know what it is? I feel as though I'm a dangerous person to know, that everyone I love—dies. I should come packaged with a warning label from the Surgeon General."

He gave her a searching look. "You're not hazardous to my health if that counts."

She nodded. It counted a lot.

"And keep in mind that whether or not you include it in that tally you hold in your head, a few days ago you saved a life."

"Thanks," she murmured. "So did you."

It was later that same day, at dusk, that they spotted the helicopter.

Ω

32

"Look, Kate, ten o'clock."

"It's heading our way."

"What's it doing way out here?"

"Searching for us. Are we closer to the islands than we think? Jeez it's flying low."

"It is. I wonder—"

They were finishing each other's thoughts at times, and Kate said, "—if we should become *Great Expectations*?"

"Exactly. But first we'd better drop the main. Otherwise they'll read our sail numbers."

That hadn't occurred to Kate and she was glad he'd thought of it. She was also grateful for the gathering dusk.

Jack raced forward and she remained at the helm and headed into the wind. The moment the sails were luffing, he dropped the main and it came down in a billowing flop of canvas. He bunched it as fast as he could and then dashed back to the stern. Kate had never seen him move as quickly. He drew the dinghy alongside and lowered himself over the side and into it with a thud and a curse. He hadn't taken the time to secure the ladder over the side and Kate left the helm to retrieve it. She fastened it to the stanchions as Jack was pulling himself around hand-over-hand to the stern.

The helicopter was closing fast. The sun had set and the aircraft's lights were visible in the dusky sky a few miles to the east. Their courses would intersect within minutes.

Jack tore strips of tape from the stern, tape that had held the mylar in place for a week. Then he rolled the thin material up from the bottom until it was bunched across the top of the stern.

"Take it, Kate!"

She reached back and held the roll with one hand and gripped the helm with the other. "Hurry!"

He pulled himself back to the ladder and scrambled into the boat, bringing the ladder up with him. Then he let the dinghy line out and told her to drop off the wind and bring them back on course. He stripped off the top row of canvas tape and tossed the roll of mylar and the ladder into the cabin.

"Oh my, that was close," he said, breathing hard.

"Do you think they could have seen all that?"

"I don't know. They were a ways off and it's nearly dark. Look, they're going to buzz us."

The helicopter's roar became deafening as it drew near and a glaring spotlight was leveled across their deck. The surrounding seas flattened beneath the downdraft of the whirling blades.

The immense olive-drab craft passed overhead and Jack looked up and waved. "U.S. Army. I don't like this one damned bit! Incidentally, I left the white plastic sheet taped across the stern. At the moment we are neither the *Espiritu Del Sol* nor *Great Expectations*. We are *nameless*.

The helicopter passed to the southwest and turned for a second pass. Their approaching spotlight illuminated the cockpit and stern. Jack waved again. "I really don't like this," he repeated over the roar.

Whatever they were looking for, the pilot was apparently satisfied because the aircraft continued flying east toward the islands.

"I think we should change course, head away from the islands," Jack said. "If we hold this course they could find us.

And let's continue sailing on the jib. Those mainsail numbers will give us away."

They headed due west for an hour, constantly scanning the skies for aircraft. At nine, they raised the main but continued west for another hour before resuming their southeasterly course. As a precaution, they sailed on through the night without cockpit or mast lights. They took turns every three hours, keeping watch at the helm and sleeping. Somewhere along the way, they pitched the "Espiritu Del Sol" mylar over the side. The course diversion added hours and miles to their sail to Grenada, but perhaps it had bought them anonymity.

The helicopter's appearance was compelling evidence that Sinclair knew the scientists had left by boat. Had Walter Jacobsen had gone back on his word?

"Any sign of the *E Del Sol*?" Michael Gregg was speaking by phone with Herb Resnick, pilot of the helicopter that had been patrolling the northern chain of islands. It was late in the evening. Since Lawrence's tip, their investigation had come up empty on every front.

"No sign of it. We did investigate a sailboat that had no name but it was growing dark and we were running low on fuel; so we had to head back."

"Why would a boat not have a name?"

"Beats me," the pilot said. "Maybe it's new. We've sure buzzed a lot of boats and bothered a lot of sailors."

Gregg's investigator instincts were piqued. A nameless boat made no sense unless it was new, or newly painted.

"How many were on board this no-name boat?"

"Looked like a man and a woman. May have been others below. They were sailing on their jib so we couldn't get a sail number."

"Do you know their course? Could you find them again?"

"Maybe when it's light. They were— Let's see, here it is. They were one hundred and thirty-eight nautical miles due west of Guadaloupe, heading south between 120° and 130°." There was a pause. "Looks like they were headed to Martinique."

Michael Gregg noted the location and course. "First light I want you back out there searching for them. A little too coincidental—no name on the boat, no numbers on the sail."

"I didn't say there were no numbers on the sail. They were sailing on their jib."

"Was it unusually windy?"

"About average. No real reason in terms of weather to drop the main. Who can explain what these sailors do? I've overflown more peculiar boaters in the last few days, observed more odd behavior—*nothing* would surprise me. I'll look for them in the morning."

"I want that boat. You're sure it was a white-hulled sloop?"

"Absolutely. You told us to only bother with white-hulled sloops so that's what we're doing."

"Call me the minute you locate them. This time don't let them out of your sight."

"Well, depending on fuel—"

When they hung up, Gregg realized he'd been clenching his jaw throughout the conversation and he now relaxed it. This could be it. He began doodling absently on a tablet, drew a picture of a sailboat. *E Del Sol.* 'Something of the Sun.' Cover the name on the stern. Easily done, hard to see from a helicopter at dusk.

ONLY GRADUALLY did Kate and Jack cease their anxious vigilance, their constant surveillance of the eastern sky for planes and helicopters. They were nearing Grenada and their apprehensiveness mounted with every passing mile. What might await them in St. George's Harbor?

Kate had described Tim's breakthrough in deciphering the transmission, and while Jack maintained a certain dogged pride in his pervasive computer illiteracy, so that the elegance of Tim's solution was lost in translation, the implications were not.

"We'd better mail that diskette from Grenada. Can't risk having it confiscated when we return the boat."

"Do you think Walter's told them about us?"

"We'll know soon enough. We ought to start monitoring our ship-to-shore radio to see if anyone mentions an investigation. And remove the plastic from the stern and clean off the spray adhesive. I brought solvent."

"Let's do it now, Jack. We're only a day out."

"Even if Walter reports us, I don't see how they can arrest us."

"Why not?"

"What law have we broken? What proof would anyone really have? And remember the snicker factor. Even if you publish the story, all they really have to do is deny it, tell people you're a crackpot. Who pays serious attention to people who go about claiming to have met up with extraterrestrials? I doubt anyone would take this seriously either."

There were some gaping holes in his logic, but Kate let it pass; it gave them courage.

AFTER THE SIGHTING of the no-name white-hulled sloop, Michael Gregg reached for the phone, intending to call Jay Roberts in St. Croix. Roberts and two other agents had spent the past two days in Puerto Rico and St. Croix, obtaining the names of every charter sailboat and passenger that might have been sailing in St. Lucia on June twenty-third. Gregg now considered that they might narrow their focus to the islands from Guadaloupe, south. It would eliminate five islands, leaving ten still to be checked—a total of thirty-one charter companies.

Gregg began dialing the number but stopped. It wouldn't do. They might have chartered the boat in St. Thomas but planned to return it in Martinique or St. Vincent or Grenada. There were simply no short-cuts.

Resnick, the pilot, had failed to sight the no-name sloop the next day. Extra agents had been dispatched to Martinique, since that had been its last known course. Gregg stood up and began studying the charts he'd ordered mounted along the walls of the converted billiards room. He needed to talk to a sailor.

He placed a small ○ on the chart exactly one hundred and thirty-eight nautical miles west of Guadaloupe. Then he drew two vertical lines through the ○, one angling across it at 120° south, the other at 130° south. What he'd created was an elongated X, whose top two points both intersected Puerto Rico in the northwest and extended southeast to Martinique. What about currents? The winds were predominately out of the northeast, and if the currents drew one west, wouldn't a sailor have to steer a more easterly course to reach Martinique? How long would it take to sail from Soufriere to Puerto Rico and back?

"Find me a sailor, Nicholsen," he snapped.

"Sir?"

"A sailor. I need to talk to someone who knows a lot about sailing in these waters."

"Yes, sir."

"Try that charter company in Marigot Bay."

Ω

33

GRENADA came into view on the morning of July first, appearing first as a dim hump-backed shape on the crest of the southeastern horizon. Jack tuned in Channel 16 on the radio to monitor the broadcasts of yachtsmen cruising in the area. Most of the messages were trivial—a lot of walkie-talkie play with plenty of over-ing and out-ing, copying and roger-ing. No gossip about an investigation or unusual activity on the part of customs officials.

"I'll listen for a while," Kate said. "I want to clean below anyway."

"It's neat enough."

"No, I mean *really* clean. If they board us in Grenada and dust for prints, they'll find a whole slew of them."

She was feeling the press of impending civilization and the enormity of what they'd done. That Sinclair was searching for them—or at least for a sailboat—was no longer in doubt, at least in her mind. The helicopter spoke volumes. As to the specifics, they'd know soon enough. If Walter Jacobsen had reported them, they'd know that almost the moment they set foot on Grenadian soil.

The cleaning took hours. She had to wipe every surface that might hold prints. She combed the fo'c'sle for the smallest traces of its recent occupants, scoured the heads, the salon and the quarterberth. She wiped every plate, utensil, pot and pan, every jar and can.

Then she started in on the empties from the beer and soft drinks they'd consumed. Partway through, she threw down her cloth, overwhelmed by the enormity of the task and a closing sense of futility. She couldn't possibly clean every bottle. Impossible. She was bound to miss one print somewhere. What about the bottoms of the bottles? Had she remembered to wipe each one? No, she'd surely forgotten some. She just couldn't. They could turn them in the moment they were ashore. But what if they were boarded immediately? She started over, wiping the bottom of every bottle.

It was stiflingly hot in the cabin, even with portholes open. She listened to the radio with mounting dread. It would look awfully suspicious if they were to find no prints at all on soft drink bottles. What? They wore gloves while drinking all that beer and Coca Cola? She felt cornered.

Hours later when she could do no more, she relieved Jack at the helm and he set to work on the boat's exterior. He wiped the mast, the winches and winch handles, the cockpit, the plastic coated lifelines.

"Don't forget the ladder."

"And the dinghy. God, this is a huge job!"

"Tell me."

After that, they took turns climbing over the boat, placing their prints on its surfaces. When they were done, the boat looked nearly new. Kate threw T-shirts around, strewed crumbs on the floor, dirtied a few dishes and set them in the sink.

At two-thirty in the afternoon, after nearly ninety hours of continuous sailing, they entered St. George's Harbor, Grenada.

"He is? Amazing! Wonderful!" Michael Gregg chortled into the phone. "Now we're going to get some answers. Send him to my office the moment you're back."

He hung up and turned to the others in the room. Ian Fitzgerald, manager of Moorings Yacht Charters of Marigot

Bay, had been delivered to Gregg's office at noon that morning and now stood before a chart of the Lesser Antilles.

Gregg announced to the room at large, "One of our missing people has just arrived at Vieux Fort on the flight from Miami." He paused for dramatic effect and then said, "Walter Jacobsen."

"He came back? Why?" Nicholsen asked, incredulous.

"Beats me. We'll find out soon enough. Let's get back to this, Ian. I want to know where that boat came from and where it's headed."

"Depends on how familiar the captain is with these waters. If he's knowledgeable he'll allow for the westerly current. In that case a heading of 125° would take him to St. Vincent, maybe even as far south as Union Island or Carriacou. Maybe even Grenada." He stepped over to the chart. "May I?"

Gregg nodded, and Ian Fitzgerald traced a faint pencil line, a gentle arc that extended from the O that Gregg had earlier marked, down to the northernmost tip of St. Vincent.

"On the other hand, if they aren't allowing for the currents they could be sailing out of either St. Croix or Puerto Rico and heading for Martinique or Dominica; but they'll find themselves too far west and having to tack."

"So their likely destination depends on how experienced they are as sailors," Gregg said.

"And how well they know the waters. Most of our bare-boat charter folks are unaccustomed to sailing under the influence of currents as strong as these. Couple that with the northeasterly trade winds and almost all these sailors, however competent, find themselves west of their destination."

"It's possible their destination is Martinique?"

"Possible. Looks like on that course they're definitely coming from either St. Croix or Puerto Rico. I'd bet money on that."

It wasn't much help. Fitzgerald had confirmed Gregg's hunch about Puerto Rico. They should double their manpower at San Juan and other Puerto Rican airports. He ordered Nicholsen to make the calls. As for the destination of the *E Del Sol*, Ian Fitzgerald had mostly muddied the waters. But perhaps Walter Jacobsen would clear things up. Why the hell had he come back?

"Okay, Ian. Thanks for your help. Appreciate your coming by. Bruce here will take you back to Marigot Bay, won't you, Bruce?"

Nicholsen stood, bristling. "Let's go."

Gregg smiled to himself as they left. He was treating Nicholsen like his personal errand boy; it gave him a perverse pleasure. The man deserved it, letting a group of scientists tie and blindfold him. What did he expect, a goddamned medal?

Twenty minutes later, Agent Kiley delivered a bleary-eyed Walter Jacobsen to Gregg's office. "Thanks, Kiley. You can return to the airport. So, Walt, have a seat." It was said disdainfully. Gregg grinned at the frail, frightened looking physicist. "Tell me what you've been up to."

Obediently, Jacobsen took a seat. "I'd really like to get some rest if you don't mind. It's been rather a long several days."

"I'm sure it has. And we're most anxious for you to get your rest, right after you tell us all about your little adventure."

"There's nothing to tell. I flew from Miami, here."

"How'd you get to Miami?"

Walter didn't reply.

"You flew there, didn't you? Maybe from Puerto Rico or St. Croix?

"I'd rather not say."

"And your wife? Where did she go?"

"I don't know."

Gregg sighed. "You don't know," he said flatly. "You can't expect me to believe that."

Jacobsen shrugged. "Believe it or not. She wouldn't tell me where she was going."

"When did you last see her?"

"In Miami."

He tells me where but not when. "And that was yesterday?"

Walter said nothing.

"So the four of you flew to Miami, and then Tim Thurmond, Rensler, and your wife left, and you were allowed to come back here? That doesn't make a lot sense, Walter. It really doesn't."

"I suppose it doesn't but it happens to be the truth."

Gregg paced. He'd admitted flying to Miami; other than that it wasn't going well. He glanced over at the other agents in the room. They appeared to be hard at work but Gregg knew they were all ears.

"I think Mister, I mean, *Doctor* Jacobsen and I would like a word in private if you all don't mind."

The agents filed slowly out of the room.

"Now, Doctor, let's see if we can't help each other out here. We know you were picked up in Petit Soufriere. We know you sailed off on a white-hulled sloop named the *E-something Del Sol*. We're pretty sure you sailed to Puerto Rico. From there you flew to Miami. How'm I doing?"

Jacobsen said nothing.

"So why don't you fill in the last few pieces of the puzzle. First of all, who picked you up, Doctor? Who helped you? I want their names."

Walter shook his head.

"Does that mean you don't know, or that you refuse to say?"

Walter slumped lower in his seat and looked down at his hands. "I'd really like to get something to eat and then rest so I can get back to work."

"Is that so? You know, Doctor, we'll find them eventually. We'll find your fellow scientists *and* your wife. With your cooperation, things could go a bit easier for her."

"They haven't broken any laws."

"Oh, haven't they? I didn't realize you were an expert in the law, Doctor. Let me enumerate a few broken laws for you. We have 'endangering and compromising national security' for starters. Dare I call it 'treason'? I'm certain some would but if you'll help us, I'm sure I can arrange it so that no one will accuse you of the T-word, Doctor."

Gregg was now lacing the word 'Doctor' with a sting of sarcasm.

"Then we have the entire arena of immigration laws to consider. Trivial, I'll admit, in comparison to treason, but nonetheless a violation of the law. Consider this: the NSA is mandated with ensuring our country's national security. To that end I can assure you we are expected to employ almost any means and go to almost any lengths. You will eventually tell us what you know, *Doctor* Jacobsen."

"I have nothing to say," Walter said almost mournfully.

"In that case I suggest you think a little harder about it and we'll talk again. Just to make sure you have plenty of time to think, you're confined to your quarters. You may go." He waved at him dismissively.

When Jacobsen had left, Michael Gregg called Jeremy Sinclair.

"They flew to Miami. We'll need to examine the guest registers of every hotel in Miami."

"Good God, Michael, you're talking hundreds, maybe thousands of hotels."

"And Grace Rensler's probably been staying at one of them and will meet up with her husband—if she hasn't already."

"What else did Jacobsen say?"

"Not much. He's refusing to cooperate. I can trip him up though."

"Try Pentothal."

"He'll talk. Trust me."

"I have no choice. I can't come down there now. I've got too many fires here. Make him talk. Drug him. Do whatever. Where do you think the rest will go from Miami?"

"How the hell do I know, Jeremy?" Then, "Sorry. I didn't mean to sound— We're not getting a lot of sleep down here."

"Neither the hell am I."

"Sorry. Here's a thought. After speaking with the manager of one of the local charter companies, I'm about ninety percent certain our people escaped by charter sailboat."

"Why?"

"Lawrence's sighting, the helicopter sighting, the type of boat."

"So?"

"So if you were going to hire a sailboat to pick up people in St. Lucia, where do you charter the boat?"

"Not on St. Lucia. Maybe a nearby island. I see where you're going with this, Michael."

"We only care about those charters active on June twenty-third."

"Interrogate returning charter groups. Pre-arrange their rooms and bug them. We'll need the cooperation of hotel management."

"You're reading my mind."

Ω

34

KATE AND JACK motored into the dogleg-shaped harbor of St. George's, anxiously scanning the scene. Cargo vessels and cruise ships clogged the bay near the main jetty and commercial shipping dock. *Avery's Guide* warned of numerous sunken or partially sunken wrecks dotting the channel, some noted on charts, most not. Kate stood on the bow, motioning them clear of hazards, and they worked their way into the Lagoon at the toe-end of the harbor. Grenada Yacht Services and customs were located near a long weathered dock, and they motored by, making a preliminary pass.

"There are empty slips," Kate called. "I'll tie on the fenders."

Jack circled and headed in. When they were alongside, Kate leapt to the dock with the bow line, cleated it down, and dashed back to catch the stern line from Jack. For the first time in days she was on solid ground. She looked around. No NSA types descended.

"I'll hoist the Q-flag," Jack said. "We're quarantined till we check in." He found the yellow flag in the chart table and hoisted it up the backstay.

As Kate gathered passports and ship's documents, she tried not to think about what might await them at the customs office. We are vacationing sailors.

Customs was situated at the end of the long, L-shaped dock, located in an airless cinder block structure that someone had painted a hideous aquamarine. A lone uniformed official accepted their forms and passports. Jack and Kate were his only customers and he appeared singularly unconcerned with their arrival. He processed the paperwork, rubber-stamped everything in sight and handed back their passports.

Kate was reeling in the close, dimly-lit room. An ancient ceiling fan labored overhead to stir the air, but she was spinning and churning as though still at sea.

"I've got to get out of here, Jack. I'm gonna faint."

"You don't look so good."

"Sea legs," the official said knowingly. "Happens all the time in this room. Needs air."

Her forehead was damp with perspiration.

Jack glanced at her, worried, and then asked about the Food Faire and Post Office.

"I'll arrange a taxi for you, no problem. And you'll want a tour of the island?"

"Well—"

"You should visit the nutmeg factory and then go inland to see our mountains. Beautiful island. My cousin has a van. He'll take you. What time?" As though it had all been decided.

"I, well, we're not sure," Jack said, recognizing that there was pressure to commit, a one-sentence sales pitch followed by the close.

"Jack, can't this wait? If I don't get out of this room *right now* you'll have to carry me out."

"Right, but we have *errands* this afternoon," he said pointedly. Then to the official, "We'll attend to our boat and then go to town. No island tour today."

"Good. My cousin will drive you to town," he said, stepping quickly to his fallback position of a lesser sale. "What time?"

"Give us an hour. Then send your cousin down to the boat. We're tied up down at the—"

"I know where you are. I watched you pull in. One hour," he said happily. "His name is Alexander."

They walked down the dock and back to the boat, both of them rolling on sea legs, stepping gingerly over sections of loose, rotting dock boards. Back on board, Jack found a hose and began refilling water tanks.

"I'm going below to take a shower," Kate told him, "a very *long* shower."

She stood in the cramped cubicle and washed away layers of salt, shampooed her hair twice, and slowly began to feel reborn. Then she gathered dirty clothes and began washing them in small loads in the galley sink.

Jack packaged Tim's diskette, protecting it in layers of the bubble wrap he'd used to transport his navigation instruments. He addressed the package to his office and enclosed a short note of instruction to his secretary. When Alexander arrived, he and Jack loaded the cases of beer and soft drink empties into the van and left for town.

Within minutes of his departure, two men arrived.

Kate was clothespinning towels and T-shirts to the lifelines when the men approached from the shore end of the dock. One of them was tall, blond and bulky in an aging-athlete sort of way. The other was dark, slighter in build, and hid his eyes behind mirrored sunglasses. Kate found their combined look menacing.

"What is this, a Morgan?" the blond inquired.

An American, Kate thought, looking up. He wore perfectly pressed khaki shorts and a new-looking Petit St. Vincent T-shirt proclaiming, "PSV's FOR ME."

"Yes, Morgan 46. Good boat," she said, wishing they'd leave.

"Where you from?" the blond asked.

"California."

The dark-haired man had a wide mustache and a superb tan. "Long way from home. Y'all chartering?"

"Yes," Kate answered wearily. "Where are you from?"

"Florida. How long you down here?"

"A few weeks." Please leave, she prayed. Jack, come back. Where are you? The steady appraisal was unnerving.

"What islands have you been to, so far?" the blond asked.

"Oh, around the Windwards," she said vaguely. "Look, would you excuse me? I need to get another load of wash."

"Here with your husband?"

"Yes," she answered, clipped.

"Maybe we could all have dinner."

"I don't think so," Kate said as she headed down into the salon.

"See you later," the blond called. From a porthole, Kate watched them head down the dock and climb aboard an enormous power yacht that was tied at the far end of the pier. No slip in the world wide enough for that monstrosity.

Jack returned an hour later with sacks of fresh produce and six-packs of soft drinks and beer. "Turned in the bottles and mailed the diskette." He lowered himself onto a cushion. "God, it's hot."

"Two men stopped by and more or less interrogated me while you were gone. Asked a lot of questions—where I was from, what islands we'd sailed to, how long we were planning to stay. They belong to that thing at the end of the pier. They said they were from Florida."

Jack frowned at the stupendous yacht. "*That* is a ship. Maybe eighty feet. Radar and every other electronic gadget known to man. What do you think? Were they government?"

"Maybe. They wondered if we'd join them for dinner. I said no. Now I wonder if it's wise to stay here."

"We're tourists. We're going ashore for dinner. Is there anything on board to hide?"

"The computer. I should delete Tim's files and programs. And wouldn't people find it odd that a local charter sailboat is carrying charts of the entire Caribbean, Atlantic seaboard and Gulf Coast?"

"We'll take them with us. I think it's vital we behave like tourists. No one's seriously questioned our presence here so far. If they were going to, I think they'd have swooped down the moment we arrived."

"Maybe they did. No, you're right. I'm spooked. I expect the NSA to pounce out of the shadows and whisk us off to an interrogation room. I can just see it—the bare light bulb suspended from the ceiling, perspiring agents taking turns firing questions at us."

"Cheery fantasy. I'm going to take a shower. I can't stand myself another minute."

The two men were back an hour later. Jack and Kate were in the cockpit watching the sunset, and Jack was reading an inspired description of Mama's Creole Restaurant, which was within walking distance of the marina. The men approached and this time introduced themselves.

"I'm Stu Simpson. This is Phil Vandervere."

"Jack Sullivan." He stood and reached across the deck to shake hands. "This is Kate. Nice to meet you." Jack's tone somewhat belied his words.

"We're off to dinner and wondered if you'd join us?"

"No, thanks anyway. Kate says you're from Florida?"

"Right. We're down here for a month of fishing. We're off to try the Turtleback Steakhouse. Why not join us?"

"We'll probably eat aboard," Jack said.

"Anything's better than that native Creole place," Phil said scornfully. "Mama's—filthy food, filthy atmosphere." The ugly American had spoken.

Jack said, "That's quite a yacht you have down there. Looks like an electronic wonder."

"It is." Phil tallied off a list of gizmos and gadgetry to Jack's appreciative grunts and nods. "Stu here says it's amazin' the damn thing still floats with all that gear. So, how 'bout dinner?"

"No."

"Aw, don't be anti-social. Gringos in foreign ports have to stick together."

Kate stood, irritated. "Look, is there some part of *no* you don't understand?"

It took Phil a moment. "Well *excuse us*," he said. The two turned and walked rapidly down the dock.

"Damn," Jack muttered under his breath. "I hate to make such a lasting impression."

"Well, some people are a little slow. *No* means *no.*" A lesson Jeremy Sinclair had taught her.

"Of course, but they'll remember us. Either they're too friendly or we're too edgy."

"I know."

"What about dinner?"

"Let's try Mama's."

Kate went below and deleted Tim's files and programs from the computer. They folded the charts and bundled them into Kate's large purse. Then they padlocked the cockpit, closed and locked portholes and hatches, and started down the dock.

Kate stopped. "Wait a minute." She returned to the boat, yanked a loose thread from the facing of her blouse and lodged it beneath the hatch-cover padlock.

"What are you doing?"

"I saw it in a movie," she said.

"The old thread-under-the-padlock technique," Jack nodded sagely, for which remark Kate came to his side and delivered a gentle poke.

Mama's was up a steep hill near the marina tucked back from the road down a stone walkway that someone had painstakingly lined with thousands of conch shells. They walked in and surveyed the room. More conch shells—conch shell candle holders, conch shell lamps. A juke box blared reggae music and nearly every seat at every table was occupied.

Mama was an enormous hulk of a woman in a muumuu with a hibiscus over an ear. "Any seat's fine," she hollered.

They settled at the end of a long table with several other patrons. There didn't seem to be a menu; food simply appeared and customers were expected to eat it. A tureen of turtle soup made its way down the table and bowls were tossed down. Kate ladled some for herself and Jack. Then came some sort of christophene cheese souffle followed by Creole curry, opossum stew, frog legs, roasted armadillos with cassava pilaf. Fried bananas with mango coconut ice cream for dessert.

Mama heaped scorn on anyone caught passing up a dish, with the result that Jack and Kate tried everything and left feeling well-entertained and seriously overfed.

As they strolled arm-in-arm down the hill to the marina, Kate said, "This place makes me uneasy."

"You think we should head north?"

She nodded. "We could sail to Carriacou tomorrow."

When they stepped aboard *Great Expectations*, the thread lodged beneath the hatch padlock was gone.

"Maybe the wind took it," Jack said.

"Right." What wind?

As Jack inserted the key, Kate thought it would have been child's play to have picked the lock. But below, nothing appeared to have been disturbed.

"What did you think of Mama's?" Kate asked as they climbed into bed.

"I could live a long full life without ever tasting another roasted armadillo."

"I suppose one armadillo tastes about like another. I was thinking I might redecorate when I get home—something in a conch shell motif."

"There's a thought."

Ω

36

AT SIX on the morning of July second, Jack and Kate cast off from the dock in St. George's harbor. As they passed the eighty-foot cabin cruiser belonging to the two fishermen from Florida, Kate noticed its name—*Southern Comfort.*

Jack figured on a nine-hour sail to Tyrell Bay on the western coast of Carriacou. To Kate it seemed a short haul after the long days at sea. By lunchtime they were abeam a graveyard cluster of rocky, uninhabited islands north of Grenada with fine names like Kick'em Jenny and Skull Rock. A few hours later they passed Large Island, then Frigate and Saline Islands and in mid-afternoon began the long tack for Carriacou's Tyrell Bay.

They spent a single night in Tyrell. Finding no customs office in the bucolic cove, Jack hoisted their Q-flag. Around mid-morning of the next day, they raised anchor and sailed around the west coast of Carriacou to Sandy Island.

Only a few hundred yards long and perhaps half as wide, Sandy Island was an oval-shaped expanse of ivory-colored sand dotted with fifty or so palm trees. Apart from the skeletal remnant of a palm-frond hut, there were no structures on the island.

"Do you believe this, Jack? It doesn't look real. It's a perfect tropical island."

He read her thoughts. "Avery says it's a terrible overnight anchorage, unprotected. We wouldn't get any sleep."

The island lay only a few miles off the northern coast of Carriacou. If sailors wanted to lay over in the area, it was recommended they put in at nearby Hillsborough Cove on Carriacou. There they might check in with Carriacou Customs. The people of Carriacou took a dim view of Sandy Island snorkelers who failed to toe the line on local regulations.

They were the lone boat at anchor and for several minutes they sat and merely stared at the idyllic spot.

"The hell with *Avery's*," Kate said. "Let's stay. We can check in tomorrow."

"We might not get any sleep."

"After what we've slept through in the last several days, we can sleep through a little chop."

Jack hoisted their Q-flag, suggesting at least a nod to local restrictions. "It's a fish sanctuary. Shall we go introduce ourselves?"

They snorkeled until the sun was low in the sky, paddling over vast stretches of coral and seaweed in colors that seemed artificial—impossible day-glo yellow, rust and chartreuse. There were massive mounds of brain coral, and clumps of a purple lacy growth that fanned out in the shifting currents. Everywhere they looked below the surface of the clear water there were fish, millions of them in silver, gold, electric blue, dandelion yellow. A vast school of silvery fish turned in unison, darting one way and then another, and the angling rays of sunlight reflected off them as they shifted directions. One moment Kate saw the school—thousands of them shining silver—and then as they turned they seemed to disappear. How could thousands of fish turn at once? It was as though they were a single organism.

The water was so salty that Kate floated effortlessly over this strange, aqueous world. In all her life she'd never seen anything more beautiful. Good planets were *very* hard to find. As the sun disappeared, they swam ashore and walked along the beach in the direction of their boat. Theirs was still the only craft at anchor.

"What are you smiling about?" Jack asked as they strolled along. His snorkel mask was looped around his neck, and he had swim fins in one hand and an arm draped over her shoulder. He looked down at her, seawater dripping from his hair and down his face.

She reached up and brushed a drop of water from the tip of his nose. "A few days ago I was thinking the whole world should set sail. Now I think they should all go snorkeling."

He smiled and nodded. When they were near the boat, they sat down and donned their fins. "Race you back to the boat," he said. "Loser cooks dinner."

"I'm too tired to race."

"Not *too* tired? I intend to ravage you tonight."

"You do?"

"I do."

She stopped and looked at him. "Actually I'm not a bit tired." She dove into the surf and began swimming hard. It was declared a dead heat; nobody cooked dinner.

"The bedding!" Jack sat forward with a lurch.

"What?" They were relaxing in the cockpit, enjoying the early stages of a brilliant sunset following a second day of snorkeling. They'd checked into Carriacou Customs that morning and returned to Sandy Island to spend a second day.

"The bedding," he repeated. "We have to wash all the sheets, blankets and towels. Walter's shoulder might have bled. All of them will have left traces—hair, skin—"

"Oh," Kate said somberly and then laughed. "For a minute there I thought we were being attacked by a swarm of bed sheets. Guess we could rinse everything off in sea water."

"And clean out the sinks and shower drains."

It was July fourth, Independence Day, with less than a week remaining of their three-week charter. Each passing day brought them closer to the inevitable. Kate's interview with Rensler had appeared in the June issue of *Science America*, and she now accepted that her association with SETI and the missing scientists was unavoidable. There was a good chance they'd be interrogated and detained in Kingstown. And if Walter Jacobsen had failed to keep his promise, if he'd spoken of their part in the rescue, they'd likely be arrested.

They blocked off the drain pipe in the cockpit floor, filled it with sea water, and washed sheets, towels, and blankets with dish soap. Then they rinsed everything in the shower with fresh water.

Removing every trace of someone was next to impossible. People left telltales of themselves—hair, skin, nail clippings. DNA testing could provide irrefutable proof that the scientists had been on board. They wondered what else they might be overlooking. There was a chance they'd be interrogated separately, and their stories had better coincide. Such daunting thoughts as these—of interrogation, criminal evidence and imprisonment—dominated their Independence Day.

THEY LEFT THE NEXT MORNING and set out across the channel for the customs office on Union Island's Clifton Harbor. They could not avoid it; they must clear British Customs there. All islands north, from Union to St. Vincent, were British, and if they failed to check in and were caught they'd surely be detained. According to *Avery's Guide,* the customs office was adjacent to an airport—which suggested the possibility of special NSA scrutiny.

By ten-thirty they were across the channel. They motored past a long jetty and tied up at the town's modest loading dock. On shore, they followed signs to a sweltering room with louvered windows overlooking a too-brief runway; the rusted tail section of a small plane was visible rising up from the waters of the bay. A more fortunate—or more skillfully piloted—LIAT Airlines twin-engine turbo-prop was on the tarmac, taking passengers aboard.

Kate and Jack queued up behind a long line of people who'd come in on the LIAT flight. Conversation was muted. The crowd, dressed in everything from business suits to bathing suits, inched forward. Jack and Kate tried to assume the air and persona of vacationing sailors; it was a stretch.

The customs official was barricaded behind a high counter. Beside him stood an expressionless, non-uniformed man with a clipboard and an officious American demeanor. His light brown hair was short and obsessively neat and his eyes were only somewhat shielded by faintly tinted prescription glasses. Kate could see that he was scrutinizing the face of each person in line as they drew near. His forehead was beaded with perspiration.

She leaned toward Jack. "Check out the guy with the clipboard. And laugh, like I just said something rather funny."

The man glanced down at the clipboard, then up at a face.

"Hilariously funny," Jack chuckled. "Could it be he's watching for our passengers, rather than us?"

"Let's hope." Her nerves were taut as she inched forward. She felt as though a cutout of a smile had been pasted across her face. As she drew nearer, she met the man's look with a direct one of her own and remembered to breathe. NSA, definitely.

"Next," the customs official said.

Jack handed over their passports and entry cards and Kate looked around. Was there was a WANTED poster with their photographs? She didn't see one. She breathed again.

The customs official seemed vastly indifferent. He stamped and paper-shuffled with the brisk efficiency of a three-toed sloth, glancing at them only briefly as he handed back their passports, concluding this apparently exhausting effort with another weary "Next."

They sighed in relief as they left the customs office. "Christ, I feel like a prisoner who's been granted a last-minute reprieve," Jack said. "We need ice and food. Where the hell is the market? I'd like to get away from this place."

"Avery says it's up the hill."

They concluded their errands and were away by noon. As they motored out of the bay, Kate said, "Oh God. Look, Jack—the *Southern Comfort*."

He turned to regard the monstrous yacht. "Small world down here. Pretty soon everyone meets up with everyone."

Right.

Their destination was Tobago Cays, a remote quartet of uninhabited islands protected from the Atlantic Ocean by a vast, horseshoe-shaped reef. They lay north and east of Union Island, so reaching them became a tacking duel against endlessly powerful headwinds and currents. By late afternoon, they abandoned the effort and motored in. Kate went forward and doused the sails and then perched on the bow to guide them through a heavily shoaled channel. They maneuvered between Petit Bateau and Baradal Islands and dropped anchor in a choppy, wind-driven spot.

"Another paradise," Jack said as he surveyed the anchorage. Some hundred yards off across their bow, waves were cresting over the rim of the reef. Beyond was the Atlantic Ocean.

They spent two days in Tobago Cays, exploring the undersea life and constructing and rehearsing a mythical sailing itinerary. They'd visited enough of the area so they could speak of it firsthand, but they needed to pad the itinerary with additional details to account for the period from June twenty-second through July first. They bargained with transient fishermen for fresh lobster, swam, rested, studied and memorized. They read up on PSV, Palm Island and Petit Martinique, all part of a group of islands near Union and Carriacou which they'd not visited. They invented encounters with other sailors and recited and quizzed each other until they felt secure with the details. It was sobering.

On July seventh they hauled anchor and sailed to Mayreau Island's Salt Whistle Bay. After a quick look-see at the cove, they continued on to Cannouan Island and arrived at dusk. Jack bartered with a father-son team of fishermen—San Francisco Giants T-shirts in exchange for fresh lobster. They remained aboard, cooked the lobster, and set sail early the next morning for Mustique.

The recommended anchorage in Mustique was in Grand Bay on the leeward side of the island. *Avery's Guide* cautioned sailors to watch for the treacherous Montezuma Shoal, which formed a barricade across most of the harbor's entrance. They furled sails and motored in, laying anchor near Basil's Bar, a palm frond-thatched structure that jutted far out into the cove.

Jack dove down to check the anchor and returned. "The water's great," he announced, and Kate now recognized this as part of his post-anchoring ritual: The Water Report. "We should go ashore for dinner," he said. "It's jump-up night."

She scanned the harbor, counting dozens of boats already at anchor for the weekly dance. To the northwest, the hilly eastern coastline of Bequia was visible, and beyond it a more distant silhouette of land that could only be the southern tip of St. Vincent. The sight filled her with dread.

She settled on the foredeck, her back against the mast, and tried for calm while Jack swam off to explore Montezuma's Shoal. A row of colorfully painted fishing boats were beached along the strip of sand near the bar, and behind them she could see hammocks suspended between palm trees. Basil's open-air platform extended out into the cove some hundred feet and was constructed of stout bamboo poles covered with a pitched roof of palm fronds. She observed lazy preparations for the jump-up. A bandstand was being assembled and a sound system tested.

When Jack returned from his swim, they showered, dressed in their best jump-up attire and rowed ashore. From the jetty, they wandered along a footpath to the bar. Someone was plinking out a Scott Joplin tune on an old upright piano, and Kate and Jack perched on bar stools and struck up a conversation with the locals. One was bragging about having recently seen Mick Jagger, who was said to own an island mansion.

"You ever see Princess Margaret?" Jack asked the beer-bellied old salt to his left.

"She's popped in for the jump-up." This man's T-shirt could not have been washed since before the Punic Wars. "Hasn't she, Keller?"

Keller, the bartender, grunted.

"Keller here's seen 'er lots," the other assured them.

"Couple a months ago," Keller said. "Havin' dinner?"

"We'd like to," Jack said. "We don't have a reservation."

"Shoulda called in on 16," Keller said. "Place'll be full, 'nother hour."

"Could you give us a table before the crowd arrives?" Jack pressed a twenty-E.C. note forward on the varnished bar.

"'Kay. Fix it for ya." Keller disappeared, returned some minutes later and motioned for them to follow, and led them to a small corner table along the railing overlooking the water.

The restaurant filled quickly. Groups from the boats in the bay arrived by dinghy. Fishermen, locals and land tourists descended over the next few hours. At nine the band arrived, a Rastafarian assortment of musically talented cutups who hammered out reggae and calypso rhythms on steel drums and guitars. Refusing to dance was both impossible and unacceptable. Everyone danced with everyone—natives with tourists, fishermen with tanned, blond Europeans, sailors with waitresses, teen-aged cooks with middle-aged matrons. Kate and Jack hitched themselves to lines of dancers and wove between the tables, stomping and gyrating to the music's percussive beat. They danced the rhumba and the cha-cha, and after the third rum punch, made a brave attempt at the lambada. Those who didn't dance were commandeered into service as gourd- and tambourine-shakers.

At one AM, Kate shouted over the music to Jack, "Enough! I'm beat!"

Jack was cha-cha-ing with a sleek, sarong-draped French woman.

"Can we go?" Her own dance partner of the moment was a fisherman named Henry, who was so transported that he wouldn't have noticed had she dematerialized on the spot.

They rowed back to their boat and collapsed into bed, but the music continued to blare across the cove until almost dawn. By eleven the next morning the cove was only beginning to stir.

Ω

37

ACCORDING TO *AVERY'S GUIDE*, the affliction plaguing them that morning had a name: PJSD—Post-Jump-up Stupor Disorder. They downed an ambivalent breakfast, swallowed assorted vitamins and over-the-counter pain remedies, and made listless preparations for the sail to Bequia.

"You ready?" Jack asked in a ghostly voice.

"I could use a day to recover."

But they didn't have a day. It was July ninth.

The sail from Mustique to Bequia revived them some, a brisk down-wind sail with following seas, but they could only half-heartedly marvel at the boat's remarkable speed, over ten knots at times.

As the Belle Point buoy came into sight, Kate broke a long silence as though there'd been an ongoing discussion. "What I don't understand is why no one's mentioned anything about the investigation. No one's stopped us. No one's said a word about unusual patrols or customs searches. Haven't they at least figured out the scientists left by boat?"

"They must have. Remember the helicopter."

"And we're what? Eighty miles south of St. Lucia? And no one's questioned us or mentioned anything. I don't get it."

Jack considered her words. "Put yourself in their place. They can't chase around to every island and stop every boat. They'd need thousands of agents and they'd still miss some. If it were my investigation, I'd question charter parties as they returned. That way I'd catch them all."

"I suppose. They'd work with the charter companies, review the schedules, focus on those that were out at the time the scientists disappeared. It makes sense." The narrow channel of Admiralty Bay lay off their bow, bustling with activity and congested with boats. "Our charter agreement shows we're from the Bay Area. That alone could raise the suspicion of a connection with Tim and Milt."

He nodded. "Could get interesting tomorrow."

"But if they'd already figured out we're responsible, wouldn't they have brought us in? They wouldn't have allowed us to sail around as we have for the last week and a half."

"True."

They motored deep into the bay and anchored to the right of the commercial pier. Later, they reclined in the cockpit to watch the sun as it disappeared amid a squallish billow of clouds. "You'll have to throw away that two hundred feet of stern line, Jack. I know it's a waste but—" Rays of sunlight streamed down through the clouds forming golden ribbons of light.

"I'll lose it over the side in the channel tomorrow on the way to Kingstown," he said.

"*And* the charts. *And* all the volumes of *Avery's Guide*. They're marked with your notes. 'Why'd you bring along a chart of Puerto Rico, Mr. Sullivan?'"

"You're right. Damn, I hate to give up those guides. They cost thirty-some bucks apiece. The charts are expensive too." He looked crestfallen. "Time to start thinking like a prosecutor again. I hate to do it. I've loved these last ten days." He reached across the cushion for one of her tanned feet, gave it a squeeze. "Hell, I've loved the whole thing."

"Me too."

Following a long silence, he said, "The only fingerprints they'll find on this boat are ours. That'll seem odd. It's an old boat; there ought to be a jumble of prints all over it." She nodded. "Better invite some folks aboard tomorrow."

"We could distribute leftovers," she said.

The following morning a succession of Bequians piled aboard *Great Expectations*. Vendors, who typically hawked their wares in the bay to visiting yachtsmen, were invited aboard and departed with free food. Word spread and a small feeding frenzy ensued. Kids arrived in droves, tying rowboats alongside. They clambered aboard and into the cabin, deposited fingerprints and left with canned goods. Kate held back enough for lunch and it was all over in an hour. Then they readied the boat for the ten-mile sail across the channel to Kingstown. Kate worked below, packing their gear.

At two PM they raised anchor and motored out of Admiralty Bay. By now they were consumed with dread. Mid-channel, Jack pitched the two hundred feet of line over the side, went below and returned with his charts and the volumes of *Avery's Guide*.

"God I hate to do this," he muttered as he flung the last volume into the sea.

"You can replace them."

"I know, but all my notes, tides, currents— What else? What are we forgetting?"

"I memorized the address in Michigan and tossed Tim's note. I've gone through all our luggage. The only things that might be suspect are your navigation instruments and my computer. I'm not about to toss my laptop computer over the side. I've erased all Tim's files, but I *am* a journalist. I brought it down here thinking I'd get a little work done. So big deal."

"And I'll be damned if I'm going to toss the RDF and sextant over the side, or my hand-bearing compass. I brought them for the hell of it—to brush up on my navigation—just in case. I like to be prepared." He was building a head of defensive steam.

Kate smiled. "It's okay, counselor." He returned her smile. He looked good—tanned, intent, his eyes, normally more gray than blue, reflecting the color of sky. She hated for it all to end. Across the bow, St. Vincent lay dead ahead like some dark monster looming up from the sea.

The charter company had instructed that returning boats radio ashore when they arrived the mouth of Kingstown Harbor. The company would then dispatch a launch with a pilot who would come aboard and moor the boats. Apparently there'd been too many mishaps involving charter groups maneuvering stern-to-dock.

Kate went below and radioed the message that *Great Expectations* had arrived. While Jack circled the entrance to the bay, Kate packed the last of their belongings. In the stern cabin, she went through clothes lockers, peered into the dark recesses of cubbyholes and drawers. She heard voices topside; the pilot had arrived. I hate this, she thought. She zipped up a duffle bag and returned to the cockpit.

Two men in matching shorts and C.C.I. T-shirts had boarded along with a third man dressed in long pants with a buttoned-down administrative look. The latter introduced himself as Cas Jenkins.

Kate extended a hand. *Mr. Jenkins has nothing to do with docking the boat.* "Nice to meet you," she said quietly.

She and Jack stood aside as the charter company's people took over *Great Expectations,* expertly speeding the Morgan 46 across the bay and into its slip. Dock lines were cast, and with that—with so little apparent fanfare or ceremony—the incredible voyage was over.

"I'll go below," Kate said, "finish looking through the salon to be sure we're not forgetting anything."

"I'll give you a hand," Jack said.

They off-loaded duffle bags and gear and noticed Jenkins huddled in conversation with two others carrying bulky leather cases.

"It's all yours," they overheard Jenkins say.

Kate and Jack stepped off the boat and Jenkins turned to them. "Would you folks come with me? There's a small matter we're discussing with all the returning charter groups. I'll need a few moments of your time."

"All right," Jack said, looking at Kate. He bent to gather luggage.

"Here," Jenkins said, "Let me." He took up Kate's computer and one of the heavier duffle bags and led the way down the dock. They followed him to a back room of the charter company's office.

"Have a seat," he said, gesturing. "Sorry it's so cramped but we have to make do." Kate and Jack took seats. "We're conducting an investigation on behalf of the United States government. What we've got here is the disappearance of a group of Americans. We're asking everyone a few questions to see if we can figure out what's become of these people."

He held forth an NSA photo-ID, and Kate took in a breath as she read: Casper Elgin Jenkins. A passport-size color photo of him was laminated onto a card alongside a written description, more fine print, and an engraved, official-looking seal. Here we go. Jenkins perched on the edge of a small table and actually beamed down on them, oozing warmth.

"What would you like to know?" Jack asked.

"First of all, we'll need your sailing itinerary. Did you folks happen to keep a ship's log?"

"No. Sorry," Jack said.

"No problem. Let's see. You folks picked up the boat on—" he consulted a folder of notes. "On June nineteenth. So you've had the boat, what, three weeks?"

If this guy got any folksier, he'd start handing out cigars and mint juleps. "That's right," Kate said. She glanced around. The room was little more than a storage closet, its shelves piled high with a clutter of marine hardware, boat lines, dock fenders and life jackets.

"So, where all did you sail?"

"We left on the nineteenth and sailed down to Admiralty Bay. We stayed there, um, was it two days, Kate? Seems like a hundred years ago."

"Two or three. Let's see— Two days."

"Okay, two days," Jenkins said, starting to take notes. "Did you meet up with anyone there, talk to anyone?"

"You mean besides the kids in the bay? The vendors?"

"Right."

"Let's see. What were those peoples' names, Kate? He was a dentist."

"The Jacobs, I think. They were at our chart briefing. They had the *Windsong*, or the *Windward Ho* or something. A Beneteau."

"That's it. Then let's see. We headed over to Mustique. Stayed there a couple of nights. Took a tour of the island. Did some hiking. Rested, swam."

Jenkins made notes. "Meet up with other sailors?"

"None that I can remember." Jack looked to Kate; she shook her head. For one unaccustomed to being on the A-end of a Q-and-A session, Jack was doing well, matching Jenkins' tone with his own good ol' boyish flavor. "Actually, we didn't come down here to be real social. We came down for a relaxed vacation and we pretty much kept to ourselves, didn't socialize much with other sailors."

"Okay. After Mustique?"

"Cannouan. Charlestown Bay. Stayed one night. Not much to see or do, just some dumpy brown hills. We swam, bought lobster from some of the locals. Then we headed down to Union Island."

"No, Jack, we stopped at Salt Whistle Bay the next night."

"Oh, right. Mayreau. One night. Had a bit of a run-in there over anchoring. We were first in the bay, and we followed James' advice, set out anchors bow and stern. Then another boat arrived and they set out only their bow anchor. So they were swinging on their hook and we weren't. I knew they'd eventually swing into us, and they did, or nearly. We fended them off. I told them they needed to set out their stern anchor but they refused. Rude, you know?" Jenkins nodded. "No seamanship. We had to pick up our stern anchor."

"Do you remember the name of that boat?"

He shook his head. "Do you, Kate?"

"No."

"They were French, that's all I know. We weren't exactly communicating real well. Let's see. We snorkeled there, went around the point in our dinghy to look at the shipwreck, the *Paruna*, a World War I gunboat. She hit the rocks going eight knots. Caught a sudden blast of wind, tore the bottom clean off the boat."

Too much detail, Kate thought. Less would have been better. "Great spot to snorkel," she said.

"Not much on shore though. We hiked around, checked out an abandoned hotel. Then we went down to Union Island."

"Okay," Jenkins said, making more notes. "How long at Union?"

"One night," Kate said. "We wanted to visit Palm Island so next morning we sailed over there, took a tour of the hotel, stopped in the gift shop. The Caldwells let us have a look at one of the vacant cottages."

"Fabulous place," Jack said.

"If you can afford $600 a night and like to sit around," Kate said with mild scorn. "After two days I'd be bored silly. Nothing to do but swim and lie in the sun."

"Pretty place to do it, though."

"Where'd you check in with customs?"

"We didn't have to at all until we got to Grenada. We'd already cleared customs at the airport in Kingstown, and until Grenada, all the islands we visited were British. After Union Island we did stop over for an afternoon at Sandy Island off the coast of Carriacou. But we didn't go ashore in Carriacou."

"But first, Jack, we stayed one night at Petit St. Vincent."

"Oh that's right. We stopped at PSV. Boy, that's another posh place. Beautiful resort hotel. We caught the end of their sailing regatta. Then let's see. Next day we got up early and went to Sandy Island to snorkel. Then we sailed back to PSV for the night and left for Grenada the next day."

"So, you spent one day at Sandy Island. Can you show me where that is?" Jenkins had spread out a small chart of the islands.

Jack pointed at the dot of island. "If you like snorkeling this is the place. We stayed there a couple more days on the way back."

"Okay, two nights in PSV."

"Right."

"Meet up with anyone?"

"No. Saw a lot of beautiful boats that were there for the regatta but we didn't meet any people by name."

"So then you sailed down to Grenada and checked into customs. Where, St. George's?"

"Right. We arrived there on July first," Kate said.

"July first? We're missing a few days here," Jenkins said. Jack and Kate traded troubled looks. "Well we sort of, um, goofed," Jack said. "Before we pulled into St. George's we sailed on down around Saline Point and put in at Prickly Bay for two nights. The thing is, we didn't realize we could check in with customs in Prickly Bay. We thought we had to go to St. George's, and everyone said not to attempt St. George's on a weekend. So we spent Saturday and Sunday at Prickly Bay and then on Monday, the first, we sailed to St. George's and checked in." Jack arranged a look of contrition. "I hope you won't bust us for that? It's not like we went ashore or anything."

Jenkins looked at Jack. "The Grenadians wouldn't like it, but I don't give a damn. If you got away with it, it's no skin off my nose."

Jack and Kate exchanged relieved glances.

"So you were two nights at Prickly Bay, and then you went to St. George's?"

"Right."

"We did meet some people in Grenada. Remember those two men, Jack? On the *Southern Comfort*?"

"Yeah, Stu somebody-or-other and another guy. *Southern Comfort*. Was that ever a yacht and a half. They said they were from Florida and were down for a month of fishing."

"They wanted us to join them for dinner, but we went to Mama's Creole place instead." Kate sighed inwardly. From now on, they could recount their actual itinerary. Everyone was silent while Jenkins scrawled more notes.

"Did you notice *Southern Comfort's* home port?"

"Pompano Beach, wasn't it, Kate?"

"I think so."

Jack concluded the itinerary, waxing a bit too rhapsodic over Sandy Island. Jenkins scribbled as Jack spoke, and finally Jack said, "That's about it. Did I leave anything out?"

"Not that I can think of. We saw *Southern Comfort* a second time in Clifton Harbor on our way north, but we didn't stop to talk with them. We passed them on our way out of the harbor." Over all she felt the questioning had gone smoothly and she allowed herself to relax slightly.

"You never headed north up the coast of St. Vincent?"

"No."

"Didn't go to St. Lucia?"

"No."

He picked up a manila folder from the tabletop, opened it and began reading. "You folks are from the San Francisco Bay Area," he said.

"Right."

"Do either of you know Milton Rensler?"

"No, I—" Jack looked over at Kate.

She froze. In all their careful practice of the itinerary, she'd never once considered being asked that question—just flat out—did she know Milton Rensler. She took a breath. " *Doctor* Milton Rensler? The SETI scientist?"

Jenkins eyed her sharply. "You know him?"

"I'm a journalist. I interviewed him in January for an article. Is this about him?" She tried to look disingenuous but her heart was racing. *Here it comes*.

Jenkins was not about to explain his question; he had a plethora of his own to ask. "You say you interviewed him in January? When was the last time you spoke with him?"

"January."

"And you've had no contact with him since?"

"No." The dimensions of her error settled over her. How could she have been so damned stupid? This man reported to Jeremy Sinclair. She should have lied, should never have admitted having met Milton Rensler.

"You know Rensler's wife?"

"No. I only interviewed him about his research project. Before that I'd never met the man, although I'd certainly read about him. I cover Silicon Valley for technical magazines and trade papers, plus I host a monthly PBS show on industry in the area."

Jenkins pursed his lips. "Interesting." He wrote something in the folder, closed it, and held it to his chest with a satisfied nod. "You know Dr. Rensler. Why do you think he might disappear?"

"Rensler disappeared?"

"That's right, Ms. Lipton. It seems a bit of a coincidence, don't you think, that you're sailing down here at the very time he's vanished?"

"I don't understand. Was he down here?"

"He disappeared from one of these islands last month."

"That's terrible. Was he kidnapped?"

Jenkins ignored the question and didn't speak for several seconds, turning his attention to the cuticle on his left thumb. "Would you folks excuse me a moment? Be right back."

He slid off the table edge and left the room, closing the door behind him, leaving Kate and Jack alone in the cramped little box. Kate started to speak but stopped. Jack rolled his eyes and shook his head imperceptibly. A ten-minute eternity passed.

Jenkins returned and shut the door. "We're nearly done. Thanks for your patience. I'll need to have your fingerprints. It's routine. We're doing this with all the returning charters."

He'd printed their names on a pair of index cards and began taking first Jack's and then Kate's prints.

"Your boat was the *Great Expectations*?"

"Right."

He had hold of Kate's right index finger and was pressing it onto the card. "Do you happen to remember seeing a boat called the *E-something Del Sol* while you were sailing?"

She caught herself stiffening, willed herself to relax. Her hand continued to rest in Jenkins'. He pressed her middle finger onto the inkpad.

"The what?" Jack asked.

"The first letter is *E*. *E-something Del Sol*. A sloop, very much like yours, in fact."

"I don't remember it," Jack said, looking to Kate. She shook her head. "We've probably seen several thousand boats in three weeks. We might have passed it but I don't remember."

Kate shook her head again, her throat too tight to speak.

"You can wash the ink off with these." He held forth a container of Handi-Wipes. "Mind if I have a look at your luggage?"

"Is that really necessary?" Jack said, scowling.

"Just routine," Jenkins' tone lacked much of its earlier warmth.

"Be my guest."

Jenkins pawed through their belongings, noting Jack's navigation equipment and inquiring about it, then exhibiting an intense interest in Kate's laptop. "Why the computer?"

"Silly me, I actually thought I'd get some work done. Never even opened it. Purely a stateside mentality."

"How do I turn it on?"

"Here, allow me." She opened a small panel in the back and flipped a switch.

Jenkins appeared to have some familiarity with computers. When the computer finished booting he listed the contents of each subdirectory, searching through files by date.

"Guess you didn't do any work," he said at last.

"Like I said."

"Okay, that's it. Ah, I hate to ask you but I'll need you folks to stay over for a few days."

"Why?" Jack said, incredulous.

"We might have some more questions. Just a day or two. Where were you planning to stay tonight?"

"At the Cobblestone Inn," Jack said, "but we can't stay over. We're due to fly out tomorrow and we have a connecting flight to catch in Miami. We both need to get back."

"I understand but I must insist. We'll rearrange your flight schedule. Use our phone to call your offices and whoever else you need to notify."

Kate and Jack stood and began edging toward the door. Kate's ears were ringing. She could barely breathe and wanted desperately to leave the cramped storage room. There wasn't enough air for the three of them.

"This is extremely inconvenient," Jack objected. "We both have obligations in San Francisco. I've got cases scheduled to start day after tomorrow. We've been gone three weeks."

"You'll have to change your plans. Now if you'll excuse me? You folks go on over to your hotel, get checked in and I'll call you as soon as I can." Jenkins stood, held the door. "One other thing. Neither of you should mention anything about this inquiry or Dr. Rensler to anyone. Ms. Lipton, I realize you're a journalist but this is not for publication. This is a highly sensitive matter and you're strictly prohibited from discussing or writing about it. Understood?"

She nodded.

It took two trips to transfer their luggage to the Cobblestone Inn. Neither of them spoke more than a few words. Kate worried that someone might be following them but was too frightened to look back, to check. When they were finally registered and safely in their room, she slumped into a chair with an exhausted sigh. "What did you make of all that?"

"Strange business." As he spoke he began shaking his head vigorously and raised a finger across his lips. "Damned inconve-

nient too. Archie's gonna be furious." He rummaged into a
duffle bag, whipped out a tablet of paper and wrote, "The room
may be *bugged*!"

Kate nodded. "Too late to call him now. We'll call first thing
tomorrow. And Nadine—she's expecting to meet our plane. I
wonder what happened to Dr. Rensler?"

"You really know this guy?"

"From the interview. I'm hungry. Are you?"

"Starved," he said with another vigorous nod.

Ω
_____

38
_____

THE MOMENT the couple from *Great Expectations* left for the hotel, Cas Jenkins placed a call to Michael Gregg to report on the interrogation in greater detail. He'd spoken with Gregg earlier, but only briefly while Lipton and Sullivan were waiting. Gregg had instructed Jenkins to detain them and call him back as soon as the questioning was concluded.

"Now, go over it again, Cas," Gregg said.

"Okay. Their names are Jack Sullivan and Kathryn Lipton. They returned the sloop *Great Expectations* this afternoon, a white-hulled Morgan 46. Miss Lipton is a journalist and she said she'd interviewed Milton Rensler last January for an article in *Science America*."

"*Science America*. Okay, I'll check it out. Overall what do you make of them?"

"Hard to say. They gave a detailed accounting of their three-week itinerary, seemed able to account for most of their time. But there are a few points you might be interested in. They both live in San Francisco."

"Go on."

"Sullivan brought along a sextant, an RDF and his own compass, not that that's unusual. Others we've talked to have brought their own navigation aids but the point is, you would need them if you were planning on navigating over any great distance."

"So Sullivan was prepared for more than island-hopping. How about charts?"

"Only those supplied by the charter company. But here's another thing: They were vague about their activities for June twenty-ninth and thirtieth, said they'd spent the time in Grenada but failed to check into customs until the first. That would just about fit as an arrival time if they sailed down from Puerto Rico, wouldn't it?"

"Definitely. Anything else?"

"Lipton had a portable computer, claimed she'd intended to work but never did. I looked at the files on the computer. Nothing was dated later than June fifteenth."

"Doesn't mean anything. You've got the bug in their room?"

"Sure do. And if they eat at the Cobblestone Inn they'll sit at the table with the wire. The maître d' will seat them personally."

"Good. This is our most promising lead. Let me know what you find in their conversations. And let's— Give me their addresses in San Francisco."

Jenkins read off the information and then gave Gregg their revised flight schedule. He'd already made the arrangements. They were booked on Delta's Miami-to-San Francisco flight on July fourteenth. They would detain the couple in St. Vincent for three days.

"How does their sailing itinerary coincide with other parties'? Did anyone report having seen *Great Expectations*?"

"They met up with two boats they could name—the *Windsong* in Bequia, which is a Kingstown charter boat, and *Southern Comfort*, a power yacht out of Florida. The *Windsong* returned a week ago and I've checked my notes. Their questioning corroborates Sullivan and Lipton."

"And *Southern Comfort*, eh?" Gregg was making notes. "Not many encounters over the course of three weeks."

"They said they weren't down here to socialize. I'll look over the other itineraries, check for discrepancies."

"Very good, Cas. This is promising. When do you question them next?"

"Tomorrow morning, separately."

"Excellent. And you'll forward all the samples and latents they turn up on the sailboat to me directly."

"Immediately."

JACK AND KATE did their best to appear relaxed as they wandered around Kingstown in search of a place to eat. They barely spoke at all and stopped frequently to look in shop windows and glance about to see whether they were being followed. It didn't appear that they were. Eventually they wound up huddled at a remote corner table in the Fishnet Restaurant a few blocks from their hotel.

When they were seated, Kate asked quietly, "Can we talk here?"

"I think so."

"You think the room's bugged?"

"I'm certain of it. Even if they hadn't learned about your interview with Rensler, I'd still bet money it's bugged."

"You realize we can't stay," she said. "It won't take long for Jeremy Sinclair to get word."

"So?"

"He'll never let us leave."

"He can't do that," Jack protested.

"Why not? Just deposit us at the compound in St. Lucia. 'National security' is all the legal justification he'd need."

"What do you have in mind?"

"Leave before he finds out, before they mobilize. Right now I think they're figuring on turning up evidence on our boat. Then they'd have grounds to detain us. But once Sinclair hears about me—"

"It's illegal for them to detain us, Kate. They can't do it. They can encourage us to cooperate, ask us to stay over, but unless we're charged with a crime and a warrant is issued for our arrest, they have no authority to detain us. We haven't broken any laws."

"Don't count on getting a chance to plead that case."

"God, you're paranoid."

She shook her head. "I just know Sinclair. Within twenty-four hours neither one of us will have any semblance of freedom left in our lives." Her eyes met his across the table. "I made a terrible mistake today, Jack. All those questions we rehearsed, all those details, and it never once occurred to me to plan a response to, 'Do you know Milton Rensler?' I should've answered *No*. Instead, I—"

Jack shrugged. "They'd have found out anyway, once they got hold of your *Science America* article."

"But that would have taken a while. Until I admitted knowing Rensler, you and I were just another returning charter party."

He nodded slightly. "So you screwed up. If we leave now, it as much as confirms that we're involved, that we've got something to hide. On the other hand, if we go along with them they'll have to release us once they realize our boat's clean."

"That's another thing. How clean *is* the boat, Jack? We can't be sure."

A waitress arrived with bread and butter and they checked their conversation until she'd disappeared with their dinner orders.

"I'm going to Michigan, Jack, while there's still a chance to get away. In a few hours you and I will be under tight surveillance. Escape will be impossible. There's a chance they'll incarcerate us in St. Lucia."

They ate in silence. He doesn't get it, she thought. The menace of Jeremy Sinclair wasn't a tangible thing to him. Sinclair was just another Washington bureaucrat who'd hassled her a decade ago. He couldn't feel it. "It doesn't matter what they find on the boat, Jack. As soon as Sinclair hears my name he'll detain us."

Jack laid his fork down and fixed her with a stare. "I think we should stay and take our chances."

"I'm leaving."

"I'm not."

"If I leave, you'll be implicated by my leaving," she protested.

"No, I won't. They can't prove I had a damned thing to do with the disappearance of their bloody scientists."

"Unless Walter Jacobsen talks. Unless they capture the scientists and *they* talk. Unless the boat yields—"

"All right! So you go to Michigan. What do you suggest I do?"

Kate could readily accept his frustration. She never should have dragged him into this. She indulged in momentary regret over what now resembled a succession of bad and worse decisions.

"Come with me," she said softly.

"No, I'll go home. I have friends, my job, resources I can draw on in San Francisco. I'll take my chances."

Kate reached down for her purse and then stood up. "I'm calling the airport."

"At least we can go back for our luggage."

She nodded. "Be right back." She found the pay phone in a dimly lit carpeted hallway near the Men's room, dialed the Kingstown Airport and asked the airline about their existing reservations on the morning flight to Miami.

"I don't show you as scheduled on that flight," the agent told her.

So it might have already started. "Never mind. Any flights leaving tonight from Kingstown?"

"Nothing to Miami."

"Any destination."

"Flight 755 is departing at nine-fifty for St. Croix."

Kate looked at her watch. Seven-fifteen. "Book two of us please."

She gave the agent their names and hung up. Then she burrowed in her purse for the tattered slip of paper with "Julius Henderson, taxi driver" printed on it and a phone number. She fed the coin box, dialed and a woman answered.

"Julius Henderson, please."

"Juuul-yus!" the woman shouted.

A moment later, "Yeah?"

"You gave us a ride three weeks ago from the airport to the Cobblestone Hotel."

"Right. You need a ride to the airport?"

"Yes, eight o'clock tonight. We're at the Cobblestone Inn."

"Okay. Forty E.C."

"Fine. We'll be at the back entrance on the street behind the hotel."

"Middle Street. No problem. Eight o'clock."

Kate hurried back to the table. Jack was absently stirring a cup of coffee and staring out the window.

"I ordered you a cup," he said.

"There isn't time. We're on a nine-fifty flight to St. Croix. That cab driver we had from the airport is picking us up behind the hotel in forty minutes."

Jack got to his feet, gulped down his coffee and tossed some bills on the table. "Let's go."

Ω

39

THE INSTANT JEREMY SINCLAIR HEARD Kathryn Lipton's name, he knew with a consuming certainty that they'd found those responsible for the disappearance of the scientists. The phone conversation had begun innocuously with Michael Gregg's description of "a very strong lead," a charter party, one of whom had interviewed Milton Rensler last January.

"Really? Possibly too coincidental?"

"It gets better." Gregg went on to summarize the couple's itinerary, the unaccounted-for days before checking in with Grenadian Customs, the fact that the couple lived in the San Francisco Bay Area, as did Milton Rensler, that they'd brought along a computer and navigation aids.

"So they could easily have managed a sail to Puerto Rico, which is where the best evidence indicates the scientists went. Excellent, Michael. What's your next step?"

"Jenkins is interrogating them again tomorrow morning, separately this time. We're going over the boat with a microscope. We'll gather and send you samples of every fiber and thread and hair; we'll lift every print on that tub."

"Their hotel room is bugged?"

"Right. We've asked them to stick around a few more days. We'll check out their story and try to catch them in discrepancies."

"We'll want to bug their homes and tap their phones," Sinclair said, making notes. "Our people will be sitting behind them on their return flight so we can monitor their conversation. Have Jenkins confiscate their passports immediately. Let's see, I'll need to— Give me their names."

"Jack Sullivan and Kathryn Lipton."

"Who?"

"Jack—"

"No, the woman. Kathryn Lipton? Are you certain?"

"Why? You know her?"

"My God, yes, I know her! If it's the same one, she used to work for me. A real ball-buster. Listen to me, Michael. Do not let these people out of your sight. Have them watched round the clock. Post guards. I'm coming down."

"There's no reason for you to— I'll need more people in Kingstown for that level of surveillance."

"Get them fast. And for God's sake, order Jenkins to confiscate their passports."

"Why are you so—"

"Never mind. Just do it! I'll be there in six hours. It has to be her," Sinclair muttered. "Son of a bitch."

KATE AND JACK hurried back to their hotel, fairly certain they were not followed. They entered the hotel by the back entrance, found the stairs and raced up to their room.

Once inside, Kate announced, "I'm beat. I'm going to bed."

"Me too. It's been a long day."

They moved about the room as soundlessly as possible, consolidating their belongings into the two largest duffle bags. They rumpled the bed and stuffed towels and pillows beneath the blankets. Then they grabbed all the luggage they could manage, closed and locked the room, hung the DO NOT DISTURB sign on the door knob and left.

At five of eight they were standing on Middle Street behind the Cobblestone Inn watching for Julius Henderson.

Kate glanced anxiously up and down the street. "Come on, Julius."

"He'll be along."

"They'll find out soon enough that we're not in our room."

"Nothing we can do about it."

"Too bad there wasn't a radio. We could have turned it on, made them think we're in there."

Jack gave her a look. "No one sleeps all night with a radio on."

"Who's going to believe we're in bed asleep at eight?"

"We were tired. So what? You're getting yourself into a flap and panic over nothing, Kate. Jenkins told us to be at the charter company tomorrow morning at ten. I'll bet they don't even notice we're missing until then."

Maybe he was right. She watched anxiously as a car rounded the corner and approached, bobbing headlights illuminating the roadway. The car lurched to a halt a few feet away and Julius Henderson jumped out.

"Right on time," he chimed triumphantly, rushing to toss duffle bags into the passenger side of the front seat. "What time is your plane?"

"Nine-fifty."

"No problem."

Kate began to breathe more easily as they piled into the back seat and zoomed down the street and up the steep road leading out of town. Julius drove like a man with a mission, for which fact Kate was now immensely grateful.

They bounded over a checkerboard of pot holes. "This has major dental work written all over it," Jack observed dryly. "I'll need all my fillings re-glued."

"Send me the bill. I'll expense it."

Julius deposited them at the airport at nine, and they assembled with their luggage in the short queue at the American Airlines ticket counter. There were a dozen or so people ahead of them in line. Kate could barely endure the wait. She constantly shifted, scanned the busy terminal, studying faces, every nerve taut. They were required to show their passports so they went ahead and paid for their tickets with a credit card. There was no way they could exit the island by air anonymously, and Kate expected she'd need every bit of their combined cash to reach Michigan. Fortunately there was the large sum Milton Rensler had given Jack to cover the charter plane and expenses. It might be enough.

They received boarding passes and set off for the currency exchange window to cash in their E.C.s.

"See?" Jack said when they'd finally taken seats near the departure gate. "No one's paying the slightest attention to us."

Her heart continued to pound. "Thirty minutes to go. I'll feel better when we're in the air. Or at least I'll try to act as though I do."

Jack picked up a discarded newspaper from a nearby seat and began reading. "President Geller's in Japan lobbying for a free-trade agreement. And he's voiced his continued opposition to the International Global Warming Treaty."

"Wonderful."

"The fighting continues in Eastern Europe."

"Naturally."

"And in Ireland."

"Of course."

"The Cubs are in last place. The Dodgers swept a three-game series with the Giants. See? The world is just as we left it three weeks ago."

But not quite. A message from life on another world had been received and at least partially translated.

Ω

40

"What the hell do you mean, they're not in their room? Where are they?"

"Jenkins says he's not sure."

Jeremy Sinclair paced off the dimensions of Michael Gregg's office in a storming rage. He'd arrived at the compound an hour earlier.

"Michael, explain how that could happen after my explicit instructions to you last night? How could you have allowed this to happen? I really need to know." His voice was venomous.

"We only had four men in St. Vincent besides Jenkins. Two were at the airport and the others are the Fibbie crime lab guys. I instructed Jenkins to call me back the moment the couple left the interrogation. After you and I spoke, I ordered the transfer of agents from Martinique to St. Vincent, but it took four hours. The helicopter was out patrolling. When it returned, it had to be refueled before they could transport our people. By the time they arrived in St. Vincent, it was evening. Jenkins had been watching the hotel, but he was alone, and he had a lot on his plate. Such as calling me. Such as bringing Agent Lemont back from the airport and briefing him. It all happened too fast."

"It happened too slow, Michael, too damned slow. Jenkins let 'em get away."

"He says they probably went out to dinner which is when he lost them. I'll get the full story from him. Right now Cas is a rather busy man."

Jeremy Sinclair slammed his fist down on a desk. "Unbelievable. Get a list of all flights that left St. Vincent last night. Get passenger lists. Alert customs in Miami. New York City. Crap. Houston. O'Hare. Oh cripe." The obvious futility of these instructions was not lost on either man. "Passenger lists, at least," Sinclair said wearily. "Damn. They could have gone anywhere. We'll need photos, descriptions."

"They might still be on St. Vincent, or maybe they left by boat. They *are* sailors."

"I know that, Michael. Why the hell didn't Jenkins confiscate their passports? Now in addition to Grace Rensler and the three scientists to search for, we have Kate Lipton. Unbelievable." At that moment Sinclair wanted very much to kick something—or someone—*hard*.

"Should we pull in agents from the other islands?"

Sinclair sighed. "Yeah, I guess. No. Lipton might show up at one of those islands. Wait till we get the passenger lists. If they left by air they have to show passports. If that doesn't pan out, we'll review manpower assignments."

"They might have false passports."

"Jenkins searched their belongings, didn't he?"

"Yeah, but he didn't do a body search."

"Not good. Well, as long as I'm here, I'll have a chat with Walter Jacobsen."

Thus far, the physicist had sullenly refused to answer questions. As the thin man was brought in and directed him to take a seat, Sinclair vowed to change that.

"Good morning, Doctor Jacobsen. Sorry to rouse you so early. I trust you've had a chance to rest up from your sailing adventure?"

"I do feel more rested, thank you."

"Fine," Sinclair said evenly. "I thought you should know that Kate Lipton and Jack Sullivan returned their sailboat." He let the statement hang there while he studied Jacobsen's gaunt face for reaction. The scientist looked at him blankly and shrugged.

Michael Gregg spoke. "We're ninety-nine percent certain these are the people responsible for getting you to Puerto Rico, Doctor. All we're asking for is confirmation."

"I can't help you."

"Damn it, Jacobsen!" Sinclair screamed, "You bloody well will tell me what happened. If you ever, and I mean *ever* want to see your wife again, you damned well better tell me what happened and who helped you!"

Jacobsen gazed out the window and said nothing. Sinclair thought he looked sad, detached, ashamed. No, resigned—that was it—resigned.

Jacobsen looked back to Gregg. "May I go now?"

Sinclair's voice was ice. "You will tell us eventually, Doctor. I promise you that. You will tell us everything. *How* is up to you. It can be easy or it can be very painful—your choice. Think about it." When Jacobsen continued to sit mute, Sinclair waved at him in disgust. "Get out of here."

Sinclair began reviewing their progress. Despite setbacks, breaks were starting to fall their way. Lipton and Sullivan were almost certainly responsible for the abduction—that is how he now viewed the scientists' disappearance—as a kidnapping. "I've got a feeling about this one, Michael. It's starting to fit."

He called his Fort Meade office for an update on the stateside teams' progress. So far there were no leads suggesting how the scientists had gotten to Miami from Puerto Rico, but there was good news. A cab driver in Miami had recalled picking up four people at the Fontainbleau Hilton—two men and two women—July twenty-seventh. The driver had studied photographs and was quite definite: These were the same people. He'd taken them to a used-car dealership in downtown Miami. A salesman had positively identified Milton Rensler and Tim Thurmond from photographs. They'd purchased a white Ford Escort for which they'd paid cash. A nationwide A.P.B. had been issued.

"So now we just have to find the white Ford?" Gregg said, after hearing Sinclair's summary.

"*Just*? We have no way of knowing where they went. They've probably left Miami. We've got the description and license number on the dashboard of every black-and-white in the country. But face it, they could've gone anywhere, and there are only a few zillion white Ford Escorts on the road."

KATE WAS EXHAUSTED. She longed for sleep, but there simply wasn't time. The flight to St. Croix would last only an hour, a fact which in itself seemed ludicrous; it had taken them all of four days to cover the distance by boat. Now she and Jack had only minutes to plan their next moves.

"If you still insist on returning to San Francisco, Jack, there are a dozen or so things we ought to consider."

"Great. Such as?"

"Well, what's the goal here?"

"Publish the transmissions," he said. "You're starting to sound like an attorney."

"Look, the fact is, if I'm in hiding there are several things I won't be able to do—*we* won't be able to do. Phone each other for instance. Your phones will be bugged."

"True. And my mail will probably be scrutinized. I'll be followed. I know, Kate."

"And passports. I'll need one in another name."

"Why?"

"To travel. I might have to leave the country. If I'm on the run, I should expect to have to travel and I'll need an identity."

"Jeez. Here we go breaking the law again. No, here *I* go. Okay. I know somebody who knows somebody— Look, none of this is difficult. I'll have Chet open a post office box for me. He or Nadine can drop by every so often and look for mail. I'll send you the box number as soon as we get it."

Kate nodded. "Care of General Delivery, Frankfort, Michigan. And have Chet and Nadine get you the numbers of some pay phones around the city and send them to me. We can arrange some sort of calling schedule."

"Okay. And I'll handle the passport thing. I know someone. Any particular name you'd care to use?"

Kate stared out the window at the night and saw her reflection mirrored against the blackness. Her hair was longer and her face seemed drawn, older. "Sarah, I think. With an *h*."

"Okay, Sarah-with-an-h. Smith?"

"Mm."

"Clark? Johnson?"

"Okay. Sarah Louise Clarke. 'Clarke' with an *e* on the end. Verisimilitude."

"She's breaking out the dollar words now. Definitely sounding like an attorney. Anything else on your list, Sarah-with-an-h, Clarke-with-an-e?"

"Cash. Have to dip into my savings. I'll write you a check. Send me cash in care of General Delivery. I can't be writing checks or using plastic. Jack, am I asking too much?"

"What? Cash a check and get you a passport? Hell, no. Look, considering what you're taking on? This is a nit. I believe in this too, you know. I'm just not quite as paranoid about Jeremy Sinclair as you." He looked at her and said, "I forget sometimes. I'll do whatever I can to help. I understand how important it is."

They held hands for the duration of the flight, leaning shoulder-to-shoulder. Kate would have given a lot, had it become possible to miraculously drop out of sight for a day, go off to Sandy Island with him—somewhere.

They touched down in St. Croix shortly after eleven. And because the island is a U.S. possession, they cleared U.S. Customs, uneventfully as it turned out, and with vast sighs of relief. Sinclair had not yet mobilized in pursuit. But it wouldn't be long.

After scanning a list of departing flights, Kate chose one to JFK International. Miami was out of the question, and a large metropolitan airport seemed safest for maintaining anonymity.

Jack reserved a seat for himself on a flight for Miami that was leaving an hour after her own. From there he would fly home.

"You could still change your mind, Jack. Come with me?"

He shook his head. "No. I've got to go back. I can be more help to you from there."

"It's possible they'll arrest you."

He put an arm around her shoulder. "I don't think so. Archie'll go to bat for me. So, I don't know where you've gone. I was just along for the ride. I'll think of something. As soon as the post office box is arranged, I'll send you the number. I'll send the cash. I'll handle the things we discussed."

"It hasn't gone very well, Jack. I'm sorry."

He touched her lips. "Don't. It went the way it went. I joined up with my eyes open and I wouldn't have missed it for anything."

"Final boarding for American Airlines Flight 1272, bound for New York City's Kennedy International. All ticketed passengers report to Gate 2A for boarding. This is the final call."

Her arms circled his waist. He felt thinner. He'd lost weight. "Watch your back, counselor," she said haltingly.

"You watch yours, and for godsake, keep away from elephants in dark places."

"At all times."

They kissed. Then she forced herself to pull away and head for the gate. She didn't dare look back; he'd have seen her brimming eyes.

She was flying under the name, "Marilyn Castillo," and she'd bought her ticket with cash. *Chew on that, Jeremy.* She settled into the window seat, buckled her seat belt and stared out across the tarmac. She was on the wrong side of the plane to see whether Jack stood at the window to watch her departure, but she knew he had. *Bye, counselor.* She swallowed hard.

Four hours later, shortly after eight AM, her plane touched down at Kennedy. She'd slept the entire way, a drugged, stuporous sleep that left her feeling becalmed and unreal. She remained in her seat until the last passenger had deplaned, then maneuvered her duffle bag and laptop computer down the narrow aisle. At least there wasn't the ordeal of customs to contend with.

She had a two-hour wait for a flight to O'Hare in Chicago, so she found a restaurant and ordered breakfast. She counted her remaining cash. Enough to buy a minimal used car. As she sat sipping cafeteria coffee, she reflected that her own prospects seemed far more auspicious than Jack's. If he hadn't already been apprehended, he soon would be. Would they arrest him? Send him to St. Lucia? Kate thought it more likely they'd place him under surveillance, hoping he'd lead them to her and the others. If they interrogated Jack, would he be able to keep from telling about Michigan? What lengths would the NSA go to, to persuade him to talk? Archie couldn't help much with the sort of problems Jack faced. This was completely beyond the small-town turf of Old Fuss 'n' Feathers.

Priorities, she thought as she boarded the Chicago flight. Keep your eye on the ball, Kate, on the goal—obtain the translated message from an extraterrestrial intelligence and hand it over to the world. Keep your eye on *that*.

In Chicago she forked over $875 of her remaining cash for a somewhat-blue Ford Pinto. The car dealer guaranteed the thing for thirty days or one thousand miles, and as Kate climbed in and drove away, she thought smart money would be on thirty days. If this rusted wreck had a thousand miles left in it, she'd kiss each one of its balding tires.

At a service station on the outskirts of Chicago she filled the tank, had them add a quart of oil, and bought a roadmap of Michigan.

"Just take me three hundred and fifty miles," she prayed over the car, patting its sun-split vinyl dashboard. "Six or seven hours. That's all I ask."

By five-thirty in the afternoon she was in Kalamazoo and in another hour she reached Grand Rapids where she stopped for dinner. She continued traveling north, up Highway 131 until she reached Cadillac, where she found an inexpensive motel for the night. She sank into the too-soft mattress and dropped off to sleep, wondering whether Jack had made it home. She'd call him tomorrow.

Ω

41

"They left on the evening flight to St. Croix," Michael Gregg told Sinclair. "In St. Croix, Sullivan caught a flight to Miami. He's en route to San Francisco. Lipton's disappeared."

"Okay. I better get back to Fort Meade then. We'll have Sullivan under surveillance. Bring in people from Grenada and the other islands. Concentrate on St. Croix. Lipton might still be there."

"They cleared U.S. Customs in St. Croix, Jeremy. From there, she can fly anywhere in the States under an assumed name. She won't have to present a passport."

"Right, but check out St. Croix's hotels anyway."

Gregg agreed.

"Sullivan's the key now. After a week or so, we'll back off, let him think we've lost interest. I'm going back to Fort Meade. There's nothing more I can do down here. Send the samples from *Great Expectations* directly to the Fibbies' lab. I want these people. The net's closing. I can feel it."

KATE ROSE AT SEVEN and ate breakfast at a roadside diner on the outskirts of Cadillac. Then she began driving northwest along Highway 115, a worn, two-lane strip that arrowed for miles through forested countryside. At ten-thirty she came to a road sign: FRANKFORT 2 MI. and under that an arrow pointing to the right indicated the turnoff to Crystal Lake.

She made the turn and wove slowly down the narrow highway. At a curve in the road she caught a glimpse of cobalt blue through the trees. The highway meandered down another mile and intersected Lake Shore Drive. She gazed ahead, across the lake. No question how it had gotten its name. It looked pristine. A ribbon of pale beige edged the shoreline marking shallows that extended several yards from shore before ending in a brilliant blue line of deeper water.

Tim's directions had been explicit, and she'd taken care to memorize them. She turned right onto Lake Shore Drive and followed the road until it ended at the entrance to a dirt and gravel drive marked by a sign: Crystalaire Camp For Girls—Private Drive. Tim's family cottage was down the road a quarter-mile, the third and last home on the right, across the gravel drive from the lake. It was set back from the road and up a gentle slope, nestled in a forest of birch trees.

She pulled to a stop in a clearing behind a Chevy pickup and climbed out of the car. As she looked up the stone steps to the cottage, the front door opened and Tim Thurmond emerged.

"Kate?"

"Couldn't stay away."

"Look who's here, Milt!" Tim dashed down the steps to meet her. "What a surprise! We figured you'd be in San Francisco by now." He draped an arm over her shoulder and they climbed the stairs.

Margo, Milton Rensler, and a woman Kate barely recognized emerged from the cottage to stand on the flagstone porch.

"Grace, is that you?"

"None other," the diminutive woman said. "It's wonderful to see you, Kate. Welcome to our retreat. Beautiful, isn't it?"

"You don't look anything like yourself. Your hair—"

"I cut it short and dyed it. Disguise, you know. Milt says it makes me look twenty years younger. I must have looked *awfully* old."

"What a great surprise, Kate," Rensler said, holding out his hand as if to shake it, but then changing his mind and wrapping her in a warm hug. "We didn't know whether you'd actually come. We've been very worried."

"I had no choice but to come. They connected us with the rescue when we returned the boat."

"We were afraid of that."

"We eluded them in St. Vincent and flew to St. Croix. Jack went home; I came here."

Margo hugged Kate. "You must have been terrified, escaping like that. Have you any word on Walter?"

Kate looked at her sympathetically. "I'm sorry, Margo. We were questioned only once and the agent didn't mention him. We were maintaining that we knew nothing so I couldn't ask. I'm certain he didn't tell them about us though. Otherwise we'd never have been able to leave. We'd have been arrested on the spot."

Tim led the way indoors and Kate found herself in a spacious family room with a wall of louvered windows overlooking the lake. Tables lined the far wall and on one of them a computer was set up.

"Our office," Tim said. "In here is the living room." The pine-paneled room had lakeside bay windows and opposite, an enormous stone fireplace. The room was crammed with cozy, overstuffed maple furniture and cushions covered in sun-faded fabric. There were two adjacent bedrooms and a hallway leading to a third room and small bathroom. The kitchen and laundry room were off the office/den, and a back door opened from the laundry room onto a porch. Behind the house, a concrete retaining wall held the hillside and forest at bay.

After the brief tour they gathered in the living room to exchange news.

Grace had made coffee and handed Kate a cup. "We're happy here. Milt and Tim have been organizing the office and assembling the satellite dish. I'm handling household chores, shopping, trips to town. Margo's working on the dictionary."

Kate looked at Margo.

"For the translation routine," Margo said. "So far, I've mostly only gathered source materials. I haven't entered much into the computer, but once the network's installed it'll go more quickly."

Tim said, "Milt and I are nearly finished assembling the satellite dish up in the woods. I'll show it to you. We've ordered a computer network with three workstations. Milt and I will be driving down to Detroit to pick everything up."

"You've been busy," Kate said. "I gather you had no difficulty reaching Miami or meeting up with Grace?"

Rensler shook his head. "Came off without a hitch. Santiago delivered us to Miami. We met Grace at the Fontainbleau, bought a used car and drove straight through. Arrived here July first."

"Have you contacted any of the other SETI groups?"

"Too risky," Tim said.

"It's likely their phones are tapped," Rensler added.

Kate looked out across the lake. The afternoon sun was reflecting off the water and light shimmered through the branches of a lakeside stand of birch.

"Beyond that boathouse," Tim pointed, "there's a dock, a breakwater and beach. And that's our leaky old garage. We keep the used car in there. Seemed unwise to leave it out for everyone to see. They might have traced it. We bought it with cash but you never know."

"Mm," Kate said. "I bought that blue thing for cash too. Prayed over it the whole way here."

"Where are your things? Did you get away with luggage?"

"It's all in the car."

"You'll stay here, won't you?" Tim asked. "I can take the sofa."

She shook her head. "I thought I'd rent a room. I might be here awhile and we might as well be comfortable. I thought I'd start looking this afternoon. Do you know of anything available nearby?"

"Possibly the Arnold's place. They don't normally rent it but they've come and gone for the season. It's on Lake Shore Drive just before the turnoff to the Girls' Camp. I'll call them. They live in Flint but they probably leave a key with someone local. Have to use a pay phone in town. We decided not to have the phone connected. Again, the risk."

Kate nodded, appreciating the caution they were exercising. Grace had disguised herself and was handling the shopping. They were paying for everything with cash, which meant Grace had to have liquidated their assets before leaving home. And no phone had been installed.

Later that day, Tim and Kate drove to town. As they crested the hill, they passed under an archway painted with, "Welcome to Frankfort." The arch spanned the two-lane road and was topped by a large replica of a black-hulled ferry boat. The town was nestled at the bottom of the hill, separated from Lake Michigan by a vast stretch of sand dunes. There was a deep-water port for car ferries and lake shipping, and Kate noticed several barges at anchor. They coasted down the highway and pulled into a service station.

"First I want to call Jack at his office," she said.

She dialed the number as Tim stood by with a fistful of quarters. She and Jack had agreed to a few signals for this call. She was to ask about the weather. If the reply was other than "absolutely beautiful," it would mean it was unsafe to talk. She waited anxiously as the phone rang.

"Sullivan." His voice was brisk and unreadable.

"Jack, it's me. How's the weather?"

"Oh, good! Ah, difficult to say. Might be beautiful out. I haven't been out in a while. It might be foggy. Changing, I'd say. I got back all right, though. I'm fine. Are you all right?"

"Absolutely. Just wanted to hear your voice and— Were you questioned?"

"Definitely. Intensely. I'm fine though. I'm at work, swamped. Archie's piling it on and I'm still wandering around with jet lag. Can't get my mind back to it."

"I won't keep you." They didn't dare prolong this conversation. The call might be traced. "Take care," she said.

"You too. Thank God you called."

"I love you, Jack Sullivan," she said.

"It's mutual."

Ω

42

ARRANGEMENTS were made for Kate to rent the Arnold cottage, and she was able to pick up the key from a neighbor and take occupancy the following afternoon. It was right on the water. From the small bedroom window she could hear the water lapping against the shore. It was rustic and comfortable and best of all, within walking distance of the Thurmond cottage, less than half a mile down the road. She wouldn't have to rely on the Pinto to take her back and forth. She found a paint-spattered tarp in the carport and draped it over the old blue clunker, giving it an affectionate pat; it had done its job.

Now she would hardly have to drive at all. Grace went to Frankfort at least a few times a week to market, check for mail, and ferry books back and forth to the library for Margo. Kate was welcome to tag along, and did so the next morning. She needed groceries and wanted to investigate the small town. They stopped at the post office and Kate inquired for mail; it was too soon for the communication from Jack, but she asked anyway. Then they breezed into Val-U-Mart to purchase warmer clothes for Kate. Her tropical Caribbean duds was insufficient for Northern Michigan weather. Last, on the way out of town they detoured to the harbor's ferry terminal and Kate picked up a schedule of the trans-Lake Michigan car ferry service.

* * *

"What have you got for me?" Jeremy Sinclair asked impatiently.

It was the morning of July fourteenth and Sinclair was back in his Fort Meade office. He'd been hounding the FBI's crime lab hourly for word on the findings from *Great Expectations*.

"I'm sending over a preliminary report."

"Any match on prints?"

"No, but so far we've only processed exterior latents. Interior should be wrapped up later today. We're matching DNA samples from the compound against boat samples. Those results won't be ready for another few days."

"Send over whatever you've got." Sinclair hung up and immediately dialed Michael Gregg.

"Michael, the lab came back negative on the exterior latents. Please tell me you've got something on the Cobblestone Inn room bug."

"The transcript's completed. A big zero I'm afraid."

"They didn't discuss it?"

"Not in a way that suggests they had anything to do with the abduction. When they first checked in, before they left for dinner, they speculated briefly about it. Lipton sounded more like a journalist who'd like to investigate Rensler's disappearance."

"Swell. Clever."

"It poses a new problem. Even if she had nothing to do with the initial disappearance, she might start investigating. They didn't eat at the Cobblestone. We're not sure where they ate but when they returned to the room after dinner, they said they were tired and were going to bed. There are sounds of packing, zippers, rustling about. Then it's quiet. That's it. Based on those conversations I'd say they had nothing to do with the disappearance."

"Impossible. They must have suspected the room was bugged. If they had nothing to do with it, why'd they skip town?"

"I don't know. Just didn't feel like sticking around? They were under no legal obligation to stay. They were within their rights."

"If Lipton had nothing to do with it, wouldn't she have returned to San Francisco with Sullivan? The fact that she's vanished is revealing, I think."

"You have Sullivan under surveillance?"

"Of course," Sinclair snapped, resenting his underling's query. "We've got his home bugged and his home phone tapped. The office phone's a little more problematic, taking longer to arrange. They're bound to slip up."

"If the scientists were on board that boat DNA tests should show it."

"If they gathered the right samples," Sinclair replied. "Has the boat gone out again on charter?"

"Yesterday, but our people were thorough. They took hairs and fibers from all over the interior. I didn't expect much from exterior surfaces. Salt water doesn't leave much. We took scrapings from the stern, looking for traces of adhesive, paint, anything that could have been used to disguise the vessel's name."

"Good. I intend to nail Lipton, Michael. And I have some other ideas. I think our scientists will set up a lab. These techie types can't survive without their computers. How's the interrogation of Walter Jacobsen going?"

"I'm on it. Nothing yet."

"Be more persuasive, Michael."

"I know."

TIM LED Kate back into the woods to view the newly assembled satellite dish. He'd cleared a forty-foot square of trees and constructed a level platform of two-by-sixes. Resting on this deck was the assembled pie-slice structure of a five-meter dish.

"It's huge," Kate commented, impressed. "How'd you manage it?"

"Milt and Margo helped. We used dollies and rigged up pulleys for hoisting. It came in a kit of twelve sections plus connecting spars and hardware. The controller unit was a separate kit. Really it was a snap to assemble. Bought the whole thing in Traverse City."

"Amazing you could find this sophisticated equipment so easily."

"You'd be surprised. These remote areas rely more and more on satellite dishes, what with TV and radio stations and amateur buffs. You're likely to find this kind of equipment just about anywhere."

Kate spotted strands of black co-axial cable snaking along the ground, leading from the dish back toward the house. "What's all this?"

"I've wired the controller to the office computer. This afternoon I'll be ready to test it. We'll have the dish orientation under program control."

She shook her head. "Really amazing. You've only been here two weeks."

"Almost three."

They walked back to the cottage, their steps muted as they tramped over the forest ground. Kate inhaled the pungent woodsy air, a lush, verdant aroma that brought back memories of childhood camping trips in Northern California.

"I was lucky growing up with all this," Tim said, sensing her mood.

"You really were." They walked along in companionable silence. "I'd like to tag along when you and Milt go to Detroit. I need a modem for my laptop."

"To dial up the SETI computer network."

"Yes. There's a phone at the Arnold place. I could—"

He held up a hand and shook his head. "Too risky. Traceable. We'll discuss ways— Incidentally, Milt has some ideas about the whereabouts of the transmitter. Ask him."

Back at the house, Tim began tinkering with his co-ax cables and Kate took a seat near Milton Rensler.

"Tim says you have a theory about where the ETI transmitter might be."

"An educated guess. When it vanished it was in an orbit concentric with Pluto's solar orbit at the edge of the solar system."

Kate nodded.

"Normally Pluto is the planet most distant from the sun. But during the course of its 248-year trip around the sun—that's in Earth-years of course—it passes inside of Neptune's orbit for a twenty-year period. The most recent of these periods began in 1979. Until 1999, Neptune is technically the planet most distant from the sun. An object seeking to establish itself in orbit at the edge of our solar system would relate itself to Neptune."

"You're saying maybe the transmitter has shifted orbits?"

"Maybe, to one synchronous with Neptune's solar orbit. At its last known location and trajectory, the transmitter was due to pass behind Pluto's moon, Charon. On St. Lucia we determined that the intersection had in fact occurred and the transmitter was lost in Charon's shadow. We were waiting for its re-emergence along its old trajectory, one concentric with Pluto's solar orbit, but it didn't happen. I've done the calculations and it works out that its passage behind Charon coincided with the moon's intercept of the orbital plane of Neptune."

"Charon. Some sort of Greek god, right?"

Rensler smiled at her. "I looked him up in one of Margo's dictionaries. Charon was the son of Erebus and Nox and his perennial task was to ferry the souls of the dead over the river Styx to Hades. In modern parlance a charon can refer to any ferryman."

The mythological suggestion gave Kate an odd chill. Considering they were dealing with an intelligent life form, was it reasonable to assign significance to the fact of the transmitter's disappearance in Charon's shadow? Perhaps it was meant to suggest the transmitter was now defunct, a dead soul, or perhaps it had been ferried elsewhere.

"Do you suppose the ETIs are up on their Greek mythology?" she asked.

He nodded. "Makes you wonder, doesn't it?"

Tim had been crawling around on the floor beneath the computer table. He stood up abruptly. "I'm going to run back and switch on the power supply at the satellite dish. Then we can try the orientation routine."

Within minutes he was back, breathing hard from a sprint. He sat down at the computer. "I'll see if I can get it to read our sequence of coordinates." He began typing and the rest gathered around the monitor, Kate with no exact idea of what she was watching for.

After a few stops and starts, Tim had his dish orientation program interfacing with the satellite controller. They could now automatically orient the dish to monitor signals on one set of coordinates and then shift to the next in a sequence of settings along Dr. Rensler's newly calculated trajectory. A second program would run concurrently to store incoming signals and analyze them for a match with the pattern of the earlier transmissions. And now they had a major advantage over earlier SETI efforts: They could confine their search to the hydrogen frequency; the cosmic haystack had shrunk considerably.

"It's working," Tim announced happily.

"Wait'll we have the network installed," Rensler said.

"Why the network?" Kate asked.

"It'll give us three workstations. Margo can focus on the dictionary, and Tim and I will each have a computer. We'll be able to share files. Otherwise we'd have a tough time receiving and translating the signal—*if* we find it, that is."

" *When* we find it," Tim said firmly.

Ω

43

"The final lab reports from *Great Expectations* are in," Jeremy Sinclair told the President. "They're negative."

"Even the DNA analyses?"

"Negative."

"Damn. Perhaps you were focusing too much on—"

Sinclair interrupted. "It looked extremely promising, Sir. I still believe Lipton's involved in some way."

"What about the scientists? Any word on their used car?"

"Nothing. They drove out of the lot in Miami and disappeared."

"The Sullivan surveillance?"

"Nothing. There's one angle we're pursuing though. Ralph, describe your idea."

Burch leaned forward in his seat. "These people are scientists. We think it's likely they'll set up a listening station and continue their work."

"Haven't the transmissions ceased?"

"The transmitter may have changed trajectories. The team in St. Lucia is operating on that assumption."

"We figure Rensler will want to continue searching, as well," Sinclair said. "He'll need a satellite dish and other special equipment. And they'll have to pay for it. We're monitoring their accounts closely, but more likely they'll pay cash. We're checking with every major outlet where they might purchase the equipment."

"Nationwide?"

"Nationwide. We'll pay particular attention to anyone who pays cash for a sizeable purchase of satellite or computer equipment."

"It's something, anyway," Geller said. "That journalist, Lipton. She hasn't turned up?"

"We lost her in St. Croix."

"And Sullivan's not talking."

"No. Our surveillance on him is extremely tight."

"So now you're looking into the listening dish angle. Ralph, any breakthrough on deciphering the transmissions?"

"Not yet, but Vaughn feels they're close. With Thurmond and Rensler gone, it's placed a greater burden on the others. Jacobsen isn't much help. He's not been feeling well, so the work of relocating the transmitter is mostly falling to Keppler, Vaughn and Alan Westlake, his associate."

"You haven't brought me a shred of good news," Geller observed dryly.

"We'll find them, Sir. I promise you that," Sinclair said, getting to his feet as the President rose.

"I view containment as extremely unlikely," Geller said. "At this point, finding these people probably won't change that."

"One thing to keep in mind, Sir: They haven't blown it open so far. Perhaps they don't intend to."

WITHIN a few days of Kate's arrival at the lake, she received the parcel from Jack containing cash, his newly opened post office box number and five pay phone numbers in a list with dates and times. Now she could contact him and communicate openly.

Life began to take on a rhythm and routine. Her day usually began with a five-mile run along the lake. After that, she spent most mornings at work on a detailed account of her involvement with SETI and the rescue of the scientists. At some point she expected to send Jack a copy; someday she might even publish it.

After lunch, unless she drove into town with Grace, she usually walked down to the cottage to check on the scientists' progress. She always took her laptop computer along in case there was anything Tim or Milt wanted stored on her machine. If there was nothing else for her to do, she continued her own writing at the cottage. More often than not, she ate dinner at the cottage; and always when she left, she was careful to take her belongings with her—computer, books, sweaters. If the others were apprehended in the night, at least the NSA would find no immediately obvious trace of her.

The scientists had their routine as well. Margo concentrated on the dictionary. During the three weeks it had taken Milt and Tim to assemble and activate the satellite dish, she had begun compiling a vast dictionary database, starting with a basic word processing spell-checker database of two hundred thousand words. Thus far she'd added another fifty thousand words to this, culled from her burgeoning library of etymological sources.

The approach they were taking, as Margo explained to Kate one afternoon, was that they would not attempt to include every word in the English language. Rather, they'd run the earlier transmission data through Tim's translation program and Margo's dictionary, isolate the untranslatable words and focus on those. Tim had developed a program to generate a series of letter combinations—anagrams—for untranslatable numeric values, and Margo could then research these word options and add those for which she found translations.

As long as Margo kept busy, her spirits seemed high. But when she stopped work for a break, for a walk along the lake or a hike in the woods, she invariable returned in a dour mood. Kate thought it probably had to do with Walter. One afternoon she joined Margo for a walk. Maybe it would help her to talk.

"I can't escape it," Margo said as they strolled along the beach. "I feel guilty for allowing him to return to St. Lucia."

"What should you have done?"

She shook her head. "That's just it. None of the options were acceptable. I knew I couldn't return with him. I couldn't imagine myself imprisoned in that compound, any more than I can now conceive of *him* tinkering here in our backwoods lab. But if I'd returned at least I'd be supporting him the way Grace supports Milt."

"In a way you are supporting him. Your contribution is significant."

"It's difficult though, watching the Renslers together. There's such a romantic passion there. I've actually caught them kissing when they think no one's watching. They've been married almost fifty years and they're still *stealing* kisses."

Kate smiled. "They're lucky, aren't they?" It made her think of Jack; she missed him a lot.

"They also have a true, practical partnership. They seem more like one person than two. They complete each other."

"I've even heard them completing each other's sentences," Kate said. "You're right, they're quite remarkable. I commented on it to Grace a few days ago and she said they're often accused of being old-fashioned—which of course they are. That sort of marriage no longer seems to be in vogue."

Margo turned to look at Kate. "It's not in vogue because it involves too much effort and risk."

Kate nodded and again thought of Jack.

"We live in a fastfood, fast-paced, throw-away culture with everyone in a great hurry. Problem is, the only places worth getting to take time, effort and risk."

"Because they're not places at all but states of mind."

"Exactly," Margo said. "People give up on their relationships and move on at the first sign of trouble."

"Mm."

"We're looking for fast political solutions, fast economic and environmental solutions, fast interpersonal solutions. "Silver bullet" is the latest slang for that. Interesting way to put it, I think, as if we could solve any problem by firing shots at it. Seems logical; we flip a switch and light a room, poke a few buttons and microwave a meal. Mostly we have no expectation that we'll understand *why* we do what we do. The qualities we seem to have lost appreciation for in all of this are patience and steadfastness. We no longer find it worthwhile—the time and care it takes to grow something that endures. Why should we? We don't value that which endures; we value that which is new, fast and different, *microwavable*, for God's sake." Margo shook her head ruefully at her own observation. "Incidentally, I added "microwavable" to my dictionary this morning—an adjective. I also added 'nuke' as the slang equivalent we've coined for the process of cooking something rapidly—as in food, or nations of people."

Kate took in Margo's soliloquy, which was not unlike some she might have had with herself, particularly when she was viewing the world as a hopeless mess. Increasingly she tried to minimize such interior musings in favor of optimism, having concluded it was essential to her well-being. "Are you thinking of returning to St. Lucia?"

"I've thought about it but why should I? Walter doesn't need me. And I don't suppose I really need him. I only need the idea of us, the playing-house pretense that I was part of a couple. I look at Grace and Milt and realize I never was. We played at it, imagined ourselves linked; but all the while we built our fences around ourselves, around the parts that mattered most. We fenced ourselves in *from* each other, not *with* each other."

Kate found herself in Margo's words and couldn't help consider her own carefully tended fences. Suddenly she felt a great longing for them to be gone. It was a costly business, keeping walls and fences in good repair.

"Being closely aligned with someone is no longer considered healthy," Margo said. "Nowadays it's called 'co-dependence.'"

"The things you're saying are sad."

"They are, aren't they?" She stared out across the lake. "God, this is a beautiful spot. And I'm just a colossal bundle of fun. Maybe I *should* go back to St. Lucia, at least make an effort at creating something that endures. Maybe when this blasted dictionary is finished—"

Freedom's just another word for nothing left to do, Kate thought to herself. "How much longer do you think it'll take?"

"The dictionary? I don't know, a month. It's become an obsession, the only real reprieve I get from the kind of thoughts with which I've just burdened you."

"You talk as though you're imprisoned—'reprieves' and 'fences.'"

Margo glanced at her, surprised. "I do, don't I?"

They were heading back toward the cottage; they'd started back the moment after Margo had mentioned the dictionary—a compulsive return to her obsession.

"I do feel imprisoned," Margo said. "Remember that song? *'Freedom's just another word for nothing left to lose.'*"

Kate stopped, smiled to herself. There it was again. "Nothing left to *do*," had been her thought, not *lose*. But no, for Margo it would be *lose*.

"I know I should feel free here," Margo said. "But ultimately freedom, like every other thing of any importance, becomes a matter of the heart."

Kate nodded at that observation.

"So probably I speak of reprieves and fences because of a badly constricted heart."

The winds that had earlier blown across the lake had subsided now, leaving the broad expanse of water glassy-smooth. There was reflected on its surface a perfect inverted image of the sky and distant hills. Insects buzzed, a razor-sharp electric sound.

"From an entirely selfish point of view, I'm awfully glad you're here and I hope you'll stay," Kate said.

"I'm glad you're here too, Kate. Do you know, you're one of only two people I've ever met who actually knows how to listen?"

"What a kind thing to say. Who's the other?"

"Grace Rensler."

Ω

44

KATE STOOD on the front porch of the Arnold cottage at dawn on August sixteenth, waiting for Tim and Milt to pick her up for the drive to Detroit. A few last bright stars lingered in the early sky. She sipped coffee and shivered, huddling against the chill under the porch awning.

She and Jack had talked by phone the previous evening. They'd discussed a range of possible outcomes and options. Most of Jack's suggestions invariably included purchase of a sailboat and their living aboard; she'd promised to give serious thought to the notion. It wasn't the first time they'd discussed it. Now however the idea held the additional appeal of offering a possible solution to the dilemma of living on the same planet with Jeremy Sinclair. It would at least give them mobility.

Detroit was a two hundred-mile drive from Crystal Lake. It took them four hours. They sat scrunched together three across in Tim's pickup, anticipating the need for the truck bed to transport the network hardware. Kate was in the middle, her thigh pressed uncomfortably against Dr. Rensler's as she leaned to give Tim access to the gear shift.

"I feel as though I've been let out of a dim jail cell," Rensler said as they drove along, "as though the light were too harsh or something. It's disorienting."

"Do you sometimes sense them closing in?" Tim asked.

"The NSA?" He considered a moment. "I can't see how they could have traced us to Michigan. I suppose they could check your family, discover your parents' history with Crystal Lake but—"

In recent weeks Kate had tried to dismiss her own mounting sense of foreboding, but it now washed over her with new force. She didn't feel as though she'd been let out of jail. More like emerging from a cocoon—raw, exposed, and vulnerable. Until now they'd mostly steered clear of discussions about their predicament, but now as they drove along the thought came home to her as deeply shocking: They were fugitives.

Tim had ordered the network hardware from Computers Unlimited in Detroit and they arrived at the store at noon. Kate waited in the truck a few moments before following them in. Once inside, she hovered nearby but kept to herself, pretending to be a lone shopper.

The order included the network file server, cabling, two additional computers, Ethernet cards for the workstations, a tape backup system and a backup power supply. With software added in, the cost was significant. Kate overheard Tim tell Milt to count out $17,425. Rensler began stacking bundles of hundred dollar bills on the counter.

The sputtering salesman stopped him, aghast. "You can't write a check?"

"We prefer to pay cash," Rensler said. "Is that a problem?"

"Well, I mean, I'll have to speak with the manager. I've never—" The young man headed off in search of the store manager.

When he was out of earshot Kate overheard Tim say to Milt, "Not good. We've become memorable customers."

"We can't use a credit card. Do you believe it? They might refuse cash?"

The store manager emerged from a back room and walked over to them, a copy of their invoice in hand. "I understand you'd like to pay cash for this?"

"Is that a problem?" Dr. Rensler asked.

"For such a large sum, you understand, I should have the bills, ah, examined. I mean, you know, they might be—"

"Counterfeit?" Tim asked, disgusted.

"Well—"

Rensler said, "You'd prefer a cashier's check."

"Yes," the man said brightly, "that would do nicely if it's not too much trouble."

"Fine. We'll get one. Where's the nearest bank?"

"Just down the street," the manager said, relieved, "two blocks down on the left side. Thanks for being so understanding."

Tim and Milt left the store and Kate stayed to make her own cash purchases, which by comparison with theirs were insignificant. She bought an external modem, cable, a length of modular phone cord and various adapters.

"I'll just look around a bit, if you don't mind," she told the salesman after he'd taken her cash and bagged her purchases.

She walked over to a color monitor and sat down, becoming quickly engrossed in a software demo. Thirty minutes later, Tim and Milt were back and began loading equipment into the truck. She joined them a few minutes later.

"Damn," Tim said.

"What?"

"Milt had to show his driver's license at the bank."

"Naturally they wrote it down. It'll be in their records."

"Was your name on the cashier's check?" Kate asked.

"No. The check was made payable to Computers Unlimited and I was allowed to leave Remitter blank. But I did have to sign their record. They have my name."

"Not good."

"I wonder how long we have?" Tim said.

"It could take months, couldn't it?" Kate said. "There are a zillion banks in this country. Think of how many people they'd have to have working on this case to unearth your little transaction."

"Not if they only have to look at Michigan banks," Tim said, "not if they have access to computerized banking records."

"Shit," Kate said. "Sorry, sailor talk."

"Yeah," Tim said miserably, "we lapse into it ourselves from time to time." He fought city traffic until they were on Highway 75 heading to Flint. "We need a plan," he said.

Over a meal in Cadillac they pieced together what seemed to Kate a rather ludicrous contingency plan revolving around the possibility that some or all of them would be apprehended. In all likelihood those apprehended would be returned to St. Lucia.

"If that happens," Kate said, "we'll need a way to communicate with those inside, a way to get information in and out of the St. Lucian compound."

"Assuming you're not caught, too."

"If I'm caught then Jack will help. Either way—"

They decided on a drop site. Phones were out of the question; there'd be no chance dialing up the compound's computer.

"We'll have to smuggle information through the fence," Rensler said. "I used to take walks along there. The jungle has been cleared back several feet on both sides. High voltage wires are strung along the top."

"We could toss a diskette over the fence," Tim said, "assuming they'd allow us out for walks."

"We could count a certain number of fence poles from the main gate," Kate suggested. "There *is* a main gate, isn't there?"

"Yeah, a gravel road leads in from the highway. Let's make the drop site ten fence poles to your left as you face the gate from outside the compound."

"Or as near to that as can be managed," Kate said. "Should we also agree on a certain day of the month? I'd rather not hang around there on a daily basis."

"How about the twelfth," Tim said, "my lucky number."

"All right. I'll look near the tenth fence pole on the twelfth day of each month." Just saying it sounded silly. And did she really dare to show up there, or ask it of Jack? "You'll be watched, of course."

"We'll manage," Milt said, "arrange a diversion. Someone can faint or something. They were awfully touchy about my medical condition, my high blood pressure."

Kate nodded. These people had proved their resourcefulness many times over. "Obviously if I'm caught— Well, I'll let Jack know of the plan."

It was a sobering conversation and they were quiet during most of the drive back to the lake. They dropped Kate at the Arnold place a little after dark, and as she unlocked the door, stepped inside, and looked around, she recognized two things—whatever sense of safety she'd had was now shattered, and it was probably for the best.

Tim spent the next two days configuring the network. He ran cable from the file server to each of the four computers, installed the Ethernet cards at each workstation, formatted the new disk, and genned the system. Kate lent a hand, following Tim's brisk directions, running cable, opening up workstations to seat Ethernet boards, and reading instructions aloud from the small tower of manuals that accompanied the components. The new backup power supply would kick in, in the event of a power outage. The printer was connected to the network, everything was tested; finally they were in business.

And none too soon. They found the extraterrestrial signal on August thirty-first.

Ω

45

THE TASK to which NSA Agent Raphael 'Rap' Sanchez was assigned involved visiting every computer hardware vendor in the Detroit area. He was to inquire of store managers as to large cash sales within the past two months. He was to carry photographs of the missing scientists to show to anyone remembering such a sale. He sat down with the Yellow Pages, looked up Computer Dealers, and began making a list of stores and addresses.

Christ, he thought as he fingered his broad mustache, why does everyone have to call themselves Compu-Something. Stupid name. Computime, Computown, Compuware, Computronix, Compupro, Compustore. Shit. Compushit. It would take weeks. This project was some kind of Very Big Deal, was all he knew. Someone Very High Up was laying on the heat. They had his boss, Tom 'Maalox' Murphy, jumping through hoops. A slew of "yessir-nossir" phone calls, a feverish pitch of closed-door huddles, part of a nationwide effort. Murphy was back to chain-smoking and guzzling Maalox. Another goddamned Maalox moment.

Murphy had assigned Rap Sanchez and two others to the project full time, one to the satellite dish investigation, and Rap and a second agent to this Compushit Detail. Rap was to set everything else aside and give this his full attention.

He finished making up his Compushit List and then he and Agent Russ Olmsted marked the locations of all the stores on a map of the metropolitan Detroit area.

"Let's split 'em in half," Sanchez said and made as if to tear the map in two.

"For crissake, don't tear it, Rap. Here, cut the damned thing."

Sanchez started in the northeast corner of the city and worked his way south and east. He was calling on between six and eight stores a day. At that rate he figured to finish by Christmas. Listlessly, he pulled up in front of Computers Unlimited and climbed out of the car. These places had all started to look alike—glossy, lots of plate glass, fancy displays of computers and colored monitors running whiz-bang demos.

It was always someone else who hit pay dirt on these needle-in-a-haystack searches, he thought to himself. Never me. How would it feel to be The One? Probably like winning the goddamned lottery. It was true. In all his years of doing the grunt work dreamed up by some brain-dead bureaucrat in Washington, he, Raphael Fernando Sanchez, had never once been the one to find the needle.

"I'd like to speak with the store manager," Sanchez said wearily to a youthful salesman.

"Frank Olkewicz. He's out to lunch. He'll be back around one." The salesman turned away.

"Then maybe you can help me," Sanchez said to his back.

"What can I help you with?"

Sanchez showed his ID. "We're conducting an inquiry. I wonder if anyone might have come in here in the past few months and paid cash for a large order of computer equipment?"

"You should talk to Frank," he said shaking his head. "I'm just a salesman. Only started here three months ago."

"S'okay. That's all we care about. The last eight weeks."

"Someone who paid cash? Lots of folks pay cash."

"For a very large purchase, maybe several thousand dollars' worth of computer equipment. Ring a bell?"

"No," the salesman said. "Oh, there was one— No, they ended up paying with a cashier's check or a money order."

"Someone wanted to pay cash but changed their mind?"

"Yeah. It was my biggest sale since I've been here. Seventeen thousand-something. They started pulling out bundles of hundred dollar bills so I called Frank over. You know, it seemed odd. No one carries that kind of cash around, not in Detroit anyway. So I call Frank over and he asks them if they mind goin' down to the bank for a money order. Pissed me off, 'cause I figure there goes my first big sale right out the door."

"And?"

"And the men agreed. They went to a bank and came back later with a money order."

Sanchez thought, damn, for a minute I thought I had it. Still, better show him the picture. "Were there two men?"

"Yeah. An older man and a younger one about my age."

"They look like these two men?" Phlegmatically, Sanchez extended the photographs.

"That's the older guy. The younger one looked older than in this picture. Might be this guy, I guess."

"You're sure about the older guy?" He tried to hold his amazement in check. He'd once bought a lottery ticket with four winning numbers on it. He'd dashed off to the store to redeem it, only to discover he'd misread the winning series.

"Yeah, I'm sure. He had that smoothed-back white hair that sticks up high like that. Quiet guy. The young one did the talking and knew about computers. The older one handled the money."

"How long ago was this?"

"Let's see. It was, oh, I remember, it was Friday, because me and Syl went out that night to celebrate my first big sale. So it was, let's see, August sixteenth, couple weeks ago."

"Can you show me the bill of sale?"

"Sure. They bought a Novell Network, file server, cable, Ethernet boards, workstations—the whole works. Nice setup."

The salesman began pawing though a desk drawer for a copy of the order. "Couldn't sell 'em a printer though. Damn, it's not here. It'll be on the computer," he said, abandoning the half-hearted search.

He walked over to the counter where a computer monitor and keyboard were set up. "Here it is," he said, "John Aiken—that's the old guy I think. Here, I'll print out a copy of the invoice if you'd like."

"That'll be a help."

When the order was printed, Sanchez studied it.

"Look, am I going to lose my commission on this?"

"I don't see why you should."

"Good. Do you need me any more? I should wait on these customers."

"What did you say your name was?"

"Chris Zabik. Here's my card."

"Thanks for your help, Chris. One other thing. Do you by any chance have a copy of the money order?"

"No. Maybe Frank does. I don't know. He'll be back in an hour or so."

"I'll stop back around later. Thanks again."

Sanchez left the store with a copy of the invoice and went to a pay phone to call his boss. When Maalox Murphy heard the news, he insisted on joining Sanchez at Computers Unlimited. That infuriated Rap Sanchez. He didn't need any goddamned help. All they were doing was talking to a computer store manager and a flunkie salesman. No weapons would be drawn.

Nevertheless, when the manager returned from lunch around one-thirty, Maalox was on hand to personally interrogate the manager about the transaction. Rap Sanchez stood by feeling profoundly annoyed.

"I remember," Olkewicz said. "I sent them down to the First Bank of Detroit. They wanted to pay cash, had a stack of hundred dollar bills. We can't take in cash sums like that so I sent them down the street."

"And they returned with a check. Did you make a copy?"

"I wrote down the check number on the file copy of the order. It's in the back. I'll get it." The manager disappeared and returned moments later. "Here it is. Check 1401223, cashier's check drawn on First Bank of Detroit, right down the street."

Maalox thanked Olkewicz and they left and hurried to the bank. After showing ID's to the branch manager they spoke with the teller who'd handled the transaction.

"You recognize these two men?" Sanchez handed him photos.

"That might be the older one. The young man— I'm not as sure about him." She glanced at the manager as she said, "Shall I get out the check register?" The manager nodded. A moment later, "Here it is. Milton Rensler of Woodside, California bought the check." The teller turned the register around to show the agents.

"You asked to see identification?"

"The one buying the cashier's check. For such a large amount, we have to. He showed me his driver's license. Here's the number."

"Bingo," Murphy breathed. "May we see a copy of the check or a copy of his signature?"

"Sure, they're in the vault. I'll get them." She disappeared and returned a few minutes later. "Here it is," she said, handing Murphy a check-sized slip of paper.

"May I take this?"

"Oh, no. Those are bank records."

The teller again looked to the manager. "We can make you a copy," the manager said.

"That'll do. Thanks very much."

Outside, Maalox turned and patted Sanchez on the back. "Good job, Rap. We got em."

Which was how Rap Sanchez came to find out what it was like to be The One who found the needle in the haystack: "Good job, *we* got em." *We*, my ass. *Rap Sanchez got em.*

Ω

46

DR. RENSLER'S hypothesis was correct; the transmitter was in orbit at the outer edge of the solar system on a trajectory concentric with Neptune. At two-thirty-five in the afternoon of August thirty-first the printer began clattering noisily.

"Milt, come quick. Look at this," Tim exclaimed. Kate, Rensler and Margo were all across the room in an instant and stood hovering over the printer as it spewed forth a stream of zeroes and ones.

"Well hello, hello," Rensler chortled. "I believe we've found you. Or you've found us. Tim, make sure the data's being captured."

Tim was already in motion, racing to a workstation to verify that the file he'd created for this purpose was growing in size. They'd tested the program with dummy data, but here was the real thing.

"It's working," Tim said.

"Wonder how much we've missed?" Margo asked.

"No way to know until we complete the translation."

"We could compare it with the earlier transmissions smuggled out of St. Lucia," Tim said. "If it's part of what we picked up before, we'll know we're listening to a re-broadcast." He immediately set to work on another program.

"When can we translate it?" Kate asked.

"It'll take at least a day," Rensler said.

Margo had finished entering words into the dictionary earlier in the week, and two steps remained to wrap up her effort—calculation of the numeric values for each word, and execution of the routine to build an index of these values. The first of these programs had started the previous evening and had been running all night. Once it finished, the indexing routine would take at least another ten hours.

There was also a binary-to-decimal conversion routine to be run, and Tim felt the data might have to be inverted. If it had come in backwards before, it was probably backwards now, though *why*, they still don't know.

"If it follows the earlier pattern it'll run for about eight hours," Tim said.

"Let's hope we can track it until it finishes," Rensler said. "I'll doublecheck the math for the next several days' coordinates."

Kate stayed at the cottage all evening. There was nothing for her to do, but like the others, she couldn't pull her eyes away from the screens, from the monitors displaying the progress of the slow-running routines that must finish before the translation could be run. Excitement mounted as they sat around the office with their feet up, drinking coffee and speculating on the transmission's content and source. *We are not alone in the universe*. The realization struck them all broadside. Certain proof was at hand.

The transmission ended abruptly seven-thirty that evening. Then Tim launched the data inversion and binary-to-decimal conversion routines, which ran until eleven-thirty. The program to calculate the dictionary word values finished shortly after midnight. After verifying a few of the values, the indexing routine was started.

"Nothing more we can do tonight," Tim said. "Shall we turn in?"

But who could sleep? Kate returned to the Arnold place and thrashed around for a few hours. She was up and out the door at first light and arrived at the cottage to find everyone already up and on edge with anticipation. This was The Day, for Milton Rensler the culmination of a life's work; but they all felt it—the enormity of what they might be about to witness.

At seven-thirty they gathered at the breakfast table for English muffins and cherry jam and at eight-fifteen moved into the office and stood around, staring at the printer. Milt reasoned that if he'd calculated the trajectory correctly another transmission could start at any moment.

As the minutes ticked by and nothing happened, the wide-eyed anticipation began to narrow. But at nine-twenty the printer once again clattered to life, spewing out a second ETI communication.

"Good morning, friends!" Milt said with a broad grin.

Tim made a fist and pounded the desk with an exuberant, "Yes! Yes!" Kate, Margo and Grace stood applauding.

"How soon till we know what it says?" Grace asked.

"The indexing routine should finish in the next hour," Tim said. "Then we can translate yesterday's signal."

"In English?" Grace asked.

"Hope so," Milt said.

At eleven-fifteen the indexing finished. Tim typed, TRANS and hit the ENTER key, and the first of the Omega Transmissions began to print.

WORD of progress in the case traveled quickly, from Detroit to Fort Meade, Maryland to Washington, D.C. to St. Lucia and California. Within an hour the President of the United States had been informed that Tim Thurmond and Milton Rensler had shopped at a computer store in downtown Detroit and purchased over seventeen thousand dollars' worth of computer hardware. Within four hours, Jeremy Sinclair had established a Michigan task force.

One team would intensify their focus on satellite dish purchases made in Michigan and surrounding states. Others would comb the records of vehicle registration departments and utility companies—phone, gas, electricity, garbage and water service. They'd search for "Tim Thurmond" and "Milton Rensler" as well as "John Aiken," the name on the Computers Unlimited invoice.

Sinclair narrowed the search for the white Ford Escort to the midwest and brought in agents from more distant regions of the country to beef up his Michigan teams. The net was closing.

Why Michigan? he wondered. If I were on the run, where would I go? I'd prefer someplace familiar, a place where I had connections.

Sinclair assigned a larger group of agents to review in greater detail the family histories of Lipton, the Renslers, Jacobsens, and Thurmond. "Watch for any reference to Michigan and adjacent states. This can't have been a random choice."

Finally she screwed up, Sinclair thought. His phone rang and he reached for it.

"Walter Jacobsen's dead," Michael Gregg said tersely.

"What the hell do you mean, dead?"

"Dead as in not living."

"What the hell?"

Within two hours Sinclair was back in the hot seat in the Oval Office facing a livid President Geller.

"I do not understand how this could happen," the President fumed.

"Sir, all I can say is the policy was always to allow the scientists to roam rather freely within the compound. It's not like they could go anywhere. I mean Michael felt—and frankly I agreed—they had to be allowed *some* privacy. We didn't want them feeling like prisoners."

"You just don't get it, do you Jeremy? This isn't a god-damned country club we're running down there. It isn't a goddamned *exercise*. It isn't even a mere interesting scientific anomaly that's occurred here. This," Geller stormed, "is the goddamned biggest, most important occurrence, maybe in the entire history of mankind. And you have just allowed Walter

Jacobsen to electrocute himself to death on a goddamned electric fence?"

Geller's face had turned vivid crimson and he paced the terrain behind his desk like an enraged tiger. "Because you felt it would be *nice* for him to have some *privacy?*" Geller froze, then turned to glare at his whipped-looking NSA Director.

"I— You're absolutely right, Sir. You'll have my resignation on your desk this afternoon."

"I don't *want* your goddamned resignation! I want solutions! I need your help, Jeremy. I need you to be taking this seriously. We are dealing here with *the* major scientific breakthrough of all time and so far all you people have managed to do is thoroughly screw it up. Now what can I think except that you have somehow failed to appreciate its importance? And that tells me that I have failed to impress it sufficiently upon you." Geller paused for air.

"Well, I'm telling you now—not one scientist is to be allowed out of the sight of your people, not one. When they go to the goddamned toilet, when they sleep, when they go for a walk, when they eat. If you need more people, tell me; I'll get them for you. More closed-circuit monitors? You got 'em. If you need, hell, pink helicopters, you'll have pink helicopters. If you need four calling birds and three fucking French hens, you'll have 'em. There is *nothing* you cannot have. Is that clear, Jeremy?"

"Yessir."

"Goooood." He drew the word out. "Now, I want Milton Rensler, I want Margo Jacobsen, I want Tim Thurmond." The President's voice continued to reverberate through the room. Passersby on Pennsylvania Avenue must have easily overheard this particular Presidential address.

Sinclair's knees were trembling so violently that his only remaining hope was to somehow collect himself sufficiently to exit the Oval Office unaided. All color had drained from his face. The most powerful man in the world was chewing him up and spit him out.

By contrast, Geller's face was the color of a ripe watermelon. "I do not care what it takes. Do you have any questions?"

"No, Sir. As for helicopters, I don't need pink ones but I might take twenty in olive-drab, standard issue. I'd like to begin combing the state of Michigan for a large satellite dish."

"Good. As long as they're used stateside. Where do you want them? I'll see to it they get there. Anything else?"

"Give me another ten of Dalton's people." Dalton Enderby was the Director of the FBI and Jeremy had thus far made good use of their assistance. He lacked the readily deployable manpower for the scale this operation had taken on.

"Very good, Jeremy. See? When you say "jump," I say "how high." Now where shall I send these people?"

"Send four to the compound in St. Lucia and the rest to our Detroit office."

"Fine. And the helicopters. We'll give that one to the Marines, I think."

Geller was calmer now, making notes. He picked up the phone and within minutes was speaking with Major General Sam Thatcher. He instructed the general to place twenty helicopters with crew on standby alert and promised to get back to him with further instructions.

"See how easy it is, Jeremy? There will not be any more screw-ups. Is that clear?"

"Very clear, Sir. I really am terribly sorry about Jacobsen. We'll put Keppler, Vaughn and Westlake under constant surveillance. I'll get you the missing scientists."

"You do that."

Ω

47

MILTON RENSLER paced. Tim drummed his fingers on a tabletop and stared blankly out at the lake. Margo was preparing copies of the first translation for each of them and the group had assembled and was waiting. Grace pretended to be busy in the kitchen. Kate sat, trying for stillness, wondering what to expect from the ETI communication. What if it turned out to be a tremendous disappointment, even gibberish? But she knew it wouldn't be. For one thing, Margo had been emitting enticing murmurs as she labored over the text.

But even if it were nonsensical, there still remained something incredibly reassuring in the fact of the communication, in the certain knowledge that mankind was not alone in the universe. If one highly advanced civilization in the galaxy had surpassed its problems, perhaps humans could also find a way. Here might be a moment marking a major shift in course and consciousness for Earth. Kate thought of astronauts who, on viewing the blue planet from space, saw in it a transforming vision, the unambiguous imperative of world peace.

Margo began distributing copies. "It appears that the same message is repeated several times during the course of the signal. Here is the text of one iteration. There are a few words for which I found no translation. Tim's program produced anagram word options, and I had to choose, mostly based on context. Otherwise, well, you'll see."

She handed Kate a copy:

Ω Transmission One:

We send you greetings. We have observed countless civilizations at various phases in their evolution. Some have survived to your approximate level; many have not. We offer observations:

Omega, the last letter of your Greek alphabet, translates as the vowel 'O', a sphere, a mark of completion, the end, the One. The symbol derived from your Hieratic glyph for death, the half-sphere resting on the horizon line and signifying the setting sun. As such, Omega represents the ultimate achievement in species evolution: the I, Iota or Individual in union with the whole.

We observe that by the Earth's late twentieth century, much of the human species had evolved to an Iotic level of consciousness, as a collection of separate, differentiated individuals, each functioning with apparent autonomy, in competition with each other and with other planetary species. Iotic consciousness, symbolized by the ninth letter of your Greek alphabet, Iota, is the I alone. We note that Iota translates secondarily as a tiny bit.
The Iotic phase in a civilization's evolution is characteristically competitive and exploitive, rather than cooperative and nurturing, and it is often at this advanced Iotic stage as found on twentieth century Earth that a crossroads is reached: The species must either transform itself beyond the Iotic or expire through the combined effects of war and planetary ruin.

For millennia, our own species paralleled yours, achieving what was considered a viable mastery and dominance over our planet, an apex of Iotic individuality. We found ourselves at the crossroads you now face. Lacking a widespread sense of our interconnectedness with each other and our planet, our viability became uncertain. We had lost our way, had become fractious, focused on inter- and intra-species differences, excessively competitive and vigilant to the faults and flaws of others. Fear had nearly suffocated all joy from the species' existence, rendering us a civilization of individuals polarized and isolated.

Some among us then began to experience an awakening, a remembrance of our connectedness with each other and the cosmos. Gradually, the entire species joined the new awareness, returning to the essential Omegan consciousness from which we and all life had arisen. We recognized ourselves as interdependent members of a larger whole, where that which affected one member would necessarily affect all. With Omegan consciousness, conflict and competition are unimaginable. When one is out of harmony with the whole, the entire species, or a relevant portion of it, rises to assist the one in need: If one is hungry, he is fed. If one is diseased, he is eased. If one is in despair, he is comforted. To do otherwise is unthinkable.

Such an awareness stands in contrast to the Iotic, where if one provides for another, it is believed there is that much less in supply for the rest; to do on behalf of another costs the individual in precise quantity that which is given.

Omegan consciousness could never be externally or forcibly imposed. Rather, we find it to be the logical evolutionary direction, inevitable when universal laws of spirit and physics are understood and a species lives in harmony with those laws.

We paid dearly for adapting ourselves to notions of conflict and competition, separation and isolation, as intrinsic to the life condition. Because such beliefs were at odds with laws of the universe, their primary manifestations were fear, self-protection, and attack, resulting in unprecedented levels of stress and disease. Our individual lifespans became greatly attenuated. Because our social constructs were predicated on Iotic beliefs, we held significant investment in their retention, and any suggestion that we reexamine our beliefs was viewed with alarm.

Yet evidence of the chaotic, self-destructive nature of our civilization was apparent even to us. We have consistently observed among Iotic-phase species a range of habitual, quasi-suicidal behaviors. Members ingest toxic, numbing substances, often convincing themselves that their very survival depends on continued use. As we ourselves passed through this phase, physical and mental disorders reached epidemic levels. We faced obliteration of all life forms, corruption and eventual loss of our planetary milieu. Brought face to face with the effects of our behavior, we looked outward to fix blame, retreated in anger and disbelief, or resorted to further chemically induced states of amnesia for solace, or to alleviate the pain caused by Iotic behavior.

Here, in brief, is a part of our own species' anguished history. But the universe is Omegan, inclusive and forgiving, and so we were assisted to reach beyond the Iotic. We come to you now with a message of hope. If members of your species were in fact separate and isolated, there would be no communication, no cooperation, no bonds of common purpose uniting you. Your species would now be at or near extinction for lack of viability. That this has not occurred underscores that humans are insepa-rably part of the vast, interconnected Omegan whole. You have merely forgotten your natural Omegan unity, an awareness we know to be embedded in the very genes of your biospinmap.

Twentieth-century humans are at the threshold of a stunning awakening. We observe that the absolute means of realizing this transformation are close at hand, inherently within each of you. You are an astonishingly wondrous species with an unlimited capacity for love, and the universe stands ready to assist you in your return. We elaborate in subsequent transmissions.
Transmission One Ω

Kate lay the last page down on the table and glanced at the others. Most were still reading. Apart from pages turning and a lot of breathing and sighing, the room was still.

"Oh, my," Tim said finally.

"Indeed," Margo murmured.

Grace and Milt nodded. "What's a biospinmap?" Grace asked.

Tim grinned at her. "The double helix structure of our DNA."

Graced nodded. "Ah. Do you suppose we'll pay attention—to their message?"

No one answered. "When do we go public with it?" Tim wondered.

"Not yet," Milt said, "If it goes out now, they'll shut us down before we can receive and translate the entire text. They speak of subsequent transmissions."

Kate considered how long they might actually have before Jeremy Sinclair found them and closed down their lab. She sensed there was little time left.

Over the next five days, they received and translated five additional transmissions. Each day the looming sense of Jeremy Sinclair grew. *He's coming.* She knew it, felt it. She began storing printed copies of the transmissions in her duffle bag which she kept packed and stashed by the back door of the Arnold cottage. She copied the text of each transmission onto her laptop computer and stored the untranslated binary data as well. Tim's translation programs and Margo's dictionary were also on the computer. Three times that week she revved the Pinto's weary engine, allowing it to idle for several minutes to be certain it could run if it had to. There was no escaping the mounting sense of foreboding. It became a tangible thing, more real at times than her physical surroundings.

When she returned to the Arnold place each evening, she concealed the laptop in the Pinto. She continued to leave the car covered beneath the canvas tarp but she now left the keys in the ignition, ready. What began early in the week as a rather vague escape plan took on increasing form and force as the days passed. He was coming.

Ω *Transmission Two:*

We explore your species' inherent ability to transform itself.

The notion of the conquest of space and of moving complex molecular structures across vast distances, is a concept typical of advanced Iotic civilizations. Space conquest is without purpose. For Omegans, there is no relevance in transporting species members through or between galaxies. Omegans are already in possession of the means for knowing all there is to know in the universe.

Thought is the means by which all matter exchanges conscious understanding. Thought transmits instantaneously and is universal. At the quantum level, thought elements cohere. At the superquantum level, coherent thought coalesces into thought-constructs. Those in accord with Omegan principles of consciousness can comprehend all, merely by listening, by attuning themselves to an instinct elemental in all four-base chemical life forms. It is cosmic synergy, the Omegan mind.

Omegans have developed their inborn ability to quiet Iotic brain activity and heed what you variously refer to as intuition, extrasensory perception or inner voice. During our Iotic phase, we typically associated such awareness with the supernatural. We equated the supernatural with the unnatural, magical, or mythical, and in doing so, abdicated to religious bureaucracies responsibility for our spiritual connectedness. We thereby relegated knowing, our cosmically instinctual inheritance, to the realm of the miraculous, superhuman, and inaccessible. We ceased to believe ourselves capable of knowing that which was within and around us.

During our awakening, we found that the quieter the individual Iotic thought, the more readily one might comprehend all that need be known. What might you learn by traversing the light years that could not be known instantly by quieting your unlimited mind?

All matter resonates. Do you require knowledge of the chemical construct of a distant star? Quiet your mind and you can know it, or you can know how to know it. The capacity of Omegan mind is as immense as the universe itself. By virtue of its holographic construct, the universal entirety is contained within its every part. You may accept that your intellect is vast, yet not entirely grasp that you are meant to use it, all of it. To know the chemical construct of a distant star, quiet your mind. To fathom the planets, hear the music of the spheres, absorb the why of a black hole or the how of a quasar, quiet your mind. The universe is not beyond your understanding because you are of it; you are like it; you are it. We elaborate in subsequent transmissions. Transmission Two Ω

Conversation at the lakeside cottage following the reading of the second transmission could only be described as muted. After the first transmission, Kate had found herself feeling slightly miffed with its senders. Now, however, she'd moved beyond irritation to a sense of wonder. If the universe itself was limitless, so were all parts of it; so was the human mind. Applied to her own life, certain truths were obvious. She'd spent a lifetime constructing walls and imagining that her safety lay in their careful maintenance. Perhaps everyone did this. Yet every moment of desolation she'd ever experienced had in some way been bound up with a feeling of separation. It sometimes became a siege mentality. How one actually moved from such a realization to the tearing down of those walls was another matter. The second transmission suggested the answer might lay in Thought, in the quiet mind. She wished Jack were beside her; but then perhaps on some level he was.

Margo said, "It's extraordinary, I think."

"We're being told to ask a great deal more of ourselves," Milt said. "I wish Albert were on hand."

"Einstein?" Tim said.

Milt nodded.

"I think he knew all this."

"What are *four-base chemical life forms*?" Grace asked.

"The phrase refers to the chemical base pairs forming the double helix structure of DNA—Adenine/thymine and guanine/cytosine—the basic alphabet of all living things."

Back at the Arnold place that evening, Kate attempted to silence her mind. It occurred to her that the transmissions might suggest an explanation for her sense over the past months of having been guided. Her awareness of the odd premonitions had become more finely attuned as the weeks and months had passed. She knew the phenomenon was beyond her conscious control; she couldn't will it but she had grown more accustomed to it and less startled when it occurred. And she did catch herself occasionally listening for precognitive thoughts. Perhaps a "thought-construct" was actually reaching to her across space and time. Was it possible she was playing some predetermined role in all of this? Was it arrogant to even consider such a thing? There was no denying that events surrounding the transmissions had unfolded—and continued to unfold—in ways that included her. She sat quietly hoping for stillness and answers, but the only thought that came was of the overwhelming imminence of Jeremy Sinclair.

THE FOLLOWING day they assembled to read the next of Margo's translations:

Ω *Transmission Three:*
We regard the unity of matter and space-time.
A rock is Omega as much as a human is Omega. Iotic consciousness categorizes and separates in an effort to conquer; Omega perceives unity, leaving nothing external to be conquered. Iotic consciousness conceives of the small as qualitatively and quantitatively apart from the vast. Yet the entire cosmos is as an organism, and a galaxy no more nor less than a cluster of star cells.

The universe is not unknowable. The peculiarly Iotic response to perceived size is an attempt to break the whole into discrete bits. Yet in its essential construct, we have found that the universe is not different, is neither more nor less fathomable than a bacteria, a microbe, a human, or any other atomic collection.

Iotic awareness of time is as distorted as its understanding of size. Iotic-phase civilizations conceive of time as a linear progression of moments strung together, rather than as a simultaneously accessible continuum. Yet we have learned that a millisecond is not essentially different than a light year, nor has the distinction any relevance except when moving atomic collections from place-time to place-time.

After reading this paragraph, Kate glanced over at Milt, gauging his expression and betting he was again wishing Albert were on hand.

When Thought, which is instantaneous and universal, is relied upon, so that the movement of atomic collections is recognized as without purpose, the constraints of space-time vanish altogether. What then is the purpose of the space-time dimension? Because Iotics believe in it, it exists as a context in which to awaken. So long as a species conceives of the universe as a thing to be divided, mastered, and conquered, that species exists within the constraints of space-time. But the moment matters of the universe are understood to be united and not in need of mastery, either by categorization or other means, the usefulness of space-time disappears and ceases to impose its limits.

Large numbers of Earth humans stand at the edge of this awareness.

You have various cultural myths to do with creation and eating of fruit from the tree of knowledge. They may illustrate to you that, having once enfolded the truth, you fled from it in fear. The shame many of you may bear, the shame that may form the basis for self-destructiveness, arises from the deep but hidden sense you have that you once knew all and discarded it. The hope we bring you now is that you have lost nothing; the truth was never yours to discard. You cannot lose that which is intrinsically and inseparably within you.

Our own Iotic civilization had long held to a belief system that was both backwards and illogical. We believed that worth was established by scarcity, that that which was abundant was without value. The air we breathed, the water we drank, the food we ate, all had been supplied to us in abundance. Yet we decimated these resources at an alarming rate. We polluted and corrupted our planet, having undervalued its resources by virtue of their plenitude. Does not your own species value the scarce diamond more than the air, the waters, the forests, and the soils that sustain life? Above even your fellow species members? But here is the ultimate abundant treasure that is discarded: universal knowledge. That it is universal could only devalue its worth to those who believe abundance the equivalent of worthlessness.

We urge you to reexamine your belief systems. In our next transmission, we will consider the power of Thought.
Transmission Three Ω

Kate read this transmission over a second and then a third time late on the night of September third. By now she'd progressed to awe and astonished acceptance of the validity of what was coming through. She also understood her earlier anger. Here were truths, many of them painful, thrust unceremoniously in her face. If humans were meant to be masters they were taking their time getting on with it. Why the delay in living up to species' potential? Laziness? Mulish intractability? It reminded her of a child caught in the *No*-phase—the "terrible twos." A part of her wouldn't have minded sinking into a long nap: *Wake me when it's over.* She felt bombarded.

Ω Transmission Four:
The creativity of the Omegan mind, at both the quantum and superquantum levels, is entirely causative.

You cannot not create. The mind is capable of receiving and processing millions of simultaneous thought-constructs, yet you block the vast majority of these. Iotic selectivity relates to choice, to free will exercised in the service of limit. You filter out that which you wish to enfold from that which you would exclude. Be aware that your every choice bears fruit. You cannot not create, and each choice amounts to a creation. The issue is not whether to create, but whether to do so mindlessly or mindfully. Every choice made and every thought beheld modifies the universe. We emphasize this not to immobilize you from choosing, but only to remind you of the power of your own free will. Those who erroneously believe themselves powerless tend to disunite. They cannot but manifest the power inherent to four-base life, yet they do so mindlessly and thus irresponsibly.

Here is an essential issue: With each choice, you affirm either Omegan love or Iotic fear, cohesion or disunity. All thought relates to one or the other, derives from the mindstate of the one choosing, and is manifest and enhanced. You even choose when choosing not to choose.

All matter, all forms of the physical universe, have these dual tendencies—to cohere and to repel. No valuative judgment attends either, but choices made regarding the physical world cause one or the other to occur. Such dualities are essential to cyclical processes of which you are an inseparable part. For example, in the choice of foods you eat, you select the substance your body utilizes as fuel. Digestion both disintegrates and absorbs, and by such process, the material universe is altered.

Yet while you may readily accept this as true, you may be somewhat less aware of the fact that your every thought is equally at cause and is tangibly manifest. Thought translates into matter at both quantum and superquantum levels. That to which attention is given is manifest. Attend fear, and fear is manifest and increased. Attend love, and love is manifest and increased.

Thought exists both within and beyond the realm of space-time. Those among you who experience prescience and retro-cognitive thought know this to be so. Every thought ever held resides in a vast sea of life-consciousness. Every four-base life mind, as it entertains Thought, selects out of that vastness that to which attention is given.

Late in our own Iotic civilization's evolution, we attempted to sever our natural bonds with this sea of life-consciousness. The most marked expression of this effort was the attempt many of us made to isolate ourselves. We wished to hide. This nonsensical effort to remove ourselves from our universe, to shield our minds from Omegan mind, arose from a sense of shame. To the extent that we withheld our thought from Omegan unity, we detracted from the collective coherence of creative thought. To amend this, it was first necessary that we set aside our shame. We began to develop appreciation for ourselves, and from this thought-construct, appreciation was extended outward to each other. Once healed, the notion of hiding was recognized as an absurdity.

As to the undoing of shame, we had developed a device by which we sought to externalize and thus eradicate that which we disliked most about ourselves. You also have such a device, which you call projection, and it is an exercise in Iotic futility. We focused in our external environment on the very things we disliked about ourselves, believing that thereby we had somehow abolished them in ourselves. We considered this possible because we believed that which we gave away, we lost. In fact, whatever is given is reinforced and retained. One cannot remove one's self from one's environment. We are all inseparable aspects in and of the universe. What is done to one, is done to all. What you perceive as external is always within you. If you find yourself disliking some aspect of your world, you would do well to look within.

With time, we learned vigilance over our Thoughts and began choosing them with consciousness and care. Gradually, fear and shame gave way to acceptance, love and appreciation. Loving thought-constructs were manifest and increased. We could then begin to treat the cosmos as we treated ourselves, with honor. Your species cannot <u>not</u> create. We urge you to be mindful creators. In the next transmission, we explore the physics of space-time universes.

Transmission Four Ω

Ω

48

"That's got to be it, Joel. They bought their satellite dish from Avatar Electronics in Traverse City. Okay. Got it. No address? Okay. Tell your team, 'Good job.'"

Jeremy Sinclair hung up the phone with an expression approximating triumph. Now they would start to close in, draw the net tighter. Traverse City.

He consulted the large map of Michigan he'd ordered mounted on the wall behind the desk in their operation control room. In Traverse City, the scientists had paid $8,000 in cash for the satellite dish kit and controller. According to the salesman at Avatar Electronics, they'd hauled the equipment away in a pickup truck.

Trace the truck. What else? Check with the bios group. Sinclair made notes.

Why Traverse City? Why not a larger city—Detroit for example? Reason suggested they must be holed up somewhere in the north. They'd found the dish in Traverse City but, unable to obtain complex computer equipment outside a large city, had been forced to travel to Detroit. Maybe.

He scribbled notes. That dish shouldn't be hard to spot from the air. Hell, a five-meter dish? A huge mother. What? Sixteen feet in diameter? Obviously it was time for the President's goddamned pink helicopters.

He reached for the phone and barked instructions to his secretary. "And send Griffith and the team leaders in here."

* * *

Ω Transmission Five:

We present general observations regarding the nature of the space-time multiverse, which is structured in quadrants of reciprocal universes or dyads.

Separate Iotic entities conceive only of the fractional; the Omegan whole is comprehensive. This is another way of saying that the entirety vastly exceeds the sum of its disunited parts. But more, it suggests that the Omegan whole is contained within every part.

As to the shape and form of the physical universe, there are many constructs, and two we invite you to consider - the quantum or triangular, and the superquantum or panogramatic. The triangle is the enclosed shape structured by the fewest possible intersecting lines; spatially and mathematically, it is expressed pyramidically. The panogram is the enclosed shape formed by the largest possible number of connecting lines, mathematically expressed as sigma lateral eight, the dimension of a bounded infinity. The outer shape of the universe of which you are aware, the spatial-temporal universe, is the panogram.

As stated, universes exist in dyads or reciprocals. Thus, for example, the reciprocal universe of the panogramatic is a refracted mirror image of your own panogramatic universe. You may conceive of these alternate universes as joined at the intersection created by an 'X' and residing in opposing quadrants therein. Two additional and reciprocal universes adjoin this fulcrum and reside in the remaining two quadrants. These are quantum or pyramidic. One is the microcosmic universe, which you may conceptualize as a universe of the infinitely small. The other is its reciprocal, the microcosmic universe of inverse pyramidic refraction.

These four universes are joined at the central fulcrum of the 'X' by Omega, a point consisting essentially of source light. The panogramatic or macrocosmic universe has thus far been explained by your laws of Einsteinian physics. The properties of *the triangular or microcosmic universe and its reciprocal are partially addressed by your known laws of quantum physics. Within the quantum, the essentially holographic nature of the universe is readily apparent, yet even there, theory itself transmutes the universe by the very effect of its origin in Thought.*

You might conceive of interstitial expanses of spatial universes as akin to quilted surfaces. The dimpled punctures in surface planes are created by and occur at the loci of structures considered black holes. It is at these fulcrums that the dyadic inversions or reciprocal universes meet and refract.

Reciprocal spatial universes exist as mirror images of one another, and time within them flows inversely.

We have said that the fulcrum is Omega, or source light. The fulcrum is the point through which Thought, traveling instantaneously, translates between universes. Thought is akin to light. One need not, indeed could not, move atomic collections between universes. Instead, communication is via Thought.

Your scientists seek a unified theory, a set of physical laws encompassing both the Einsteinian laws of the macrocosmic, and the quantum physics of the microcosmic. That Unified Theory is to be found in Thought.

In addition to these four spatial-temporal universes, there exist adjacent fulcrums with quadrants containing universes whose dimensions and properties are non-spatial-temporal. These are linguistically inexplicable to those whose consciousness resides in the panogram; your language lacks tools for an expression of their characteristics. If you would conceive of them, quiet your mind. In the next transmission we will discuss communication beyond the limits of space-time.

Transmission Five Ω

Receipt and translation of the fifth transmission occasioned a ranging conversation among the scientists. Kate listened as they considered the notion of "dyadic" or "reciprocal" universes. The discussion left her spellbound.

"Under this construct should we expect the Big Bang as the prespatial event?" Tim looked at Milt.

"What if the Big Bang is a single event, on either side of which exist these opposing quadrants? The transmission calls it 'Source Light.' We might conceive of it as the seminal moment, but outside our linear experience of space-time, perhaps that event occurs simultaneously with every other."

"How in the world is that possible?" Kate asked.

"It isn't, not *in* the world. From our vantage point within a linear-time universe, the Big Bang might only appear as the terminus of an expanding/contracting universe."

"One that is conceptually like Einstein's theorized universe of a bounded infinity."

"But perhaps we should conceive of it more as a hologram where everything is continually undergoing. The Big Bang would then be an omnipresent flashpoint."

"The source light necessary to the illumination of the hologram," Tim said.

"Precisely."

"Here's the way I make it," Sinclair said. His team leaders had assembled around the conference table in the control room for the second time in as many days. "Three scientists plus Grace Rensler holed up, I'm pretty sure, somewhere in the vicinity of Traverse City." He jabbed a finger at the Michigan map. "They bought a satellite dish in early July, a kit. The odds are they've got it deployed by now. Should be a lead pipe cinch to spot from the air."

Sinclair turned to Agent James Griffith, head of the biographical research team. "Grif, have you found anything linking these folks to Michigan?"

The agent nodded. "Tim Thurmond's parents—born and raised in Michigan, attended the University of Michigan. So far,

Thurmond's family is the only one of the group with any ties to the state."

"What about northern Michigan?"

Griffith sifted through pages of notes. "Family summer home, mother's side—that would be the Huddleston family—on Mullett Lake, address Indian River."

Sinclair held up a hand to the agent while he pressed a red pushpin into the Michigan map. "Right here. Go on."

"Father's side—the Thurmond side—family summer home at Crystal Lake, address Frankfort. Grandparents, Huddleston side, Saginaw—"

"Wait. Okay, here."

"Grandparents, Thurmond side, from Grand Rapids. All grandparents now deceased. Parents survived by two sons and one daughter. That's about it," he said, looking up. "We interviewed all of Thurmond's siblings weeks ago and came up empty. The brother resides in Seattle, one sister in Memphis, another in Phoenix."

Sinclair squinted at the map. "Crystal Lake. Well, will you look at that! Crystal Lake is only thirty miles from Traverse City. Address Frankfort?"

Griffith nodded.

"Right here. I'd say it's time to pay a visit to the Thurmond homestead at Crystal Lake. Yes indeed. And we might not need those pink helicopters after all."

"The what?"

"Never mind. Let's plan it. It's ten-thirty. Boynton, Drexler, Seagler, we fly out of Andrews at one this afternoon. By then I'll want your detailed plans for going in, and teams and equipment ready. You'll want Frankfort to fax surveyor's maps detailing the Thurmond property and surrounding areas. Anything else? Questions?"

They exchanged looks.

"Good. Meet back here at noon. Grif, you'll be going, too. Distribute copies of your notes. Get to it."

* * *

"Here's the next one," Margo said, handing Kate, Milt, Grace and Tim each a printed copy of the sixth transcript. "What can I say?" Her tone held the sense of inadequacy they were all feeling by the end of that remarkable week. "It's quite incredible."

It was the morning of September fifth.

The room became silent as everyone read the next ETI message.

Ω *Transmission Six:*
We summarize observations and reveal the manner in which these transmissions are sent.

As you reach toward Omegan consciousness, Iotic forces may seek to draw you back from the awakening. You may find you long for sleep and the ingestion of numbing substances. You may feel inclined to busy yourselves with distraction and, discouraged at this habitually amnestic behavior, may retreat from the awakening. It is essential at this stage that you persist, despite these distractions, in your effort. Do not permit yourselves to become discouraged. There is no greater challenge nor safer path for you to follow, and nothing can ultimately prevent your success. As previously stated, you hold the inevitability of Omegan consciousness in your biospinmap. You may delay, but you cannot alter your natural longing for a return to instinctive unity. It is your journey home.

So long as Iotic thought prevails over Omegan, individuals among you awaken separately. However, you may look forward to the achievement of a collective, critical mass thought-construct, wherein the cohesiveness of Omegan thought produced by many minds combines to form impetus sufficient to launch the species into a broader phase of awakening.

Iotic forces may amass in opposition, but if you have learned well, you will not attempt to conquer the Iotic fear. You will unify with Omegan love. Love is the only means by which you may step across the line, the only bridge from the Iotic to the Omegan, the uniting force of the universe. Do not be concerned that your power might become too vast, for it is in the nature of the universe that true power is only commensurate with love.

Care for and regard every life form with appreciation. Perform each task, no matter how seemingly insignificant, with devotion and assurance of its worth. Do not disregard or diminish that which lies before you. To do so is to demean yourself and your creations. Nothing appears to you by accident. You are too powerful a creator to generate accident. Practice listening. Practice quieting your mind. Choose your thoughts consciously. Resist negative judgments against your fellows.

We are certain you can succeed, and our certainty is emphasized by what we share with you now: that we come to you from future-time. Our messages, the source of which you are eager to identify, are transmitted via a cathyon beam technology. As you grasp the full implications of that statement, you will also recognize that your success must be assured. Omega is your inevitable journey home. In the next transmission, we will discuss our own position in space-time. Transmission Six Ω

"Have you read the last paragraph?" Milt interrupted Tim's concentration.

"Yeah. As Margo says, incredible stuff. Tune in tomorrow—"

"About the cathyon beam? You read that?"

"Yeah."

"That's the only translation you could come up with, Margo? *Cathyon*?"

She looked at the line to which Milt was pointing. "It's not in my dictionary. Tim's program produced twelve anagrams, none of which were in our dictionary. I selected *cathyon*."

"Let me see the list," Milt said, and Margo handed it to him. "Achyton, cathyon, chanoty, chatony, chyonat, hatoncy, nachyot, nochyat, tachyon... That's it, Margo. *Tachyon*, not *cathyon*. My God! Do you know what this means? It means they're transmitting outside the constraints of the speed of light!"

The group stared at Milton Rensler.

"They're circumventing time. Just as it stated, this is a signal transmitted in the future!" His face filled with awe. "Which explains why we haven't been able to locate the inbound signal. It's moving faster than the speed of light. Incredible. Carried on a tachyon particle beam."

"Of course!" Tim said. "There'd be no way to pick up a tachyon beam signal coming into that transmitter. Amazing. I wonder how they managed to de-accelerate it?"

"At the transmitter site, maybe using some sort of gravitron field adjoining the transmitter." Milt shook his head.

"That would explain why the signal comes in backwards, why we have to invert the data stream," Tim said.

"Right! The transmitter receives the signal inverted. It has to; it's traveling faster than the speed of light, so it ends before it starts." Milt's face was lit with an infectious grin. "How the hell did they get the transmitter here? Can they translate complex matter over their tachyon beam? Tunnel it in somehow, pop it into our slower-than-light universe?"

Tim shook his head. "And if they can beam a transmitter here, why not just drop a message intact, instead?"

Milt held up pages of text. "They have, and maybe in the only way that would really get our attention. And they might avoid the transmitter problem altogether by utilizing an object already positioned."

"Such as?"

"A celestial body. A derelict space probe or—"

"A moon?"

"Pluto's Charon," Kate said quietly.

"A moon, or a cratered asteroid might make a good transmitter."

"Something with a stable orientation, predictable orbit. They'd have to calibrate their amplitude modulator to accommodate the asteroid's metallurgical construct. It might work."

Margo said, "They seem to suggest they'll reveal their identity in the next transmission." The matter of these ET's identity did remain the tantalizing unanswered question.

"Who might Charon be ferrying?" Rensler murmured. His face again held an enigmatic look, an expression of amusement and comprehension. Finally he said, "Tim, prepare Kate's copy."

Tim made the diskette and handed it to her. Then he looked over at his boss and grinned. "A tachyon transmitter."

At that moment, Kate felt what could only be described as an unsettling lurch followed by another intense desire to sleep. She'd had two such spells that week but hadn't mentioned them to the others. Was it only that her mind felt too small? No. *He was coming.* That was it. Jeremy Sinclair was coming. What should she do? Tell these people? What proof did she have? Should they dismantle the lab mid-signal, race off somewhere, all because she was having a premonition? And where could they go? She felt caught in a web of indecisiveness and fear, the very thing these Omegans cautioned against.

"Who do you think is sending this signal?" she heard Grace asking. "You know something you're not telling us, don't you, Milt?"

Rensler only continued to smile enigmatically.

Kate stood up abruptly. "I'll be back in a few hours, sometime after dinner." She needed to think. With her laptop and Tim's diskette in hand, she followed the lakefront path to the Arnold place, but her mind was elsewhere, far from the lapping water and the sharply angled afternoon sun.

Ω

49

WALKIE-TALKIE IN HAND, Agent Joel Seagler turned to Jeremy Sinclair. "All teams in place, sir."

Seagler and Sinclair, along with Agent Griffith, stood leaning against the front grill of a silver minivan containing communications equipment and a miscellany of supplies and weapons. The van had been parked to block passage down the narrow gravel road. Just beyond their position was a tennis court belonging to the now-deserted Crystalaire Camp for Girls. A quarter-mile past that stood the Thurmond cottage. It was dusk.

Seagler spoke softly into the walkie-talkie. "Hold your positions." He nodded to Sinclair. "Ready on your word."

Sinclair knew many would accuse him of micro-managing this operation but it was one exercise he could not delegate. Too much was at stake, not the least of which were his livelihood, his retirement, his reputation, his entire future. With any luck they'd apprehend Lipton with the rest. Gregg and Geller seemed to place less emphasis on her capture. In Sinclair's mind, her crimes were no less than treasonous.

The Sullivan surveillance had been a notable failure. Sullivan had been circumspect, avoiding suspicious contacts, making use of pay phones and carrying on with a normal life and case load. No leads had emerged. They'd only recently arranged the phone taps in the D.A.'s office, so if Sullivan had contacted Lipton immediately following his return to San Francisco, the NSA could not have known of it. Now, however, they could scrutinize D.A. office phone records and transcripts from bugs recently installed and pay special attention to calls to Michigan. After today, though, that effort would probably be moot.

"All right," Sinclair said. "No one's to be harmed unless it's the only way to prevent their escape. There's computer equipment on site; it must not be damaged. If force is needed stun guns should be sufficient. If any one of these people is injured without good reason, we can all start reading want ads for bank security jobs." Sinclair was still smarting from the President's catastrophic reaction to Walter Jacobsen's death.

Seagler spoke again into his walkie-talkie, repeating the essence of Sinclair's words. They'd gone over it but a reminder couldn't hurt.

"Let's do it!" Sinclair said.

There were three teams of agents, a total of fifteen men, deployed to encircle the Thurmond place. Two teams converged from the woods behind the house. The third team approached from the front, concealing their movements amid the trees lining the roadway. Sinclair and a team of four command agents maintained the obstruction across the private drive to prevent unauthorized persons or vehicles from venturing down.

As the operation was set in motion, it quickly became almost anticlimactic, over within minutes. Seagler relayed the walkie-talkie message to Sinclair: "All secure, sir."

"Who'd we get?"

"The three scientists plus Grace Rensler."

"Not Lipton?"

"No, sir."

"Damn. Okay. Joel, you stay here with the van and the others. Absolutely no one's allowed down this road."

"Yes, sir."

"I'm going in. Grif, you're with me." When Jeremy Sinclair reached the cottage, he found the subdued foursome handcuffed and seated in the living room. Jakes reported that none of them had offered any resistance.

"Where's Kate Lipton?" Sinclair asked tersely, looking from face to face.

"She's in the area, isn't she?" No one spoke. "Isn't she?" Sinclair barked. Dead silence.

"Jakes, examine everything. Look for any trace of Lipton— purse, notes, anything."

Milton Rensler held up his cuffed hands. "Is this really necessary? None of us has any intention of escaping."

"Now why would I find that difficult to accept? Sorry, Doctor. When did you last see Kate Lipton?"

Rensler shrugged.

"Grif, organize disconnection of the computer equipment. Get it loaded into the vans, but do it carefully, understood?"

"Yes sir."

"Boynton, Drexler, have your teams scour the area. Find Lipton."

Tim spoke up quietly. "It would be unwise to disconnect the computers. We're receiving an important signal. It should finish in a few hours, but if you disconnect now, information will be lost. It's the extraterrestrial signal."

The news caught Sinclair by surprise. "Damn. Okay, Grif, post a guard on the computer equipment. How long will this signal last?"

"Probably until sometime this evening," Tim said. "But it might start up again in the morning."

"What time?"

"Possibly as early as eight-thirty."

What now? If they hauled these people away, they might lose vital data; if they kept everyone here, they risked attracting attention. "Who's in residence along this road?"

"Everyone's left for the season. These are all summer homes except for the Girls' Camp, which is closed. We're the only ones here."

"You're sure the signal will start up in the morning?"

"It has for the past six mornings, but we can't predict the exact time nor how long it'll continue. It has started each day a little later than the day before and ends eight hours later."

Sinclair exhaled, folded his arms, drawing into himself. He wandered into the scientists' office, glanced around at the impressive array of equipment. One computer monitor displayed a steadily flowing stream of data. He shook his head.

He returned to where the scientists sat and spoke to Agent Jakes. "We'll secure the area for the night. If the signal continues in the morning, we'll move the operation tomorrow night after it's ended." His glance fell on the scientists and Grace Rensler. "Meanwhile, the four of you—well, I guess we can't keep you cuffed. But there are a few dozen agents surrounding this place. Let me make it as plain as I can: If any of you attempts an escape, my people have orders to shoot. Clear?"

His captives nodded somberly.

Sinclair reached for the walkie-talkie and spoke with Seagler at the command van. "Post two guards on the road. Bring the van down here. Bring the communications gear into the house. We're staying the night. We'll initiate road blocks on every highway leading out of the area. Lipton's still at large."

KATE LOADED the sixth transmission onto her computer, stored the printout of the text in her duffle bag with the others, and returned the computer to the trunk of the Pinto.

Now for dinner. She wasn't really hungry; it was just something to do. The information about the tachyon particle beam was fascinating. All that about fulcrums, multiple universes and dyads was beyond her; her mind could scarcely contemplate the vastness of a single universe, let alone the several implied in the last transmissions. Then there was the fact that the signal had been sent from the future. Take that in, she thought with an awed sense of inadequacy.

What was it Dr. Rensler had been considering? He'd been grinning—practically ear to ear. Had he deduced the source of the messages? Today's translation had hinted at the senders' identity. What was it they promised to reveal in the next transmissions? Their own "position in space-time?" She ought to return to the cottage to discuss it with Rensler. Soon, Margo would start the translation of today's signal. Grace would be preparing dinner.

She made a sandwich for herself, gobbled it down, and grabbed an apple to take along. As she started out the door, she thought of a sweater. It was dusk, chilly outside. Fall was beginning to settle over the lake and foliage was tinged with fiery-orange premonitions of the new season. She grabbed a sweater, locked the house and strolled along the shoulder of Lake Shore Drive toward the cottage.

Then she saw the van. It was parked some fifty yards ahead, obstructing the entrance to the private drive. Three figures were visible nearby. She squinted through the darkness. Two people were moving now, taking up positions on opposite sides of the road. The third climbed into the van and as he did so, the interior light flickered on momentarily. She heard the rumble of an engine starting and watched as the van executed a bouncing turn and zoomed off, down the pitted road toward the Thurmond cottage.

Her heartbeat lodged like a knot in her throat. Who were these people? But she knew. It could only be Sinclair and his agents. Her eyes strained to see. The van's tail lights had disappeared but she was quite certain at least two men had been left behind at the entrance to the road.

She had to get away.

She flew into action, raced back to the Arnold place, unlocked the door, dashed through the kitchen and into the bedroom, and grabbed her duffle bag. There were a few things strewn about—toiletries, a pair of shoes, a wind breaker. She gathered them and stuffed them into the bag. What else? Her eye scanned the room.

In the living room she grabbed her purse, opened her wallet and extracted several bills—the second month's rent—and placed them on the coffee table. Then she locked windows and doors, slid the key under the mat by the back door and dashed to her car. She yanked off the canvas tarp, tossed her bag into the back and climbed into the driver's seat with a prayer: "Please start." She turned the key and pressed the accelerator. The engine sputtered and caught and started.

"Thank God." She looked at her watch. Seven-fifteen. How long since she'd left Tim's cottage? An hour and twenty minutes perhaps. She should figure at minimum Sinclair had an hour's headstart—sufficient time to have established roadblocks. But he might not know of the car ferry. It was a long shot but she had to take it. If she hurried, she might still catch the last ferry of the day.

She drove to Frankfort, careful to keep to within the speed limit, not wanting to attract attention. She descended the hill warily, alert for roadblocks. At the turnoff to the harbor she passed the gas station and looked in; it was closed for the night. She'd have to gas up after the crossing. What she could see of Frankfort town seemed unnaturally hushed. She turned left and headed slowly down the road in the direction of the ferry dock. She was in luck; the eight o'clock ferry was at the dock with several cars in line to board. She drew to a halt behind a Dodge pickup. She opened the glove compartment and found the ferry schedule, double-checking her memory of its daily routine. This one was due to depart in thirty minutes. It would cross Lake Michigan and deposit its passengers in Manitowoc, Wisconsin. She glanced at her watch, wishing the boat would leave early, wishing time could suddenly collapse on itself.

The wait was maddening. She sat in the Pinto with the engine idling, afraid to shut it off for fear it might not start. She continually glanced in her rear-view mirror. Ten excruciating minutes passed, time in suspension during which she tumbled through a roller coaster of emotions. She might actually escape; she might not. What would they do to her if they caught her? What would they do with the Renslers, with Tim and Margo? The thought brought an onrush of guilt. She should have warned them. She'd had such a strong sense that Sinclair was closing in, yet she'd said nothing. But what could they have done? Rensler wouldn't have been willing to leave, not in the midst of receiving the transmissions. Neither would Tim. And if she'd told them, it would have taken several days to dismantle, move, and reassemble the equipment, even assuming they knew of a safe place to go. Would they have been willing to do all that based solely on her premonition? It would have been too late anyway. Sinclair had already been zeroing in.

A car drew to a stop inches from her rear bumper and Kate held her breath. The headlights were extinguished. She rolled down her window to listen. The driver shut off his engine. No one got out.

At seven-fifty they began allowing cars to board. When her turn came, she rolled the Pinto up the steel ramp and onto the ferry's lower deck. A crewman directed the flow, distributing the weight. He waved her to the starboard side where she nudged into a tight parking spot, shut off her engine and climbed out.

She glanced around and spotted a stairway. It led to the upper deck and signs directed the way to the ticket window. Her footsteps echoed metallically. She emerged onto a corridor with starboard windows that looked out on the night and the darkened harbor. Shore lights were receding; they were underway.

She found the ticket office and joined the short line at the window, glancing ahead at the ticket seller. She inched forward, looked ahead. And suddenly for the briefest moment she believed she might faint dead away. Her knees became rubber and she could scarcely breathe. For directly behind the ticket seller's head, painted in stark black letters against the pale yellow of the ship's bulkhead, was the vessel's single-word name: *Charon*.

The ticket-seller was speaking to her. "The crossing takes ten hours. You want a cabin with sleeping accommodations or seating in the main passenger salon?"

"What? Oh, a cabin please."

She paid and was handed a receipt and cabin key. Shaken, she hurried away and wandered back downstairs to retrieve her duffle bag. Her cabin—more a cubbyhole really—was on the port side of the ship near the stern. She closed and locked the door and collapsed onto the narrow bunk. It would be a ten-hour crossing at ten miles an hour. One hundred miles across the lake to Manitowoc, Wisconsin. They'd arrive at six AM. Would Sinclair's people be waiting for her on the other side? She set her travel alarm for five AM, curled up beneath the blanket and fell asleep.

Ω

50

SINCLAIR'S agents completed their search of each room in the Thurmond cottage. They examined the scientists' belongings, clothing, toiletries, food. No sign of Kate Lipton. Fingerprints would no doubt reveal her having been there but that analysis would take time. Sinclair didn't have time. He *must* assume she was in the area and deploy his manpower accordingly.

Search parties returned and reported no sign of Lipton.

"She's been here," Sinclair said firmly. "She might show up any minute. Joel, our people at the entrance to the road are well-concealed?"

"Absolutely."

"Good. We'll work them in four-hour shifts. Rotate in Kelly and Driscoll at midnight."

"Right, sir."

Roadblocks had been set up on all highways leading out of the area. If Lipton headed north toward Traverse City or south to Cadillac, she'd be stopped. What else? What was he missing? What if she stayed in town? At a hotel? First thing in the morning he'd dispatch teams for a door-to-door search. It was a small town; he'd find her.

He wandered into the scientists' office to consult a map of the area. He'd taken over a table with his own gear, moving aside books, papers, and mugs of cold coffee.

He spread the map out, and his elbow nudged a ceramic coffee mug, nearly toppling it to the floor. He looked down into the cup. Coffee with cream. Disgusting. There were a succession of scummy brown rings lining the inside of the cup. What did that remind him of? Which of these people drank coffee with cream? His own people were drinking from styrofoam. A memory of another decade filled his mind—Kate Lipton in the computer room, himself standing behind her, looking down into a stagnant, forgotten cup of cold coffee with cream, partially evaporated, a residue of beige rings lining the cup. It had spilled when she grabbed for the pencil. She'd stabbed the back of his hand. A small fragment of graphite was still imbedded there, still visible beneath the pale skin of his right hand. Unconsciously he rubbed at the spot.

The transmission ended at seven. Grace Rensler had prepared dinner for the scientists and they filed slowly into the kitchen to eat.

As Milton Rensler entered the small kitchen, he gave his wife a squeeze. "It'll be all right, honey. I know they're not going to hurt us."

Sinclair moved to stand in the entrance to the kitchen, leaning against the door jamb to watch as the group sat down. They ate in silence.

Tim Thurmond pushed bites of food around on his plate, listlessly corralling peas against his pork chop, jabbing them angrily with his fork. When the meal was over, Rensler's wife automatically poured coffee. Sinclair observed very carefully as they all accepted cups of coffee. None of them doctored it with cream.

AT FIVE AM, Kate's alarm sounded. She'd slept in fits and starts, awakened periodically by the motions and sounds of the ferry and the mental gyrations of her mind. She dressed, washed her face, brushed her hair and teeth, and felt somewhat human as she made her way down to her car. Other passengers were already in their vehicles, sitting with engines idling.

There was a soft jolt as the forward motion of the vessel ceased. She started her own engine and offered up a prayer that the old Pinto had enough left to give. The ferryman collected her ticket as she rolled down *Charon's* ramp and onto Wisconsin soil. It was early, still dark, and she looked around as she drove slowly through the outskirts of the small town. There didn't appear to be roadblocks; no one stopped her.

She came to a road sign for Highway 43 South and decided to take it. She drove carefully, watchfully. In Sheboygan she pulled off for gas and bought a Wisconsin road map. She saw that if she continued on Highway 43 along the lakeshore, she'd pass through Milwaukee, and by her calculation, reach Chicago within two hours.

AT TEN AM, Sinclair's call was put through to the President. Based on Geller's clipped responses, Sinclair thought he might not be alone.

"Sir, we've apprehended the missing scientists," Sinclair reported. "We didn't get Kate Lipton. She's been here but unfortunately she'd vanished by the time we moved in. We've got the others though, plus Grace Rensler. They've been receiving the ETI signal for the past week. It looks as though the signal's ended. They tell me it runs for about eight hours each day, but this morning it hasn't started up at all. They claim to have translated it."

"Excellent! They believe it's ended?" Geller asked.

"The signal? Yes sir." Sinclair proceeded to outline the steps taken to apprehend Kate Lipton.

"Fine," the President said. "The foursome goes to the island immediately."

"Sir, you're saying I should send the scientists and Mrs. Rensler to St. Lucia?"

"Yes. I want them incarcerated and interrogated."

"And Kate Lipton?"

"An intensified hunt. You've got everything sealed off; she won't get far."

Across the room, Agent Drexler was waving frantically. Sinclair nodded and quickly concluded the call with, "Sir, I'll keep you informed."

They hung up.

"Damn it, Drexler, that was the President of the United States. What's so damned—"

"Sir," Drexler said, holding a cellular phone in his hand. "It's Seagler calling from town. There's a regular car ferry service out of Frankfort that crosses Lake Michigan. He's concerned Lipton might have left by ferry."

"You're kidding? Where does it go? How long does it take? Give me the damned phone. Joel, you have the ferry schedule?" He fired questions and orders into the phone, listened to answers and hung up.

"There are ferries into Kewaunee and Manitowoc. Get me a goddamned map of Wisconsin!" Across the room, Tim Thurmond suppressed a smile. "Call headquarters! Dispatch agents to Kewaunee and Manitowoc and to airports in all major cities in Wisconsin—Madison, Milwaukee. Where else?"

"Sir, Chicago is just south of Milwaukee."

"O'Hare too! Crap. And pack up all this gear—carefully. We're moving out. Thurmond, lose the smirk."

Ω

51

KATE ABANDONED the rusted blue Pinto in a parking garage at Chicago's O'Hare Airport on the morning of September sixth. She paid cash for a ticket on a noon flight to San Diego, and while waiting, telephoned Jack at his office.

"Hi. We've decided to move into Apartment C," she said when she heard his voice.

"You are? Okay. Give me five."

She smiled as she hung up. He would be rummaging through his mind for which was Plan C as he dashed down the hall to another phone. They'd planned for this call with care. She waited five minutes and dialed a second number.

"Pete," he said.

"Hi, it's me again."

"Apartment C?"

"Right. The rest of the family's already moved. Sarah wonders whether you ever found that *blue book* you were looking for?"

There was a long pause while he pondered the question. Light must have dawned—she was asking about her passport.

"It's taking a while. I'm to pick it up this weekend. How soon will you move into Apartment C?"

"A week from yesterday."

"The twelfth. You couldn't wait a month?"

"No. The landlord has turned on the heat. Delay wouldn't be wise."

"Oh. Well then, tell Sarah I'll bring her booklet."

"Thank you."

"Good luck."

"You too."

They hung up. For the time being, Kate would be forced to travel on her own passport. It changed her strategy. But waiting a month created a far worse set of problems. As of now she had a head start on Sinclair but the edge couldn't be hers for long.

At four PM she arrived in San Diego. She taxied to a motel near the San Diego Airport, registered as Lisa McNulty, and killed an anxious evening in a drab room with the curtains drawn.

At four-thirty PM the next day, September seventh, Kate crossed the border from San Diego into Mexico by bus. She noted with satisfaction that Mexican Customs officials appeared completely indifferent, accepting her entry card and barely glancing at her passport. They were equally disinterested in the fifty or so forms and passports of the other bedraggled throng of bus travelers. Even Jeremy Sinclair could not have whipped this bunch into a state of readiness. It was too hot, too crowded, too noisy, and probably only the thought of a cold Dos Equis, once this busload had been dispensed with, kept any of them at their posts.

From the bus depot, she taxied to the Tijuana Airport and caught an 8:05 PM flight to Mexico City, arriving there three hours later. She checked various airlines and reserved a seat on an early morning flight for Caracas, Venezuela. She had eleven hours to kill before it departed. She was discovering how vastly inconvenient it was to travel under the passport of a fugitive. She would approach her destination with tremendous caution and by the most circuitous of routes. At one-thirty AM, she found a quiet corner of the airport and curled up with her duffle bag, computer, and purse to sleep. She was bumped and jostled throughout the night by members of her own species. Couldn't they see she was trying to sleep? At five AM she gave up and sought out the airport cafeteria. *Huevos rancheros* seemed like the thing to have.

She catnapped during the flight to Caracas. After disembarking, she endured another nail-biting round of customs, forms, passports and officialdom. She was waved through solely for the purpose of changing planes. Finally she boarded a 7:15 PM flight to Martinique and landed in Fort de France two hours later.

Now her risk of arrest was enormous. She followed arriving passengers down a featureless corridor and into the customs check-in line, keeping her head down as she walked and wishing she could somehow become invisible. How alert would French Martinique's officials be? Would Sinclair have dispatched agents to Martinique? He couldn't possibly monitor every Caribbean entry point, could he?

She worked her way forward in the line. People spoke in muted tones, disheveled and weary from traveling, as was she. When her turn came, she smiled at the official and handed over her entry card and passport. He looked at her, studied her face, matching it with her passport photo.

"You are staying in Martinique how long?" he asked in French-accented English.

"A week."

"Vacation?"

"No, business. I write travel articles."

"Ah, yes. Excellent. You will find this a beautiful island. Have a pleasant stay."

She blinked at her good fortune and hurried through the terminal. With a sigh of weariness and relief, she loaded herself and her luggage into the back seat of a taxi.

"I'd like a hotel in Fort de France," she told the driver. "I don't have a reservation."

"Anse Mitan's Hôtel Méridien is very nice."

"Anse Mitan?"

"Across the bay from Fort de France."

"Fine," she said.

JEREMY SINCLAIR strode into the Oval Office. "Mr. President, I've brought the translations." He lay his briefcase down on the President's desk, unlocked the wrist chain, dialed the attaché's combination, and raised the lid with an important flourish.

President Geller took the pages from Sinclair and walked over to the sofa, sat down and immediately began reading. Twenty minutes later he looked up. His words surprised Sinclair. "Who else has seen this nonsense?"

Nonsense? "Well, sir, the Renslers, Tim Thurmond, Margo Jacobsen, the team in St. Lucia, and probably Kate Lipton. You, me, Ralph Burch, of course. He's in St. Lucia right now with everyone else."

"Margo Jacobsen's down there?"

"Yes, Sir."

"Obviously she's learned of her husband."

"Yes. She told Michael Gregg he could go straight to hell."

"Yes, well— Is this it?" the President asked, "or will there be more? Have the transmissions continued?"

"No. We think we've got the entire message now. It might be repeated but the transmitter either disappeared again or is no longer transmitting."

Geller was silent for several more minutes, rereading the pages. "You want my opinion, this stuff is hogwash. Well, no, that's not entirely fair. Maybe dangerous is a more accurate description. Thought-constructs? Christ. Manifesting instantaneously? That *is* what it appears to suggest. Is there anything in here that could be considered technologically significant?"

"Well, I don't know, I mean—maybe the stuff about the tachyon beam. I don't know. Ralph would be the one to answer that. I just—"

"But what do *you* think? Mostly it's a lot of psuedo-mystical religious crap in my opinion."

"Well, it does have a spiritual flavor to it."

"All this about a single species, universal knowledge, Omegan consciousness. Jeez. Just what we need is another goddamned religious cult. Can you see me getting reelected if we publish this? Can you imagine what the churches'll say? The religious right? They'll roast my hide. I'll be laughed right out of office." He said this with a wave at the room that had come to be synonymous with the apex of world power. "And maybe it's just plain dangerous. What do we do if people begin believing themselves this, ah, powerful? It could result in panic, even anarchy." The President nodded at the sagacity of his own observation.

"So you want to continue to keep a lid on the project?" Sinclair asked with what Geller must have recognized was either disingenuousness or blazing stupidity.

"Damned straight I do. Now more than ever. Not one of those people in St. Lucia is to be allowed out of that compound."

"For how long?"

"Until we can come up with an acceptable alternative."

"Such as?"

"I don't know, Jeremy," Geller said irritably. "This is coming at me out of— There are considerations that surpass the needs of a few scientists. Political and economic considerations. There's a lot to evaluate. Meanwhile, they all stay put."

"Burch too?"

"No. Send Ralph back. I'll talk to him. I want to hear what his scientists make of this."

"All right."

"Let's get Doleman in here to see how he reads it," Geller said, referring to his Chief of Staff. He reached for his phone. "Send in Doleman... Cancel it... No... And the lunch with the Attorney General. Reschedule."

When Doleman appeared moments later, the President said, "Chip, sit down. There's a complicated and delicate matter I need to go over with you, and then I'll want your opinion on— well, you'll see what I mean. It's to do with that matter you were questioning me about last January. It's still on a strictly need-to-know basis. You are not to discuss it outside this room. Clear?"

"Yes, Sir."

For the next forty minutes, Geller and Sinclair briefed the Chief of Staff on the SETI Project, on Code Shepherd, the receipt of the transmissions and the status of the scientists. Doleman's face grew incredulous as he took in the information.

"So that's what was so damned secret," he said at last.

"Now read these transcripts."

Doleman read, glancing up at the President, and occasionally at Sinclair, and shaking his head in amazement. Finally he set the pages down on the coffee table.

"Incredible stuff. Amazing."

"The question is, what do I do with it? Can I use it? Politically, I mean? Does it guarantee me a second term or should I scuttle it? Is releasing this mumbo-jumbo tantamount to committing political suicide? Maybe worse, might people take it seriously, act on it? What would that do to our institutions, our international standing, existing delicate balances of power?"

Doleman chewed his lower lip and stared across the room. "Yes, I see what you mean. On the one hand you could be the President responsible for tracking and releasing an astounding communication. A hero, even a statesman. A place in history such as no president before you."

"And on the other?"

"You're the laughing stock of the industrialized world. People claim you invented it, that you've lost your mind, that you're sitting up here in the Oval Office conversing with imaginary space aliens."

"Exactly," Geller groaned.

"They might even seek your impeachment on mental health grounds," Doleman added. No one spoke for a moment. Finally Doleman murmured, "The churches would have a field day."

"They'd hate it, wouldn't they? They'd call it heresy. And that part about competition? Economic heresy. I'd be labeled a Communist. Or worse, a nihilist."

"I suppose you could convene some sort of council of religious and secular leaders—scientists, economists. Allow

NASA to publish it, keeping your distance, of course. Then you invite the world's religious and scientific elite to meet, analyze and comment on it. That way you appear detached and impartial, statesmanlike."

Sinclair was taking in this conversation with a certain open-mouthed astonishment. He'd never before observed the President as backroom politician.

"Does it help me get reelected?"

"Hard to say. Depends on how it's handled. I can easily see it getting out of hand, a panicky public, every nut case from California to Nepal rising to predict the end of the world."

"I know. Falling down on their knees to worship Omega, for crissake."

"The question is, do you have any choice? Is it even possible to contain it?"

"It was airtight until the scientists escaped from the compound in St. Lucia. From then on, we have no way of knowing who they might have contacted with the information. Rensler's participated in international SETI symposia and is a strong advocate of the sharing of any SETI contact. It's possible he contacted his counterparts in Europe and notified them of the signal."

"Wouldn't you have heard about it?" Doleman looked from his boss, over to Sinclair.

Jeremy nodded. "I believe we would have by now."

Silent moments passed. Chip Doleman had been Geller's campaign manager through Geller's two successful races for the Senate and then in his Presidential campaign. He'd been the man behind the Man, exercising a ruthless political acumen on behalf of his boss, shielding Geller from the seamy, mud-splattering side-effects inevitable in a man's rise to the pinnacle of world power. Behind the back of his stockily built, dogged Chief of Staff, Geller often referred to Doleman as "Buster Mud Flaps."

When Doleman finally spoke, it was to serve up a blizzard of metaphor, cliché, and doublespeak. From it, Geller might pluck laconic pearls. Sinclair closed his open mouth and listened.

"We lack sufficient information to formulate a coherent, politically strategic response," Doleman began. "Who knows of these transmissions? If it's limited to those on St. Lucia, plus Sinclair, Burch, you, then it's foolish to announce it. You're riding high in the polls at the moment. Barring some disaster you're a shoo-in for reelection. Conventional wisdom dictates you not rock the boat. Announcing news of these transmissions could backfire badly for all the reasons we've discussed and probably for many that we have no way of anticipating. In my opinion the optimum strategy is to keep the lid on. Huddle with your experts. Siphon off whatever scientific and technological utility exists and exercise extreme discretion over any dissemination of the data. The payoff will come if and when that utility exists and we're in a position to control its application."

Geller considered this verbal melange. "The national interest is served. Yes. That is the justification."

"If others get wind of it, we're that far ahead of the game in the application."

"And the scientists in St. Lucia?"

Doleman shook his head. "They have to be considered expendable when an issue of this magnitude arises that so broadly impacts on the national interest. It just so happens that a don't-rock-the-boat approach to your political well-being coincides nicely with the need for continued security and protection of the national interest. The bottom line, the net-net, is that you continue playing it extremely close to the vest."

Ω

52

ON THE MORNING of September ninth Kate awakened, climbed out of bed, crossed the elegant hotel room and gazed out at the vast bustling harbor of Fort de France, Martinique. She contemplated the day ahead.

She had four days to work with, four days including the twelfth in which to find a way to reach Soufriere *unnoticed*—the operative word—to locate the compound, and if all went well, retrieve a diskette at the agreed-upon drop site. There was at least one translation she was missing, the seventh, that they'd received the day the scientists were apprehended. And there might be more. The ETI broadcasts might have continued for several more days or even weeks.

She hoped Tim would include instructions on the diskette for how and when she was to dial up the SETI network. Regardless of whatever other publication arrangements she made, her primary approach would be to transfer the data to the international SETI group's computer network and rely on them to handle the announcement.

Even if that effort was successful, Kate wondered whether the story's authenticity would be questioned. Tim had dismissed that concern. He had a solution, he said. She could dial up the SETI network on her computer, log onto the system using his personal ID and password, and copy the translation files via the phone line and modem to a special account. Coming in that way, it would be believed. The problem was that Tim had not given her the phone number, account ID or password. He'd withheld the information from her, probably, she surmised, as a way of ensuring she didn't break the story before the entire signal was received and decoded. Fleetingly she'd wondered whether he mistrusted her that much. Without his instructions her hands were tied.

First things first. Find a way to get to Soufriere undetected. She might arrange for a private plane, but then she'd be arriving at the airport in Vieux Fort, and she had no intention of going anywhere near that place. Sinclair's people would be all over it like ants at a picnic.

What about ferry services between Martinique and St. Lucia? No, the NSA could scrutinize disembarking passengers. Which left private yachts. Maybe she could hitch a ride.

She dressed carefully. She already suspected from the briefest glimpse of Martinique that it was a posh place. She wandered out the hotel lobby and onto the main drag of Anse Mitan and was met by the sound of revving speed boats.

She ambled along, taking in the atmosphere, and eventually came upon the Hotel Bakoua and the marina. There were hundreds of boats at anchor, sailboats and power boats of every conceivable size and description, from the blatantly opulent to the marginally seaworthy. Sidewalks teemed with sailors and tourists.

A duet of catamarans sliced through the harbor, passing within inches of each other, one arriving and one departing from a passenger loading dock. She ambled over and read the sign: Anse Mitan/Anse l'Ane Ferry. Boats departed on the half-hour transporting people between Anse l'Ane and Fort de France. The arriving catamaran slid to a halt and disgorged twenty or so passengers. Kate sidled up to an English-speaking foursome and lacking a better plan, trailed along behind to see if they might be yachtsmen. Or might *know* yachtsmen. She was desperate.

They made their way to a sidewalk café a few blocks away, took a table, and Kate sat nearby to eavesdrop. She couldn't hear a word over the general din. She caught the eye of one of the men at the table and smiled at him. Screw the subtlety, she thought. There wasn't time to do this gracefully.

She walked over. "You folks from the States?"

"Yes, we are," said one of the women, eyeing Kate.

"I was just wondering, ah, I just got here myself. Are you sailors?"

"No," one of the men replied.

"Oh. I was looking for a marine hardware store but I don't speak French. You wouldn't happen to—"

They shook their heads and murmured, no, they had no idea where the hardware store was. Feeling foolish, Kate thanked them and hurried away.

She spent the rest of the day wandering the streets, browsing in marine hardware stores and striking up conversations with strangers. No one was the least bit inclined to offer her a ride to St. Lucia. By that evening she was thoroughly discouraged. By late the next morning she was edging on panic. Out of sheer frustration she ventured into a cheesy-looking bar across from the Anse Mitan ferry dock, waited for her eyes to adjust to her dim surroundings, and perched on a barstool between two men. She ordered a Coke and looked around. Maybe this was more like it. Folks were belting back beer at eleven in the morning.

"Hi there, little lady." The very large, T-shirted man next to her stretched out his hand. "Frank O'Dell."

She read his T-shirt: "Don't Sweat the Small Stuff."

"Hi." A Texan? "Sarah."

"Nicetameetcha, Sarah." He pumped her hand vigorously. "Where y'all from?"

"California. Bet you're from—" She held up a hand. "No, let me guess. Texas?"

"Bingo," he said, jabbing the air with an upraised index finger. "Y'all sailing or hotel-slummin'?"

"Actually I'm here on business. How 'bout yourself, Frank?" She could so easily lapse into a Texas twang. It was the most contagious accent on the planet.

"Purely pleasure. A little fishing, a little drinking. Jus' me-n-the-missus this trip."

"On your own boat?"

"You bet. The *Allemande Left*, the most gorgeous hunk a yacht in the gulf. My opinion, y'understand."

Kate gave him an appreciative smile and tried to rein in her twang. "I believe you. I love your T-shirt."

"'Don't sweat the small stuff.' Words to live by. Check out the back." He twisted on his stool and Kate read: "It's All Small Stuff."

"I want one," she said, a little surprised that a Texan would wear such a message, especially so close to his heart. "Are you traveling around the islands or just in Martinique?"

"Actually me-n-the-missus was planning on heading north this week to the Iles des Saintes. Hear there's great fishin'. The Missus likes the snorkeling."

He'd pronounced it, "Ill-ees-dee-saints," which brought another smile to Kate's face; even she couldn't slaughter French so mercilessly.

"I was about to head down to St. Lucia," she said. "I write travel articles."

"Y'ought to cover Domenica. Columbus landed there, second voyage. Beautiful spot."

"Next trip. This time it's 'Martinique and St. Lucia—A Study in Contrasts.'"

"No kidding. This place is too posh for my blood. St. Loosha, eh? I don't know that island. Never got that far south."

"It's charming, not fancy at all and only twenty miles south. Probably a piece-a-cake for the *Allemande Left*."

"Two hours max. Probably ought to try it sometime."

"I'll be flying down later today. LIAT Airlines—you know, Luggage In Another Terminal?"

He awarded her with a guffaw. "So they say. Care for a beer?"

"Well, it's awfully early. Oh, why not. Better than wandering the streets of Martinique in search of travel news."

"Nice work, y'ask me." Frank caught the waiter's attention. "Heineken all right?"

She nodded. "Thanks. Yeah, I'm lucky. I get to travel around, write off my expenses, explore tropical paradises, meet nice people—" Lay it on a bit. What the hell.

"Me, I'm in awl."

"In what?"

"Awl. You know, the black stuff. O-i-l."

"Oh, *oil*."

"Right. Rest a the world can't pronounce the stuff but they sure know how to guzzle it."

"Things haven't been so easy in the Texas oil business, or so I've heard."

"Nah. The price of a barrel drops, I don't pump. The price goes up, I start pumpin'. Nothin' to it. Lot easier than farmin' or cattle or most other occupations you'd care to name."

Kate nodded. How was she going to prod this man into a ride? "What time do you have? My watch seems to have stopped."

"'Bout noon."

"Darn. I've got to go. My flight's at two."

"Too bad. Unless— Whyn't me-n-the-missus take y'all down to St. Loosha?"

"Oh, that's awfully kind, but I really couldn't impose—"

"Course ya could. Be lots more interestin' than losin' your luggage in another terminal. Be my guest. Price is sure right."

"I'd insist on paying you."

"You could try but you'd never get away with it," he said with a wide grin.

"You really mean it?"

"You bet. I got charts. Can't leave today, though. Evenin' plans. Tomorrow do?"

"Wonderful! First thing in the morning?"

"Sure. Let me check with The Missus."

Kate had envisioned The Missus as a corpulent, middle-aged apricot-blond aboard a *Southern Comfort* yacht, possibly reclining on a stratolounger. Wrong. The Missus was a leggy ash-blonde, easily twenty years Frank's junior. She was astride a stool at the end of the bar near the window with her nose in a paperback. Bet it's a rippling-smoothie, Kate thought uncharitably.

"Hon, how'd ya feel about a little trip down to St. Loosha?" Frank called to her.

The young woman looked up. "What, Frank?"

"This here lady's desirous of a little boat ride."

"Whatever," she said with an indifferent wave.

"Come on over and meet The Missus." Frank heaved himself down from his barstool with a soft grunt. Kate followed.

"Jennifer Sue, honey? I want ya to meet Sarah—"

"Clarke," Kate supplied. "Nice to meet you, Jennifer Sue. Frank's been telling me about your trip."

"Pretty soon we're heading home, right honey? 'Fore the hurricanes hit?" Jennifer Sue laid her book face down on the bar and Kate got a look: *Great American Political Thinkers, Volume One*.

Frank chuckled. Kate chuckled. "Jennifer Sue's not much of a sailor. Hates weather. Sarah here's a travel writer. Ya know, 'Travel 'n' Leisure' in the Sunday paper?"

"Oh, that's nice. An' you'd like a ride where?"

"I'm actually booked on the afternoon flight to St. Lucia, but your husband has very generously offered to take me on your boat if you have no objection?"

"Fine with me. When do we leave?"

Frank looked at Kate. "How early, Sarah?"

"Is eight too early?"

He nodded happily. "Meet you right across the street at the ferry dock in my launch. Seven-forty-five sharp. Jennifer Sue, we can do that, can't we?"

"I won't be up but y'all can do whatever you like. Don't wake me before ten. Ah require my sleep."

Kate smiled at Jennifer Sue. "I really love your hair. Do you use anything to, um, help the color?"

"Why, Ah do. Ah use Lo-re-al."

"I was thinking of changing my hair color."

"Look real nice on you, too. Blondes have lots more fun."
She patted her hair happily.

Kate left Frank and Jennifer Sue at the bar. She had errands
to run before morning. She needed to alter her appearance and
change hotels. Jack had advised her to keep moving to evade
Sinclair. At the very least there was a Martinique Customs form
with her name on it, and a cabbie who might remember her. By
mid-afternoon she'd checked out of the Méridien and into the
Hotel Bakoua. By dinner time she'd taken the scissors to her
hair, resulting in a rather ragged-looking shag-do. And she'd
dyed it ash-blond.

She rose at dawn the next morning, breakfasted and checked
out of her room, and presented herself at the ferry dock with her
luggage at the stroke of seven-forty-five. Frank breezed up in a
twenty-foot launch, the *Do-si-do*.

"That you, Sarah? Could a fooled me. You women. Why you
can't just leave what the good Lord gave ya alone is beyond
me."

"You don't like it?" Kate ran a hand over her bristly crop of
hair.

"'S okay. Liked it fine the way it was."

He helped her aboard with her luggage and motored them out
to one of the largest yachts Kate had ever seen. So much for
sneaking into St. Lucia unobserved.

He led her to a bridge perched high above the deck. "Make
yourself at home, Sarah. I'll have us away from this fool's
playground in a shake." He took a seat in a cushioned leather
swivel chair and consulted a chart. "Got to watch out for Idiot's
Reef." He pressed a button to start the engines and another to
activate the anchor windlass.

"Would you like me to watch at the bow?"

"Nah. I'll just keep an eye on this here sonar screen."

This was looking a great deal easier than sailing, and just
maybe a lot less fun.

Ω

53

"Lipton arrived two nights ago in Fort de France, Martinique." Michael Gregg tracked Jeremy Sinclair down at nine-thirty AM at his home in Georgetown.

"Is she in custody?"

"No. Our people came across her entry card this morning. She flew in from Caracas."

"Caracas! Michael, I'm on my way. She's headed for St. Lucia. You realize that."

"Of course. I've dispatched a team to Martinique to search and I'm calling in everyone else from the other islands to beef up security."

"Post extra people at the airports."

"It's done. What can she hope to accomplish here, Jeremy? We're locked up tighter than an ant's ass."

Sinclair pondered the question. "Beats the hell out of me. Maybe there's another escape plan afoot, though I can't quite imagine they'd be foolish enough to try. You'll want to check every vehicle in and out of the compound. They might try leaving on a laundry truck or disguised as one of your food service people or—"

"I'll institute a general lock-down, Jeremy. As of this moment no one will be allowed in or out of the compound. Then we won't have to worry about laundry trucks."

"Good. I'll arrive later today, after I clean up some things
here. I'll bring another three dozen men. We'll need coastal
patrols. Look into that. We'll need at least ten power yachts. See
if they're available for charter."

"We'll get 'em."

"What about ferry boats between islands? Is there a Martinique ferry service?"

"There is and it's handled. What's the status with Sullivan?
Has he disappeared?"

"No. He's going to work each and every day like a good boy.
This time we're going to nail her, Michael. No screw-ups."

THE *ALLEMANDE LEFT* sliced through the heavy chop like an
arrow, indifferent to the broadside currents and seven-foot
swells. Kate could only marvel; it was like cruising on an ocean
liner. If she and Jack had been sailing this course to St. Lucia,
they'd be on a stiff port reach, bounding along, hair tangled and
faces damp with spray. The crew of the *Allemande Left* would
arrive looking as though they'd just stepped out of a bandbox.

By ten-thirty they'd reached the northern tip of St. Lucia. The
winds and chop soon subsided in the lee of the mountainous
green island.

"Awful pretty," Frank said. "Look at this, Jennifer Sue."

Jennifer Sue had made an appearance fifteen minutes earlier,
a model in stature dressed in skin-tight white shorts and a barely
adequate red and white striped halter top.

"Pretty island," Jennifer Sue concurred, cuddling up to her
husband at the helm.

"Sarah, any place in particular you'd like to put ashore?"

"Would it be too much trouble to go down to Marigot Bay?"

"No trouble 'tall. I'll just have a look here at the chart. Looks
like a nice deep little cove. Hon, would you hand me *Avery's*?"

Jennifer Sue handed her husband Volume III of *Avery's
Guide, Martinique to Trinidad*, and Frank read about Marigot,
"a picturesque hurricane hole."

If this description didn't exactly thrill his wife, the sight of Marigot Bay did. It was a thin finger of cove lined with palm trees and white beaches, cut deep into a jungled valley. The *Allemande Left* glided smoothly into the quiet harbor. Frank steered wide of the sandbar that bisected the cove midway, dividing Marigot into front and back anchorages. On the left as they entered was a yacht charter company complete with docking facilities, slips, buoys and offices. On the right was the British Customs Office and farther back, the Hurricane Hole Hotel and Restaurant. A canopied launch ferried people back and forth across the narrow channel.

Frank pressed an anchor release button and held it until a rode of eighty feet was payed out. There'd be no diving down to press anchor flukes into sand, and definitely no delivery of a Water Report. He'd just payed out a ton or two of heavy-gauge galvanized chain and they weren't going anywhere.

"That's got it. Say, whyn't we all have lunch ashore at that pretty restaurant?"

"Oh let's do!" Jennifer Sue was game.

"We'll have to clear customs first," Kate said uncertainly, scanning the cove.

"So? Let's do it. I'm famished. A rum punch would go down real good. You gals all set? I'll just hoist the Q-flag."

Kate gathered her things at the ladder while Frank lowered the launch. He climbed in and Kate handed down her duffle bag and laptop, making her best effort to conceal a mounting anxiety. She scanned the bay. She could not check into customs under her own passport. There had to be an alert posted. And what if Jack— Skip it, Kate. You'll have to take the chance. And you have not broken any laws. Right. Small comfort. And what would these nice people say when they realized she'd been using a false name? *Well now, Kate, what Mr. and Mrs. Frank O'Dell think would seem to be at the bottom of your pile of problems.*

They docked at a small pier near the simple white wood-frame structure that was the customs office. A rooster and some chickens pecked in the dust near the dock and a golden mongrel lay snoozing on the wooden porch. Inside, a native man sat behind a desk dressed in a spanking white uniform emblazoned with black and gold chevrons and epaulets.

"Ah, yes. Good day," he greeted them in a crisp British accent.

"Well howdy," Frank replied. "We just arrived from Martinique and figured we'd best check in with y'all. Plan on havin' a bite up the way."

"Very well, I'll ask you to complete these forms," the official said, getting to his feet to take up position behind the varnished wooden counter.

Kate looked about as she accepted the form. Her gaze lit on a bulletin board mounted on the wall beside the counter, and she scanned it for her photograph. It wasn't there. Out of the corner of her eye she caught sight of a bearded man in dark glasses who was striding toward the customs office. He stepped onto the porch and his sharp footsteps echoed through the clapboard walls. Her heartbeat resembled the kettle drum section of the "William Tell Overture." What the hell could she do?

She rummaged in her purse for a pen and bent to complete the entry form. The door creaked open and closed. She scarcely breathed.

"Sarah, is that you?"

She turned to face the bearded man. He'd removed his dark glasses and was walking toward her now. She searched his face—and found herself staring into the smiling eyes of Jack Sullivan.

"Oh, thank God! I wasn't sure if you'd—"

"Here it is," he whispered, slyly slipping her the passport in the same motion that he engulfed her in a great hug. Then he stepped back. "Almost didn't recognize you with your new look."

"Oh, thank God you're— Any difficulty with the, ah, boat?"

"Nope. All set."

"Sarah, who's your friend here?" Frank asked.

Before "Sarah" could answer, Jack stepped forward with his hand outstretched. "Pete Ballard."

"Frank O'Dell. Big surprise y'all meeting up like this. Small world. This here's my Missus, Jennifer Sue."

"Actually, Frank, we planned it," Kate said. "Frank and Jennifer Sue have been awfully kind, Pete. Let me just get this form filled out, and we'll—" She eyed Jack's beard. It completely transformed his appearance. Still trembling, she printed the date on her form: September eleventh.

KATE AND JACK insisted on buying the O'Dells lunch at the Hurricane Hole. It was a tricky affair. Jack was at pains not to say anything that might contradict whatever Kate might have told the O'Dells, and Kate kept her own conversation so vague as to be inane. They both had to catch themselves mid-syllable a few times, almost calling the other by the wrong name.

They were able to extricate themselves around two in the afternoon. By then, Kate was knee-deep in Texas twang and Jack had exhausted his repertoire of questions about Texas awl. Jack paid the tab over Frank's protestations and they separated with hugs and hand shakes and pats and "y'all take care's" at the ferry dock near the customs office.

Jack loaded Kate's things onto the launch and gave her a hand aboard. "Our boat's called the *Peak Experience*," he told her, "another Morgan 46."

"That's great, J— Pete." She laughed. "I'm not good at this. God, it's wonderful to see you."

The small canvas-topped motor launch ferried them across the narrow channel and let them off at the charter company's pier.

As Jack led the way down the dock he said, "I left them in San Francisco following the wrong guy."

"How'd you manage it?"

"You know Spencer Macmillan? Looks enough like me. He agreed to become me for a few days. We swapped clothes, I put on this beard and he shaved his off—"

"It's not real?"

"Not yet." He fingered it. "Maybe I'll grow one of my own."

"Sure looks real."

"Here we are. Feels like home, eh?"

Kate stepped onto the stern of the *Peak Experience* and looked down into the cockpit. "It really does. Did you remember the bicycle?"

"Nope."

"What do you mean, *nope*?"

"Look in the foc's'le."

She climbed below and hurried through the salon. Wedged in and secured with bungee cords between the locker and forward head was a bicycle contraption with pedals, mountain bike wheels, and a small engine mounted on the crossbar.

Jack stood behind her. "A motorized bicycle. I figured you might need power if the road's steep."

She turned and hugged him. "It's wonderful. Thank you. Thank you for all of this. I was so relieved when you walked through the door of the customs office."

"So, we've got a few hours before we have to leave. Tell me the latest. Did they find the signal?"

" *Did* they! Read the transcript." She retrieved the pages from the bottom of her duffle bag and Jack sat down in the salon and read slowly.

After several minutes he said, "It's miraculous, isn't it?" He lay the last page down on the table. "I hardly know what to say." He didn't need to say anything; his eyes told it well enough.

Kate took a seat beside him. "I've been doing quite a lot of thinking over the past few weeks, mostly about when this is over. It seems to me those transmissions apply to the two of us. I want to talk to you about—crossing the line, I guess. I'm tired of the way we back off, the way *I* back off. I figured something out: It's never been *your* walls holding me back; it's been my own and I don't want them anymore."

She watched his eyes widen as he took in her words. "That's amazing. It's almost verbatim the speech I'd been rehearsing." He took her hand and laughed suddenly.

"What?"

"Chet and Nadine will be so relieved."

She started to speak but he stopped her, kissed her. "There's another stern berth that needs inaugurating."

"Part of the pre-cruise shakedown."

"Essential."

The intervening weeks since she'd seen him suddenly seemed like years. She had wanted him with her in Michigan at the lake, reading the transmissions, hiking in the woods. She'd watched the Renslers with the same envy and admiration as Margo had, and with some of the same regret. Now they drew out each touch and look and word and their lovemaking became a celebration of walls falling away. Maybe they'd finally reached and crossed the threshold, and wonder of wonders: the world hadn't fallen in at all; it had come together.

Ω

54

JEREMY SINCLAIR stared at a full-color, eight and a half by
eleven photo of Kate Lipton. It was a recent one taken from
KQED's files, originally used in a promo piece for Lipton's
"Focus" show. The thirty-six-year-old Kathryn Lipton had
smiled forthrightly into the camera, a girl-next-door type,
slightly tomboyish perhaps. Curly brown hair framed the round
easy face. Almost pretty, Sinclair thought. She hadn't changed
that much in eleven years. Still the look of the innocent, though
as Jeremy well knew the woman whose friendly face smiled up
from the glossy print had the cunning of a fox. Hardly your
average girl next door.

He shuddered with revulsion. He'd changed too. He no longer
cared as much for college girls. He preferred them younger now,
adolescent. By seventeen they'd lost something. Worldliness had
crept in. It showed in the eyes, a cynicism and fatigue in the
expression, a studied sophistication. Breasts too large, hips too
broad for his taste. He liked them budding, on the edge of
womanhood. He closed his eyes.

The FASTEN SEAT BELTS sign came on with a soft chime and
he took out his handkerchief and patted his brow. As he tucked
the photo back in his briefcase, an image of Lipton's face came
to him, this one ravaged by fear. A thin smile crossed his lips.
He'd see that face again very soon. He tightened the seat belt
against his hips with a soft sigh. Maybe there'd be someone at

the compound, maybe a native girl. He needed someone. The pressure had become intense.

Within moments the plane touched down in Vieux Fort. He was bringing Gregg his three dozen agents and they deplaned and piled into vans and taxis for the ride to the compound. Sinclair rode alone with Gregg in a Ford Escort.

"Bring me up to date," Jeremy said when they were underway.

Gregg drove slowly. The road was winding and narrow, badly potholed in sections. "A Martinique cab driver recognized Lipton from the photo and remembers taking her to the Hôtel Méridien in Anse Mitan. From there the trail's cold. We have six boats patrolling the west coast of the island, from Castries to Vieux Fort, and another six on the eastern coast. We've got our people in town—in Soufriere—as well as all around the Hummingbird in case she tries to come ashore there. We'll use the new people you've brought to spell the coastal patrols. Some have been at it nonstop for fourteen hours."

"Are they stopping every boat?"

"Absolutely. They're checking passports and boarding whenever it seems appropriate."

"And the Brits are cooperating. Good. And the compound?"

"Locked up tight. No one in or out for the past twelve hours. That'll remain in effect until she's found. Can I ask—"

"What?"

"Why so much attention on Lipton?"

Sinclair turned away to stare out the window. They were passing through a vast banana plantation. "She's the leak. If we can silence her before she blows it open, we may still achieve containment."

"Oh."

"How about the scientists?"

"They're all right. Margo Jacobsen's still quite distressed over her husband's death."

"To be expected," Sinclair said without emotion.

"The others are subdued. Ralph told them they're to keep searching for the transmitter."

"And you've got people watching them every moment?"

"Twenty-four hours a day. And closed-circuit monitors."

"And Rensler's wife?"

"Same thing, Jeremy. I tell you, there isn't any way they can pull anything."

"Good." Sinclair stared out the window again, shook his head. Somehow he couldn't summon Gregg's supreme confidence. She'd won too many early rounds. "I'll be attaching myself to the Hummingbird team, though of course I'll remain in touch with you at the compound. Michael, we can't let her get away this time."

AT FOUR O'CLOCK on the afternoon of September eleventh, Kate and Jack left Marigot Bay and headed due west, out to sea. Two hours later the sun was beginning to set. They were sailing on their jib, killing time. Kate had unpacked and then fixed them a light dinner which they ate in the cockpit with Jack at the helm.

"Where are the second set of passports?" she asked after they'd eaten and the galley was straightened.

"In the bottom of my duffle bag."

She went below and returned with another set of bogus passports, these depicting "Peter Edwin Ballard" and "Sarah Louise Clarke" as Afro-Americans. She held them under the flashlight beam. "They're outstanding. How'd he do it?"

"She. Petra Eichorn, one of the best counterfeiters on the West Coast. She took our photos and darkened the skin tones, superimposed Afro hair styles. Pretty impressive, eh?"

"Amazing. No trouble finding my leftover passport photos?"

"Nope. Right where you said they'd be. How do you like the other passport, the blond version?"

"Can't see how she did it. It's great. The Afro wigs are outstanding. I'll try mine on." She disappeared below and returned moments later. "What do you think?"

"It'll look better with skin to match," he said. "How's it feel?"

"Tight, though I suppose that's better than too loose."

BY THREE-THIRTY PM on the twelfth, Kate and Jack completed the second long leg of a giant triangular course. Now they turned and headed east for the final run into St. Lucia. Jack estimated they'd arrive around eleven-thirty. During the long hours, Kate's nerves had grown increasingly ragged. She knew they couldn't have thought of everything. Nothing ever went exactly as planned.

At ten-thirty PM, she went below to change. Jack had already become Peter Ballard, a black man. When she returned to the cockpit she shone their spotlight on her face.

"Pretty good," Jack said. "We make a handsome couple. If I can just keep from scratching, from messing up this grease paint."

"It's difficult."

When they drew into the lee of St. Lucia they were eight miles south of Marigot Bay and two miles north of Soufriere. Almost the moment they'd doused their sails, Kate's eyes were blinded by a sweep of flood lights. There was a roar of a high-powered engine drowning the hum of their own small engine, followed by the static din of a loudspeaker hailing them through the darkness.

"Request you halt! We'd like a word and will come along-side."

"A request," Kate murmured. "How polite."

"Looks as though Sinclair's laid on a small reception," Jack noted dryly.

"And damned thoughtful of him, too. You look sensational, Mr. Ballard."

"You do too, Sarah Louise. Let's hope it's sensational enough. Better tie on the fenders."

The thirty-foot power yacht closed in and hove to, and three agents stood on the deck and shone spotlights on Kate and Jack. The three wore matching caps and navy jackets imprinted with "USDEA" in white block letters. Drugs would be the obvious cover for Sinclair's operation. They flashed badges and made a big show of holstered weapons.

"You folks are arriving awfully late," one observed.

"Long haul from Bequia," Jack said. "Shouldn't have tried it in one leg. What's up?"

"Mind if we have a look at your passports?"

"No problem. Sarah, would you?"

"Sarah" went below for their Afro passports. They have no actual authority to be doing this. Otherwise, they wouldn't be quite so polite. They'd come aboard and search our belongings. She touched her wig and winced. It was giving her a sharp headache. She climbed up to the cockpit and handed the passports across the lifeline to the agent.

"Where you folks from?"

"Chicago," Jack replied. "Down for a few weeks of sailing."

"Bare-boat charter?"

"Yes."

"Out of?"

"Kingstown, St. Vincent."

"Where you putting in tonight?"

"Soufriere."

"Guess you overshot the course a little."

"How far is it down to Soufriere?" Jack inquired.

"Two miles. Okay then," the agent said. He handed back their passports. "Have a nice vacation."

"Thanks."

As the boats separated, Kate watched as the patrol circled them, probably checking the stern and noting the name of their boat. They'd note it in a log. And instead of writing down *Peak Experience*, they would be recording the name *La Luna*. They'd made the switch that afternoon. Jack had chosen it for its brevity. Easier to paint, he said.

"Whoow," Jack said as the patrol disappeared into the night. "Makes me wonder what Soufriere will be like?"

"If they're in communication with each other, maybe they'll leave us alone."

Kate went below to change again. She stripped off the light-weight cotton slacks and blouse and hooked herself into a padded bra that made her look extremely buxom. Then she stepped into a faded cotton print dress with a sash that tied around the waist. Jack said he'd found it at a garage sale. It looked it. A pair of worn sneakers completed the outfit. She checked her appearance in the mirror and touched up a few spots of grease paint. With luck, in the dark, she'd pass for native.

There were sounds of another patrol boat approaching and drawing alongside. This time she remained below and overheard Jack telling the agents they'd already been stopped two miles north. Nevertheless they insisted on checking passports. "Sarah" handed them up to "Pete" and then stood on the cockpit steps so the agents could see her darkened face. Once again they were questioned and rather politely dismissed.

Twenty minutes later, at midnight, Jack steered into Petit Soufriere Cove. The bay was utterly dark and still. "You're sure you want to do this," he said.

She touched his shoulder. "There's no choice."

"There's always a choice." He looked into her eyes. "God this is nuts."

"I know. Don't screw up my makeup," she said, swallowing hard.

"Here, I'll give you a hand. Try to get back before daylight, by four."

She slipped her arms through the straps of a small backpack. In it were a mirror and grease paint for touchup, a flashlight, Zip-loc plastic storage bags and the ignition keys to the motor-bike. She climbed into the dinghy and Jack lowered the bicycle to her.

"Good luck, Sarah Louise," he whispered. "No boiled eggs this time."

"And no elephant."
"What elephant?"

SINCLAIR had deployed the minivan to the Hummingbird Restaurant parking lot. The van had been reconfigured as a mobile command post. All land-based teams including those in town, at various airports, and posted to other islands, would continue reporting to Michael Gregg at the compound. But all shore patrols plus the agents detailed around Hummingbird Cove were to report to Jeremy. He was in constant contact with Gregg by radio. Agent Jay Roberts was seated in the back of the van, monitoring marine communications.

Sinclair stared out across the dimly lit parking lot. Restaurant patrons had departed, and the only remaining vehicles belonged to Hummingbird staff and the hotel's few overnight guests. Coastal patrols had been instructed to report to Sinclair hourly, and immediately if they came upon anything suspicious.

Manpower was his main headache. Six shore patrols, each with three agents working in twelve-hour shifts—that alone entailed thirty-six men, plus another thirty-six on the windward side of the island. Three at each of the airports, twelve guarding the scientists, another dozen at the compound assisting Gregg with general security, communications and control, plus all those deployed in and around the town of Soufriere and at the airports on nearby islands. Then there was the score of men detailed to search for Lipton in Martinique. It was all too much. They could have used another hundred men, but communication, coordination, and manpower redeployment were all next to impossible. Rapidly changing developments called for quick movement. It couldn't be done. It was too likely their people were in the wrong place, or the wrong island, or the wrong end of the right island.

When would Lipton make her move? She was coming, of that he was certain, though why he couldn't imagine. Unless it was because *he* was involved. She had to be aware of that. Perhaps that had been her motivation all along—revenge.

"Aqua Sector B Patrol reporting in. Over," crackled over the radio speaker in the back of the van.

"Aqua Command here. Over," said Agent Roberts.

"Report Status A, repeat A. Stopped two boats in the last hour. One sailboat crewed by a couple from Chicago. Powerboat crewed by locals. Nothing more to report. Over."

"Copy Status A. Report for crew shift at 0100 hours. Over."

"Roger that. Aqua Sector B, Out."

Sinclair stood outside the van on the driver's side, listening to the exchange and staring out into the night. Where was she? He could almost feel her presence. He caught the distant din of a small engine receding into the night over the steady backdrop of sounds, nocturnal jungle sounds. The air was sultry but he shivered, nonetheless. Did it ever really cool off in this pl— *A small engine??*

Sinclair scrambled into the van and raced back to where Jay Roberts was sitting before the radio microphone console. "Roberts! Contact the Soufriere patrol. Now!"

"Terra Sector C, come in. Over."

"Terra Sector C here. Over."

Sinclair grabbed the mike. "Sinclair here, I mean Aqua Command. I just heard a small engine of some kind. Small vehicle probably. Check it out. Should be headed your way."

"Copy that. Small vehicle engine. Over."

"Go. Aqua Command Out!"

After that Sinclair could only wait and listen and pace and endeavor to read the mind of Kate Lipton.

Ω

55

KATE HAD located a narrow path climbing up from Petit Sou-friere Cove and leading back into the valley. She had walked her bicycle up the steep incline until the path intersected a wider one which she followed to a dirt road. She kept to this road until it joined a steep, paved but narrow two-lane highway. There she began pedaling the bicycle.

Within minutes her legs were trembling with fatigue. She should have exercised more. She continued laboring up the hill until she could go no farther. She climbed off and walked the bike. Did she dare risk the noise of an engine? She had to. It was already nearly one o'clock. She pressed the ignition and the engine revved, a buzz-saw sound that sliced through the night. But as she rode up the valley slope she was grateful for the burst of speed.

A sliver of moon afforded some light but she turned on her headlamp to illuminate the roadway. Tim had told her the town of Soufriere was two miles north of the cove, and the compound another mile inland from that. He had advised her to watch on her left for a dirt road just past town, just beyond a white house with chartreuse trim.

As she crested the hill, she shut off the bike's engine and began pedaling down a long steep incline. She passed a slew of structures, ramshackle affairs painted in random screaming colors. The ruling standard could only be the brighter, the better.

Minutes later she spotted faint neon lights and thought she must be nearing the town of Soufriere. She slowed at an intersection and glanced down a street dimly lit and lined on both sides with modest commercial establishments.

"Stop right there!"

She froze.

"Your name!"

"Avila." She kept her eyes downcast; they'd be a dead give-away.

"What are you doing out so late?"

"Delivering medicine to my mother," she answered in a reedy voice. The words sounded absurd in her ear, a Little Red Ridinghood exchange.

A flashlight beam blinded her. Behind it two men dressed in fatigues were dark forms against the darker night. They shone their light over her and then her bike, huddled a moment and dismissed her with a wave.

Were they stopping everyone in this way? How dare they? If these were Jeremy's people, they had no authority. Obviously the local gendarmes were cooperating or looking the other way.

She pedaled on. Moments later she saw a white wooden structure on her left and turned her bike so that her headlamp illuminated the building in all its chartreuse-on-white glory. Beside the structure was an outbuilding and beyond it an unmarked gravel road. She turned onto the road and stopped.

The bike would have to be left. Tim had told her the main gate was at least half a mile—maybe as much as a mile—from the highway. She'd cover it on foot, hugging the edge of the jungle in case she needed to duck for cover.

She led the bicycle into the dense growth beside the road and left it there. Stepping back, she saw it was so well concealed she'd never find it on her way out. She found a fist-sized rock and laid it on the road to mark the spot. Then she began walking. She had a flashlight in her knapsack but didn't dare use it. She tried to make each step as soundless as possible.

It was an extremely dark night. Jungle brushed her arms and she imagined insects and crawling things. She longed to swat at them but resisted; her makeup would smear. How ridiculous she thought she must look, a native woman with odd eyes and uncharacteristic features, done up in an old plaid dress and sneakers creeping along in slow motion at the edge of the jungle. Every step was a labor, every footfall measured to mute the touch of her soles on the gravel roadway.

At this rate it would take hours to cover the distance. She'd begun the walk at one-thirty and she estimated her progress. Could she possibly make it back in time for them to make good their escape under cover of darkness? Everything was taking too long.

She forced her mind back to the present. *Keep your mind only on this*, she told herself—this step and the next. *Quiet your mind,* the Transmissions counseled, and one could know all that need be known. At the thought her nerves grew calmer and she took another step. It would be all right. Another thought occurred to her—that even if she were to die, it would be all right. Death would be soft, hardly more than an exhaled breath, another in a lifetime of them.

After that the walk—she thought of it as The Walk—took on a dreamlike quality and the darkness ceased to hold terror. At each step she saw that she was safe and took another until she'd was finally within twenty-five yards of the compound's main gate.

A man in camouflage fatigues was clearly visible, standing beneath the awning of a covered guard post, illuminated in the bluish beam of an arc lamp. She stopped, crept back into the undergrowth and wondered fleetingly what creature's habitat might lay underfoot. Were there snakes? Scorpions? Multi-legged crawling things? She had no choice but to cover the last yards through the dense growth. She took a few steps, rustled giant leaves, and cringed at noise. Perhaps the guard would dismiss the sounds as those of a jungle creature. Maybe. She stood as still as possible and allowed the sounds of the night to enfold her. It was not a silent place. All sorts of chirpings and rustlings filled the night. She tried to convince herself that even here she was at home and more or less succeeded.

The progress was painstaking, working her way toward the compound fence in a direction she hoped was roughly parallel to the roadway. Time ceased to have meaning; she couldn't allow her mind to consider it at all. Only this step and this moment. It occurred to her she could easily become lost, could wander in circles indefinitely. She dismissed the thought.

She finally came to the narrow clearing edging the fence and took a moment to get her bearings. The chain link rose several feet in the air and above it the high voltage wires stretched taut and horizontal between fence poles.

The jungle had been cleared back from both sides of the fence for a distance of five feet, just as Tim and Milt had described. Now she had only to count fence poles from the main gate—ten of them. To her right beneath the arc lamp, the guard stood alert and motionless and appeared slightly absurd in his camouflage, especially considering their relative positions—she in her old plaid dress so much less visible that he. She counted three vertical fence poles from the gate.

She crept in the direction opposite the gate keeping to the edge of the jungle and counting poles. Four. Her muscles would definitely feel this in the morning. Five. It was like *t'ai chi*, an exercise—almost a dance—of meditation. Six. Seven.

At the eighth pole she began searching in earnest for the package. Her eyes were more accustomed to the darkness and with each step, she scanned from jungle to fence. At the ninth pole there was nothing. At the tenth still nothing.

Then she saw it lying near the eleventh pole—a four-inch-square package sealed in plastic. She bent down, picked it up and reached back and behind to tuck it into her knapsack. Then she straightened and turned.

There were voices; someone was coming. She ducked back into the jungle and willed herself to silence. Men were patrolling the fence's inside perimeter. They passed within feet of her position. She held her breath as they moved on. Would they retrace their steps or circle the entire compound?

When they didn't reappear after a several moments, she concluded they must be circling. She stepped back out into the clearing and began the journey back in the direction of the main gate, counting fence poles as she went. When she reached the third pole she submerged herself into the jungle for the painstaking journey back to the highway.

With each step her sense of safety grew. Now the most difficult challenge became the effort it took to resist running headlong, to be away from this place. She forced herself to slow, picking her way a footfall at a time until she'd retraced her steps and was back to where the road met the highway.

She retrieved her bike from the undergrowth and took a moment to shrug off the knapsack. She took out the mirror and studied her appearance in the dim light and risked using her flashlight for a moment to touch up a few spots of makeup on her face and arms. Then she sealed the diskette into a Zip-loc storage bag, and that into another, and returned it to the knapsack. With the pack on her back she mounted the bike and began pedaling back toward town.

Again the patrol intercepted her. This time it was well past three AM, and if her story had sounded silly before, it now seemed preposterous—delivering medicine to her mother indeed.

"It's Avila again," she said, eyes downcast. "I'm on my way home."

The agents scrutinized her, running the beams of their flashlights over her. She felt invaded. Her skin crawled. The walk through the jungle must have wreaked havoc with her makeup. These men would see all of it. Before they could register and react to the sheer absurdity of her presence and her story, she was on her bicycle and pedaling away, acutely conscious of their eyes on her retreating form.

Past town the road began angling sharply up the hillside, so much steeper now than it had seemed coming down. Again she knew she must risk the ear-splitting noise of the motor; she was

nearly out of time. Dawn could not be far off. As she crested the
hill there were headlights approaching, an oncoming vehicle. She
cut her own engine and began pedaling hard. The vehicle drew
even with her and stopped.

"You! Who are you? Halt!" The voice belonged to Jeremy
Sinclair.

Kate said nothing.

"What are doing out at this hour?"

There was no time for this. Jack was waiting. She didn't dare
answer; he'd know her voice. He'd kill her. Her legs burned
with fatigue but she demanded more of them, tearing down the
hill toward the cove. She felt and then saw the beams of
headlights closing fast from behind and heard the sound of the
van as it gained on her.

THE MOMENT he saw the odd figure in the van's headlights
pedaling up the hill, he knew. She was all wrong. It was past
three in the morning. It was too incongruous, so much so in fact,
that they'd very nearly dismissed it.

"That's her!" Sinclair shouted at Jay Roberts. "Turn around!"

"That's the native woman reported by the Soufriere team."

"No! It's Lipton!" he bellowed.

There was a scream of rubber on asphalt as Roberts wheeled
the van around and roared down the hill in pursuit. Sinclair
strained forward in his seat, hands clenched, peering through the
darkness. She'd vanished. Where had she gone? She could not
elude him this time.

"There! She left her bike. Stop the van! Where's the flashlight?"

"Behind the seat." Roberts drew the van onto the shoulder
and screeched to a halt and both men leapt out.

Sinclair scanned the area with the flashlight. "This way!" He
patted his holstered firearm as he ran, Roberts close on his heels.

KATE had tossed her bike aside and was careening through jungle like a frightened animal, running on instinct and nearly out of control. He was following. Where was the damned path? She kept on, knowing she'd stumble onto it any moment. When she did, she turned to her right and began the descent to the cove of Petit Soufriere.

Or so she thought.

But it was all wrong. Instead of dropping down to the beach, the path was angling upward. It was too dark. She could barely see where she was going. Her breath caught in her throat and a stitch of pain grabbed at her side. She kept running. Definitely, the narrowing path was switchbacking upward. Her breath was coming in bursts and she stopped to fill her lungs.

There was the sound of him thundering behind her on the footpath, unmistakable. And voices. How many were coming? She felt him nearer and began running again. Her limbs were limp and trembling from the bike ride, the painstaking walk to and from the compound. The path had become steeper and narrower. Where the hell was she?

And then she knew—it was Petit Piton. She was climbing up the Piton and there was probably no other trail down, no choice now but to continue up. Moments later she had the sense of stars and sky overhead, of the cover of jungle receding and safety left behind. Worst of all, she could hear the footfalls of him behind, outstripping her pace.

She kept running. He'd kill her if he caught her.

SINCLAIR had never actually played out in his mind the details of what he'd do when he captured Kate Lipton. He only knew she was quarry. She must be ensnared. In some abstract way his own life seemed to depend on it. When he reached the path he stopped. His flashlight beam lit on a small sign. To the left was Petit Soufriere Cove and to the right, Petit Piton. He steeled himself into silence and listened.

"Jay, she's going up the hill." He was breathing hard. "Take up position on the beach in case she doubles back. I'm going up. Call in reinforcements."

"The walkie-talkie's in the van."

"Shit. Go back for it. Radio for assistance. Have the coastal patrols converge on Petit Soufriere. Wait for me down at the cove. Radio Michael at the compound. Let him know we're closing in. There's got to be someone offshore waiting to pick her up. I'll bring her down."

As he ran, the sharp beam of his flashlight illuminated the narrow footpath ahead. So long as he could hear the sound of her ahead, he knew he could press on. But if there was silence, if she stopped and concealed herself, he might pass right by her. Would she be that clever? Every few steps he paused and forced himself to listen. He was gaining on her.

This woman had nearly brought him down. Years of devoted sacrifice to country and career and she'd nearly destroyed it all. She must have been planning it for years, sought him out with the obvious intention of ruining him. How carefully she must have schemed, stalked him, lying in wait until he'd attained the pinnacle of his career. She'd chosen her moment and closed in. His own President had lost faith in him. She'd kidnapped the scientists right out from under his nose, eluded his people again when she'd returned the charter boat. And then just as he was certain she was within his grasp, as he'd drawn the net over their Michigan hideout, she'd eluded him again. She damned well wasn't getting away this time. No one would ever humiliate him as Lipton had and live to tell of it. How would he punish her? He'd start slowly, draw it out, make her feel each moment, a protracted anguish, just as she'd done to him for the past several months. There were many ways he'd make her pay. She'd resist, of course, cry, plead with him to stop. But he wouldn't.

His chest burned with rage and exertion—the chase, the hunter and the hunted. She was almost his.

* * *

SHE WAS FALLING. It might have been a sudden switchback in the path, unseen in the dark, or a rock that caught the side of her shoe and threw her off balance, or the thought of him gaining on her, a feeling of him crawling up her back, behind her—like the computer room— Her feet were no longer her own. She was on her stomach sliding down. Her fingers grasped for any purchase and found a rocky nub, dug in and held. Her toes came to rest on a thin lip of ledge. Below—a sheer drop to the waters of Petit Soufriere Cove.

She had no sense of how far she might have slid. The crescent bit of moon was scarcely adequate to see by. She drew her head back and looked up at the featureless darkness. There were sounds—her own gasps for breath, the faint heaving surf hundreds of feet below and overhead, Jeremy Sinclair thrashing up the narrow path. Her only hope lay in total silence but though she willed herself to be still, her hands clawed for purchase on the rockface. Her breath came in bursts. There were sounds above—footsteps. She saw the flickering glow of a flashlight beam. Maybe he'd continue up the path. How much farther might it wind? If she could somehow climb up and regain the path before he realized she'd fallen— Her legs felt over-cooked spaghetti. She could get no footing, no traction. It was mostly sheer will—an intense yearning for life—that held her against the face of Petit Piton.

Now she thought she could hear him retracing his steps; he was drawing nearer. She tried for silence but her own breath betrayed her. The beam of his light bounced over the trail edge, scanning methodically until suddenly it caught and held her.

And she knew he'd won.

"Your luck's run out, Kate. Rather clever actually, disguising yourself as a native." His own breath was coming in short, gatling-gun bursts. "Thought you'd even the score, ruin me, didn't you? Ha!" The tone was laced with gloating triumph.

She didn't speak. Her right foot had wriggled its way into a small crevasse but she didn't know how long she could hold it. The nub of rock to which her left hand clung seemed loose. It could break away any moment. She needed a better grip. Her hand brushed across the rock and felt out a nodule of rock at shoulder height. Better. She looked up and saw his looming form, head and shoulders an ominous shape framed behind the piercing beam of light.

"You blew it, Kate. We were always one step ahead. Clever but never clever enough. You always did fall slightly short of the mark. Remember when you ran away from me that first time—in the computer room? Quite a study in cowardice. I frightened you, didn't I? You always did want to play in a league larger than your talents. Must be hard to accept you don't have what it takes." His breathing had almost returned to normal and he was warming to his subject. He laughed. "Your reach definitely exceeds your grasp."

"Cut the crap, Jeremy."

"Ah, so testy. And here I am about to save your life. Given our relative positions here, I'd expect some manners. Here's my belt. Grab hold and I'll pull you up."

Her shoulders and arms tensed. How much longer could she hold on? "What'll you do, Jeremy? Rescue me so you can kill me? Finish what you started in the computer room?" Her mind ranged frantically over her abysmal options.

He gave a sharp laugh, spoke in a voice sluiced with disgust. "You should see yourself. You're a mess."

"You'd prefer a co-ed. Or a child maybe." She leaned with all her heart and will into the cliff. "You're sick, Jeremy." Her fingers ached. Her nails felt as though they'd tear off with the strain of digging in. Somehow she must hold on. "How the hell does someone like you get to be head of *national security*? How many have you terrorized?"

The hot moisture of tears surprised her, scalding a trail down her cheeks, wetting her face against the rough grit of rock. "Too many," she whispered. The tears were salty. She didn't try to hold them back. She imagined they would meld her to the rock. She let them fall not only herself but for others he must have assaulted, for the fear he induced and thrived on and for the sheer frustration of it all. She had no more to give.

The silence was broken by Sinclair's easy laughter. "You whine about basic laws of nature. Power belongs to the fittest, Kate; the rest learn to deal with it. Take hold of the belt. It's there by your hand. You can't hang on much longer. Take it. If you don't, you'll die. Pretty simple choice."

The belt buckle dangled just above her right hand, reflecting glints from the flashlight beam.

"Take it, damn it!"

If you don't, you'll die. She knew what she had to do. Only one of them would leave this place alive. When she lunged for the belt, it was with such force and abruptness that he was caught offguard, startled by the sudden downward tug of weight. And then suddenly the belt was limp in her grasp. She let it go and felt his hand graze hers, was conscious of him sliding past headfirst, slowly but then faster and faster down the cliff. A piercing scream accompanied his long fall, echoing for an endless stretch of moments and reaching her from farther and farther below until it was finally cut off by a stunning silence.

Long moments passed before she could either move or breathe. Tentatively her right hand felt about, found a grip and took it. She began easing up the rockface, her toes testing each small hold, trying her weight before giving herself to it. Inch by excruciating inch, stomach and face and legs pressed to the Piton, she made her way up until she could hoist herself onto the footpath. She exhaled a vast sigh of exhausted relief.

She fumbled through the knapsack for her flashlight, started descending the switchbacking trail and minutes later found herself on leveler ground. When the trail widened she found the sign and the path angling down to the cove. At the edge of the jungle, her legs were ready to fold, and it was adrenalin alone that propelled her across the ribbon of sand to the water's edge. Frantically she panned with her flashlight beam; the dinghy was gone!

"Halt or I'll shoot!" The male voice came like a shot out of the darkness. Someone was running toward her. For a moment she stood locked in a frozen confusion. It couldn't be Jeremy Sinclair. He was dead. The endless sounds of his dying still echoed in her ear.

Whoever this voice belonged to, she couldn't be bothered. She flung the flashlight aside. "The hell with you!" she yelled and dove into the surf.

She swam for her life, spurred on by muted popping sounds she assumed must be gunshots. She clawed at the water, arms churning, legs kicking, distancing herself from shore. She looked up and caught sight of the mast light ahead, shining like Arcturas against the black sky. Then she dove and swam submerged. The sodden weight of her backpack, dress and sneakers were a terrible drag on her progress. When her lungs seemed about to burst, she breached the surface to risk another breath.

Finally her hand met the smooth surface of the hull. She felt along for the ladder and scrambled up. And there were Jack's strong hands gripping her, dragging her into the boat.

"Let's go!" she gasped.

"My God! You got it? You're okay? You're not hit?"

"Yes! No. Let's go!"

Ω

56

THEY STOLE out of Petit Soufriere under cover of darkness. All around them were the lights and throbbing engine sounds of Sinclair's patrol boats converging. Somehow they got away. Somehow they weren't seen.

Silent running was how Kate thought of the long sail to Mustique. Long after the St. Lucian coastline was behind them, they continued to scan the dark night for patrols. They didn't dare risk raising sails until they were well miles from the island's southern end. Even then Kate remained hyper-conscious of the patrols. There'd been that man on the beach who'd fired at her. He'd seen them leave. Would it ever end? Would she ever again feel safe?

She took the helm while Jack removed *La Luna* from the boat's stern. They sailed on as the *Peak Experience*. Kate slumped down on the cockpit cushions and was silent for a long time. Finally she said, "Jeremy Sinclair is dead."

Jack sighed. "That's who I heard."

"A good prosecuting attorney would make the case that I murdered him."

He shook his head. "Self-defense. How did he— How'll we—" So many questions needed asking that no single one came out.

"He chased me up the trail that wound up Petit Piton. I thought I was on the path down to the beach but I'd taken a wrong turn. I was running so hard. I slipped and nearly slid down the face of the Piton. He fell as he was trying to reach me."

"That's not murder."

"He extended his belt to me to pull me up. I grabbed it and yanked as hard as I could. I *intended* for him to fall."

The defense attorney stepped in. "Impossible to prove malicious intent without substantiating evidence, witnesses or some other—"

The words sounded absurd, far away. "His screams were— It was horrible. They went on and on and ended with—a nightmare."

"The nightmare's over."

She rose wearily. "I'll clean off my war paint and see what's on the diskette."

Jack remained at the helm while Kate went below and became Kate again. Then she sat in the salon and listed the contents of Tim's diskette. There were three files—DATA7, README, and TRANS7. She typed SCROLL README and read Tim's words:

"Here is the seventh and last of the transmissions. You must get them all transferred to the SETI network as quickly as possible. Some tragic news—Walter Jacobsen is dead. We do not know for certain how he died. Authorities here claim it was either an accident or suicide but we'll probably never know. They're insisting we remain here indefinitely to search for the transmitter—which we all agree has sent all there was to send—and analyze the data. It's a waste, especially without better proper facilities, and mostly the freedom to do research away from closed-circuit monitors and ever-present guards. Enclosed are

SETI network dial-up and file transfer instructions. God speed, dear friend."

Then she read the text of the final Omega Transmission:

Ω *Transmission Seven:*
Naturally you wonder who we are, yet perhaps you already know the answer: We are your children, a generation of your own species yet to be born, residents of planet Earth. We come to you across time, from your future. Our message spans the centuries via the tachyon beam, accelerated by means of a reciprocal universe fulcrum positioned at the gravitational limbus of a black hole. Yet our message to you and the minds that send it are as near to you as your next breath.

As inhabitants of the blue planet, we send to implore you to learn about love.

You have achieved great mastery over forces and means by which all life on Earth can be extinguished; yet also within you is the capacity to save it. You might assume, and with reason, that there could be no true urgency to this plea, that life must have survived, for how otherwise, could you receive a message from Earth humans, sent millennia hence.

That observation is only somewhat accurate. Our history records that a shift in human consciousness occurred, an evolutionary species transformation that began during Earth's late twentieth and early twenty-first centuries. This shift is said to have been prompted in part by messages received on Earth from Earth-future. Our reach to you now with these transmissions is in fulfillment of that historical imperative.

Messages from Earth-future led in subsequent centuries to a species-wide awakening of Omegan consciousness. We came to a full reassessment of ourselves and our place of responsibility in the cosmos. We accepted the necessity of embracing a new path for humanity, one reestablishing Earth as a sanctuary and haven for all of life. The human species transformed itself from competitor and exploiter to shepherd and steward of Earth and its treasure. The harmony of humankind within the cosmos was reestablished.

For each of you, it becomes a simple matter of choice. Beginning now, choose a new way; from the immense power of your own free will, from which we neither can nor would detract, choose only love. Your children send you this plea along with an assurance that you are not at all alone in the universe. You are master creators embodying an unlimited potential for love that joins you in timelessness with all living consciousness. Your choice for love abolishes every sense of separation and loneliness, every manifestation of fear. We call on you to awaken to that force. When you do, you will enfold the universe. Consider the duality of the Omegan symbol: the image of a setting sun is equally an image of a rising sun. As such, Omega is a beginning.
Transmission Seven Ω

Kate nodded to herself. Part of her must have known all along. The messages had been sent back in time by Earth's own human descendants. Dr. Rensler had guessed as much. There'd been that gleam in his eye, that look of comprehension and wonder. It made sense. It wasn't that life elsewhere in the universe was not to be found but that such life would keep its distance until earthlings had cleaned up their act, stopped warring with each other, stopped ravaging their planet.

Self-healing would be the membership fee for joining the cosmic talk circuit, before humans would be invited to sit at the table with a universe of intelligent life. There had been an epidemic raging on Earth, Kate thought, not so much of body as of heart and spirit. She thought of Margo's comment about the constricted heart. Freedom was a matter of inner shackles far more than anything externally imposed. At hand were—and had always been—the means to release those shackles and mend it all. The Omegan whole was contained in every part.

Kate returned to the cockpit. It was dawn. On the eastern horizon the tip of the sun was a brilliant blaze of orange emerging from the dark expanse of ocean.

"I'll take the helm, Jack. Go wash off your blackface. Then read the last transmission."

As she stood at the wheel, the memory of a pair of objects came to her, the silicon wafer resembling a small mirror, and the black postcard beneath it with the white arrow, the caption *YOU ARE HERE*. The mirror above the galaxy, reflecting back an echo of ourselves. Three years ago she'd fixed those objects to her office wall. Now, looking back, she thought that might have been when her mind had first become quiet, when she'd first had a sense of being led. There was a symmetry to the events that followed and possibly an explanation for all those premonitions. Perhaps she'd had the briefest glimpse of the realm described in the transmissions as beyond the context of linear time.

EPILOGUE

THEY ARRIVED in Mustique at two-thirty on the afternoon of September thirteenth. With their dinghy lost somewhere in the cove of Petit Soufriere, Jack had to swim ashore, returning in a small rowboat which he said he'd rented from a local fisherman. Quickly Kate handed down her computer, modem and cords and climbed into the boat. Would anyone attempt to stop them? If the NSA had tapped SETI's network phone, would they be able to trace the phone call she was about to make? The transfer of data might take hours. They tied up at the dinghy dock and walked the short distance along the ocean front to Basil's Bar.

In a back room sitting at a dusty table, her computer open amid piles of papers, Kate connected the modem and dialed the international SETI computer network.

She typed:

LOGIN THURMOND
PASSWORD:
AMETHYST, she entered, followed by
CD\SIG_ALERT and then FILECOPY TRANS*.* C:

The transfer of the seven text files, the binary transmission data, Tim's notes and translation routines, and Kate's own written account, took ninety minutes. Every moment of it was anxious. Jack paced and stood watch at the door, knowing full well that his presence would do nothing to deter the NSA— "about as much as a traffic light would halt a buffalo stampede," as he'd put it. When the file transfer was completed, she called Marilyn Rosewald, her editor at *Science America*, and told her to expect a diskette in the mail, "the story of the Omega Transmissions."

"And Marilyn, if you publish the story, it must not be under my name. It's— You'll understand. Attribute it to an unnamed but reliable firsthand witness. In exchange for that favor, I'll decline payment. Otherwise no deal."

Marilyn Rosewald finally agreed.

Then Kate called the operator and asked for the charges. She emerged from the tiny room and wandered over to settle the bill with Keller who happened to be tending bar.

"All done," she said to Jack. They perched on barstools. "How about a rum punch?"

"Sounds reasonable. Keller?" He held up two fingers.

"Thank you," she said.

Jack gave her a knowing look; she was referring to much more than the drink that was placed before her.

"No need," he said.

"You've given a lot."

"So have you." He stirred his drink. "Now don't be insulted."

"What?"

"Next time you feel the need of a vacation just speak up. It's not necessary to stage anything this elaborate."

She burst out laughing.

"So what now?"

She looked out beyond the bamboo-and-palm-frond structure to the bay. There weren't many boats, fewer than there'd been on jump-up night in June. It was hurricane season and most sailors steered clear of the Eastern Caribbean until November or December. "I can't understand why I should feel safe but I do. You realize we're probably fugitives, at least until the transmissions are announced. How long do we have the boat?"

"Three weeks. I know of a smugglers' cove where we could hide out. It has a terrible reputation and lousy weather."

She made a face. "I know of a snorkeling spot with terrific weather and a reputation as a very good place on a very good planet. I could use a vacation—nothing elaborate, you understand." She tilted her head until the hollow of her cheek came to rest against his shoulder. Her finger traced a vein over the back of his hand. His palm opened and their fingers locked.

"I suppose we could move down here," he said, "maybe work in a paper route at some point. I have it on good authority that the gods do not deduct from one's allotted time the hours spent delivering newspapers."

"While sailing?"

"Especially while sailing."

Ω

ACKNOWLEDGMENTS

I am deeply indebted to a great many for encouragement, support, and assistance with this novel:

Sharron Forrest, literary agent; Gene Olson—writer, friend, mentor and bipedal encyclopedia; Judith Cope, editor extraordinaire; Dr. Donald Erbschloe, physicist, U.S. Air Force Academy, Colorado Springs; and eagle-eyed proof-readers Lou Lyman and Joan Spear.

Thanks also to past and present members of my writers' group—Esther Bell, Beth Coye, Barbara Jones, Sue Milburn, Kathleen Sullivan McCarthy and Sandy Summerhays—friends aboard the roller coaster.

And many others who took the time to read and comment on early versions of the manuscript: Jean Bakewell, Margaret Clark, Gail Coufal, Patricia Garlan, Mary Greer, David Hartwell, Teddy and Heber Holloway, Laura LeMarr, Sara McCracken, Lucien McGuire, June and Bill Parker, Mary Perry, Damaris Rowland, Ellen Schaefer, Sue Schilling, Karen Siefert, Don and Becky Smith, Judy Voruz and Lorna Wuertz.

And Alice, the four-legged definition of a friend.

With special thanks to Ann Robertson and
Georgia Otterson, crew mates, along with
Captain Bill, aboard the *Peak Experience*.

About the Author

NANCY PARKER was born and raised in southern California and lived most of her adult life in the San Francisco Bay Area. After a career in freelance art followed by another as an independent computer programmer, she began writing fiction. *The Omega Transmissions* is her first published novel and she is at work on the next—a follow-on Caribbean sailing adventure/thriller. She currently resides in southern Oregon and shares living space with an unruly Jack Russell terrier named Alice.